PRAISE FOR

"An insightful and timely ta̲̲̲̲̲̲̲̲̲̲̲̲̲̲ : and illuminating book shows us h.... has changed in three and a half thousand years. How do women wield power? In the shadows, like scorpions. With cunning and guile and through alliances and solidarity. She shows us true power is not found in dominating others but in the simple freedom to live and love as you choose."

—Nikki Marmery, author of *Lilith*

"*Neferura* by Malayna Evans explores the tense political landscape of ancient Egypt through the eyes of Neferura, princess and high priestess of Kemet. Neferura's story is excellently researched, and I especially enjoyed Evans's close attention to detail, demonstrating her impressive knowledge and background in Egyptology."

—Rosie Hewlett, author of *Medusa*

"Set in ancient Egypt, *Neferura* plunges the reader into a fascinating world of unfamiliar beliefs, traditions, and social mores. At the same time, its focus on the trifecta of power, ambition, and desire feels very modern indeed. As Neferura surrounds herself with potential allies, she must struggle to decide whom she can trust—with her kingdom, her love, and in the highest stakes of all, her life. A compelling and intriguing read."

—Liz Michalski, author of *Darling Girl*

"A lively reimagining of one of the most intriguing women of ancient history, all set in the context of the author's deep knowledge of Egyptian history, culture, and religion."

—Peter F. Dorman, Egyptologist, University of Chicago

"This fast-paced novel takes us through the illustrious Eighteenth Dynasty of Egypt's New Kingdom when a woman pharaoh sought to have her daughter succeed her on the throne! This tale, both murder mystery and love story, shares a coming-of-age story in which the power of women's friendships, women's wisdom, and women's autonomy combine in the surprising conclusion."

—Solange Ashby, Ph.D., Egyptologist and nubiologist

NEFERURA

THE PHARAOH'S DAUGHTER

MALAYNA EVANS

sourcebooks
landmark

Published by Sourcebooks Landmark, an imprint of Sourcebooks
P.O. Box 4410, Naperville, Illinois 60567-4410
(630) 961-3900
sourcebooks.com

Library of Congress Cataloging-in-Publication Data

Names: Evans, Malayna, author.
Title: Neferura : the pharaoh's daughter / Malayna Evans.
Description: Naperville, Illinois : Sourcebooks Landmark, [2024]
Identifiers: LCCN 2023025048 (print) | LCCN 2023025049 (ebook) | (trade paperback) | (ebook)
Subjects: LCGFT: Novels.
Classification: LCC PS3605.V36867 N44 2024 (print) | LCC PS3605.V36867
    (ebook) | DDC 813/.6--dc23/eng/20230602
LC record available at https://lccn.loc.gov/2023025048
LC ebook record available at https://lccn.loc.gov/2023025049

Printed and bound in the United States of America.
LSC 10 9 8 7 6 5 4 3 2 1

To the girlfriends I've cherished and the remarkable women I've never met, those who keep pushing forward, fighting age-old battles, taking care of others as they march on. Keep going, ladies. The world is better for your efforts.

GLOSSARY

Throughout the book, I sometimes use terms an ancient Egyptian would have used, rather than employ more classical or recent word choices that may be familiar to today's readers. The glossary below should shed light on some of the less familiar terms used generously in the book.

Aaru: The heavenly "Field of Reeds" is ruled by Osiris. If one's heart is found light enough for the scales to balance, they may begin their journey to Aaru where they might enjoy a peaceful afterlife.

Djeser-Djeseru: Hatshepsut's mortuary temple on the west bank, across from the modern-day city of Luxor. Djeser-Djeseru translates as "Holy of Holies."

Heka Khasut: These "rulers of foreign lands" are more commonly referred to as the Hyksos. The Fifteenth Dynasty kings ruled part of Egypt from Avaris in the delta until they were defeated by Ahmose, founder of the Eighteen Dynasty, in which our story is set.

Iteru: We call it the Nile, but they called it Iteru, "the great river."

Kemet: Meaning "the black lands," Kemet is a colloquial way ancient Egyptians referred to Egypt.

Kush: Nubia, known as Kush for much of antiquity, lies south of the first cataract. It was home to a rich culture and was the gateway for luxury products such as ebony, ivory, and incense.

Men-nefer: Hellenized as Memphis, this is one name ancient Egyptians used for this sometimes capital near modern Cairo. It translates as "enduring in beauty" and is adapted from the name of the nearby Sixth Dynasty pyramid of Pepi. During the Eighteenth Dynasty, Men-nefer functioned as a kind of second capital and was home to the important temple of Ptah.

Shedeh: This popular drink was probably made from red grapes and first appears in texts during the Amarna period, just after our story takes place.

Ta-sekhet-ma'at: Generally translated as "the Great Field," the Valley of the Kings on the west bank, across from the modern city of Luxor, was home to royal burials throughout the Eighteenth Dynasty.

Wadj-wer: "The Great Greenery" is both a fertility god and the personification of bodies of water. It has long been read, as in our story, to refer to the Mediterranean, although some scholars suggest it would be more properly read as the Nile delta and/or the Red Sea.

Waset: Modern-day Luxor is more commonly referred to as Thebes from the Greek Thebai. The ancient Egyptians called the Eighteenth Dynasty capital Waset, "city of the was scepter," the scepter of the pharaoh. It is home to the temples of Karnak and Luxor on the east bank, and the west bank hosts cemeteries and funerary complexes.

PART
ONE

ONE

I N THE END, EVERYONE'S HEART WILL BE WEIGHED.

Some will be heavier than the Feather of Truth. Those hearts will be crushed by the sharp teeth of the goddess Ammit, the Devourer. For the poor souls whose lives have rendered their hearts heavy, death is a sad ending. But for those whose hearts are light enough to balance the scales, death is a beginning, a door to a new, eternal life—a life free of unruly bodies and controlling mothers and cruel boys who think they're men.

Fortunately, as the god's wife of Amun, I'm rich in opportunities to serve my people and lighten my heart, especially on sacred festival days like today.

"Gut in, Neferura," Mother jeers, although I'm not sure why—the tight shift dress I wear already squeezes my stomach in as far as it goes. Plus, she's standing in front of me, as usual. She can't possibly see me with that towering crown balanced on her head.

I swallow the angry retort that stings my tongue and shift my shoulders back, looking out at the crowd of raucous revelers that fill the streets of Waset, waiting for the procession to begin. Amun, the god I serve, faces me and the high priest as we stand side by side behind Pharaoh, my mother. The god's golden statue is hidden inside a shrine that rests atop his ship-shaped float, which is covered in gold foil and encrusted with gemstones. Golden ram figureheads are fixed on the prow and stern. Behind Amun, his wife, Mut, and son, Khonsu, wait, hidden inside their own lavish shrines.

The crowd stretches behind them as far as I can see. The divine triad will soon be carried by priests in parade, cheered on by the crowd and musicians and acrobats. They'll cross the river to visit the mortuary temples of the ancestors. Their ultimate destination is Djeser-Djeseru, Mother's Temple of Millions of Years.

To prepare Amun for such a public spectacle, I spent my morning bathing the golden statue in precious aromatics and dressing him in the finest linens and most extravagant jewels. All the while, the people were enjoying bread and beer as dancers and musicians entertained them.

It's been a long day already.

Finally, the priests lift the gods onto their shoulders on long cedar poles and the parade begins. The musicians redouble their efforts. A cacophony of trumpets weaves around the chanting of priestesses who work for my estate, their bodies cloaked in white linen robes, lotus flowers tucked into braids and belts, their chins held high. The air is heavy with scents—a heady mix of cooked meat, perspiration, and blossoms. Amun, Mut, and Khonsu will be doused in a rainbow of colorful flowers as they move through the city. The ankh-shaped bouquets, fashioned by hand and thrown by the people, will soak up the gods' spirit before being gathered back up and placed in tombs and at grave sites in private family celebrations later tonight.

"It took them long enough to get moving." Mother turns to me as the parade shifts away, wiping her face with a linen cloth. Imagine the scandal if someone spotted Pharaoh with a dewy brow. "I do hope you're prepared to service the god again tonight, Neferura?"

"Of course, I am, Mother."

As a woman, Mother is a rarity among pharaohs. And I'm no typical princess. My mother, the great Hatshepsut, has no queen. So it falls to me as the king's eldest daughter, lady of Upper and Lower Kemet, and mistress of the Two Lands to perform the queenly duties, which include serving as Kemet's most powerful priestess, a role I've managed since I was a young girl. At first, I didn't believe I could succeed as the god's wife of Amun. But over time, I've earned the trust of the priesthood and expanded the wealth and influence of the House of the Adoratrice beyond even the lofty heights it reached during Mother's tenure, before Father passed and she climbed onto the throne. Mother has no reason to doubt my abilities or my dedication. It's not as if this is my first festival.

"We're in for a night of revelry." Senenmut strides up wearing a friendly smile. A handsome man with long legs and a lean build, Senenmut is my royal tutor and Mother's steward, treasurer, and lover. I'm not supposed to know that last bit, but their love affair is the worst-kept secret in a court full to bursting with poorly kept secrets. "Kemet will be teeming with new babies by the time we celebrate again next year."

"Let's hope the lands are as fertile." Dimples slice through the priest's chubby cheeks as his eyes follow a remarkably nimble acrobat, her bare body flipping so fast it makes me dizzy to watch.

"They will be," Mother intones.

If she says so, it must be true. Mother takes good care of the gods, so they take good care of Kemet. She's worked to ensure festivals like today's are more opulent than ever so the land will be bountiful when the river rises again.

"We have some time until we meet the gods at Djeser-Djeseru," Senenmut tells Mother. "The royal pleasure barge is prepared to serve us while we cross back to the west bank."

Mother nods, just enough to agree to Senenmut's agenda without tilting the two large plumes rising from her gold diadem, one of several headdresses she'll don throughout the day.

The four of us walk toward the sacred parts of the temple, reserved for the priesthood, to let the crowd disperse before we venture to the barge. Senenmut and the high priest are both gifted at meaningless chitchat. I'm barely listening to the priest babble about the tomb he's building when Mother's old handmaid breaks protocol, rushing up to slip a scroll into Mother's hands, then dash off again.

Mother scowls as she rolls it open, reading it with pursed lips. She curses under her breath, then crushes the papyrus in her fist. "Thutmose is coming to Waset." Her tone is icy.

A chill runs down my spine. My half brother has rarely visited the primary palace since Mother tossed him from court as a child.

"Is he?" The high priest is blissfully unaware of the enmity that brews in my family. "What a shame Thutmose wasn't able to make it for today's festival. Imagine both pharaohs together before the gods."

"Yes." Mother is droll. "Imagine."

I clasp my hands behind my back, trying to mask the tingle of trepidation that flows from my head to my toes. Although we were once close, Thutmose decided years ago that he'd rather be enemies than friends. Our early childhood comradery, playing in the kitchens and running the grounds, turned hostile and cold. Now he hates me, which is one reason Mother keeps her co-pharaoh—in name only, bless Amun—busy training with the army and hobnobbing with low-level foreign bureaucrats in Men-nefer so he's isolated, both from the court and Kemet's true political power: the rich priesthood

I serve. After all, Thutmose is not Mother's son. He's the heir of my father, dead more than a decade. And now, apparently, my perpetually aggrieved half brother is ready to come home.

"It will be good to have him back," Senenmut lies while, with the diplomatic skills that led my tutor from the lower rungs of society to the top, he puts a hand on the priest's shoulder and steers him away from me and Mother with talk of wine from the islands of the great green sea awaiting us on the barge. My tutor is giving me time to gather myself and act the proper god's wife. I suspect he's worried Mother will break out her crook and flail and beat me if I don't calm my breathing and settle the jitters running through my limbs.

I'm managing well enough until the priest, who's toddled a few steps away, rubbing his bald head, turns back to me and says, "Don't worry too much about him, Adoratrice. You are an excellent god's wife. The priesthood will stand up for you. We won't back down."

The tingles swell. The priest returns his attention to Senenmut, and I turn to Mother. "Back down from what?"

In lieu of an answer, Mother glares at me. Her flinty eyes are ringed flawlessly in kohl, a nod to her vanity and a failed effort to pull attention away from her double chin and crooked nose—a nose I have the misfortune to share.

"What is the priest talking about, Mother?" I push forward, testing my luck. "Is Thutmose up to something?"

"That boy is always up to something, Neferura. You know how desperate he is to pull power away from us, your estate above all. If it were up to Thutmose, the military would feast while the House of the Adoratrice—and the people—starve."

She's right, of course. It's no surprise that Thutmose wants to diminish my power—he detests me, and he blames the position I hold for Mother's rise to the throne. For good reason. She was able to take and hold power in large part because of the riches and loyalty she earned as god's wife, a loyalty I have only nourished.

I curl my hands into fists and breathe, reminding myself that the heart pulsing inside my body will one day determine my fate, its blood and tissue made light—or heavy—by my lifetime of decisions. I squeeze my eyes shut and see an image of the Devourer examining my heart, blood dripping from her razor-sharp teeth. Thutmose stands before the goddess, pressing his fat thumb on the scale, forcing the pan to dip. Ammit, realizing my heart now outweighs the feather, snaps her sharp teeth, and my eyes fly open.

Mother lifts a haughty brow as if she's seen my vision and judged it unseemly. Perhaps she has. She is the embodiment of the god on earth after all.

"What aren't you telling me?" I try again.

"There are many things I don't tell you, Neferura. And still, miraculously, you seem to know all you need to know." She turns away, beckoning for Senenmut and putting an end to another futile conversation. As my tutor and the priest wander back toward us, she shares a final piece of advice. "Do tread carefully around Thutmose, daughter. He is reckless. And reckless men are never to be trusted."

I feel the frustration grow in my chest, the potent irritation at missing information and unsolved riddles, and I turn to Senenmut. His eyes are warm with concern as he lifts a hand to his ear and tugs once—one of our secret signals. We concocted them when I was a child: tapping your forehead three times means someone is lying; tugging both ears means you know something about the topic at hand you'll explain later, in private; scratching your head with your left hand means you think the person speaking is a fool. The ear tug is unique. It doesn't translate easily into words. It's more of a feeling, a kind of pep talk. It means something like *We can do this. Let's make it work.*

But I'm not a child anymore. Small gestures won't satiate me. And news that Thutmose is on his way certainly can't be quashed by an ear tug.

Mother, Senenmut, and the high priest jabber about some small skirmish between two venerated priests at the temple of Ptah in Men-nefer as my head spins, worrying over what Thutmose could be up to. My half brother's plans may be opaque, but they're also imminent. He's probably sailing toward Waset now as we chant hymns and pour wine and cater to the needs of the gods, as the people gather flowers and drink beer and visit the tombs of their ancestors, begging the dead to give them wisdom or revenge, money or fertility.

The thought reminds me how important the work we do today is. The regeneration of the land depends on me, especially on festival days. If I fail the god, creation could collapse, the sun could vanish, the river could run dry. Plants and animals could wither and disappear, leaving nothing for the people to eat. I can't waste time worrying about Thutmose now.

I take a final deep breath and banish him from my mind. Thoughts of my rogue half brother won't hijack the day. Closing my eyes, I utter a quick prayer.

Mighty god, I am your servant. Forgive my mind for wandering.

Amun, sacred of arm, regenerate the land we love, show the people Mother's rule is right and blessed, and let the crops be bounteous.

Also, powerful Amun-Ra, bull of your mother, if it pleases you, let Thutmose choke on a chicken bone and drop dead before he gets here and disrupts the good work we do together.

The clickety-clack of Iset's sandals slapping against the stone floor grows faster and closer at my back like my handmaid is rushing to catch up before I pass through my quarters' doors and leave her behind. As if I could. With few exceptions, Iset is glued to me like tar to a ship's hull.

Kamut's presence, on the other hand, is less predictable. I suck in my gut and lift my head higher when I see him standing guard at my door. He doesn't notice me—not in the way I wish he would—but I see him. Only a year older than me, he's the youngest of my guards. And he's handsome—tall and broad, eyes deep and dark when they flicker my way. Even the scar that crosses his cheek from the corner of his left eyebrow to the bottom of his left ear is interesting. That doesn't stop me from squirming every time I see it. The scar is my fault after all.

He drops his eyes as I approach: eye contact between a princess and her guard is forbidden. He and my pretty handmaid, on the other hand, are free to gaze into each other's eyes all they like. I imagine Kamut and Iset smiling at each other behind my back. I'm so certain they're mocking me, I almost whirl around to confront them. But of course I don't. Mother says lashing out is a sign of weak character.

The door shuts behind me as Kamut's staff bangs against the floor: twice fast, once slow. It's another of the signals Senenmut and I invented years ago. This one means my tutor is in my study, waiting for me. Finally, my questions will be answered. If I'm lucky, the god heard my prayers and Senenmut is about to announce that Thutmose was gored by a crocodile, or drowned in the river, or got stung by a particularly vicious scorpion on his way here.

I move faster, rushing past my receiving room, weaving around cedar chairs and golden stools, through my bedroom, where Iset busies herself with my wardrobe, and into the small study I've set up in the back of my quarters. It used to be a dressing room. Now it's stuffed, floor to ceiling, with scrolls. Like my bedroom, the study is open to my pool and deck with its picturesque view. The blue of my small pool, surrounded by palm trees and drenched in lotus blossoms, contrasts with the calm, green waters of Iteru, the river that gives Kemet life, floating past two stories down. My desk is situated so that the breezes keep me cool as I review ledgers and copy the words of our wise men, dipping my brush into water, then wetting the ink cake—red or black—before painting onto papyrus.

"You're late." My tutor is perched in his favorite high-backed chair that sits facing my desk, one leg propped on the other so his ankle rests on his knee. He wears his favorite wig, falling in wavy black curls to his shoulders, and a sheer top with intricately pleated sleeves that match his skirt. A broad gold collar, inlaid with a carnelian scarab beetle, girdles his neck.

"You've been avoiding me," I retort, sinking onto the stool by his feet, still cross that he turned away from me after yesterday's parade to disappear into the revelry.

His smile is sly. "Never."

"You have been. And you know it. You knew I wanted to speak with you, so you dashed off. I tried to talk to you again last night, but you were stuck to Mother like sand to the desert. I'm surprised you didn't cancel today's session."

"You would have tracked me down," he deadpans.

"Yes," I agree. "I would have. I hope this means you're ready to tell me what Thutmose is up to."

Senenmut's sparkle dims. He lifts his slim shoulders. "The same as ever. Chaos and spectacle."

I think of Thutmose's usual antics—poking foreign bureaucrats to create drama Mother must manage or siphoning resources from the temple of Ptah to reward his band of petty followers—and I shake my head. "I don't think so. His spectacle usually occurs far from court. He's coming here without even being summoned. Mother was surprised he's on his way. That's new. She seemed more bothered by news of him than usual. And she refused to tell me what the priest meant when he said they'd stand by me. Why would I need that?'"

Senenmut folds his arms. "It can hardly come as a surprise that Thutmose is interested in your position. He's always working against you, even when he's doing nothing at all. There's nothing new about that. But he's no match for you and the god. You know you're going to serve Amun faithfully, running off to temple at dawn each morning, no matter what Thutmose does. Remember when you were ill? The doctor ordered you to sleep in and you simply ignored him."

"The doctor is no pharaoh."

Senenmut's smile turns snide. It says what he'd never say aloud. Thutmose isn't much of a pharaoh either. In theory, the throne belongs to Thutmose as much as it belongs to Mother. In reality, Mother rules every cubit of the Two Lands, every peasant and patrician. Even the gods no longer outrank her: she's declared herself their equal, the living conduit through which Amun speaks. Thutmose is a mere soldier in comparison.

"Stop avoiding the question," I snap. "You can't distract me with compliments anymore. You know the specifics around Thutmose's visit. Is there a reason you think I don't deserve to know as well?"

Senenmut sags, reaching out to cup my cheek in his palm. Although touching a royal is punishable by death for most people, the rule does not apply to Mother's paramour. "You are correct, as usual, dear one. But it's nothing really. We've just heard word that

Thutmose has been making the rounds. He's visiting nobles. He's whispering in their ears. We believe he's attempting to poison them against your influence. He tells them the god's wife estate has too many priestesses, that the House of the Adoratrice has too much power, that you spend too much—"

"Feeding the people," I interrupt, bitterness rising in my throat.

"Correct. But since when has Thutmose cared about the people?"

I stand to pace, fingers digging into my palms. "Is Mother planning to stop him? Or is she going to let him damage the estate she once managed?"

"I'm sure she has a plan—"

I pivot. "What plan?"

"She is the omnipotent one, dear one. Not me. We both know my abilities to predict her are"—he pauses—"limited."

I scoff. Senenmut is Mother's one true love. She didn't love my father, who was, by all honest accounts, a weak man with a fragile hold on power. The court pretends Father was a mighty pharaoh just like they pretend not to notice that Senenmut and Mother are lovers.

Still, it's clear Senenmut doesn't know what Mother intends, so I try a different approach. "Are the nobles swayed by his arguments?"

Senenmut taps long fingers against his bony knees. "A few agree that the resources you wield are excessive. But most see only the good you do. It doesn't hurt that you've managed to promote women from virtually every noble family in Kemet. You've earned loyalty from Swenett to Per-Wadjet. I don't believe the nobles will side with Thutmose over you and your mother, and the priesthood is fiercely loyal to you both."

"And the military?"

Senenmut pauses, weighing his words. "The military respects Thutmose. But they also respect your mother. They won't take sides, not now anyway." He crosses his arms. "Thutmose can't hurt you, dear one."

"Yet." I twirl and march back across the small room, only to spin and pace my steps again. "But it's only a matter of time until Mother has to give Thutmose some real power. He's not a child anymore. And we both know he'll use whatever influence he gathers against me."

"He may try." Senenmut's head swivels back and forth, tracking my march. "And you are right—your mother does have some difficult decisions to make. Her current strategy—treating Thutmose like the spoiled little boy he once was—is unsustainable. I suspect that's why news of Thutmose feels more salient now." He sighs. "You may not see it, but your mother's hardships—"

"Hardships?" I interrupt.

His eyebrows inch up. "You can't believe it was easy for her to capture the throne. Hatshepsut faced more battles than you can imagine. The pressure to be perfect pushes her forward still. Unlike the pharaohs before her, your mother has no room for mistakes. You can't imagine what she's been through, from the vitriol she faced as a young woman to a painful marriage—"

"Why doesn't she tell me this herself?" I slow my steps, curious.

Senenmut's eyes soften, his voice turning tender. "Because she can't afford to show weakness. It's entirely possible she's forgotten how."

"Talking to her daughter is weakness?"

He shrugs. "She protects you in her own way. If it weren't for the trials she survived when she was your age, I suspect she'd have followed the family tradition and married you off to your half brother years ago."

The thought stops me in my tracks. I lean against my desk, steadying myself. "What a terrible custom."

It's true, although the gods themselves invented it, of course. Every pharaoh is the embodiment of the god Horus, son of brother-sister duo Isis and Osiris. That doesn't mean I want to marry Thutmose. I don't even want to think about where I'd be if Mother hadn't put an end to the brother-sister marriages my ancestors survived. Thutmose and I are both past marriageable age. But if he were married to me—the only princess, daughter of two pharaohs, and the god's wife of Amun—he'd have an immediate link to the priesthood. Were I to give him a child, a future pharaoh, Thutmose's prestige would outshine even Mother's, which is, of course, the reason she put an end to the family tradition.

Senenmut turns pensive. "It kept power in the family, to be sure. But yes, it was an unfortunate custom."

I'm tempted to ask what he thought of my father, a subject we generally avoid. But before I form the words, Senenmut stops brooding and leans forward.

"I know it looks gloomy, dear one. But it has been a long time since you and Thutmose spent time together. You're both older now. Perhaps it's not as bad as it seems and word from the nobles is just silly gossip. Maybe the two of you can find a way to work together. He is a pharaoh. And as you say, he won't be powerless forever. In spite of his recent activities, I'd advise you to try and make peace. He might surprise you." Senenmut rubs his chin, signaling that he's about to impart some riddled wisdom. "Remember what the great wise man Ptahhotep said: No one can be born wise."

And some who are born never become wise, I think. But my tutor wants to cheer me, and I don't want to let him down. So I swallow the words, offer him a smile, and hold out a palm to receive today's scroll.

Iset's brown eyes sparkle with delight as she runs her fingers over the gossamer fabric of my newest gown. "The linen is so thin. And all these pleats. It's perfect." She drapes the diaphanous material over my arms, fastening it just under my breasts, which, to my horror, seem extra plump today.

She spins in a circle. Her eyes roam over my large bedroom like it's the first time she's seen it. Iset has always been one to marvel at pretty things, and the lavishness of the palace inspires awe even in those of us who were born to it. I glance around at the painted scenes of Kemet's plants and wildlife on my walls, the eight marble pillars stretching from my floor, drenched in rich carpets, to the ceiling, spotted with golden stars, wondering what Iset's old house was like.

Most royal handmaids are old noblewomen. But Iset, presented to me by Senenmut on my fifteenth birthday, is common. Her mother, a peasant, died birthing her second child, a brother Iset only knew for a day, and her father is an artisan who works at Djeser-Djeseru, Mother's mortuary temple. How Senenmut convinced Mother to let Iset serve me has been a mystery since the day she arrived. But my tutor insisted I have a handmaid my own age. I suspect he chose a girl who was raised far from court for personal reasons. Our esteemed steward was lowborn; he has a soft spot for commoners.

"Let's try the new wig," Iset squeals, fingering a delicate diadem with rosette inlays and a golden uraeus designed to sit on my brow. The birds playing in the pool, just outside my open wall, erupt in song, as if they're as excited about my new clothes as she is.

I plop into the chair facing my large, polished bronze mirror with a stony stare. I'm brewing over Thutmose's imminent arrival. Iset's small talk doesn't help my mood. The truth is, I'm only truly comfortable when alone in my study or, better, surrounded by the temple's stillness. I'm calmed by the cool stone walls, the sounds of chanting, the low cries of sacred cows, the smells of incense. Senenmut claims I didn't spend enough time with kids my age as a child, so I'm not used to it. Mother says the royal blood running through my veins makes me better than others, rendering me as haughty as her, even if I don't want to admit it.

I think the truth is much simpler. I just like being alone more than being with people, which might say something about the people I'm too often stuck with. The god is silent, but he's also reliable and predictable, unlike the vipers who fill the court. Not that Iset is one of them—she's nice to everyone, even me when I'm at my worst. But if Mother saw the familiar way my handmaid speaks to me, Iset would be carted away with no chance of return. And while I've never admitted it aloud, I'd miss her if she were gone.

"We should redo your braids tonight." Iset ignores my pursed-lipped scowl. Finished rubbing perfumed oil into my scalp, she pulls a heavy black wig with long, full tresses over my braids. Two long curtains of hair frame my face, falling to my breasts, while the back of the wig laps at my shoulder blades. "I once knew a woman who gave her hair to the wigmakers. She had beautiful, long locks. Then one day, she was bald." Iset giggles. "Wouldn't it be amazing if her hair was in this very wig?"

I grunt. Iset knows I prefer silence. She just can't seem to stop herself from chattering.

"You're like a goddess in the flesh." Iset pats my perfectly situated wig.

"More like a hippo dressed for festival," I mumble, inspecting our reflections in the mirror. Iset's heart-shaped face and plump lips look so elegant next to my sharp cheeks and hawkish nose. I imagine swapping places with her, letting her try on my wigs and jewels and feel the soft fabrics against her flesh.

"Stop that." She tugs a lock of hair. "You're so cute. And I'm not the only one who thinks so. One very handsome palace guard notices you too. Kamut—"

Panic seizes through me. "Don't say that." It comes out like a hiss.

Her smile in the mirror is wide and happy, her eyes curious. "Why not? He's—"

"No!" I spin around and grab her wrists, pupils darting across the room, desperate to confirm we're alone. We are. But Iset's joke is dangerous, even between the two of us. "Never say that again. Do you hear me?"

Her pretty face crumples in confusion.

"Iset." I breathe deeply, determined to make her understand. "I'm chosen by the god himself. My loyalty to Amun must be absolute or…or…" I can't say exactly what would happen if I was unfaithful to the god, but surely his punishment would be severe, and it wouldn't fall on me alone but on the country I love. "Surely you understand that?"

She nods, but I can tell she's not getting the point.

"That means I can never be touched by a man. The very idea of…of…" I stutter, scared to repeat Kamut's name. "Amun is my partner. My only partner. I must devote myself to him so he can be reborn each day. The perpetual re-creation of the cosmos depends on it. So do the people of Kemet. You know how many people depend on my estate for food to feed their families, for their very liveli-hoods. The idea of me with anyone but the god, even something as

16

innocent as your joke, puts all that at risk. It's dangerous. If a man was interested in me…in touching me"—I swallow hard—"his life would be forfeit."

Her eyes, which have grown wider as I've talked, fill with tears. She shifts her hands so she's holding on to mine. The intimacy is uncomfortable. I want to pull away, but I need to drive my point home.

"Never joke like that again. Promise me?"

She sniffles. "I'm sorry—"

"You didn't know." I squirm my hands out of her grip and turn back to the mirror, heartbeat slowing to normal. I consider telling her the timing is especially bad for such talk since Thutmose is drawing closer, whispering lies with his forked tongue. With a rumor about my fidelity in the wind, even our fiercest allies might listen to Thutmose. But Iset is my handmaid, not my confidant. She has never understood how tenuous and vital the relationship between the nobles and my family is. Mother empowers the nobles, it's true, but mostly because she has to—she takes her power from them and could lose it to them if they united against her.

"You're right. I didn't know that." Iset shakes her head. "I mean I knew it, but not really. I didn't understand what your relationship with Amun means to you. Or for you. That's the thing." Our eyes meet in the mirror. "I mean I'm sorry you can never be with a man."

I scoff. "There are worse fates than that." It's a thought I've turned over in my heart a thousand times, but I've never voiced it aloud. Mother's unconventional path to power led to me not only stepping into the role of high priestess as a child but also stepping out of the role most princesses play. I'm not chattel to be married off to enrich the royal coffers or solidify a power base like the princesses before me, or worse, to be married to a blood relative so there are no pesky in-laws competing for my family's power. Indeed, Mother used my ritual position to justify not marrying me off at all.

It's irrational—she was a married god's wife herself not so long ago. The estate came to power when the rulers of Waset drove the Heka Khasut from Kemet's borders, securing rule over the country. The estate has always been managed by a queen, a move cleverly designed to ensure the royal family wields control over the powerful priesthood of Amun. Of course these women were married. But the gods speak through Mother, and she claims Amun now insists on a virgin god's wife. Who can argue with the commands of gods and pharaohs?

Of course, the justification also means I'll be single for life. Mother says that just makes me like her. She never mentions the fact that she has a partner, a perk I'll never enjoy. I am a young woman— I'm not uninterested in romance and passion. It stings a bit to know I'll never be with a man, not in the way Iset and virtually every other woman in Kemet will be.

"There are worse fates than a life of chastity," I repeat, although I'm not sure which one of us I'm trying to convince.

"Of course there are worse fates. A woman was fished out of the river half-eaten just yesterday. That doesn't mean you don't deserve love. I mean, I haven't done it yet, but it does sound fun, doesn't it?" She giggles and I relax, searching for a change of subject.

I brush my already clean shift dress, finding a stray hair to pluck off. "I'm not the one attracting the palace boys." I force my voice to jest, my tone light. "You have more than your fair share of charm, Iset. And you don't need piles of gold to accent it." I push away the large jasper eye of Horus amulet a prestigious local jeweler dropped off this morning. "In fact, that bracelet you wear is lovely. I don't think I've ever seen you without it. Does it mean something to you?"

Iset bats her eyes prettily, and I swallow my envy.

"It's nothing compared to your jewels. But..." She pauses, dropping her eyes. "It was my mother's."

"Oh." I squirm, embarrassed that my attempts to lead our conversation into safe territory have landed us on another painful topic. "I see. Well, the blue of that turquoise is unique. And the amulet dangling from it. It's a...?"

"Scorpion."

"It's sweet," I lie. In truth, a scorpion is a deadly thing to dangle from a wrist, but that hardly matters. "It's perfect on you."

"My mother was perfect." Iset's voice is low. "She was kind and thoughtful and powerful." Iset's eyes dart to mine and she shakes her head, sending her braids wriggling. "Not powerful like your mother is, of course. But in her own way. She was free and open. And she was like you—she lived to help people, to make a difference in the lives of everyone she touched. It's not the kind of power you and your mother and tutor wield, of course. But it's equally potent, in its own way. You know?"

Is it? I've never imagined a peasant woman with power before. Is that even possible? How potent could the power of the powerless be?

"How about these?" Iset holds up soft leather sandals, adorned with a lapis lazuli djed pillar, for my consideration, effectively ending the conversation.

I watch them swing back and forth, dangling from her fingertip, and manage a small grin, just wide enough to let her know I'm ready to discuss the pros and cons of festooned footwear if it means we never have to revisit the topic of my sex life—or the eternal lack thereof—again. "They're perfect," I lie.

Her smile is wide and knowing as she leans down to shove them on my feet.

TWO

IT TOOK ONE WEEK FOR MY FEARS TO BE CONFIRMED. AT LEAST I expect they'll be confirmed once I reach the throne room. Mother never summons me there at this hour. It can only mean Thutmose has arrived.

My sandals clack against the stone floors as I march toward my doom, Iset trailing me. I don't need to look back to know she's gawking at the brightly painted palm fronds creeping up the mudbrick walls as if it's the first time she's strolled through the palace halls. She's lived in the palace for three years, and still she acts like the awkward teenager who arrived wearing a tattered shift dress and a sunny disposition.

"Does this mean he's here?" she whispers over my shoulder. "The blind stable boy told me—"

I hush her. Mother summons. She doesn't explain. And Senenmut has been busy at Djeser-Djeseru all day, so I'm left to guess where Thutmose is now. Clearly Iset's guess is as good as mine. Who even knew we had a blind stable boy?

She falls silent. I pick up the pace and chant the words of this morning's ritual in my head, trying to summon the peace of the temple to ease my mounting unease.

A few footsteps later, the peace I've won is shattered.

"Neferura."

I halt my steps, blood running cold. It's been nearly five years since I last saw him, so of course he looks older, eyes like the night and skin as smooth as the sacred lake on a windless day. His black braids barely kiss his broad shoulders. He was shorter than me then, but now I have to tilt my head back to look up at him. Still young, but no longer the child I once loved.

"Thutmose." Stiff with emotion, I force myself to meet his gaze.

His eyes run down to my toes, then back up to my crooked nose. "A pleasure to see you looking so"—one side of his perfect lips quirks up—"sturdy."

I hate myself for the blush I feel creeping up my neck. It takes all the will I possess not to rearrange my dress or cover the flesh of my arms with my hands. I search for a clever retort, but all I can think is how I'd like to wipe that smirk off his face before curling up alone in my study, surrounded by papyrus and silence.

"You're really back," I say, settling for the obvious.

"I am."

"I hear you've been busy of late."

He grins. "Always. I have important work to do."

"Yes. I understand you're spending more time with the nobles. It seems you have a lot to say to them." I study Thutmose's face, hoping for some sign of discomfort.

His smile only grows wider. "That's a very small part of my workload, I assure you." His eyes glimmer in the torchlight. He's happy I know what he's been doing, pleased I'm bothered. He wants me to believe his moves against me go beyond what I've heard, which may be true, but I can't do anything about that now.

I force myself not to squirm. I hear Senenmut's words like he's standing next to me: *Try and make peace. He might surprise you.* I'm skeptical, but my tutor is wise; his advice is worth a try. After all, the path Thutmose and I are on now surely leads to no good.

I take a deep breath and make my best effort. "We are on the same side, you know. You as pharaoh, me as god's wife. Our responsibilities are similar."

"Are they?" He crosses his arms, resting his fingertips against the gold cuffs that ring his thick biceps, raising an eyebrow in mock surprise.

I bristle and my voice comes out hard. "We both serve the people. We're both chosen by the gods. We keep them appeased so the sun continues to rise and fall, the river irrigates the fields, the—"

"I know my responsibilities." His grin falters. "I don't need one of your lessons in piety."

"I'm not—"

"You are."

I sigh, twining my fingers behind my back. He may be right, but so am I. "I'm simply saying I'm ready to put the past behind us, to work together."

"How noble of you." He glances at the throne room door, secured by two guards at the end of the hall.

A group of nobles stands before it, drenched in pleated linen, their gold collars and bracelets glittering in the light of the lanterns that pepper the walls. They stare at us while pretending not to.

Thutmose leans into me; he's so close I smell the fish he had for lunch on his breath. "We've tried working together before. We failed."

"Not always." I hold his eyes, dredging up memories of a sweet little boy, nervously holding on to my hand as we stood side by side, staring up at Mother on her throne. We were so excited the first time she summoned us to the throne room, proud when she sat us down atop cold miniature thrones, leaving us to hear the made-up stories of palace workers who pretended to be angry spouses and wronged villagers and abused merchants. Thutmose and I listened to each one, deciding how each story put before us should be resolved. We returned money to a prostitute who had been robbed by a client, punished a man who tried to blame a servant for the death of his cow, and forced a man to return the dowry of his estranged wife. The day went on and on. And as royal children, we performed well. That is, until little Thutmose lost control and peed himself on the sacred seat. At the time, I felt awful for him, tried to protect him from Mother's wrath. It only made him angrier.

Thutmose drops his eyes, perhaps stung by the same memory, as I search for a hint of that hurt little boy. But the young man standing before me now is full of malice. It may be aimed at me and Mother, but my stomach churns thinking of the others who could be hurt if this enmity spills over. Not that Thutmose cares. He's reckless and negligent to the core.

"Together then?" He shifts his shoulder back and motions toward the throne room, the smirk back in position.

I swallow my rage and nod, then follow a step behind.

The throne room is not large, but it has a towering ceiling. The walls are painted with images of Mother. But instead of the woman

I know gracing the walls, she's portrayed with a false beard and a lean, masculine body, looking like every pharaoh who came before her. My real mother leans back against her intricately carved wooden throne, her faience-beaded tunic neatly arranged to hide the extra pounds she carries. Her gemstone-studded sandals rest on a carved limestone base that depicts Kemet's traditional enemies—Mother literally stomps our foes each time she sits her bottom on the throne.

I stand next to Thutmose on Mother's orders, a swarm of nobles crowded around us. She intends my position at his side as an insult. He outranks me. I should stand behind him if I must be here at all.

"Thutmose." She nods. "Welcome to court. It is always our pleasure to host the second royal child." Thutmose's eyes narrow at the barb as she continues, "It has been too long. Yet I do not recall summoning you."

Thutmose shrugs. "I don't recall being summoned."

Mother leans forward. "Well then, perhaps you can explain why you are here rather than training with the military in Men-nefer, where I sent you?"

"As a pharaoh, surely you know it is the pharaoh's job to inspect the court from time to time. I came to make sure my kingdom is running smoothly."

The crowd of nobles is silent as a tomb but Mother chuckles. "That is kind of you, child. I have everything in hand, as you must know. Men-nefer isn't so far away after all. The peace and prosperity I've established reach far beyond—"

"You must be referring to the prosperity my father established."

Mother settles back into her throne like she's readying to watch her favorite singer trill her best-loved songs. "It is true that, ruling by my side, your father made some progress. It is an honor to have made so much more since he passed. But of course"—she waves a bejeweled hand—"you are so young. Who can blame you for not knowing the many details one must master in order to lead the most powerful country in the world so successfully?"

Nobles stir. A few titters and one "hurrah" echo through the crowd. I'm stuck like a planted mushroom facing Mother. The fact that no one else can move either is some consolation. As long as Mother is talking, the court must be still and attentive.

"I'll happily return to Men-nefer, as soon as the country rights itself."

Mother's amusement is waning. "For now," she intones, "let us settle for righting you, shall we?"

I hold my breath, hoping she'll order him to leave court. From the hush that settles through the room, I'm not the only one waiting to see what she'll do next. Mother and Thutmose gaze at each other.

"I'm already righted." He shrugs.

That's a lie. Nothing has been righted. Indeed, the tension between Kemet's two pharaohs feels heavier than ever. I look away, longing for relief from their tedious griping, and my eyes land on a servant girl, dipping and weaving through the crowd. She looks light, her every step buoyant, especially compared to the rigid nobles she prances past. Her gauzy dress and even the beehive-shaped hat she wears—made of wax that douses her in sweet-smelling perfume as it melts—look weightless on her. This girl doesn't have to worry about power struggles and court intrigue. She can choose to ignore all that, knowing others fight those battles, if she gives it any thought at all. I wonder what it would be like to enjoy such expansive liberty.

It's enough to make me wonder if I've had it wrong all these years. Perhaps Amun doesn't favor me. Maybe he's saved his greatest gifts for girls like this light-footed servant with a wide mouth and eyes that sparkle with secrets, girls who can come and go as they like, girls who don't have every moment of their lives planned out and controlled by others, girls who will live and marry and bear children and work and die knowing at least some of their choices are their own rather than duties of their station. At a minimum, she has more power over her body and what she does with it than I ever will. On paper, I'm the most powerful girl in Kemet. Could the power she wields be more real than mine?

The girl flips her hair and I notice a small tattoo on her neck, just below her ear. I see a flash of a stinger, an armored body. A scorpion. The image brings to mind Iset's bracelet and the description of her mother as powerful. Is this what Iset meant? Was her mother like this girl, free and light? Or was there more to the power Iset described?

The girl wanders out of my view, and I imagine the freedom she must enjoy. I envision being in her lithe body. I go with her as she weaves through the crowd and out a narrow side door that leads to the kitchen. I visualize traveling the halls without drawing a single glance. I stroll outside and take off my shoes, walking through warm sand with bare feet. I head for the market where my fingers slide over rough textiles and my tongue lingers on coarse foods loaded with spices. A boy—he looks suspiciously like Kamut—flirts with me, and I let him hold my hand. He points toward a tent with suggestive eyes. I pull my hand away, suddenly shy, but he—

"Neferura."

Mother's voice sinks into me like a snakebite, snapping me back to reality. Her assembly has ended, and Thutmose has vanished. Nobles now talk in small groups, buzzing about today's barely shielded confrontation. I wish I knew who among them was swayed by Thutmose's whisperings, enthralled by his novel presence at court. I make a note to ask Senenmut later as I make my way to

Mother. I attempt to replicate the servant girl's lightness, lifting my legs delicately, stepping softly on my toes, but my feet are as heavy as my heart.

"Mother."

She motions me closer, and I lean in.

"Stay away from him," she warns.

I meet her eyes, weighing my words. I decide on honesty. "He's trying to poison the nobles against me. Do you expect me to do nothing?"

"I expect you to focus on your duties. I expect you to serve the god. And the people. And above all, me. Thutmose is only aiming at you because he doesn't have the strength to come at me. Let me handle him."

I pause, a shiver running up my spine at her words. I want to ask what she intends to do, how she plans to stop him from taking the power that is, if we're honest, rightly his. He is a pharaoh too, chosen by the gods just like Mother. She can't keep him from power much longer. Once he has it, he'll use it against me, against us. What can she do to stop that?

But nobles are swarming, some inching closer, hoping to earn Mother's attention. This is not the time or place. So I nod my agreement and retreat, happy for Iset's presence at my back as I rush toward the tranquility of my quarters, wondering all the while if I simply imagined the wicked gleam in Mother's eye.

THREE

OTHER'S PRIMARY PALACE SHIMMERS UNDER A SCORCH-
ing sun. Bright white with high windows designed to
catch the breeze, the entire complex faces the palm tree–
lined river, Iteru, which flows into Kemet through Kush and the
lands beyond, leaping over the cataracts to wind its way past the
palace, eventually emptying into Wadj-wer, the great green sea. The
palace's three levels are each brightly painted with the colorful flora
and fauna sprawled out below. I've gathered five of my priestesses on
the large, third-floor deck, just above my quarters. We sit in a circle,
shaded by tall blue-and-red-striped pillars, while servants attempt to
alleviate the day's heat by waving ostrich-feather fans. Guards hold
attention at every entryway, while others grapple and squirm in the
practice yard that abuts the river.

Iset stands apart, leaning over the rail to watch men swing and
shout and wrestle in the yard. Her back is to me and my priestesses
as she stares down at Thutmose and the retinue of young men who
followed him from Men-nefer. Usually, I host the five priestesses who
help me lead the troupe on my deck when they visit the palace, but

I wanted to keep an eye on Thutmose today. So we're gathered here, where the view from the palace's highest wall is most expansive.

I'd like to join my handmaid so I could watch Thutmose myself, but there's work to be done, so I sit with the priestesses, hoping Iset's penchant for chatter means she'll share anything interesting that happens later. Not that giving my troupe leaders an update on goods expected to spill into our coffers from abroad is boring, exactly. Resins and lapis from distant lands are scheduled to reach Kemet next week, riches that will be added to the revenue from my estate's production of honey, oils, grain, and beer. Nebtah, who was not born to a family with roots in the priesthood like most of the other leaders, wants to use a portion of the profits to increase the royal herd.

"Slaughtering a few more cows a day won't hurt." Nebtah's argument pulls my attention back to the matter at hand. "It will provide more food—"

"Of course. See to it," I agree, cutting her off before she launches into a new diatribe. I'm sick of talking about bloody cows. I turn to the other women. "And the new priestesses? Any problems to report?"

One by one, the troupe leaders fill me in on the recent additions. Following in Mother's footsteps, I'm determined to give more women roles in the priesthood. Providing the women of Kemet with more resources and status in the court and country is one of my favorite parts of the job, though some say Mother and I only advance them to curry favor. But what's wrong with solidifying loyalty to the royal family while we're growing the ranks of the well employed? Plus, the priestesses share my passion for Amun and the people of Kemet. I trust them. And in a court teeming with intrigue, that's not nothing.

As Satiah, Nebtah's dearest friends and the only other troupe leader who doesn't come from a family of priests, begins entertaining the group with the not-so-pious antics of her favorite new priestess, Iset clears her throat, catching my attention. Curious, I excuse myself, weave past servants and their enormous fans, and join my handmaid to stare down at the yard.

Below, a man just older than Thutmose—a man who appears more scribe than soldier with a wiry frame and a scribal kit tucked under his arm—talks animatedly to my half brother. I watch the exchange before Thutmose turns his head, eyes trained directly up at my quarters.

I press a hand to my stomach, willing away the nerves.

"I think they're talking about you," Iset whispers. "That man just handed Thutmose a scroll. He read it, and now he keeps looking up at your deck."

"Who is the scrawny one?"

I wince at Satiah's voice. I didn't realize she'd left the others to stand next to me.

Iset and I ignore her, keeping our eyes aimed at Thutmose as he walks away from the young man to disappear beneath the palace balconies. The man wanders toward the river. He doesn't leave, just sits cross-legged and watches as a skiff carrying a lonely fisherman floats past.

"I've seen him before. He's a scribe in the House of Life," Iset answers. "I don't know what he said to…Pharaoh," she says, the word sounding like a curse on her tongue. "But they were talking about you, Mistress. I know it. You saw him look up at your quarters, right?"

I shake my head, processing.

"Why is that interesting?" Satiah watches the scribe, who has no idea he's under surveillance. "You're the god's wife of Amun, king's eldest daughter, lady of Upper and Lower Kemet, mistress of the Two Lands. Don't people talk about you all the time?"

She's right. There are a million things that young man could have said to Thutmose, most of them innocuous and none of my concern. Yet…

"I'm sorry." Satiah takes a step back. "I'm overstepping here. I was simply curious, but this is none of my business. I'll go back—"

"Wait." The word slips out before the plan in my mind crystallizes. Satiah happens to be the most stunning woman I've ever laid eyes on, with flawless skin, pouty lips, and large bright eyes. Even in her plain white priestess robes, she's a striking figure. She's as kind as she is beautiful, spending most of her free time caring for the orphans of Waset. I also know she's much cannier than most give her credit for. I've watched her deploy her beauty to move men and women alike, and she once told me she has no qualms using her appearance to her advantage. I look at her now, feeling a flicker of hesitation within, then I let out a sigh. "Never mind, Satiah. Please return to the others—"

"No, wait." Iset sets her hand on my arm, and I'm certain the plot my handmaiden mulls matches mine.

A smile blooms on Satiah's lips. "Is there something I can help with? What's going on, exactly?"

Iset turns to me. "This woman could tempt sweet words from a tiger or I'm a dung beetle."

Satiah's grin grows wider. "I do excel at tempting tigers." She looks down at the man. "Do we need to know what that man said to the little pharaoh?"

I examine Satiah, grinning at the use of *little pharaoh* before wondering if the connection to Thutmose will scare her off.

She reads the thought behind my eyes and shrugs. Satiah is the first to raise her voice when she disagrees with me. She's proven again and again that she's not intimidated by royals.

"I would like to know what he said to Thutmose," I admit. "But truly, Satiah, this is not your responsibility—"

"I'll do it." She nods happily. "But I need Nebtah and the others to join me to make our outing convincing. If we go now, we can be back soon. I can't promise to return with the information, but the odds of my success are good." Her perfectly arched brow inches up, confidence oozing off her.

Moments later, I've agreed, and the priestesses have made their way down to wander past the practice yard. Men turn to watch them as the women strike up a conversation with a gaggle of guards. Satiah peels off from the others and approaches the scribe. Soon enough, she's seated next to him, talking animatedly. She laughs and tosses her hair, then turns serious, resting a hand on his arm to whisper low as she leans in close.

"Poor man," Iset chuckles. "He's like clay on Khnum's wheel."

I nod absently. I should feel guilty for using Satiah like this. Instead, I'm captivated by her power. It's not her beauty that interests me but the skillful way she puts it to work for her. If she doesn't mind, I suppose I won't either. After all, Thutmose did insinuate that he's been up to more than whining about my estate to every noble who will listen. I have no idea what he meant—it's entirely possible he was simply trying to provoke me—but if there's more to his threat and this scribe is involved, perhaps I can learn more.

Too anxious to watch, I turn to pace, wondering how many ways personal characteristics can be harnessed to advance one's objectives. Kemet, it seems, is full of invisible powers. I crisscross the deck a few times, thinking and worrying, and suddenly the priestesses are back, cackling, a flushed Satiah in the center of the throng.

"Success," she crows.

32

The four priestesses return to the chaises they occupied earlier while Nebtah summons the servants, and soon enough, they're sipping honeyed wine and being fanned by servant girls, trilling with the adventure of it all.

Satiah joins me and Iset near the rail. She leans close so only the two of us can hear. "He was sweet. Nebwawi." She swirls his name around her mouth like she can taste it. "He's young. He's a simple scribe. He received anonymous instructions and a payment at the House of Life. He took the job because he wanted Thutmose to see him—he had hopes that it would lead to some improvement in his status. Apparently the little pharaoh wasn't unduly impressed with him, but Nebwawi did have the sense that Thutmose was pleased by the message."

"Did the scribe read it? Does he know who sent it."

"Yes and no. The letter didn't name the sender, and he didn't meet the addresser. Another scribe transferred it to him, and Nebwawi knew nothing about the original author. But he did read it." Satiah flashes a catlike smile. "He's a curious sort."

My breath catches. "You know what it said."

"The exact words—he memorized it, since it was destined for the ears of a mighty pharaoh and all—were, 'I almost have him convinced. He fears it would ruin her, but I'm certain he'll do it soon. I'll meet you in your quarters after sun fall tomorrow night.'"

My skin buzzes as I run the words through my mind. *Ruin her.* It refers to me, certainly. But how?

"Is that helpful? Can I do anything else for you, Adoratrice?" Satiah bites her lip. Surely she knows I'm the "her" the note refers to.

"You've done more than I should have asked you to do already." I put a hand on her shoulder. "Thank you, Satiah. I hope you didn't have to promise anything…"

Her grin is naughty. "I promised nothing. And truly, if I had, that would be fine too. I wouldn't have offered anything I haven't done before and nothing I don't enjoy. I'm honored to serve. In fact, if you ever need me again, please don't hesitate to ask."

She bows, that small smile still lit across her face, and returns to the others.

I turn toward the river, watching a heron skim the surface. "We need to know who visits Thutmose's quarters tomorrow night," I whisper.

"Or better," Iset, still at my side, retorts. "We need to know what is said inside them."

"Are you sure about this?" I examine the servant's clothes Iset hands me, surprised by the linen's rough texture.

She pulls her braids under a cloth cap, looking uncertain. When she finally speaks, her response is unconvincing. "Yes?" She grimaces, then nods. "I'm sure servants sometimes gather outside Thutmose's quarters. They've been empty for so long, and it's on the back side of the palace with a view of old rocks, so it's private." She shakes her head, and a long black braid falls loose. "I'm not an expert on disguising princesses, but who is going to be looking for you dressed in this?" She holds up a plain servant's smock. "Once we're free of your quarters, we should be left alone. There's a hidden spot just below his windows." She shakes out the dingy tunic and glances up at me. "Do you think this is a bad idea?"

"Terrible," I say, wrenching the material over my head.

"What if I go and you stay? I am a servant. If I get caught, I'll play dumb, act like I've sat there before, like it's a thing I do, even if no one has noticed."

"You're my royal handmaid. People watch you wherever you go."

"Not disguised like a kitchen maid."

"When is the last time you wore something like that?" I point at the headcloth covering her small shiny braids.

A smile spreads across her face. "Three years, two months, and six days ago."

I grin at the mention of our first day together, suddenly aware of how different Iset's life might be if she were not in this station. And conversely, how different mine would be if one of Mother's old noblewomen still served as my handmaid, with loyalty only to Mother. The same person who just warned me to stay away from Thutmose.

I turn the what-ifs over in my mind. Maybe I should let Iset go alone, or, wiser still, take Mother's advice and keep myself and my handmaid away from Thutmose altogether. But how can I protect what I've built if I don't know what Thutmose is up to?

"I'm coming," I say. "But I do hate putting you in danger. And Kamut."

"Don't be. He's as anxious to help as I am. He swapped with the guard who was on tonight's schedule to be at your door when we leave. He did threaten me though." She flashes a lopsided grin. "I will be in danger if something bad happens to you. That threat comes directly from Kamut. But with my promise to keep you safe and bring you back soon, he's fine letting us slip out."

Kamut's involvement doubles my trepidation. "If I get caught, the two of you will pay the price."

"Well then." Iset pulls the tunic down over her body. "Let's not get caught."

I follow Iset out, past Kamut, who ignores us as if we truly are the lowly servants whose garments we wear. We weave through the mazelike servants' halls, heart hammering with every step. I haven't walked these plain, undecorated passageways since I was a child. I think of the servant girl flitting through the throne room, that tattoo behind her ear. Does she walk this way? What secrets might she glean as she glides through these halls, light and invisible?

My musings accompany me until we reach the back of the palace, and I inhale sharply as we pass the large pool bordered by palm trees, then slip by a small group of laughing servants hidden just beyond the tree line. They pay us no heed as we tiptoe to Thutmose's receiving room window. He has the only bad view in the royal wing. A gift from Mother, who has never once passed up an opportunity to punish him for existing. The window is open. It's so close I could touch it from where we finally perch on two gray boulders.

"I don't hear anything," Iset whispers.

I shush her, then close my eyes and concentrate. Thutmose is inside. I know it. I can barely make out his low hum over the distant chatter of servants and the chittering of insects. But it's enough to confirm he's alone, and better, confirm we'll hear him once he's not.

The wait is painful. The boulder is hard and unforgiving beneath me, and my knees groan from crouching in this uncomfortable position. Slowly the group of servants disbands, their laughter fading with the sun's rays. The purr of the river and low hum of insects lull us into a stupor. The sun's light is nearly gone when new noises from the other side of the window finally trickle out. Iset sits taller, stiff as a mast. I squeeze my hands into fists, heart banging so hard I'm worried I won't hear the visitor. In the end, it's not my heartbeat so much as her voice that proves challenging—its pitch too soft to glean anything beyond the fact that whoever has arrived in his quarters is a woman.

I close my eyes, straining to hear, catching bits and pieces of Thutmose's response. "...she mixed...must be certain...find...tell him...write...witness."

Then her unintelligible whispered response.

Finally, Thutmose raises his voice. A few clear words ring out, bringing everything to a halt.

"She poisoned my father. That old hag..."

Poisoned Father.

Old hag.

I hiss. Thutmose has called Mother old hag since we were children. But would he truly dare accuse Mother of murdering our father?

My heart sinks.

What if the note wasn't about ruining me? What if he's gunning for Mother, for the throne itself?

I push my hand against my chest, trying to still my pounding heart. It's one thing to fight for his share of power. It's another thing entirely to attempt to dethrone Mother. Thutmose must know any effort to do so would tear the country apart.

Iset sets a hand on my trembling knee. She motions for us to leave, eyes round as the full moon. She's right. We should go, but I don't trust my body to budge without my clumsiness alerting Thutmose we're here. I'm taut with shock, immobilized by dread.

Accusing Mother of murder would be a staggering plot. Mother's heart would be as heavy as an obelisk if she was guilty of such an offense. But of course she's not. No one in Kemet believes in the sacredness of pharaonic rule more than Mother. Besides, if Father died of poison, rumors would echo through the court to this day.

If I haven't heard such tales, how could Thutmose, who grew up far from court and was a mere child when Father died? Thutmose can't possibly remember him; even I have only vague memories of a weak and sickly man. Mostly I remember his pockmarked skin and his breath, so putrid no amount of resin could cover the stench. And of course, I remember the hours I spent comforting Thutmose in the days after Father's death, when the court was filled with whispers. The few tears that were shed reflected not love but the fears of nobles worried about being displaced if an unfriendly family came to power.

Iset pulls at my hand, pointing back toward my quarters.

I'm about to give in and tiptoe away when Thutmose's footsteps draw close. I hold my breath and press my body against the wall. Iset stills next to me, hands slapped over her lips. He's just above us now. He's looking out his window. He must hold a lantern: light flickers on my skin. If he leans forward, he'll see us. I keep my eyes shut tight. When he speaks, his words are as clear as the pyramids on a windless day.

"I need the wisewoman. She's the key."

His footsteps move away, and Iset tugs my hand again, harder this time. Quietly, I stand, willing away the trembles. It doesn't work, but it's enough to get one foot moving, then another. Finally I curve behind a tree and look back, but I can't see Thutmose or his mysterious guest through the window.

If it weren't for Iset, I'm not sure I could find my way to my quarters. But we make it, unspotted, and even in my confused state, I notice Kamut sag in relief as we slip past him and back into my rooms, where I strip off the servants' clothes and step into my bathroom to douse my burning head in cool water, reliving the sharpness of Thutmose's words and trembling at the chaos they herald.

"You think he was accusing your mother? You don't think she really…" Iset pauses, eyes wide.

The moon still creeps across the sky, but sleep is impossible, the events of the evening too heavy on my mind. I slump at my desk, watching Iset shove the servants' clothes we peeled off our bodies into a bag she'll throw away later.

"Mother would never," I vow. "If she were guilty of such an awful crime, the gods would have punished her by now. She wouldn't still be in their favor."

"Right," Iset says. "If one pharaoh accused the other of murdering a third, that would be bad, right?"

"Very bad." My stomach turns at the mere thought. "With a credible witness or some kind of evidence to back such an accusation up, the peaceful transition of power would turn to chaos. People would die, nobles and artisans and peasants alike. And I'd be…" I don't finish the sentence. Surely even Iset understands that if people were tricked into believing Mother murdered Father, I'd likely suffer for the crime along with Mother. Given Iset's position, she'd be lucky to escape such turmoil alive.

Iset thinks a heartbeat, then says, "You have to warn your mother."

I release a strangled laugh. "How? If I admit what we did, you'll be sent far away from court, and Kamut will be buried alive. I can't tell Mother what I know."

"So what are you going to do?"

"I must find a way to protect Mother from this lie before it spreads through the country. The truth is Father was weak. He died.

Mother stepped into the role since Thutmose was too young to rule, and by all accounts, Mother was wielding power in Father's name long before he passed."

"That may be true. But it doesn't mean Thutmose can't use the accusation against her. And you. You seem worried about some rumor that a few nobles like Thutmose more than you. Just wait until a woman is accused of stealing power through murder. I might not understand the nobles like you do, but I understand that."

I sigh, heavy with dread. My eyes find Iset's—she looks as anxious as I am, though I'm not sure why. "You don't have to be part of this, you know. I could help you find another position, perhaps even at court. You'd be wise to get away from me before things turn dangerous."

She crinkles her brow as she sinks into Senenmut's chair. "You can't believe I'd abandon you now when you might finally need me for more than just braiding your hair? Mistress, I…" She pauses, eyes roaming over my face like she's seeing me for the first time. "I know my place."

My bark of laughter surprises me as much as her. Just sitting in that chair breaks protocol. She smiles at my amazement, and I grin back.

"I do," she insists. "But being your servant doesn't mean I can't also be your friend. Before I came here, I was…alone. Always. Father is…" She stops to stare down at the bracelets that ring her wrist. She's wearing a dozen thin bracelets crafted of gold and turquoise and small beads, but only one bauble draws her thoughts. After a heartbeat, she looks up again. "What I'm trying to say is I think of you as my closest friend. I care about this because I care about you. But also, as you say, if things do go bad, everyone is at risk. So I'm not going anywhere. I'm here, and I'm going to help you figure this out."

I let my head fall back and stare up at my ceiling, blue with gold stars. The truth is, I may not say it aloud, but Iset has become a true and cherished friend in the years she's served me. Mother would lock Iset in a dungeon if she knew I thought of her as more than a handmaid. But I do. I suppose I've thought of her that way for some time. I don't want to send her away. But I don't want her to be in danger either. It's my duty to protect her, isn't it?

Inexplicably, the girl I watched wander through the throne room shimmers before my eyes. Perhaps I'm fooling myself. Maybe Iset doesn't need my protection any more than the light-footed servant girl does. Iset does more for me than I do for her. And I've no doubt the girl from the throne room is tougher than I am. She probably needs to be. Maybe she's like Iset's mother: poor but powerful. I wonder what she'd do if she were in my shoes. I close my eyes, imagining what it would be like to be her. If I were a girl who was free to move about without guards trailing me everywhere I go, and if I had the kind of power Iset claims her mother had, what would I do?

Finding no answers, I open my eyes and ask Iset, "What would your mother do in a situation like this? Not in this exact situation," I clarify. "But when your mother was in trouble, where did she turn?"

Iset fiddles with the scorpion amulet. "She turned to friends. She had a few close friends. They socialized with a larger group of women. They were always whispering and plotting and laughing. Those women were fierce. If Mother was in trouble, she'd lean on them. Together, they'd find a path forward."

I visualize Iset peering down into the yard yesterday morning, bringing me servant's clothes and convincing Kamut to help earlier today, sneaking around with me this evening even though it could cost her her livelihood. "Friends," I parrot.

"It's not like I'm your only friend," she says. "You have Senenmut. And that old noblewoman you linger near at court, Thuiu. And your priestesses. Satiah and Nebtah would do anything for you. The others are as loyal."

"Loyalty isn't the same as friendship," I say.

"Maybe." She shrugs. "But good friends are loyal. And you need loyal friends now."

I sigh, thinking through her words, then dredging up everything we heard Thutmose utter, working through the implications. "If Father was poisoned, people would gossip. The court would be blathering still. I need to find out if there really are rumors or if Thutmose invented them himself. And we need to figure out who sent Thutmose the letter. We could start with the scribe. His name was..."

"Nebwawi," Iset reminds me.

"Right. We need to talk to him. And who is this wisewoman Thutmose mentioned? He said she was the key. Maybe we can find out who she is. Surely people would whisper about a mysterious wisewoman lurking around the palace."

Iset nods. "People do like to talk. It's a good start. More knowledge is always good, no matter where it comes from. Doesn't that wise man you like so much say something like that?"

"Talk with the ignorant man as with the sage," I say, echoing Ptahhotep's words, learned on Senenmut's knee as a child. It's excellent advice. "Can you question the other servants? Find out what they know? Discreetly." I tap my fingers on my desk. "Kamut's brother is a scribe. He'd know this Nebwawi."

"Kamut also has more connections at court than I have. He's been here longer. If there've been rumors about your father or poison or an evil wisewoman, he'll know."

"I don't want to involve him any more than—"

"We're relying on your loyal friends now, remember? Besides, Kamut is a grown man. He can be the judge of which risks he's willing to take."

Before I can stop her, Iset jumps up and marches out of my study. I fly to my feet, strangling a cry when I stub my toe against my desk. By the time the pain dims, they're before me, Kamut standing behind Iset.

He stares at me.

And I stare back.

It's not the first time I've looked into Kamut's eyes, but we were children then. I can't recall if they were dark and dreamy years ago, though I've often imagined them as such. But I do know that no one could have misinterpreted our relationship back then, young as we were. Kamut was in no danger. Standing in my quarters now, in the middle of the night, is reckless.

I search for words, finally managing, "This is dangerous."

"Well then, maybe I should sit for it?" He waits for my nod, then perches stiffly, eyes shifting from Iset to me and back.

My stomach roils. This is the second risk Kamut has taken on my behalf today. If someone happens by and finds my door unattended, he'll be fired before the sun rises. Put to death if Mother discovers he's inside my rooms. I should order him to leave, warn him never to enter my rooms again. But I can't find it in me. We were never friends, exactly. Our stations didn't allow that. But he was the closest thing to a friend Thutmose and I had growing up. And of course, he's starred in my dreams and every one of my fantasies for years now. I blush at the thought and lower myself back into the chair facing him.

"Thank you for helping us today. We couldn't have done it without you."

"I'm here to serve you." His eye contact is bold but welcome as he adds, "little princess."

The old nickname makes me grin. Kamut's father was the court sword master. I spent countless hours watching him order Kamut and Thutmose around. He always referred to us as the little prince and princess. Kamut followed suit until Thutmose threw a fit, insisting Kamut address him by his proper titles: good king of Upper and Lower Kemet, the lasting one of Ra's manifestation, image of Amun, king's eldest son... Kamut used them all, feigning innocence when Thutmose complained about that too.

"I haven't heard that nickname in years." I don't look away. I should. But I don't. "I am sorry about your father."

He drops his eyes. "Thank you. We're adjusting to the loss. It's been just over a year. The funerary gifts you sent made his death more manageable. Thank you for that."

I nod, forcing my body to stay still. My skin is hot and tingly. But in spite of my misgivings, Kamut is here now, and he may know something. Best I make this risk worthwhile. "Speaking of fathers, have you ever heard rumors about...about my father's death? Any suspicion that it was...unnatural?"

His eyes crinkle in confusion, and he shakes his head. "Never. Why do you ask? That was so long ago..." He pauses, then sags. "Ah, I see." He doesn't name Thutmose. He doesn't have to. I've always suspected Kamut saw the truth I avoided long before I did.

Kamut's father often pitted Thutmose and Kamut against each other as children. Kamut was older and stronger, but Thutmose was always wily. An awkward moment passes as if Kamut is thinking of the many battles he lost to my smaller half brother before he continues.

"I've never heard a single rumor of your father's passing. He died naturally, and everyone knows that. Whatever you've been told to the contrary…" He takes a moment, choosing his words carefully. He can't speak ill of a pharaoh, even a powerless second pharaoh. "Well," Kamut adds, "I wouldn't lose sleep over it."

I unclench. Thutmose must be making up stories. If only I knew who was whispering in his ear. The girl I heard in Thutmose's rooms is our only clue, and the scribe is our one path to her. "There's a scribe in the House of Life," I continue. "His name is Nebwawi. Have you heard of him?"

"No, but my brother would know him. Why?"

"I'd like to talk to him. Discreetly. Could you ask your brother to find out if Nebwawi is willing to meet me? If he's trustworthy, would you help me arrange a time? You can bribe him if it helps. I'll find him a position in my estate, some kind of promotion to buy his cooperation."

Kamut nods. "My brother is away on scribal duties for a few days, perhaps longer. I can ask when he returns. Or I can talk to another scribe friend—"

"That's soon enough. Let's keep this between you and your brother. I trust you both." I lean back against my chair, lingering on the last thread I overheard from Thutmose's window. "Have you ever heard whispers of a wisewoman at court? I believe she would have been around late in my father's life. If she exists at all."

The question lands. I can tell by the way his jaw tenses. Apparently my hours of dreaming about Kamut's face have made me an expert in his expressions.

"So it is true," I press. "There was a wisewoman?"

"Your grandmother's wisewoman was here when your father passed. She was rumored to be skilled at many things."

I lean forward, anticipation coursing through my body. "What kinds of things?"

Kamut sighs, a nervous edge to his voice. "Some say healing, some say poison. She was a…mysterious figure."

My stomach plummets and I squeeze my hands into tight fists. "She used poison? At court?"

He shrugs. "I'm not sure about that. I know she was feared and respected. I was a child. I don't know much about her, although I know my father studiously avoided her. He always seemed a bit superstitious about her. If she truly was poisoning people, well, I couldn't say."

I sigh. I want more, but the last thing I should be doing is putting Kamut at risk a moment longer than I must. Besides, he's told me all he can. "You should go."

He pauses, watching me. "Are you sure? Is there anything else I can do?"

I shake my head. "I fear I'm pushing my luck today. It's been quite an adventure already. I don't want you to get caught. Go now."

He stands, nods, and turns to go.

"And, Kamut."

He turns back.

Our eyes meet and the world slows down. A flush creeps up my neck, so I drop my eyes, utter a thank-you, and let my head fall into my hands as he leaves, wondering if Kamut will ever have cause to enter my quarters again and how I'm going to learn more about Grandmother's wisewoman.

I turn to Iset as Kamut disappears through my study door. "You know what this means?"

She nods, tight with tension. "Thutmose thinks your mother used this wisewoman to…to…"

"To poison my father," I finish. "It's up to us to uncover the truth before Thutmose finds a way to make this lie stick."

46

FOUR

RE YOU READY TO SEE THE SURPRISE?" SENENMUT ASKS AS HE leads me through the palace hallway, Iset on our heels.

"I am."

It makes Senenmut happy to plan surprises, and his revelations rarely disappoint. Sometimes my favorite treats sit waiting for me when I return from temple early in the morning. He's surprised me with amulets that hide small bits of papyrus inside them. Their sacred signs spell out my favorite maxims, or the tiny, beautifully decorated scrolls explain a dream I had or offer a well-timed blessing. He once sent me on a treasure hunt using clues from a story I adore, the battle of Horus and Set. At the end, I found a golden collar I treasure to this day. The nefer symbol, the heart and trachea, the root of my name, which means good or beautiful, repeats itself again and again in thick rows. It fits my neck perfectly. I wear it on days when I need an extra dose of confidence.

But today I asked Senenmut to meet me so I can question him about Grandmother's old wisewoman. He showed up at my quarters happy and anxious, chattering about his latest surprise.

At least it's just the three of us so I can mine him for information. I assume.

"Mother isn't joining us, is she?"

"Pharaoh is meeting with the high priest. There's an uproar regarding an errant priest and some missing gold."

"Sounds dramatic. Has she seen the surprise?"

Senenmut turns to me, eyebrows jiggling humorously. "Pharaoh sees all, dear one." His smile widens. "We're here." He pushes open a cedar door, ushering me and Iset into a small room off the forecourt. The door shuts with a clunk behind us.

The sight that greets me triggers a smile that seeps into my heart. It's a new statue of me as a child on Senenmut's lap, head poking up through his cloak so that the top of my royal headdress rests comfortably under his chin. It's endearing but hardly unexpected. Senenmut has loads of statues depicting him as my protector. They're housed in temples throughout Kemet so that we're constantly dedicating ourselves to the gods. He even had a stele of the two of us erected as far off as the mining camp at Biau, where it sits in the temple erected to honor the goddess Hathor.

My tutor is famous for many things, but his innovative statuary tops the list. Breaking with tradition, placing statues in forms never before seen along temple processional ways, comes as naturally to Senenmut as breath to the living. He must have more statues of himself carved and strategically placed throughout the country than any man before him.

His statues of the two of us are my favorites. Some whisper that I should be offended. They say he uses me because my position boosts his. There's no denying the truth of that. No man is above ambition, certainly not my tutor, who clawed himself from humble beginnings to the top of elite society. Why should that mean they're not also a genuine reflection of our close relationship?

Of course, displays like the one before me, carved in smooth, gray stone, do nothing to stop the gossip that I'm the child of Senenmut's body. I've never given the whispers much thought. But now, staring at the sculpture's smooth curves, a thought comes unbidden. What if Mother isn't the woman I've always believed her to be? What if she's the evil ruler of Thutmose's imaginings? Could she have done the unthinkable to pull herself onto the throne? If so, could Senenmut be...

No. I shake away the doubts Thutmose's vile accusation has planted in my heart. I can't validate the chatter of idiots. *Mother didn't murder Father or cheat on him*, I tell myself as I wind my way around the statue, admiring it from every angle.

"You look tired." Senenmut examines me as if I'm a statue on display.

"Do I?" It's hardly a surprise—I barely slept last night. "I had a long night," I admit.

He leans closer and drops his voice. "You're not still worrying about Thutmose, are you? I told you. The nobles will not be swayed. And your mother is making plans for him."

My ears perk at this, dread pooling somewhere deep inside, the question again vibrating through me: what is Mother capable of? "What plans?" I ask quietly.

He ignores the question and rests his hand against my cheek. "Everything will be fine, dear one. But you need your sleep. Your headrest is inscribed with the proper spells, yes?"

"Of course," I promise. My headrest is carved of acacia. It's covered in protection symbols, and an inscription ensuring my dreams are peaceful runs its length. It works fine. Usually.

"Are you dreaming?" He wears the same look he has when considering a troublesome passage in some text we're worrying over. "Have you been bitten by a dog or seen yourself in a mirror in your dreams?"

I grin at that. Senenmut and I studied the dream scrolls diligently when I was younger. The topic fascinates me. I love the straightforward explanations they offer. Like if a man sees himself looking into a well, it's bad and means he'll go to prison. Or if a man sees himself in mourning, it's good and means his possessions will increase. But the answers I seek aren't found in a scroll.

I shake my head. "None of my dreams are worth sharing."

"Well," he says as he crosses his arms, "I'll send chamomile to be taken this evening with honey. If that doesn't do the trick, the doctor will know incantations that might help. If you dream of anything odd, you must tell me. You understand?"

I promise to do as bid and steer us toward the subject I really want to discuss. "The subject of dreams reminds me—I've been meaning to ask you about Grandmother's old wisewoman."

Senenmut's eyebrows inch up. "You've heard tale of your grandmother's tattooed wisewoman, have you?"

"Tattooed?" Visions of a woman covered in tattoos, dark ink swirling around her arms and legs, covering her from head to toe, erupt before my eyes. Schooling my face, I shake my head. "I had not heard of her tattoos, no. Only that Grandmother employed a powerful wisewoman. Can you tell me about her?"

He closes his eyes like he's summoning up the memory of her face. "The wisewoman and your grandmother, Ahmose, were close. The wisewoman was lowborn, perhaps even more lowborn than me. But she was also—aside from your mother and grandmother—the most powerful person I've ever known. She was living proof that one's knowledge can trump one's sex and birth." A hint of reverence thrums in his voice, perhaps appreciation for another who pulled herself up from humble beginnings like he did.

"What was so powerful about her?" I edge closer to him, eager for more. Imagining another woman with the grit and potency of Mother and Grandmother feels sacrilegious. Knowing she was born a peasant makes me wonder again if there are powers in the world I've ignored, so focused have I been on gods and royals.

Senenmut taps his chest, just above the heart. "Knowledge. Education. Secrets. She always knew more than everyone else in a room. And she knew how to use the knowledge she hoarded to advance her agenda."

"What was her agenda?"

He grimaces. "That's a very good question. I wish I was sure of the answer. What I do know is that the wisewoman could turn the tides in whatever direction she wanted. If she was on your side, good things tended to happen. If not..." He trails off.

"Was she...bad?" I ask.

He narrows his eyes but doesn't answer. I search Senenmut's face, wondering if he's heard darker tales of this woman. Perhaps even that she poisoned my father, at Mother's behest no less. I wait for him to say more, but when he doesn't go on, I give up on the wisewoman's motivations and ask what exactly she knew so much about.

"Medicine. The gods. Spells. Above all, she understood people. She was, unofficially, the court doctor and magician. Incidentally, you may not want to mention tattoos to Inhapi unless you want to cause the poor doctor discomfort." Senenmut smirks. "The tattooed woman was more capable than our good doctor—she lived in his quarters during your grandmother's years, actually. And beyond her considerable skills, she had access to something mysterious that amplified her power."

"What was that?" I twine my fingers together, hoping to mask my impatience.

"I'm not sure. A tool of some sort. She called it her scorpions."

"Scorpions?" My skin prickles. It's as if the god is trying to tell me something—something that has to do with scorpions. The treacherous little creatures are suddenly everywhere. "What does that mean?"

"No idea." Senenmut pushes himself away from the pillar, then trails his hand over the statue of us. "Whatever it was, it helped her solidify her power and expanded her knowledge. Hathor knew more about what happened at court than anyone else here, so the rumors say."

"Hathor." The wisewoman has a name. I wait a moment, the information arranging itself in my head, before asking, "What happened to her?"

Senenmut sighs. "She vanished," he says after a beat. "Why are you interested in her?"

I shrug, but my insides squirm. I'm not accustomed to lying to my tutor. "Just curious."

"Well, be careful with your curiosity," he warns. "It can be dangerous. Now is not the time for risk-taking, especially with Thutmose at court. You are steering clear of him?"

"He's a snake," I hiss.

Senenmut shrugs. "Snakes bite, dear one, especially if they believe they're cornered."

Hoping to lead us back to safe territory, I turn back to the statue. "You should pay the artists a little extra."

"For what?" His smile creeps into to his eyes.

"For capturing our bond so faithfully." I cringe as I say it, embarrassed by the sentiment, but Senenmut just laughs and agrees to increase the artist's fee, his hand reassuring on my shoulder.

The hum of Iset's feet brushing against the stone floors thunders in my ears. This is the third time in my life I've crept through the palace like a thief, the second time this week alone.

The first time was with Thutmose. Once, when we were children, he insisted on sneaking into the kitchen to steal sweets. It was ridiculous—they were his for the asking. But I was desperate back then to keep him happy, believing we'd one day serve side by side. The adventure ended fine—he got his treats and we got away clean—until I learned later that a servant girl was blamed for our crime. I felt awful. I begged him to confess and save the girl. He refused. Thutmose was always careless about other people. And I was too worried about crossing him to confess without his agreement. I never did learn who she was, but I know she was whipped. She's probably wearing scars still today. I've lived with the guilt of not stepping forward ever since. And here I am now, adding more sins to my heart, rendering it even heavier. I can practically hear the Devourer gnashing her teeth, and a shiver runs up my spine.

"We shouldn't be doing this," I whisper to Iset, even though visiting the doctor's quarters, where the old wisewoman once lived, was my idea. Now, in the tightness of the plain corridors, I'm second-guessing myself.

"Of course we should," Iset argues. "More information is good, right? It's like those texts you read. You don't know what you're going to learn until you roll the scroll open and read it. But sometimes to learn more, you have to put down the scrolls and actually do things."

"I do things," I argue.

"Rituals don't count."

I grunt, annoyed, mostly because I suspect she's right. Perhaps a life confined to my small zones in the palace and temple has limited me in ways I haven't quite understood. I'm considering the implications when we reach a hall running perpendicular to the one we're in. I spot a cedar door on the left, distinguished from the other doors by the large lock appended to it. According to the old kitchen maid Iset questioned this morning, the doctor's door is the only one with a lock. I put my hands on the carved wood, envisioning a woman covered in tattoos coming and going from this room.

"Knock," Iset prompts.

Bang, bang, bang. I act without hesitation. If I hesitate, I might change my mind and make a more responsible decision.

I'm not sure if I'm relieved or disappointed when we're met by silence.

"Try again," Iset says. "Mistress," she adds, as if the honorary, a shortened form of one of my more prestigious titles, mistress of the Two Lands, will somehow render our behavior appropriate.

When a second effort brings no response, I consider turning back. I'm not sure what I hope to find in the rooms the old wisewoman abandoned more than a decade ago anyway. I doubt she left a confession inside. And Senenmut said the doctor is cagey about the wisewoman. It's unlikely Inhapi will help us. Still, this is the lead we've got. And I have to do something.

"Now what?" Iset glances back down the hall we just tread.

I ignore the question, unsure of the answer. But we've come this far. If I'm going to unravel this mystery, I can't give up at the first sign of resistance.

I fiddle with the enormous lock. I've seen every type of lock imaginable. My tutor has a passion for mechanisms—a passion he's shared by bringing me boxes with hidden compartments and containers that spring open when you trigger a secret latch. Even the seal ring he wears has a secret interior. The variety of tricks and traps enjoyed by Senenmut is endless.

"Can you open it?" Iset whispers.

"Not without the key," I say and pout, staring at the rectangular, wooden lock. I tug the pinlock's latch and gasp in surprise when the door opens with a click.

"You did it," Iset squeals.

My stomach squirms. Dropping by the doctor's quarters unexpected is one thing. Breaking into his rooms is something else. "We can't just walk in uninvited," I whisper even as I push the door open.

"Great holy goddess." Iset's face is lit by the alabaster lamp she holds high.

We stand side by side, staring up at the vast shelves that cover the entire wall, from floor to ceiling, stretching the length of the room. There must be hundreds of small nooks and crannies bursting with thick glass jars, alabaster vases, and ointment jars shaped like amphorae and pitchers, some with handles—one or two—and others without. There are pottery vases shaped like women and monkeys and fish and scribes. Dried plants hang from hooks dangling from cubby holes and the ceiling.

I step into the room—I need to get closer—and feel Iset just behind me. I flinch when the door shuts with a faint thud.

"These must be Hathor's ingredients," I mutter.

"How do you know they're not Inhapi's?" she whispers back.

I shake my head. Inhapi is conventional and common. This collection is anything but. The room reeks of forgotten spells and guarded secrets. Literally. I smells herbs and... I sniff, trying to place the competing scents, both familiar and unfamiliar to my nose. I'm momentarily overwhelmed, taking in the mix of herb and smoke, flower and brine. The dim lighting from Iset's lantern casts an eerie light on the shelves. The jars and containers squirm like they're full of living things, wriggling to be free.

"It's a good place to keep poison." Iset tiptoes across the room to pluck a small glass jar from a tall, thin compartment. She pulls off the top and sticks it to her nose.

"Stop," I warn. "You may be sniffing poison right now for all we know."

She wrenches the jar away from her face and stares at it like spiders are crawling beneath the lid before placing it back in its spot.

I move closer to examine vessel after vessel, my fingers trailing over the shelves. I pick up an alabaster jar for inspection, then make an effort to set it back as it was to hide the dust-free circle its absence left. They're all old—they look like they haven't been touched or moved in years. I pick up another to read the inscription, then notice a symbol inscribed on the bottom of the small glass jar. I look closer, peering at the curved outline, the pointy end.

"More scorpions." I show it to Iset.

She shrugs. "Maybe she used scorpions in her potions."

"Maybe." My mind turns back to Senenmut's words about Hathor's power. A tool of some sort. She called it her scorpions. Could this be what he meant? "Maybe these potions *are* her scorpions."

Iset chews her bottom lip, thinking, as I lift another, then another. We find a few more containers marked by scorpions, but most are unmarked.

"Whatever she called her concoctions, it's safe to assume the woman who stocked these shelves had the ability to mix whatever potion she chose," I admit.

"That doesn't mean she poisoned your father," Iset argues.

"No," I agree. "It doesn't. We're no further than we were before. We need more." I twirl in place, searching for something that could shed light on the mysterious woman and her enigmatic pursuits and, more importantly, Thutmose's current plans.

"Why are they all still here?" Iset holds a small alabaster pigment pot in one hand, lantern held high in the other. "The doctor doesn't use them, it seems."

I'm about to admit I have no idea, again, and suggest searching the next room, when the door opens with a creak. I struggle to recall the words I practiced—words intended for the doctor—but they've vanished. It doesn't matter anyway. It's not the doctor but his daughter, Teena, who enters the room, eyes round with surprise.

We stare at each other until Teena gathers her wits. "Adoratrice." She closes her mouth and bends forward in submission, eyes on the floor, skin flushed. Teena is even older than me and still unmarried. She's plain and a bit dull, but given her connection to our family, it's odd that she hasn't yet made a match.

"We're looking for your father." Iset steps forward, feigning a boldness I should emulate. I'm the princess and high priestess after all. These may be Teena's quarters, but she's living in my family's palace.

Determined not to be outdone by my handmaid, I shift my shoulders back and do my best impersonation of Mother. "Your father is not here." I say it like Mother would, with a coldness in my tone like the man should magically know to be waiting for me whenever I choose to bless him with my presence.

Teena stands tall and glances at the door I was about to enter. My blood chills. Is Inhapi in there now? Has he heard everything Iset and I have said?

"Father is not seeing people at the moment," Teena stutters. "He's been...ill."

"I'm sorry, Teena. I didn't realize your father was ill." I sigh, feigned confidence gone. "We shouldn't have... Is there something Mother and I can do for you?"

She looks up at me and I step back, surprised by the glint of anger in her eyes—anger so intense it's tangible. Why? Is it directed at me? Is she mad that we've invaded her space? Probably. I'd be furious too if someone broke into my rooms, especially if I were burdened by a sick parent. She's already lost her mother. Perhaps she's just frightened and her emotions are getting the best of her.

"We will leave you to it then," Iset says. Her hands are behind her back, an alabaster jar clutched in her fist.

"Right," I add.

Iset slips the jar in a pocket, grips her lamp, and steps toward the door.

I don't need nudging—I'm right behind her, back stiff, a pose I manage to maintain the entire way back to my quarters. The walk feels eternal.

Finally safe in my receiving room, I drop onto my chaise and moan. "That was a mistake. What if the doctor was in the other room the whole time? What if he heard us?"

Iset drops down next to me with a relieved sigh. "We didn't say anything revealing. And we did learn something. We know for sure the wisewoman lived there. And that she had more than one could possibly need to mix poison."

"We need to find her," I blurt. "Thutmose said she was the key. He must need her to advance his scheme. Maybe he's not sure she really poisoned Father. Or maybe he plans to force her into claiming Mother ordered her to do it. She could be his witness—"

"He did mention a witness."

I nod, mind focusing. "If we can find Hathor before he does, we can disrupt his plan."

"How are we going to do that?"

"I don't know," I admit, thinking again of Senenmut explaining how Hathor simply disappeared. "But we must find a way. We need to know what the wisewoman did and why she did it. And we need to figure it out before Thutmose finds her and uses her as a weapon against us all."

Iset nods, approving of my boldness. She shifts sideways to face me. "I wonder if Kamut's brother is back."

In the events of the night, I've forgotten about the scribe. Hope rises in my chest. "I hope so. We need to talk to that scribe. Even if he didn't see the woman who sent the message, he may know someone who did."

"Or the man," Iset points out. "Maybe the message sender was a man. Maybe one person sent the message, and another met with Thutmose."

"Maybe." I sigh. There are far too many maybes for comfort.

Iset plops the small jar she stole on my golden chest. "At least we have a memento to remember our adventure by."

I pick the jar up and twirl it between my fingers. My body is still buzzing as I read the signs. The jar is marked with the symbols for crocodile excrement. "I won't need this ingredient anytime soon. Or ever." I hand it to Iset.

"What is it?"

"It's used by women who want to rid themselves of an unwanted pregnancy. Hold on to it. Who knows. One day, you may find yourself in need of an abortifacient—"

The door separating my receiving room and my bedroom squeaks open, and I jump up, worried Mother is about to find me sitting next to my handmaid. Ever since I realized Iset is the closest thing to a friend I have, the fear of Mother sending her away is a constant. But instead of Mother's demanding presence in my doorway, the chambermaid enters, looking more alarmed than me. She drops her head, mumbles an apology, and rushes out the door before either Iset or I can speak.

I turn back to Iset. "Do you think she heard us?"

She looks up at me with wide eyes, shaking her head. The silence between us suddenly feels dizzy, like a secret, the evening's antics finally catching up with us. Slowly, a smile spreads across her face. Without my permission, my lips follow suit, and we double over in uncontained laughter.

There's a moment of lightness, as if we're simply two girls free to whisper and gossip and trade stories in the light of the evening. But as our laughter dies down, I remember that the stories we're trading have dire consequences and that Thutmose is in this very palace, plotting to accuse Pharaoh of murder.

"I need to stop Thutmose's lies from taking root. He could destroy everything with this story."

Iset puts her hand on mine so our fingers are twined together. "I know. And I know how much it hurts to lose a mother. I'll do everything I can to make sure you don't have to go through that anytime soon. And certainly not at his hands."

FIVE

THE SUN BEATS DOWN, HARSH AGAINST MY SKIN. MOTHER AND
I are visiting her mortuary temple, which is eternally under
construction. She invited Thutmose to join us, though I
don't know why. He trails behind us, bored and moody.

I shield my eyes as sweat pours down my back and glides under
my pale linen gown like a centipede. Mother's face is beaded with
perspiration. She masks her discomfort with a haughty temper,
and the scent of eucalyptus fills my nose from the linen cloth she
taps against her head, careful not to spoil the kohl that outlines
her dark eyes.

She looks as bored as Thutmose, but I'm amazed anew each
time I see the colonnades and statues that sprout up from every
slope and corner. One of Senenmut's many innovations, the
construction of Djeser-Djeseru is inspired by the nearby temple of
the old pharaoh, Mentuhotep. But Senenmut's version is unique in
its tiered design, with three layers fronted by porticoes and statues
of Mother depicted as the god Osiris, wearing the red and white
crowns of kingship, the crook and flail crossed over her chest,

cleverly integrated with the ankh and scepter. Trees bloom in the desert here. Some were miraculously brought back from Mother's expedition to Punt, the bountiful land of the gods where only the most successful pharaohs have sent expeditions. Proof of Mother's divine birth is all around us. Everything about this space, from its construction to the scenes that cover the walls to the plants that blossom around it, is designed to remind the people that Mother was chosen by the gods.

I'm guessing the majesty of the site is what prompted Mother to drag Thutmose along. She's reminding him that she's the one with the resources and power to command such an ambitious construction project, while he'd be lucky to erect a shack and is dependent on her to include his name and image within her opulent reliefs, something she rarely chooses to do. I can be found gracing as many of Djeser-Djeseru's walls as Thutmose and, at times, assuming more powerful poses, which is an insult he no doubt feels deeply.

But we're not here to admire our own depictions or Mother's publicity campaign, clever as it is. We're here to view her newest statue. She's shown larger than life, an enormous man with a king's body and a king's false beard. I like her older statues better. They showed her as a woman.

"Looks just like you," Thutmose smirks at her back.

She grins. "It captures the truest me."

"Bearded?" he drones.

She turns to him, head tilted, lips curved into a grin. "I see you need a lesson in royal iconography. I'm happy to help you, child. Let's start with the basics. People don't care what we look like. They care what we are. And what I am is the god Horus on earth. This"— she motions toward the statue—"displays my power, not my appearance. That's rather the point."

His sarcastic smirk melts as she talks. "Horus is a man, like my father. And me," he spits.

She shrugs. "The gods are what they choose to be. They're not limited to your little categories." Her grin spreads across her face. "Nor am I."

His calculated blasé guise returns. He dips his head in a caustic bow, muttering something about lying to oneself, then turns to wander down the ramp to the lower court.

"Do you like it?" Mother asks me, as if the confrontation with Thutmose isn't worth another moment.

I keep my eyes on my half brother, anxiety simmering in my gut. Thutmose nears the spot where Senenmut talks with some workmen, and he greets a familiar-looking young man. The man whispers in Thutmose's ear. My half brother smiles and nods, patting the man on the back, shifting from dour to cheery in an instant. My anxiety simmers. Am I letting my imagination get the best of me, or did that man just say something terrible—something bad enough to make Thutmose smile?

I watch him turn away, steps jaunty, then my eyes find Senenmut talking with two men I don't know. My tutor nods his head, and one of the men, older with a pudgy belly and droopy eyes, peels away and heads toward Mother's sedan chair, near the bottom of the ramp, where my royal handmaid waits in the shade of a myrrh tree.

Iset stands next to Mother's four attendants, her gaze glued to the ground. Odd. The scene here is raucous enough to shatter anyone's concentration, especially Iset's. She marvels at the opulence of our royal surroundings daily. And here, men are shouting and hammering and pushing and shoving, all to craft Mother's oasis in the desert, yet Iset acts like she's never seen sand before. The man draws closer, and she lifts her chin to greet him. The move looks forced. Is it her father? I search for some resemblance, but he's too far away for me to find it. Iset visits her father once a week, but seeing these two together, I wonder if she should. I make a note to ask her about their relationship.

"Neferura?"

I turn my attention back to Mother and her statue.

"I asked what you think of the depiction."

I consider the statue. Do I like it? In truth, I don't like her pretending to be something she isn't. She may be the embodiment of Horus, but she's also a woman.

"I think..." I pause. I'm tempted to lie, but it's hardly worth adding weight to my heart over. So I decide on the truth, dropping my voice so only she can hear me. "It's lovely, Mother. But I do miss seeing you with breasts."

"Neferura!"

"You are an exceptionally good pharaoh, Mother." That's true. Under her rule, new trade routes have opened, bringing a steady stream of gold from the south, copper from Biau, wine from Keftiu, poppies from Susa, and luxury goods from Hattusa and beyond. The quarries and mines are more productive than ever. Temples burst with activity throughout the land. Festivals once ignored have been brought back, and thousands more workmen and priests and priestesses are employed, ensuring the gods are pleased with her rule. The gods clearly approve: the Two Lands haven't known a single famine or flood since Mother ascended the throne. Her reign is truly blessed. Even Thutmose must know that, though I doubt he'd ever admit it, especially if he believes she murdered our father.

"Yes, I am an excellent ruler. Yet it is never quite enough." She grows pensive. "I suppose having my body displayed as if I were a man, like most of the pharaohs before me, is a small price to pay—smaller than many other prices I've paid, I assure you. It comforts the country's nobility to see me fit neatly into the old mold. I'm afraid you'll find, daughter, that breaking with tradition requires a never-ending program of justifications."

Her sex, Mother had determined, is simply another fact of life, bendable to her will, as so many realities are. If only Thutmose were so malleable. I turn to find him, worried when I can't spot him. What's he up to now?

"How long are you going to let Thutmose stay at court?" I ask, sounding petulant.

"The gods will take care of Thutmose. With a bit of fortune, we won't need to worry about him much longer."

My skin prickles. "What does that mean?"

A hint of a smile graces her rouged lips. "The world is dangerous, Neferura. You and Thutmose were both lucky to survive childhood. My father had five children. I'm the only one alive today. Thutmose may face threats we can't imagine soon."

What she says is true, for royals and peasants alike—many babies don't make it past three, many children don't survive to become adults, and many my age never make it to Mother's decade. Still, her certainty is alarming.

"Don't tell me you'd be sorry to see Thutmose come to an unpleasant end," she adds.

I look for him again, but he's vanished. I turn back to Mother, thinking about her question. I may dread Thutmose taking the throne, but the country would suffer if the line of succession was broken. I can picture the upheaval vividly in my mind. I may be the king's eldest daughter, god's wife of Amun, mistress of the Two Lands, lady of Upper and Lower Kemet, but I'm not the heir. Mother's not going to have another child, so with Thutmose gone, there would be no clear heir to the throne. I'd be the most likely candidate but not the only candidate. I haven't been named by Mother or chosen by the gods, and there are plenty of resourced men who would convince themselves they deserved the job. And just like that, ambitious nobles and Thutmose's allies would begin to circle like packs of jackals hunting the riverbanks. Court would devolve into schemes, and the people outside the palace would suffer for the aspirations of the affluent.

"No. Not sad," I say. "Not for myself anyway. But it would be bad for the country. Our duty is to put the needs of the people over our own."

She looks away. "Whatever happens to Thutmose will be exactly what the gods will."

When she turns back to meet my eyes, the air stills. The sun shimmers around Mother like an orb framing the moment. A chill settles on me, creeping into my core in spite of the day's heat.

"You should think less about him and more about yourself, Neferura. Thutmose is not the only royal child. He's not the only one who could rule after me."

The hair on my arms stands up. It's one thing to think it, but saying it aloud is blasphemy, even for Mother. The gods chose Thutmose, just as they chose her. Literally. Both Mother and Thutmose were singled out by Amun when the priests carrying the god's statue bowed before them, marking them as his chosen ones in public. To suggest I could take the throne, unchosen, is a desecration.

"You shouldn't say that, Mother. The gods chose Thutmose."

"Perhaps," she admits. "But you are my child, Neferura. He is not. The gods may one day make a different choice. After all, I'm a god too, and I'd choose you over him."

My hearts hammers as I study her face, wondering if Mother would or could force her will on the gods. I hope not. The thought of sitting on her throne, spending my days squabbling with petty nobles, repels me. I close my eyes and see Ammit, her crocodile mouth lowered to my heart, beating as it rests on her scales. The balance is perfect until the red and white crowns of Upper and Lower Kemet fall onto it, forcing the scale to tilt, rendering my heart too heavy. I force my eyes open before I can watch the Devourer snatch my heart up.

I don't want to rule. And as much as I detest him personally, I don't want Thutmose to die and send the country tumbling into chaos either. Above all, I don't want Mother to be guilty of murder—Thutmose's or Father's. The idea of her heart weighed down by that violence terrifies me.

Mother is untroubled. She raises an imperious brow, then turns back to stare up at the statue.

I squeeze my hands into fists so tight my nails dig into my palms. Rather than the comfort I hoped for, her words only add to my worries. Is she insinuating that she'd cause Thutmose harm to put me on a throne I don't want? And if she'd dispatch Thutmose on my behalf, what would she have done to Father to advance her own power? What if there's some truth to Thutmose's suspicions?

Stop!

I shake my head, flinging off these evil thoughts. If Mother were a killer, Thutmose would have dropped dead years ago. I'm letting him infest my heart with doubts. Mother is simply planning like any good pharaoh would. Until Thutmose has an heir, I am next in line, even if it would mean war if it ever came to that. Maybe admitting the fact out loud isn't a sin. Maybe it's another reality Mother has grappled with—a reality I've ignored because I'm less experienced than her. If I had lost as many people as Mother has, I'd have redundancy plans in place too.

Yet a chill sits in my gut. It feels like doubt. And doubting Mother now, in the face of Thutmose's threats, is as dangerous as a swarm of angry cobras.

Days later, the royal pleasure barge rocks gently as it moves against Iteru's current. I watch an osprey dive for a fish as I sit next to Thuiu, who gulps beer. She's the only noble I know who prefers the thick beer our workman drink to the rich, red shedeh popular at court. She's also my favorite noble, as old as the gods and with even more education than me. We're an odd pair, bonded by our passion for the wise men and their maxims. Conveniently, she was at court in Father's final days. Her knowledge may be a gift that gives, especially today.

"How's Ineni?" I ask.

Thuiu has aged since her husband took ill. He's rallied in recent weeks, and we all pray he'll be back on his feet soon.

"He can no longer hunt," she admits as she shoos her old handmaid away.

The old woman, Benerib, has served Thuiu for as long as I've been alive. I watch Iset sidle up to her, knowing she'll try to tease the same information out of Benerib as I hope to get from Thuiu: a better understanding of Grandmother's wisewoman, a bit of clarity to move us forward.

Thuiu and Grandmother were friends. I've heard stories of the two of them pulling pranks on the nobles. If the tales of their escapades are true, they once convinced old Ahmose Pen Nekhbet that his family tomb had been robbed, only to return his treasures the next day after he'd roused my father from his bed to complain.

Thuiu was as close to Grandmother once as she is to me now. It's only logical to turn to her next in my quest to find the wisewoman.

"Neferura." Thuiu calls my name, drawing me back to the moment. She taps a finger against the golden cuff bracelet that circles her wrist. She wears one on her other wrist too; two more ring her upper arms.

"I'm sorry. I'm tired lately." I turn in my chair to face Thuiu so my view of Iset doesn't distract me, although if I'm honest, Kamut, still as a statue near the ship's rail behind my handmaid, is even more diverting. "Is Ineni uncomfortable?" I force my voice to sound light.

"Oh, you know Ineni." Thuiu waves away my concern with gem-studded fingers. "He never complains. He is not uncomfortable enough to stay away from his garden, although I've scolded him for it, I assure you. Do you know he has seventy-three trees now?"

"So many?" I grin. Ineni is known for his lavish gardens. From the berry-dotted sycamore fig to the flowering date palm to the aromatic myrtle, if it grows, Ineni will plant it.

Hoping my interested smile hides the anxiety I feel beneath, I try not to squirm as I listen to Thuiu's stories, biding my time, watching the shoreline, speckled with men fishing and boys leading water buffalo to drink and women cackling in large groups. They all stop as we sail past to bow and prostrate themselves. One little girl braves a wave until her mother grabs her hand and pulls her to her knees. Between the fresh air and the view of Kemet's people living and thriving, my worries recede. I almost don't want to broach an unpleasant subject, but who knows when I'll have Thuiu to myself again?

When she's finished complaining about some scribe who can't read the rarer signs, the worst offense imaginable for my old friend, I fix my eyes on the small shrine we're passing and ask, "Thuiu, do you remember Grandmother's wisewoman?"

She studies my face. One side of her thin lips finally lifts in a crooked smile. "No one who met her could forget her."

She doesn't offer more, so I prompt her. "Can you tell me about her?"

"Why do you want to know?" Her eyes narrow, and her grin falls.

I look away, unnerved by the intensity of her gaze. I consider telling her the truth, but Thuiu has enough to worry about with Ineni's illness, and I don't dare whisper such an awful rumor aloud, even to dear Thuiu. Yet she's too canny to fool easily.

"Neferura." Her voice is tense. "Is there something you want to tell me?"

My eyes catch Iset's, and I decide a half-truth suits the moment. "You can't get angry. And you can't tell Mother."

She leans in, eager for my secret.

"Iset and I went to Inhapi's rooms. Iset wanted to talk to the doctor—she hasn't been feeling well. He didn't answer, but the door was open, so we snuck in. We saw the wisewoman's old collection of potions. It was…impressive."

Thuiu grins at that. She loves an adventure, and an adventure that breaks decorum is the best kind.

"The wisewoman was impressive," she admits. I freeze, waiting for more, relieved when she goes on. "She was brilliant. She was covered in tattoos, you know. She had the head of the goddess Hathor tattooed on her chest, complete with horns and a sun disk. Two more depictions of the goddess decorated her thighs. She enjoyed displaying them too. She shared the goddess's name after all. Although I never did discover if she was given that name when she was weaned or adopted it later in life. All I know is she made a striking figure. And she was the most adept doctor and magician I've ever known. Your grandmother adored her." She shifts her gaze away from me, aiming it at the water swirling past.

I know all this. I need more. "And can you tell me…" I pause, feeling inexplicably nervous. But if I can't question Thuiu, one of the few people in Kemet I truly trust, how will I ever figure out what Thutmose is up to? The enmity between Thutmose and Mother feels more and more dangerous as his childhood recedes. Mother may be thinking up contingency plans, which only makes the situation more precarious. So I sit taller and spit out the words. "Is she still alive? Can you tell me where she is?"

"I am no expert on the wisewoman's status, dear." Thuiu shrugs. "I don't know where she is now. Few do, I suspect."

"You said 'now.' So she is alive?"

Thuiu doesn't answer, but her silence is answer enough.

"All right." I catalog all I know thus far of Hathor and briefly think again of the marked ingredients in the wisewoman's old chambers and the scorpion inscribed on the bottoms of mysterious jars. "Thuiu, can you tell me about Hathor's scorpions? What are they?"

Thuiu leans back, swirling her beer in one hand. "You are very interested in her. All this because you saw a few old bottles in the doctor's quarters? Really?"

I keep my gaze steady. "I've asked around since I learned of her, and the few whispered rumors I've gathered only make her more intriguing. Some even whisper that she wielded some kind of tool that gave her more power. Of course I'm interested. Why should that surprise you? Women with power and education fascinate me. That's why I like you so much."

She laughs and takes a swig of beer. After a pause, she gives in. "Do you remember the story of Isis and the seven scorpions?"

Of course I do. Senenmut and I studied the legend when I was young. But I want to hear what she'll say, so I ask her to tell me the story.

She nods. Thuiu is a consummate storyteller and always eager for an audience. I listen intently as her measured voice recounts the story of the scorpion goddess Selket, who sent seven scorpions to protect Isis, the first daughter of the earth god and the sky goddess, as she hid her newborn son, Horus, from her vengeful brother, Set. The tale is one I know well, but I become enchanted by it all the same as Thuiu weaves the story together.

Selket's seven scorpions became Isis's companions, her protectors, her watchful eyes during her hiding. They followed her into the local human town as she begged for food and necessities. One day, the goddess, disguised as an old hag so as not to be discovered by her ever-searching brother, ventured into one such town for assistance. There, she came across a wealthy woman. The woman saw Isis in all her misery and slammed her door, refusing aid. As Isis turned away, a modest woman caught sight of the goddess, and although the woman had little to give, she welcomed Isis into her home and gave her food to eat from her hearth.

But Selket and the scorpions were upset by the wealthy woman's affront. Combining their poison, they stung the wealthy woman's child in vengeance. The poison seeped in, and the woman cried out, taking to the streets for help from anyone who could hear. Isis answered. Mercifully, she saved the child, earning the appreciation of the wealthy woman and of Selket, who'd begun to regret letting her pets harm a young boy for his mother's mistake.

It's a tale of morality and of powerful women. It's a tale that positions the scorpion goddess as a protector and scorpions as her spies and executioners. It's a tale of a woman who used scorpions as her eyes, extending her vision far beyond her own. Does that mean…?

"The scorpions are people?" I ask.

Thuiu nods. "Marked people."

"Marked how?" I remember the girl from the throne room with the scorpion tattoo just below her ear. "With tattoos," I gasp.

Thuiu doesn't say yes, but she doesn't say no either. She simply stares at me, still curious about my interest.

I should be cautious, but I'm desperate for the information, so I press forward. "Hathor used these tattooed people as her eyes and ears?" *Perhaps to kill for her,* I think, but I don't say that bit out loud. "That's what you're saying?"

Thuiu grunts and beckons one of the servants lurking on the other side of the ship with an ostrich-feather fan to come closer, the old woman's polite way of putting an end to my questions. "I said that Hathor was smart, capable, and loved by the powerful. One of the powerful anyway. You said those other things. Well, most of them."

The servant girl begins fanning Thuiu, who leans back and closes her eyes. I think back to the girl in the throne room. Could she be one of Hathor's scorpions? If so, that means Hathor still has spies in the palace. Does that mean she's nearby? I search the young servant girl's nearly bare body for tattoos. She's unmarked, as far as I can tell. But perhaps another on this ship is tattooed. A rower? One of my guards? And if one is so marked, what does that say about their loyalty? Is it to my family or some shadowy group created by a wisewoman who left court long ago?

I want to ask Thuiu about Hathor's motivations. If she did create an organization of spies, what was its purpose? How large was it? Who was part of it? Was it made up of palace servants alone, or do scorpion tattoos stretch the length of the country? But clearly Thuiu is done answering my questions, at least for now.

The discomfort of not knowing makes me squirm. My gaze lands on Kamut, and I act without thought.

"Excuse me," I say to Thuiu as I signal to Iset, walking to meet her midship.

"Benerib is a rock," Iset mumbles grumpily as she approaches. Apparently she had less luck with Thuiu's handmaid than I did with Thuiu.

"You have papyrus and ink?"

Iset fishes a small blank scroll and reed pen from the bag hanging over her shoulder—it's not the first time I've asked to write something down unexpectedly. I take them from her and rest the papyrus on the ship's rail, dipping the pen in the ink cake Iset holds to scribble rough signs on the page.

Come to our quarters after the palace sleeps. Come only if safe to do so. Make sure no one knows.

I roll the scroll tightly. "Slip this to Kamut. Is his brother back?"

"I haven't had a chance to ask."

"Let's hope so," I whisper, handing her the scroll. "We can't waste any more time."

Kamut lives with his brother, and the two have always been close. Kamut will know better than to show a note from me to anyone but the brother he trusts, assuming he's returned. And in spite of the risk, I need to look Kamut in the eyes when I ask how many scorpion tattoos are walking the palace halls, if the scribe is willing to meet with me, and if Kamut has heard rumors of Hathor's whereabouts.

It's the last time, I vow.

Even I don't know whether I'm sending the promise to my divine husband, Amun, or the goddess who may devour my heart, Ammit. Nor can I say for certain my vow is true.

I've often imagined Kamut appearing in my bedroom in the middle of the night. The reality is nothing like my fantasies.

He stands facing me, fidgety. Iset yawns from the cot she set up next to my bed so she'd be nearby if he arrived. I was wide awake, listening to Iset snore softly and fretting over asking Kamut to return, when he walked in through my bedroom's open wall. I give Iset a shove as Kamut explains that he switched schedules with the guard who should be standing outside near my rooms tonight after Iset gave him my note. Forcing myself to stop staring at his arms, sweaty from the night's heat, I ask if he's noticed scorpion tattoos wandering the palace halls.

"Scorpion tattoos," Kamut repeats.

"Hathor, my grandmother's old wisewoman, seemed to…I don't know, collect people maybe? Mark them, with tattoos," I babble, staring up at Kamut, marveling at the way the moonlight makes the curve of his jaw and the muscles rippling across his abdomen even more pronounced. "Senenmut told me Hathor knew things. He thought her scorpions were some kind of tool that extended her power. I think they're people—people marked by tattoos. And I might have seen a servant girl with a scorpion tattoo on her neck, and I thought maybe she's…" My words fizzle out as his dark eyes search mine.

"Please sit." Iset pats the cot next to her.

My anxiety swells at the familiarity. "He can't stay."

"We're safe, little princess." His small smile sends a drove of ibises flapping through my body.

With a nod, he sinks down next to Iset so they sit side by side, facing me, stiff on my bed, feet planted firmly on my cold stone floor as if my body needs grounding. I'm so anxious I feel like I could vomit. Our friendship is risky, and his presence here at this hour could doom them both.

"I don't want to put you in danger. I won't summon you like this again. It's too risky—"

"I'll come."

"No." I shake my head. "We both know what it could cost you." I look at him. And he looks back. And the wings rustle inside me again. I order them to be still. When I'm in control, I continue. "Just tell me what you know. I assume your brother is back?"

He nods.

"What did he say about the scribe?"

Even Kamut's grimace is appealing. Light from the lantern sitting on the table next to him dances across his scar; his eyes glitter in the candlelight. "I'm afraid it's bad news."

I hunch my shoulders, nervous.

"Nebwawi is dead."

"Dead?" I stutter. "How?"

Kamut shakes his head slowly. "A cobra bite. Nebwawi was copying a scroll when a cobra struck his toe. They tried the usual cures, but nothing worked. He died a few days ago."

"When did this happen exactly?" My body hums with worry.

"He was bitten five days ago. He survived a day more, in agony."

Five days. That's the day Thutmose and I joined Mother at

Djeser-Djeseru, the day Thutmose was cheered by some secret whispered in his ear. What if...

The silence simmers as I consider the possibilities. Surely I'm being paranoid. The man is hardly the first scribe to succumb to a snakebite, although a snake in the House of Life is a curious thing.

"I'm sorry," he says.

I shake my head, banning suspicions from my mind. They'll only lead me astray, and I can't afford that now. After all, aside from the fact that the poor man is dead, he was our only lead. Without him, we have no way to discover the identity of the woman in Thutmose's quarters, which means the only path forward leads me back to Hathor. "Have you heard anything more of the wisewoman?"

"I've made discreet inquiries since last time we spoke. People are either scared of her or they hold her in high esteem and won't say much. I have heard rumors of her and your grandmother..." His eyes find the floor.

"Go on," I prompt.

"People say they were close. Very close."

"Lovers?" I ask, searching my memory for any clue, beyond the existence of her children, that Ahmose had a sex life at all, let alone one that involved a powerful wisewoman.

Kamut blushes, which makes Iset smile. I clutch the linen throw underneath me on my bed, where I've imagined Kamut more times than I can count.

"So they say." He's worrying something in his fingers. It's the note I scrawled on the ship. Noticing I've spotted it, he drops it on the gold stool next to the lantern. "I don't know if it's true. I'm just telling you the rumors I've heard. As for scorpion tattoos, I've never noticed any. But I don't..." He shakes his head. "I don't look much, so perhaps..." His words fade.

Iset's smile grows wider.

I ignore her and the dark fluttering wings. "Is there anything you can tell me? Do you have any idea where this wisewoman might be?"

His gaze is steady. "I'm sorry. I'm afraid I'm not much help."

Another dead end. I try a different approach. "What about people with a grudge? Does anyone in the palace despise me or Mother so much that they'd wish us harm?"

Kamut and Iset share a glance. She shakes her head, but he pauses.

"Kamut?"

He shrugs. "Teena, the doctor's daughter, is forever angry. She still blames you for what happened."

I remember the anger in Teena's eyes the day Iset and I snuck into the doctor's quarters, the palpable hatred I couldn't understand. I shake my head in confusion. "What did I ever do to Teena?"

"She was whipped when we were children. Unjustly, she believes. Something about stealing treats from Cook. For some reason, she blames you—"

I gasp as pieces click together. A young Thutmose with date loaves between his fingers, hiding in the kitchens. An unnamed servant later blamed for the crime. "Teena was the girl who was punished." Iset looks confused, so I explain. "Thutmose stole sweets from the kitchen when we were children. I begged him to confess when I learned some servant girl was to be whipped for what he'd done. He refused, and I stayed silent. I didn't want to make him mad. My entire life at that point was about not making Thutmose mad." I turn back to Kamut. "Teena has known it was us all these years? No wonder she hates us."

"Well," Kamut says and grins, "mostly she hates you."

"You don't think she'd…" I pause, realizing she lives in the rooms Hathor worked out of. What could Teena know about Hathor's actions, growing up surrounded by evidence that the wisewoman once brewed mysterious concoctions where she and her father now live?

"What if Teena was the voice we heard talking to Thutmose?" Iset leans forward so far I fear she'll topple over.

I shake my head. I have no idea. One would think if she blames me, she'd detest Thutmose even more. He was the true culprit. But at this point, it feels like anything is possible.

I'm staring at Iset when my eyes snag on her bracelet. "Iset, do you mind if I borrow your mother's bracelet?"

She touches it gently, possessively even. "Of course you can. But why?"

"Maybe I can draw the attention of one of Hathor's scorpions if I display a penchant for their symbol."

"What are you going to do if you find one?" Iset asks.

"If I could get just one of the tattooed servants alone, maybe I can get them to help me make contact with the wisewoman. I need to discover what Hathor did and who was involved. I can offer something in exchange for the information I need to get ahead of Thutmose—" I stop, realizing I've said too much in front of Kamut.

"Do you want to tell me what's really happening here?" Kamut asks, his smile from earlier now replaced by a worried frown.

I shake my head. "I'm afraid you've heard too much already. More will just put you in danger."

"I like danger. I'm made for danger." His eyes sparkle with mischief.

I roll my eyes and hold my hand out to Iset, who slips off the bracelet and hands it to me. I stand as I pull it on. "You should go."

"Fine." He's on his feet, so close I could touch him. "I'll search the palace for scorpion tattoos and see what I can learn about your grandmother's old wisewoman. I'll get word to Iset if I hear anything useful. But, little princess." He purses his lips, weighing his words. "Don't let him send you off chasing myths and stories. Don't give him your time or your energy. Unless you want to? Give him your time, that is."

His eyes are wide, inquisitive. I wonder if he's curious about my feelings for Thutmose, a subject that suddenly feels more delicate than my grandmother's sex life.

"Of course I don't. I don't want to give him any part of me."

He relaxes a bit, and Iset's smile is so wide now it's a wonder her face doesn't split open.

With a final glare at my handmaid, I thank Kamut and head for my study without looking back. The last thing I need is for either of them to see that the smile on my face matches Iset's.

The table groans beneath the weight of our favorite foods. Spiced milk, goose egg custard, and savory bread for me. Date tarts, pistachio pudding, fig cakes, and wine spiked with honey and exotic spices for Mother.

"Are we celebrating something?" I ask. The weekly dinner with Mother and Senenmut, hosted in Mother's private quarters, is always delicious. But tonight's spread is more extravagant than usual.

"Do we need an excuse to dine well?" Mother responds.

I shrug and reach for the still-warm bread, wondering if my plan might fare better with full bellies and empty cups. Since learning of the scribe's death, I've been flashing Iset's scorpion bracelet around the palace, hoping to draw the attention of someone who might lead me to the wisewoman. But with the hunt for Hathor and the scorpions stalling as time slips away, I have no choice but to approach Mother for answers. It's not a plan I relish, but it would be less awful with Senenmut at our side. He's like the river between disparate shores, bridging us like the calm waters of Iteru. "Is Senenmut coming?"

"He's tied up for the evening."

I blow a heavy breath, disappointed, and we fall silent, both distracted by our own thoughts. The *tap, tap, zing* of Mother's signet ring against her cup, which is made of turquoise glass and adorned with lotus petals, punctuates the stillness. I watch her eat, wondering how she'll react to questions about Grandmother's wisewoman and her poison. The thought is terrifying, but I need to know what Mother knows and what she meant about Thutmose meeting a deadly end. So I sit taller, prepped for battle, and begin. "Mother, I want to ask you—"

"Move or I'll do it for you!" Thutmose thunders from the other side of the door, sending a handmaid scurrying and a tense-looking guard turning to Mother for orders.

"Let him in." Mother's smile suggests she expected Thutmose, which explains the extra care she took with tonight's repast.

I cringe as Thutmose storms in, the composed demeanor he usually dons replaced by rage.

"You won't get away with this." He leans over Mother, snarling.

Her eyes glitter in the candlelight. Even looking up at him from her chair, Mother is a more imposing figure. "What is this hysteria about, child?"

He steps back at the moniker, struggling for some semblance of control. He pauses a beat before speaking. "What are you going to do if I reject your bidding? If I refuse to lead the men, my men, into this fool battle you've planned? It's suicide and you know it, which is no doubt the point."

She ignores the accusation and answers his question. "You can refuse, of course. You are a pharaoh after all. If you're too afraid to lead, simply stay here at court and be pampered. I will let the nobles know you don't have the courage to take up arms when it matters, when our domination is at risk."

Thutmose's scowl deepens. "The dominance of Kemet is secure. Grandfather—"

"My father," Mother interrupts.

"The first Thutmose, after whom I am named, saw to that. This campaign only serves as an excuse to get rid of me. And you do realize the alternative you're threatening is the same lifestyle you indulge in."

She shrugs, delighting in his anger. "My reputation is built on peace and prosperity, on understanding the ins and outs of the court, on my unwavering dedication to the gods. Avoiding battle does nothing to harm me. You've chosen to set yourself up as the brave military man. An attempt at contrast, I suspect."

"Or a rational response to the situation you forced on me. You may recall sending me off to the military barracks as a child, Pharaoh." He spits out this last word with venom. "I excelled where I was allowed to excel."

"Then you should welcome the opportunity. War will be good for you."

He leans in, the smirk finally returning to his face. "You are right about that. I will lead the men, and I'll do it well. So well nobles will finally start to see that I'm the better choice to rule. And if I'm lucky, I might even have a window to enjoy my triumph before a well-paid friendly arrow finds my back!"

He twirls and flees. I gape after him, a chill prickling my skin. I turn to Mother, and her smile stops my heart cold.

"What did he mean? What friendly arrow?" I ask, dread and confirmation in turn staring me in the face.

"Eat your food, Neferura," she answers, raising a date to her lips.

"But, Mother—"

"I said eat, Neferura. I told you not to worry before, and I'm saying it again. Do not make me repeat myself a third time. Amun will be displeased."

Bile rises up my throat, and without thought, I stand from the table to follow in Thutmose's path. He's well ahead of me by the time I spot him down the corridor.

"Thutmose!" I shout after him, my voice echoing off the bright walls.

He slows his pace but doesn't turn around. I catch up to him and push open the nearby door to yank him out onto the deck.

"You can't honestly believe Mother intends to have you murdered," I whisper, aching to believe my words are true, even with Mother's smile lingering behind my vision. I glance around to ensure we can't be heard. We're alone but for the large ship sailing past and the silent guards sprinkled around the complex, too distant to eavesdrop.

Thutmose's bark of laughter is part fury, part indignation. "You cannot still be this naive, Neferura. You can't be so blindly loyal you're unable to see who she is. She's a vicious serpent, a sharp-toothed crocodile. She always has been. She'll kill me without thought. And it won't be the first time she's tried. But clever as I've become at avoiding your mother's traps, if she lays enough of them, one day she'll succeed." He pauses, jaw tight, eyes boring into me. "But maybe you already know all this. Maybe you feign this childlike naivete because you also want me out of the way. You've built up your own estate. Perhaps you plan to use it just like she did—to take my throne."

"No." I grab his arms, digging my fingers into his skin, desperate to make him see. "Thutmose, this has to stop. This is dangerous. I don't want your throne. I've never wanted anything but to serve loyally—Mother, yes, but mostly the god and the people and, one day, you."

"Then I advise you to switch sides before it's too late."

I feel my frustration grow. "I'm not on anyone's side. I never wanted to take a side."

"That is taking a side, Neferura. Only you are too childish to see that the choice not to stand up to her means you're standing with her."

"Childish?" I scoff. "I was a child."

"And now? Are you ready to do the right thing now? Even if it means betraying your own blood?"

I sag. His words hit me like the winds of a sandstorm, sharp and unrelenting. I consider telling him I know he believes my mother murdered our father, but I'm trying to quell the flames, not fan them. "I'm not going to betray anyone. I'm simply trying to get you to see that it's in everyone's best interest—mine, yours, Mother's, most importantly the people's—for us to find a way to make peace and work together. If you'd only—"

"You're preaching to the wrong pharaoh." He wags a finger in my face, that brutal smirk back in place. Twirling away, he yanks the door open, pauses, and says over his shoulder. "This is not our final goodbye, Neferura. Don't expect me to make this easy for you. I will survive your mother's current attempt on my life, and I will be back. When I return, the score will finally be settled."

I watch him go, heart pounding, faith shattered. I want to cling to the hope that Mother is innocent, but she's sending Thutmose to war for a reason. And whether she merely hopes he'll end up dead or is actively working to ensure that it'll happen, she's the one at the helm. She wants him out of the way, and she doesn't care if it costs him his life. Would a woman who would intentionally harm her nephew and stepson, no matter how awful he is, really think twice about harming the husband she never loved? Could all of it be true, exactly the way Thutmose has whispered?

I suck in fresh air, then, with heavy feet, return to Mother. I find her tearing into honey-roasted fish as if the display from moments ago never happened at all.

I slide into the chair next to her and say, voice low, "He thinks I want to use my position as god's wife to follow your path, to take his throne."

She hums. "It's no more than you deserve. And it is the legacy I deserve—my child ruling Kemet."

"And if I don't want that?"

She drops the fish, chewing slower, to stare at me. "My legacy is your legacy, daughter. You want what I want, because what I want is what's best for us all. And what I want, I will get."

I stare at the woman who raised me, my pharaoh, and a thought crosses my mind with the force of Iteru rushing over the cataracts: In a court full of vipers, I truly don't know which one I should fear most.

SIX

S ATIAH AND NEBTAH, MY TWO MOST TRUSTED TROUPE LEADERS, flank me as I march through the temple pylon gates, passing images of fierce gods and reverent rulers. The sun has risen, announcing another scorching day. Iset waits for me, leaning against the enormous obelisk erected by my grandfather. She waves an ostrich-feather fan in front of her face and ignores the guards loitering at her back. Satiah stops to speak with a small girl—there's not a child in Kemet the priestess can resist—and Nebtah peels away to join her.

Our duties are done anyway, so I turn to wave goodbye and stop dead in my tracks.

A mousy-looking young woman stands next to the child's mother. She disregards the beaming woman and giggling little girl, both entranced by Satiah's attention, to stare boldly at me. It's so unexpected I flinch at the eye contact, rarer than Kushite gold when one is the princess and high priestess. Then I notice the inked pincers reaching out from the top of her white linen sheath dress, cut in a straight line across the chest and held up by two thick straps. I follow the pincers to find a tail curving up and across the top of her left breast.

She knows I see the tattoo. I can tell by the way she smiles before turning to march away.

I follow, heart banging, as she waltzes deeper into the temple, through one of Grandfather's pylon gates, curving around one of Mother's twin obelisks and disappearing into the columned hall with its gold-leaf papyrus columns and mummiform statues. Panic creeps down my spine. This is my chance. I can't let this girl slip away.

I catch a glimpse of Iset, rushing toward me, just as I spot my prey, lingering on the other side of the next pylon, near the red quartzite shrine Mother is building for Amun's bark. I stumble when the girl shrugs and glides inside. The shrine has not been consecrated—it's still under construction—but still she has no business going this deep into the temple.

I pick up the pace, rushing into the chapel, then stop so abruptly Iset, who has caught up to me, bumps into my back, then gasps at the young woman standing in the shrine's vestibule, clearly feeling at home in the space designed to one day house Amun's ship-shaped portable shrine.

"Who are you?" I ask the girl. "Why are you here?"

"I'm here to answer your questions." She motions toward the scorpion inked into her chest, stinger raised in warning. "You've been asking about my mistress, and you've flashed that amulet at every servant in the palace." She motions toward Iset's bracelet, dangling from my arm, her tone sardonic. I have been rather zealous with it. "As for who I am, I'm just another member of the nest."

"Nest," I repeat. "You mean your little group of spies?"

"We do far more than spy." She glances at a sketch that marks where my image will be carved. I'm traced on the wall, offering wine and milk to the god, a diadem encircling my short wig. A grid of straight lines runs side to side and top to bottom, ensuring the artist's proportions stay true.

I quell the anger and study her. She's young, plain, and dripping in confidence.

Iset asks the girl her name. I'm surprised when she gives it: it's Senseneb. The name fits her. Senseneb was the name of my great-grandmother, who is rumored to have been common and arrogant as well.

"What exactly is it your nest does? Who are you people?" I ask.

"We're a group of women—"

"All women?"

"Men are allies." She rubs a hand against the wall absently. "Many help my mistress because they care about the same things we care about. But the scorpions, yes, we are all women."

"The spies, you mean? Are you all in the palace?"

She eyes me thoughtfully, her voice steady. "We're where people need us, which means we're everywhere."

"People need you?" I scoff. "Do you feed them? Care for them? Appease the gods to keep them safe?"

I'm being sarcastic—those duties are mine and Mother's alone—but the girl's response is serious. "We feed and care for them, yes. Appeasing the gods is, well, everyone's job, no? It's a lofty one at that. We're happy to leave the sacrifice and ritual and theatrical ceremony to the god's wife." She says it almost with a sneer, so removed from the reverence my position usually earns. Her eyes glitter with derision as she reaches out to touch the sketch of me in ritual. "While you're busy with…whatever this is"—she lifts a brow—"we're engaged in more tangible work. We get the people of Kemet jobs. We help them find care when they need it. My mistress spreads cures. Little of what she does for the people is political, but when it is, she uses her power and resources to see that your royal squabbles don't spill over and hurt the subjects you're meant to serve. That's her goal anyway." The girl pauses, tipping her head to the side. "She's not always successful, I'm afraid."

I cross my arms, shielding the goose bumps that dapple my skin in spite of the day's heat. "And if quelling royal battles requires murder? Would that fit into her agenda?"

The girl's face is still. "I'm not the right woman to answer that, but it may be necessary at times, no?"

I think through her point. Murderers and thieves and enemy soldiers must be punished. But putting a criminal to death is not the same as poisoning a pharaoh. "Who is your mistress to decide who to punish?"

She shrugs. "Who is yours?"

"Mother, you mean? Pharaoh? Her authority comes from the gods—"

"My mistress would say the same."

I release a strangled laugh, wondering if this woman I've been searching for is more mad than wise. But as fascinating as this girl's answers are, they're not the answers I need most. "You say you're here to answer my questions."

She nods.

"Fine. Then tell me if Hathor is working with my mother."

"No, my mistress is not aligned with Pharaoh."

A chill runs through me. Does that mean she's aligned against her? That could be even worse.

"Did she ever work with Mother, perhaps during the end of Father's reign?" In spite of all I've learned about Mother, I still want to believe she's innocent of this brutal crime—the death of a pharaoh, my own father.

Senseneb shakes her head; her blunt bangs swish over her face. "I will tell you the truth, as much as I'm able—those are my orders. But I cannot tell you what I do not know. And I do not know if my mistress once worked with your mother. Only that she is not doing so now and has not in the past decade. Before that, I was not involved."

"And Thutmose. Is Hathor working with him?"

She grins at that. "That's a question I can answer with confidence: no. The young pharaoh is volatile. And capricious rulers put people in danger."

"By your logic, that means you and your mistress would be fine with putting him in danger?"

"He's already in danger. He may not survive the battle to come. But that is by another's hands, not my mistress's."

"My mother's, you mean."

She doesn't answer directly, but the tilt of her chin is all the answer I need.

"Is Hathor near?"

She shrugs. "Sometimes she's near. Sometimes she's far. I cannot tell you where she is now."

Frustration burns at the girl's flippancy. "I need to speak with her. Can you bring her to me?"

"The palace is too dangerous for my mistress."

"Here at the temple then. Or in the market. I'll meet her in a tomb if that is her choice."

"I can pass on your request. I can't say if she'll accept your invitation." She pauses a beat, then adds. "I will tell you that in all the years I've worked for her, I've rarely known my mistress to respond to the summons of another like this."

"Would she accept an invitation from Thutmose? Because he's

searching for her too. And if he finds her before I do, your aim to, how did you phrase it, ensure royal battles don't overflow and hurt the people? Well, that's exactly what will happen if he gets to her first."

"Don't worry," the girl says gravely. "My mistress is used to being hunted. She won't be caught unless she wants to be."

"Can I…" Iset interrupts, then pauses, looking to me for permission to continue. I nod, and she turns back to Senseneb, glancing down at the amulet still clasped around my wrist. "Was my mother one of you?"

Senseneb shifts to press her back against the wall like she's bracing herself, then nods. "They say she was one of the best." Her small smile turns naughty. "If you ever want a place among us, you're welcome to join our nest, Iset."

I freeze at the sound of deep voices, just outside. The workmen have arrived to resume their work. Before I can react, Senseneb pushes away from the wall and glides out of the shrine.

"Senseneb," I hiss at her back. "We're not done here."

She pauses just beyond the doorway, turning back. "Nothing is truly done until Hapi lets Iteru run dry and Anubis calls us home. That's what my mistress says." She wags a finger from me to Iset and back again. "You two should be careful too. Thutmose isn't the only one dancing on the edge of disaster."

With that, she disappears into the morning. What she meant or whether her visit will lead to more is a mystery for another time.

"Well, that was interesting," Iset sighs when we're alone.

"Yes," I agree. I realize Iset is looking at the bracelet, so I slip it off and hand it to her with thanks, wondering how she feels about her mother's role in the nest, just as one of the workmen steps inside, stiffening when he sees me.

I nod as he bows low, stepping forward to slip past him and lead Iset out. Thutmose is leaving for war today, and I'm duty bound to be there as the troops march away. My stomach squirms as I wonder again if Mother's plot will succeed and he'll be gone for good or if he'll return and use the rumor—true or not—that Mother murdered Father to tear down everything we have achieved.

SEVEN

THE OLD WOMAN'S NEARNESS IS LIKE SHARDS OF POTTERY shoved beneath my henna-tinted nails. Rather than Iset, my friend and confidant, at my side today, I'm joined by one of Mother's handmaids. To make matters worse, I have no idea where Iset is. After weeks of quiet—weeks spent wondering how Thutmose fares and if Hathor will agree to see me—I woke this morning to find Iset gone. Her mother's bracelet was on the ground by my door as if she'd dropped it for me to find. My worry only doubled when I spotted the old woman waiting by the small boat I ride across the river each morning. She took Iset's spot at my side, but even when pressed, she refused to explain Iset's absence.

Finally done with the morning ritual, I march toward Mother's quarters.

It's only when I enter her room and find her coiled like a cobra, the note I wrote more than a month ago now asking Kamut to come to my room in the middle of the night in her tight fist, that I understand how dire the situation is.

My anger vanishes, replaced in an instant by fear. "I can explain," I begin.

"Did you believe I would not find out?" Mother throws the crumpled papyrus at my feet, and my head spins, wondering how the scroll found its way to her.

"It's not what it looks like. I was trying to—"

"I should have known better than to let Senenmut install some peasant in your rooms. But even if that girl doesn't know better than to mate with some man in your quarters, you should."

"That didn't happen," I cry.

"You are the daughter of two pharaohs, Neferura, not some village housewife, helping girls rid themselves of unwanted pregnancies for extra cabbage."

"Unwanted pregnancy? What are you talking about?" My mind spins, turning over the words. I remember the crocodile dung, and my heart sinks. Mother must know about the jar Iset took from the wisewoman's old rooms. "That's not what—"

"I deserve more after all I have done for you. Who is the man?"

I almost sag with relief. At least Mother doesn't know Kamut was the man in my rooms. But how can I convince her Iset did nothing wrong? "You've got it all wrong, Mother. Iset did not—"

"Do not tell me I am wrong. Or was it you dallying with a man in the middle of the night?" Her voice is low, but it thrums with danger.

"Of course not. You can't possibly believe I would betray the god. I know my duty."

"You are too old for such naivete," she snaps. "You are not in this position at the behest of the gods. You're unmarried, Neferura, so that you'll be in a position to rule after me. Any man you marry would suck power out of your body like a baby suckling milk from its mother. We cannot have that. Above all, we cannot have Thutmose claiming the power you carry. It's not that the god demands your virginity, child. It's that I demand your loyalty. Unfettered. Until it's time for the throne to go to you."

I gape at her, shocked speechless. I've spent my entire life believing the gods demanded my virginity. And it wasn't true? Ever? It was Mother's greed this entire time?

In spite of everything I've learned about her, I never imagined she'd use the gods like this, lie about their will to advance her schemes—schemes I want no part of. Ironic from a woman whose throne name, Maatkare, pronounces that the soul of Ra is truth.

"I don't want the throne, Mother," I cry, desperate to make her see how wrong she's been. "The country would rebel. And they'd be right to. I don't want to rule. I don't want people to die just because you think I should. And I certainly don't want you to murder Thutmose to give me a throne I've never wanted."

Flames flicker in her eyes. "I am Pharaoh, Neferura. I will decide who rules and when. I will decide how, where, and if."

I deflate, worn down by too much unwanted information coming at me too fast. I weigh my words. There are so many things to say and too many said already. I ask about the one thing I need to know most. "Where is Iset?"

"Gone."

The word makes my blood run cold. I twine my fingers together, the panic mounting. "Please, Mother. Don't hurt her—"

"She's been sent from the palace."

I exhale. Sent from the palace is better than dead. It's better than being whipped or tortured or locked in the dungeon.

"And her father has been stripped of his position," Mother continues. "Perhaps you'll think twice before you attempt to betray me again."

"I didn't betray you. She did not sleep with a man in my rooms. You're wrong. And not just about Iset."

"You think you know better than Pharaoh?" She runs stubby fingers over her slick, black wig, cropped at the shoulders with a shroud of impenetrable bangs. "If you're so clever, daughter, perhaps you no longer need a tutor. Consider Senenmut's position rescinded."

"What?" My heart hammers in my chest, a chill creeping down my spine. "Why? What does Senenmut have to do with this?"

Mother's glare is as venomous as an asp's. "Senenmut can keep the title. But he's to be your tutor in name only. You will no longer study with him. You are to keep your distance—"

"You'll stop me from seeing Senenmut out of spite?"

"Spite and insight," she says cryptically.

"Insight," I repeat. I have no idea what she means, but I do know the two people who bring joy to my daily life are gone. I may never see Iset again. And the hours I spend with Senenmut, reading the words of the wise men and studying my ledgers together, hours that fill my heart with peace and knowledge, are to be no more.

"You chose to host a man in your rooms, and now we cannot afford to let rumors simmer."

"What rumors?"

She doesn't answer, but there's only one rumor she could be referring too—the rumor that I'm Senenmut's child. It's a rumor I've ignored my entire life. Of course that was before I knew Mother was capable of such staggering lies, plotting even against the gods. All these years, all the machinations and scheming, to put me on the throne, no matter how many people get hurt.

Mother yells for her handmaid, and I lean down to pick up the note. I can't stop the tears from flowing, wiping tracks down my skin. I can't imagine who gave mother the letter and told her about the ingredient we stole from Inhapi's rooms. I don't know who or how, but someone discovered my secret and sent the information right into the hands of the one I needed to keep it from most.

I sob quietly as Mother marches into her dressing room. I stare at the blurry scroll, then drop it on the stone floor before running toward my quarters, praying to Amun as I run: *Great God, mighty Amun, please hear me. Help me unmask the one who betrayed me. Grant me the power to punish them and bring Iset back.*

EIGHT

I SPEND THE NEXT MONTH MISSING ISET, SEARCHING THE PALACE
for tattooed girls, wondering if Thutmose is alive or dead, and
watching Senenmut from afar at dinners and palace affairs. I'm not
allowed to speak with him. And I can't translate his enigmatic glances.

Mother's handmaids see to my toilette, a different one each day
of the week. They barely look at me, much less speak to me. They've
been trained by Mother to be utterly invisible. I long for Iset's inces-
sant chatter. My world is finally silent. I once thought I wanted that.
The reality is lonelier than I could have imagined.

I worry constantly about Iset's safety. Her father's anger must be
great. How will they eat? Where will they live? I twirl her mother's old
bracelet, staring down at the scorpion amulet. I imagine Iset being
dragged from my rooms, dropping the bracelet as a final farewell to
me. I wish she'd taken some of my gold to remember me by or, better
yet, to trade for food when times turn desperate. I'd give all the gold
in my estate to know how Mother got her hands on the note.

I hold my breath each time I pass Kamut. I don't dare look at
him, lest someone suspect he was the man who snuck into my rooms.

At least he's safe. I hold on to the thought. It's the only good news I can find in a pile of catastrophes.

I can't stop myself from suspecting Thutmose is right, as much as it pains me. Maybe Mother did poison Father. It's clear she'll kill Thutmose soon if she can. I obsess over news from his campaign, the deadly mission she's sent him on. He's somewhere near the coast of the Wadj-wer now, fighting enemy troops along the shore. It's hardly surprising he'd want to ruin Mother after all she's done to him. And if he believes I want his throne, why wouldn't he come after me as well?

I can't shake the belief that Hathor is the key. Thutmose himself once called her that; perhaps in that he was right too. I remember Senenmut once saying Hathor could turn the tides in whatever direction she wanted. Does that mean the wisewoman could help me keep Thutmose safe and craft some solution that keeps us all in our roles and, more to the point, alive? That assumes what Senseneb said about working to protect people from royal squabbles is true. It's equally possible that the girl lied. For all I know, the scorpions gave Mother the note I wrote to Kamut.

I can't risk talking to Kamut, and the only other person who might know how Mother learned of his midnight visit is banned from my presence. I have no idea if Senenmut wants to talk to me. At a dinner last week, I lifted my hand to my ear. For a moment, I thought I could tug it and our secret sign would make everything all right. I paused and someone distracted him before I found my courage. But the truth is I don't care how he feels. He has answers to the questions that plague me. One way or another, I'm going to get them.

Tonight's festival is as fun as a scorpion's sting. I'm dressed in my finery, a broad golden collar circling my neck, falcon-headed terminals facing left and right. Its carnelian and obsidian beads match the beads that adorn the belt I wear, so long it nearly touches the bottom of my narrow, ankle-length gown.

I'm expected to charm the nobles by showing off my extensive learning during dinner. That's an enormous task under the circumstances. Thutmose is outperforming even the highest expectations. He's taken to war like a crocodile to the waters of Iteru. Although young, our fearless pharaoh is leading men in battle and securing victories none thought possible, his success talked about with awe throughout the great hall. Plus, the nobles have heard me quote the wise men a million times. If they ever were impressed with their learned princess, their enthusiasm has faded by now.

I'm hoping to escape the moment dinner is over, but Mother makes her expectations clear with a royal glare: I'm not going anywhere. I console myself by spying on Senenmut. He keeps his distance, but I can tell he's aware of me by the way he skirts the room, as if there's a rule that he has to give me a predetermined amount of space. For all I know, there is.

"Adoratrice."

I turn to find Thuiu. "Thank the goddess, someone I actually want to talk to."

"I'm not the only one," she retorts. "Senenmut and Nehsi are worthy. And they appear to be having a good time."

"Are they?" My ignorance is feigned. I've been watching Senenmut talk animatedly with Nehsi through the harpist's past three songs. Nehsi is famous throughout Kemet for leading Mother's expedition to the far-off land of Punt. He's also one of the nicest men at court. Like Senenmut, he's self-made, having risen from nothing to power under Mother, which means, of course, his loyalty to her is unquestioned. At the moment, they're face-to-face, wearing similar wigs; black curls hang to the napes of their necks, hugging their heads, and blunt black bangs nearly touch their eyebrows.

"I'm happy to see you tonight, my dear. I've been meaning to talk to you about a passage I've reinterpreted..."

Thuiu's words fall away as a tall guard with a square jaw interrupts Senenmut's conversation to hand him a scroll. Senenmut unrolls it, scowls, nods at the guard, then says something to Nehsi before turning to scan the room.

His eyes find mine, and for a moment, even the harp fades. It's just the two of us, alone in a crowded room, gazes locked.

I reach up and tug an ear. It's more of a question than a statement. I wait for him to tug his ear in response, confirming everything will be all right.

He doesn't do it. He bites his lip, then sags. A heartbeat passes before he pivots to march away.

My heart throbs. The old inquisitiveness, once stoked by Iset—it's faded since her departure—returns with force. That scroll has something to do with me. I saw it in Senenmut's eyes. And his unwillingness to engage in our old game tells me he has no intention of telling me about it. Not anymore.

"Neferura." Thuiu lays long, wrinkled fingers on my arm. "Are you all right?"

I turn to her, anger creeping up my spine. "I need to leave." If Senenmut is not going to tell me what he knows, I'll find out for myself. For all I know, that scroll contains the names of every scorpion in the palace, or details of Mother's or Thutmose's plans, or information about Iset. Or any of the number of things that haunt my dreams—the spells carved into my headrest no longer keep the terrors at bay. I'm sick of sitting in my study, thinking and wondering, waiting for some mysterious band of women to rescue me. I hear Iset's words. They're as real as if she were here with me, speaking them in my ear. *"You have to put down the scrolls and actually do things."*

She's right. I've been still since she left. But if I'm to move forward, I must start moving now.

"Neferura," Thuiu repeats.

"Can you hold Mother's attention so I can sneak out?"

She scrunches her eyes together, deepening the crevices that crisscross her face. Her pupils dart to the handmaids who line the wall. They're whispering with each other. She glances at Mother, talking to a bevy of hairless priests, then nods at me. "Fine. But go quickly. And do be careful, my dear."

I try to make myself invisible. I cast my eyes down and pull my arms close, keeping my steps light as I weave my way out of the great hall to follow Senenmut, praying none of the handmaids tasked with following me notices my escape. I pause inside the hallway, listening, but aside from the chatter and the melodious harp, there's nothing, not even footsteps.

It doesn't matter. I know where Senenmut is headed. His quarters are this way. I rush toward his rooms, stopping just before I turn the corner into the hallway where the guard stationed at his door stands.

Peeking around the corner, I find my old tutor speaking with his guard. Their voices are too low to make out, but Senenmut beckons at his door and the guard opens it and follows him inside.

I rush to the door, stopping it just before it bangs shut. I listen through the crack but there's nothing to hear. One deep breath and I peek inside. Senenmut's elegantly furnished receiving room is empty. I slip in. The door shuts behind me, and a longing for Iset hits me like a sandstorm. I'm not sure how I turned into a sneaky rule breaker. But I do know that sneaking around with Iset at my side was if not fun at least less terrifying.

I hear voices in Senenmut's study—his study door is one of the three openings that spot this room. I jump behind a wooden armoire and shove my back against the wall, then hold my breath until Senenmut and the guard leave.

The door clicks shut, and I exhale. I'm alone. But I'm not safe. The guard will be stationed in the hallway on the other side now. And there are more guards outside, beyond Senenmut's open wall, one room over. There's no way for me to leave without being seen. I drop my head in my hands and think. If I were a scorpion, Iset's mother perhaps, what would I do? For that matter, what would Iset do if she were here with me?

I know the answer to the last question: my old handmaid would be bold. She'd make the risk worthwhile.

I step out of my hiding spot and head for Senenmut's study. If there's anything in his quarters that will shed light on what he knows and what the scroll he just received has to do with me, that's where it'll be.

I sink into the carved wooden chair behind Senenmut's cedar desk. I pick up his glazed steatite cylinder seal and read the inscription etched into it: *Great Steward, Senenmut, Overseer of the Cattle of Amun.* Only my old tutor bothers with this old-fashioned seal form anymore, although he has plenty of stamp seals and scarab seals as well. I set it aside to riffle through piles of scrolls, searching for the one Senenmut just received. There are eight rolls of papyrus on the desk—two about small military skirmishes with the Naharin, three tracking temple goods heading to Kemet from Alashiya and Kush, one from a priest informing Senenmut of his views on recent infighting in Amun's temple, and two listing Djeser-Djeseru workmen and the supplies needed to keep them fed and paid.

I lean back, mimicking a pose Senenmut often strikes, peering over steepled fingers. Unless the scroll is still on him, it has to be here. Where would he put it? The one the guard gave him was smaller than any of these, with darker papyrus. Perhaps…

I scan the room. Somewhere in here, there's a secret hiding spot. And knowing Senenmut, it won't be easy to detect. He'd put it within arm's reach. I run my hands over an alabaster box and two wooden trays. Nothing. My fingers skip across the desktop, then around the sides, before running down the legs.

There.

I drop to my knees and inspect the three small pegs protruding from the back of the desk's left leg. Fiddling with the buttons, I release a door that opens to reveal a small compartment inside the hollow leg. The scroll is inside. I pull it out and unroll it, heart hammering. The missive skips over the usual naming of the scribe and titles of the addressee and mention of gods and list of well wishes to get right to the point, as if whoever penned it writes Senenmut often enough to dispense with the formalities.

In life, prosperity, and health, I have much to report.

First, you'll be pleased to learn that the plot to end him once he reached Retjenu failed. I can't say if more attempts will be made, but I can assure you Set survived. The man who had been paid to kill him now floats in the great green sea.

Second, your guess is correct. Though lowborn, the chambermaid's nephew is often by Set's side. I suspect the boy gathered the information from his aunt, then reported Isis's behavior to Set. I believe Set reported it to Nut in an effort to sow chaos between them. If rumors are to be believed, it worked. But that, dear friend, is a problem for you, not a lowly servant like me. Thank the gods for small triumphs.

Finally, our man followed up on the rumor you passed on. He went to Sap-Meh to investigate and met the woman. He swears it's not her. If the lady of stars is still alive, she remains in hiding.

I'll report more when I have worthwhile information. Until then, stay well, old friend.

My hands are trembling so violently I have to press the scroll against the desk to read it again. On the third pass, the pieces fall together. Set, the god of chaos and discord, must be Thutmose. Which leaves Isis, his sister—that must be me—and Nut, their mother, presumably Mother. Fire races through my blood. Knowing the risk I took sneaking into this room paid off is a rush. Because of this note, I know Mother actually did make an attempt on Thutmose's life, and it failed. So far. Hathor could be the lady of stars. If so, Senenmut is looking for her. Does that mean he knows about Thutmose's plan to accuse Mother of murder? Why else would he be looking for the wisewoman? But who is the chambermaid's nephew?

I read it again, then slump in the chair as my world spins. A series of pictures flashes before my eyes: the chambermaid walking in on me and Iset side by side on the chaise; the words I spoke as she entered—*"You may find yourself in need of an abortifacient"*; Kamut dropping the note I wrote him on the table in my bedroom for my chambermaid to clean up later. Who else would know about the crocodile dung in my rooms? My chambermaid could have seen it all. And she is the one person alive who absolutely had access to the scroll that made its way to Mother.

I can barely breathe. If my chambermaid's nephew is close to Thutmose, then Thutmose must have given Mother the letter I wrote to Kamut, along with information about the abortifacient. He wanted to—I turn back to the scroll—"sow chaos."

My mind reels. I did not think for one moment that Thutmose was behind this, that he is to blame for Iset being sent away. I didn't even consider my chambermaid as a suspect. I'd barely recognize the woman if she walked into the room right now and sat down next to me. She usually comes when I'm out, invisible and efficient.

I nearly jump out of my skin when voices ring out from the other side of the door. Heart pounding, I shove the scroll back into Senenmut's secret compartment, my eyes searching the room for someplace to hide. With no good option at hand, I sit tall in Senenmut's chair. I'll have to pretend I snuck in to talk to him.

"Thank you for seeing me, sir."

Kamut?

"I'm sorry to disturb you in private like this…"

I rush to the door. Pressing my ear against it, I hear Senenmut's response.

"…anytime you have concerns, son. Worrying about her is one thing we have in common."

"If you can just look at this?" It's Kamut's voice, but loud. Too loud. "Can we step into the other room, where the light is stronger?"

Footsteps move past the door, into the next room, which is open to the outside. I crack open the study door and peer out to see Kamut, standing in the other doorway, blocking Senenmut from view. Kamut glances back at me and scowls.

He knew I was here.

He jerks his head, instructing me. He's keeping Senenmut busy so I can escape. But what's the point? Senenmut's guard will see me the second I open the door.

"Are you sure?" Kamut turns back to Senenmut and stands wide, shielding me. "I can't shake this feeling. Would you mind taking one more look?"

He glances back at me, lips pursed. He looks angry. He nods his head toward the door again, more insistent.

With a deep breath, I rush to the door, open it, and nearly faint from relief when I find the hallway empty. I slip out and let the door close behind me. My legs are so shaky I can barely stand. I force them to move—one foot, the next, the first again—until I'm back in the great hall with its loud music and the smell of too many bodies. Dinner is just being laid on long flower-covered tables.

I spot Thuiu speaking with Mother. The handmaids are lined up against the wall. No one has noticed my absence. I'm safe. And more importantly, I know just who to blame for stealing Iset and Senenmut away.

I'm dying to confront Kamut about rescuing me from Senenmut's rooms, but that feels impossible when I'm not allowed to talk to him. Finally, I break down and force the opportunity.

I'm entering my quarters, one of Mother's treacherous handmaids trailing me, when a servant boy, the son of a guard who rows me to temple each morning—a boy I paid handsomely yesterday—runs up and whispers my well-crafted message in the old lady's ear. She excuses herself with a cry and a quick bow my way before following the boy down the hall, leaving me standing alone next to my handsome guard. I feel a little guilty—her grandson is fine, as far as I know—but desperate times demand innovative solutions. The lady glances back once, and I step forward and let my chamber door swing shut behind me, stopping it with my heel before it closes.

I wait a few heartbeats, then step back and turn to Kamut. "How did you know I was there?"

He meets my eyes boldly. "Are you sure you want to have that conversation? I thought you were scared of a little danger?" His lips twist into a grin.

"Oh, Ra, help me." I drop to the floor. I intend to fall with finesse, but I have the grace of a hippo, so even my dramatic, fake faint is clumsy. I roll onto my back, ignoring the flush creeping up my skin, enthralled by the dimple curving down Kamut's cheek. "Better?"

"I don't know. Is it?" He drops to one knee and leans close—close enough for me to inhale his scent: beer and cinnamon.

"I'm fainting," I explain. "If someone comes, say I dropped and you're checking on me. Tell them to run for the doctor. Act hysterical, or…or…I don't know, do whatever you have to do."

His crooked smile sends the familiar flock of birds soaring around my belly. I slow my breath, determined to ignore the tingly feeling filling my chest.

"How did you know I was in Senenmut's study?" I repeat.

He shakes his head, defeated. "You're more stubborn than you were as a girl, you know?"

"Yes," I admit, surreptitiously studying the lighter-colored speckles in his dark eyes. They're even more astonishing up close. "I'm working at it. Now talk!"

He glances down the hall. Finding it empty, he turns back to me. "I saw you follow Senenmut. I've been keeping an eye on you both since Iset left. I've been trying to tell you—"

"Someone told Mother Iset had been in my quarters with a man."

"I'm sorry, little princess. I shouldn't have—"

"Stop," I whisper. "I asked you to come. You came. We did nothing wrong. I hate that Iset is gone, but I'm glad you're still here. And safe." I swallow, willing my heart to stop banging. "But why were you watching? Why did you follow me?"

"I have news for you. I was plotting a way to get to you when I saw you trail Senenmut. I knew you were in his quarters. I was talking to the guard, planning your escape, when Senenmut returned. What was I supposed to do? He was going back inside. The best I could do was go with him."

"What were you showing him?" I ask.

"Nothing." Kamut shrugs. At my glare, he continues. "I was doing whatever I had to do, as you say. I pulled an old clay tablet out of my pocket. I keep it because it's the first thing my brother ever wrote. I'm superstitious about the little tablet. I asked Senenmut to read it. I implied I had some reason to suspect it had something to do with you."

"What does it say?"

"It says 'Writing is more enjoyable than a basket of beans.'"

I laugh, the words clicking together instantly. "Nebmarenakht's advice to his pupil, Wenemdiamun. Most scribes study it in school."

Kamut smiles wider. "And you studied it at five years old, I'm guessing?"

I roll my eyes, mostly because staring into Kamut's is making me dizzy.

"I just needed to get Senenmut's attention so you could slip out. It's not like I had a lot of time to plan. His guard owed me a favor— he'd agreed to leave his post for a few moments—but I knew he wouldn't stay away for long."

"But why? Why take the risk?"

The birds in my belly flutter their wings faster. Kamut looks into my eyes, and I'm scared he can see the flock, my fears, my secret fantasies.

"Look, Nefer—" he stops, instantly tense.

My heart is in my throat. My skin is hot. Suddenly, there's nothing in the world I want more than to hear my name on his tongue. "No one will hear you," I whisper.

A heartbeat passes, then, "Neferura." He swallows hard.

I watch the Adam's apple in his throat jump, suddenly alive with the knowledge that the god does not, after all, demand my virginity.

Mother does.

But Mother is not here.

My hand reaches up like it has a will of its own.

He's perfectly still as I touch my fingers gently to the scar.

My skin tingles at the touch.

"I'd do it again." His voice is husky.

The god may not require abstinence from me, but that doesn't change the fact that this simple touch could cost Kamut his life. My eyes are suddenly blurry. "It's not worth your life."

"I honestly think it might be." His eyes are steamy.

I act without thinking, leaning up, stretching toward him.

He meets me in the middle.

The kiss is soft and sweet. Gentle but full of desperation and danger.

When he pulls away, too soon, I want to yank him back to me. But his eyes widen and I hear the footsteps.

Kamut grips my shoulders, speaking fast. "I found one. There's a kitchen girl with a tattoo on her wrist."

"A scorpion?" I didn't think it was possible for my heart to race faster.

"Yes." He glances down the hall as the footsteps draw closer.

Any second now, someone will turn the corner, and this moment will be lost to time, gone forever. I have to make it count. I must convince Hathor to help me before Thutmose finds her and uses her against us all.

"Bring the girl to me." I lie back down and squeeze my eyes shut. "And please," I whisper. "Bring her soon."

PART
TWO

NINE

TIME FEELS LIKE A COILED SNAKE READYING TO STRIKE. Months creep past. Every day is agony, waiting to learn if Thutmose survived another day, hoping Kamut will deliver the scorpion girl to me, worrying about Iset.

If it weren't for my temple duties, I'd have gone out of my mind. My priestesses have been extra attentive. I suspect Satiah and Nebtah noted Iset's absence and decided I need cheering. They're studiously optimistic, perpetually armed with compliments and hands ready to help. I appreciate their efforts.

Plus, Mother has relented and agrees to let me speak with Senenmut again. He now joins us for dinner once a week. He's still not allowed to tutor me, but we can talk when Mother is feeling tolerant. So far, we've had exactly one opportunity to speak alone. I used it to ask him to replace my chambermaid, who, it seems, reports my every move to Thutmose. Predictably, Senenmut had already sent the woman packing. If he wondered how I knew the chambermaid was disloyal, he didn't ask. It's entirely possible he knew exactly what Kamut and I were up to the whole time. My former tutor is nothing if not shrewd. And for once, I'm almost grateful that Senenmut is so adept at seeing through me.

I wish he were here tonight. Dinners with Mother are at least tolerable when he's with us. Pretending we don't both know the villainy she's plotted, what she might have done before, makes small talk laborious. Yet in spite of all the accusations, if her rule comes to a bad end, too many will pay the price, including myself, my priestesses, and my estate. If I could find some way to broker peace between Mother and Thutmose, power might transition peacefully, the people would be safe, and I could continue my work.

But with each day that passes, the possibility feels more remote.

I'm playing with my food, worrying over my mound of troubles, when Mother takes a large swig of her wine and announces, "The doctor is dead."

I drop the fruit I just plucked off a golden plate, and it careens across the stone floor.

"Leave it," Mother orders as I kneel to scoop it up. "The fool man is probably having his heart weighed against the feather right now."

I close my eyes and whisper a quick prayer: *Let his heart be light.* I should probably pray for his daughter as well. After all, I owe Teena for the scars she bears, the justified anger she carries in her heart.

Unless, of course, she was the voice Iset and I heard in Thutmose's rooms. Iset once wondered as much aloud. If the voice was Teena's, she may have already forced my payment in full. It's possible. Teena hates me, and she lives in Hathor's old quarters. Who knows what information she has access to? I've imagined confronting her, but how? Mother's old handmaid is always by my side. And unlike Iset, she's not there to help me but to spy on me. Teena is one string I haven't yet pulled. Perhaps this is my chance.

"We should do something to help Teena." I place the pomegranate back in the bowl. Maybe if I approach the girl carefully, I can offer something valuable in exchange for information. "We can help her find a good match. We could marry her to…" I pause, ticking through unmarried noblemen in my mind. None seem a fit for such a drab girl.

Mother chortles. "Even I might have trouble bribing a man to her bed. She is slow and plain. That girl is trouble. Always has been. Some girls never learn."

"Perhaps the lessons need adjusting," I mumble, handing my gold-rimmed faience cup to the servant girl lurking at my side, waiting to refill my spiced wine.

I notice her closeness and assume she's new to serving in Mother's quarters and unfamiliar with the rules of invisibility. I glance at her, surprised when she holds my gaze. As she returns my glass, she tilts her wrist, revealing a small, unmistakable mark on the delicate skin.

Blood courses through my body as I watch her walk out onto Mother's deck.

Kamut's scorpion has finally come.

"Excuse me," I stutter as I stand to follow. "I need air."

"Neferura!" To Mother, dinner is like a ritual, with a tempo that can't be altered lest one offend the gods.

"I'm sorry, Mother. I need a moment. Please stay. I'll be right back."

I'm awash in relief when Mother turns back to her roasted duck, mumbling something about the many things unruly daughters have in common with Apep, the demon of chaos, beneath her breath.

The girl turns to me as I step outside, just beyond Mother's view. "Your guard is persistent." A heartbeat later she adds, "Adoratrice," as if my status is an afterthought.

"Why should he have to be?" I ask. "Is it so much to ask for you to have a conversation with your princess?"

The girl nods like she's agreeing, but her words say differently. "I am not authorized to speak… I should say I was not. I sent word of your summons to my mistress. I'm sorry it took so long to respond to you. But my mistress told me to tell you that she knows you're searching for her. And to alleviate the risk your continued questions pose to her and to you, she is willing to meet with you."

I feel the momentary sting of embarrassment at her words, immediately smothered by relief. Hathor is coming. Finally.

"When?" I ask.

The girl shrugs. "When she gets here. I can't say how long, but she will make contact when she's ready to meet you."

I press my hand against my stomach, trying to bind my impatience.

"My mistress also wants you to know she's not the only one on the way to the palace. Thutmose is close—closer than your mother knows. Pharaoh is tracking his body double—one of the few that still breathes. But the real Thutmose will be back within the week."

"He's survived another day," I mumble, half in thanks, half in dread.

"He is resilient." She nods.

"That's not all he is," I grunt. "Is your mistress coming to meet with him too?"

"No."

"Will she help me?"

"I do not speak for her."

"You just did."

She smiles. "I speak her words when she tells me to. But I wouldn't go beyond my instructions."

"So your mistress demands great loyalty."

"I would say she earns it."

"Earns it how?"

The girl looks out at the river, then glances at the door to confirm we're alone before her voice picks up again. "My family was killed when I was a child. I'm from Per-Wadjet, but after the men killed my parents and brothers, they took me hostage. I was taken down south, far from my home, forced to serve them against my will. I was abused and alone. A child, although the men didn't care about my age.

"One night, when the moon was high and bright, Hathor appeared like a goddess, manifesting as bloodthirsty Sekhmet, punishing the men who abducted me." The girl pulls in a shaky breath, her eyes misty. "After all she's done for me, all the healing and caring and time she gave me, doing what she asks in return is a small price to pay. She gave me my purpose." She pauses, and her grin returns. "Plus, she is very funny. I love her for rescuing me. But I like her because she's likable."

Likable? I've imagined Hathor as many things—shrewd, mysterious, deadly. Funny and likable weren't on my list of possible attributes.

"I must go." The girl bows and steps toward the door. "Stay ready," she says as she steps in, leaving me alone with the wind and, finally, a tiny, nascent spark of hope.

I lead Satiah through the temple. The spaces expand as we leave the innermost sacred areas. We weave past Mother's two enormous red granite obelisks that tower over us, their pale gold tips casting shadows under our feet, and walk, at last, through the final large pylon and across the outer courtyard, which is open to all believers. It's late morning. A smattering of worshippers gathers in small groups to gossip or sit alone in silent prayer. One young man is selling amulets to the faithful. He drops a handful of Horus's eye charms as Satiah sashays past, not the first man to lose his bearings at the sight of the troupe's most beautiful priestess, I'm sure.

We wind our way to the small office I've set up in one of the administrative buildings, butting up against the enormous wall that rings the temple. It smells of cow and fertile ground—the sacrificial herd is just beyond the wall—but I'm rarely here anyway, and it's convenient for a private conversation. It sat empty for years, but since Iset was sent away, I've spent more time outside ritual with my priestesses. Sometimes I wonder if this is what Iset meant all those months ago when she said her mother had a group of women to lean on. The thought adds warmth to her cold absence.

"Sit." I motion Satiah into a cedar chair and fall onto the room's only chaise. "You asked to speak to me?"

"I did."

"Because you're worried about me?" I ask.

"Not worried." She shakes her head. "Although I will remind you that I'm here to help. If there's anything you need…"

"Are you ready to spy for me again?" I smile.

Her eyes sparkle. "I'd be thrilled to. Anyone new I can spy on?"

I laugh, but then I remember the poor man Satiah spoke to that day, the scribe, Nebwawi, died shortly after he whispered the contents of Thutmose's scroll into Satiah's ears. Perhaps he died because of it. Or not. Who knows what happened to that poor man? I do know that if it weren't for Satiah, I never would have known to spy on Thutmose. I wouldn't have overheard his accusation against Mother. I'd be in the dark, blissful but ignorant.

I've had more than enough ignorance for this lifetime.

"Thank you again for that," I say sincerely.

"You've thanked me many times, Adoratrice. And you know I was happy to do it." Satiah leans forward eagerly. "Honestly, it's the most exciting thing that happened to me in years. I may not look it, but I'm pathetically boring."

I laugh at that—it is hard to believe. "You didn't mind me using you like that? Using your looks against some poor man we didn't know?"

She shrugs. "The gods made me like this. I see no harm in using what they gave me to my advantage. Those born with intellect don't hesitate to use their skills, or those with physical prowess. Why shouldn't I make the gift the goddess Bastet gave me work in my favor? Do you think that's wrong?"

"No." I lean back against the chaise, considering her. Now that I think of it, the comparison between Satiah and the fierce goddess of beauty and pleasure makes sense—catlike grin, sistrum in hand, beautiful but deadly. "I think you are as wise as you are lovely. But I wonder about you sometimes, Satiah. If you don't mind me asking, what is it you want? You've been given beauty, yet it seems unimportant to you, except as a means to an end. If Amun appeared to you now and offered to fulfill a wish, what would it be? And don't waste your wish on helping the orphans—you do enough for them. I want to know what you want for you."

She looks down shyly. If I didn't know her so well, I'd suspect it's artifice. Because I do, I'm certain she's embarrassed of the answer. "I envy you," she says finally. "Your position, I mean. If I could change what I've been given for the gifts of another, I'd have been born to lead. I don't mind being lowborn. Not really. Not for the reasons others do anyway. But if I had been born to power, I could make a real difference. Yes, for the orphans, but also the priestesses. And for me too. Others see only the way I look, not what I can do. Most don't expect much of me. They certainly don't expect me to be wise or clever or competent. My beauty masks my capabilities, except when it enhances them." She flips a braid over her shoulder. "I would very much like to be in a position not only to reward the worthy but to punish the greedy and selfish."

"You really are good at so many things," I say honestly. "And you're right—rewarding the worthy is one of the best things about my position. Thank you for telling me. I'll keep your goals in mind. But that's not what you wanted to talk to me about."

"No. I wanted to give you this." She pulls a gold chain over her head and hands it to me. "In private."

"What is it?" I take the necklace, admiring the long, narrow, rounded chamber that dangles from a gold chain. It almost certainly holds a small scroll—a blessing for the wearer. "A gift? You really are worried about me."

"It's the best gift: a message from Iset," Satiah whispers. "She found me in the market. She asked me to give it to you. I can return it to her if you like. Anytime. Truly." She stands as I stare down at the golden cylinder, eyes blurry with tears. "Return it to me if you want to write back to her. I'm happy to be of service. I'm also remarkably discreet," she says with a wink before bobbing her head and leaving me alone with my pounding heart.

The moment the door clicks shut behind her, I unlatch the end with trembling fingers and unroll the tiny scroll inside.

In life, prosperity, and health and in the favor of the gods and goddesses, I write in the hope that you don't mind me asking your priestess for help. She was so lovely the first time we put her to work to advance our schemes, and I knew you wouldn't want me to bother Kamut with this. But I am desperate to communicate with you, so this seemed the wisest course. Our friend's brother is the one writing down my words, by the way. I had to trust someone, and I'm betting this handsome man—truly, he's as adorable as his brother—is trustworthy.

Iset is safe.

And close.

Relief thrums through my limbs. I close my eyes, whispering a prayer of thanks to Amun.

Clever girl. She knew to leave Kamut out of this. Satiah is a much better choice and more ambitious than I ever would have believed. If I knew where Iset was, I might have initiated this plan myself. I'm not thrilled to learn Iset turned to Kamut's brother to write for her. I suppose that means Kamut will know what passes between us, which feels oddly intimate. The memory of our stolen kiss rises, and I push it away and return to her letter, hungry for more.

I've been praying for guidance since I was tossed out of the palace, unfairly, of course, although I can't figure out how this information, along with some misinformation it seems, reached Pharaoh. Did she tell you she had me woken in the night and pulled out of your quarters bound and gagged? I barely had time to drop Mother's bracelet for you. I do hope you found it and knew I was saying goodbye the only way I could.

But that information is old news. You'll want to know that I'm safe. Father is safe too. And angry, predictably. But our situation should improve soon. Two tattooed girls have been in touch. Incidentally, if they know who framed me, they aren't saying. They did offer to pass a letter to you—I swear by Thoth they read minds—but if I agreed, then they'd know every word that passed between us. I haven't yet decided if we can trust them, and I'm not sure how you'd feel about it, so I refused that offer.

But I have agreed to join them. They promise to find me and Father jobs, which we desperately need. It will also put me closer to the wisewoman. Perhaps I can get her to speak with you if I'm working from inside the nest. I haven't been asked to do anything yet, but I promise to report everything I learn to you through Satiah, unless you order otherwise. I may be a scorpion now, but my loyalty is to you, not Hathor. That will never change, even if I one day cover myself with tattoos.

That is all there is to report about that.

But there is more. I have personal news. You'll want to sit down for this part.

I'm to be a married woman, the mistress of my own house!

I'm still quite shocked to say the words aloud, as it's so new and everything happened so fast. I was still reeling from being exiled from the palace when I met him. His timing was perfect. Now I'm moving into the home of Meriptah, who works as an artisan decorating the tombs at Ta-sekhet-ma'at. He has a home in the village.

My husband—the word feels strange on my tongue—promises me a new milk cow as a wedding gift. I plan to name her Bast. I do hope she'll keep me company. (I'm accustomed to quiet companions after all.)

I wish you could meet him. I've convinced myself that you'd approve. He's quite stern and serious and rather ambitious. I think of you and of my mother. I'm convinced you'd like his solemn and earnest nature, and she'd be drawn to his kindness and efficiency.

And that thing we once discussed, the thing neither of us had done (although I was released from your service for suspicion of doing it!), I can tell you it's every bit as wonderful as I hoped. He's sweet and patient. I do hope you get to enjoy true love one day, Mistress. It's unfair that your position could strip you of the pleasures I'm enjoying now. (I'm imagining you now, blushing more than Kamut's brother, who just figured out what I'm talking about! Is it wrong that the thought of you squirming as you read this makes me smile?)

Anyway, enough of my romance. I do hope you'll write back. In the meantime, stay aware. He will return eventually, and he is not to be trusted. He'll hurt you if he can. Be brave. And know that I miss you. I miss the hours spent working through your braids and deciding which linens to pair with which jewels. My warmest thoughts go out to you, not to mention a ridiculous number of cheap trinkets left at Hathor's shrine on your behalf.

I read the scroll twice more before burning it in a lantern, determined it should never reach stray hands like the letter I wrote Kamut did. Then I drop my head in my hands and breathe in the cloying air, releasing the fear that's lived in my gut for the past months.

Running the words of Iset's letter through my mind, I hurry to the palace, ordering the old handmaid out of my study. I clutch the necklace, running the strand through my fingers. I pause only for a moment before dipping my pen in ink and scrawling minuscule signs on a small piece of papyrus ripped from a larger scroll. I jot down just a few short sentences congratulating her on her match, praising her for choosing Satiah as go-between, and telling her to keep me informed. I roll the scroll up and wiggle it into the necklace's hiding place, then rethink my words and worry the papyrus out again. Rolling it open, I add a small note:

By the way, Set, a name I've learned Senenmut uses for him, is the one who told Mother about our late-night visitor. My chambermaid found the note I wrote and perhaps mistook a conversation she overheard, which explains why Mother took the visit to be something it wasn't. I wish you were here to help me work through these unwelcome mysteries. I miss you too. But you don't need to worry: I have no intention of letting him hurt me. I too spoke with one of your scorpion sisters, and she says the wisewoman is coming to me soon. It wouldn't hurt for you to pass on my wishes too, if you have the chance. I'm running out of time, and Hathor seems to be the one person who might be able to help me. In the meantime, I'm hoping to learn something about the woman we heard talking to Set through his window. I have a hunch. I plan to follow up and will let you know what I learn.

I shove the small scroll back into the chamber, then string the necklace around my neck so the chamber lies close to my heart, more resolved than ever to get to Teena and uncover the truth of the woman in the window. Knowing Iset is safe and still an ally, even if she's working from afar, fills me with determination.

TEN

I'M MISSING ISET MORE THAN EVER AS I RETRACE OUR PATH through the mazelike servants' quarters toward Hathor's old rooms, the rush of escaping Mother's handmaid still coursing through me. I took advantage when she was distracted by an old nobleman who arrived this morning—an old friend, I gather. Iset would be proud.

I finally find the door and pause. My plan is to offer Teena a large dowry out of my god's wife estate in return for any information she may have. I'm about to knock when I hear noises from inside.

I lean closer, pressing my ear against the door. The moaning intensifies and I jump back, then take a breath and step close again. The sounds are unmistakable. The heat of the revelation crawls up my skin. I should leave. Teena is in her rooms with a man—perhaps she doesn't need help finding a husband after all. But I so rarely manage to escape my keeper. And Thutmose will be back any day now. If Teena knows something, I need to know what it is. According to the scorpions, I may not get another chance before Thutmose returns.

So I ignore the groans of delight and knock quickly, schooling my face. The least I can do is let the poor girl pretend she wasn't…

The door opens. And lurking behind a half-dressed Teena is Thutmose himself, bare-chested and disheveled, dark eyes misty with lust. They land on me and clear as his perfect lips spread wide in a smile.

I stand gaping. I swear I'd be less shocked if I woke to find a tiger sleeping peacefully in bed next to me.

I didn't even realize he'd returned to the palace. And he's the last man I'd expect to be bedding Teena. It's not Thutmose's womanizing that surprises me. If it weren't for Mother's stubbornness and gender, he'd be married to a bevy of women by now. But Mother wants to keep Thutmose away from potential allies just like she wants to keep me an eternal virgin. She can't grant Thutmose a boon she doesn't have herself. So although he's old enough, Thutmose is a pharaoh without wives or children. In that, he may be as singular in our country's long history as Mother is. That doesn't mean he's a virgin. He has—and will always have—his pick of women. And unlike me, he's free to do whatever he wants with them.

But the woman he's picked is, well, unexpected would be an understatement.

I inch away from the door, heart sinking. Teena has already chosen a side. She's not going to help me no matter how much gold I offer. I step back again, bumping into the far wall, speechless as I process the scene.

She pulls her shift up. On instinct, I search her body for tattoos. I don't see any, but her rounded stomach is impossible to miss. It makes my heart sink further.

She's pregnant. With Thutmose's child, it seems.

She turns toward him, and I catch a glimpse of her back,

crisscrossed with scars. As if she needs instructions on how to handle me, she looks up at Thutmose with puppy-dog eyes. His pupils are glued to mine, grin stuck in place. He's proud, whether of the affair or the pregnancy or merely to have made it back alive, I can't say. And I'm not about to ask.

I turn and flee. Teena must have been the woman I heard in Thutmose's quarters, which means he already knows everything she knows, her words whispered into his ears beneath the wisewoman's own curatives and potions.

My plan to learn from her was as ignorant as a mouse in a pile of scrolls.

And what's more, I've run out of time.

Thutmose has indeed returned to Waset. And I have yet to speak with the woman I've spent months seeking.

I dream of scars—legs and breasts and backs and faces covered in hard, sinuous tissue. I wake gasping for breath. Unlike the dreams Senenmut and I once studied together, this dream is not a mystery but a warning.

Too many people bear the scars of the childhood Thutmose and I shared.

Teena is not the only one mutilated by my past. Kamut's scar is also a result of our royal infighting with Thutmose's dog, Anubis, leaving its mark behind. He followed Thutmose everywhere. Aside from me, that dog was Thutmose's only friend.

It all ended one day when Thutmose and I were playing senet. I usually let him win the board game, but that day, sitting near the yard so Thutmose could watch the men fight, I flubbed the play and beat him. He flew into a rage, hitting me with both fists. Kamut saw us and ran to help me. The dog attacked Kamut, shredding his face with sharp teeth.

Later, I lied to Mother, blaming the whole incident on the dog. As terrible as Thutmose's attack on me was, I knew if I told Mother he'd struck me, his punishment would be severe. Mother was cruel to Thutmose even then. And there was no way to explain Kamut putting his hands on a royal without that context. So I said the dog attacked for no reason and that Kamut shielded us. I had to protect Kamut, who'd put himself in danger to protect me. And I wanted to protect Thutmose because I believed that was my duty.

The effort earned me nothing. Thutmose blamed me for the entire thing. It drove him to even more extreme behavior, which eventually got him booted from court.

I relive the day as I lie in bed, plotting a path forward. I'm still convinced Hathor is my best hope. But I can't wait for her any longer. Thutmose is back. Who knows what he'll do or how soon he'll do it? I have to try to reach him, with or without the wisewoman.

By the time I rise for temple, one thing is clear. The enmity between me and Thutmose has endangered too many people. It has to end. And until the wisewoman appears, my best hope of ending it is to embrace the confrontation I've spent years avoiding.

I find Thutmose on the palace's top deck. I stop and watch him. He sits on the wide rail, fondling a dull dagger. Its simple, unadorned grip contrasts sharply with his gold-studded goatskin sandals and heavily beaded tunic. He stares out at the river as three ships float past, large rectangular sails whipping in the wind.

I take a deep breath and walk toward him, bidding the old woman behind me to stay put. The last thing I need is for the words we exchange to enter Mother's ears. Mother was enraged by Thutmose's surprise appearance. Presumably, she believed she knew where he was, unaware she was tracking a body double. Mother's anger must have stemmed in part from being played a fool by the young man she's so easily fooled for years. I can't stop her from knowing we spoke—and being mad at me for it—but I can mask our words.

Thutmose twirls toward the sound of my footsteps. His reaction is lightning fast.

"It's just me." I put my hands up, pausing only a heartbeat before closing the distance and climbing up on to the deck rail to sit next to him. We sit side by side, feet dangling precariously over the edge.

"Lucky me," he says and pouts.

I sigh. I'm sick of him already, and this conversation hasn't even started yet. "I'm glad you're home safe."

"Surprised to see me?"

"Not as surprised as I was yesterday. Congratulations are in order, I guess. Will it be your first child, or are there other royal babies I should know about?"

That earns a familiar snide smile. "What do you want, Neferura?"

"Peace," I say. "I want to find some way to cure this rift between us. The path we're on is dangerous for all of us. One of us is going to get hurt if we don't make a change. You and I were close once. Mother won't hold power forever. You will be pharaoh one day. I want to find a way for us to work together."

"So now you want to be my ally? After all you've done to me?"

I'm tempted to point out he was always the aggressor, but we've had that fight before. I didn't track him down to revisit old arguments. So I take a deep breath and say what I came to say. "I know you believe Mother murdered our father."

"Do I?" He tries to hide his surprise, but I see it in the curve of his cheek, the furrow of his brow.

"You're trying to prove it. But you're wrong."

He snorts, puffed up with disdain.

I stop and start again, honestly this time. "I hope you're wrong anyway. Because if she did and it came to light now, our family would be ruined. And if she didn't but enough people were convinced she did, our family would be ruined. Either way, we're damaged. And if we're damaged, the country is damaged."

Thutmose picks a rock off the rail next to him and throws it. We watch it sail through the air. It's too far away when it lands to see it splash into the river. "You tracked me down today because you think your mother may have murdered our father and you want me to let her get away with it? Is that what you're asking me to do?"

"I'm asking you to put the future above the past. I don't know what happened. Nor do you. But, Thutmose." I turn toward him, balancing on the rail. I pull my knees to my chest and wrap my arms around them. "We must find our way toward peace, all three of us. In time, she'll be gone, and you'll rule. You and I must reconcile."

"Finally you're making some sense. I'll rule in time. That's true whether I work with you or not. How does it benefit me to partner with you? What's in it for me?"

"Your safety, I hope. She tried to have you killed. If we work together, perhaps we can make Mother see that she was wrong. We can convince her that transferring power to you is the best course for everyone."

"If your mother wanted me to have power, I'd have it. Why would she do anything different than she's done before?"

"Because Mother has never faced you and I together. If anything, she's stoked the animosity between us. If we act together, we can convince her this is the only path to security and prosperity, for us and the country." He's listening, so I go on. "You're an excellent military leader. The soldiers look up to you. But you haven't spent enough time at court to understand the people here. I know them all. I can help you. And my estate is second only to Pharaoh's. The House of the Adoratrice is a powerful ally. My role grants me its riches and influence over the priesthood. You won't rule well or long if the priesthood doesn't approve of you. That won't be a problem with me as an ally."

"That would be one way to earn their approval."

His words invite the question—what other way is there? But I don't voice it. Reminding him of the powers I hold is a double-edged sword—I can help him, yes, but I could hurt him as well. I must make him believe I don't want to. "You said yourself I should align with you—"

"I said you should switch sides. That's different."

"But what if there weren't any sides? What if we were all on the same side?"

"What if this bright picture of our happy future is another fantasy you've convinced yourself is worth believing in? It wouldn't be the first time you were delusional." He scoffs. "No. No, I will not join forces with you so we can beg the woman who killed my father, stole my throne, and tried to murder me to play nice." He turns to face me, leaning forward to inch into my space. His face is calm, but his voice is dripping with contempt. "I will explain this to you one time only, Neferura. This court is not big enough for all three of us.

I know that. Your mother knows that. It's absurd that you still can't admit it. But I promise, you and I will never share power. You will be under me or in a tomb with your mother, or I will be in a tomb and your mother's wish to put you on my throne will be fulfilled."

"I don't want—"

"I don't care what you want," he hisses. "Nor does your mother, by the way. You're offering me nothing I can't get without you. If I decide I need to add your power to mine, I'll make that happen on my terms." He climbs off the rail to walk away. "You'll be the first to know when I make that choice. Until then, stay away from me. And from Teena." He spins on his heels and marches toward Mother's old handmaid, who watches us from afar, her mouth round with surprise.

I watch him go, heart throbbing. The conversation wasn't what I hoped for. But it was illuminating. Excruciating as it is to admit, Thutmose is right. This court is too small for the three of us. Turning to him was a waste of time.

I could join Mother, perhaps even agree to take the throne one day. But the price I'd have to pay, the price the people would have to pay, would be too great. My heart would be too heavy. I can't agree to Mother's way. I must find my own path forward.

I look out at the river as a rowboat makes its way toward the palace's ramp. I imagine the wisewoman sailing within it. Hathor is my last hope. I must pray she's not another delusion. She could appear any day now. When she does, I need to make the most of my meeting with her. Perhaps if I knew more about her, I'd be better prepared to convince her to help me. Fortunately, I have a friend who knows more about the wisewoman than she's let on. I'll just have to be more convincing than the last time I asked her for information.

Thuiu pulls a leather throw over her lap. The light of the lantern perched next to her gleams on her wrinkled face.

"I'm sorry to come to your quarters so late, my dear. I received your summons and, well, this was the easiest time for me. I do hope you don't mind."

I smile at her concern. "My evenings aren't exactly in high demand. I'm happy you came. How's Ineni?"

After an update on her husband's health—it's the same as it's been for months now—she turns to the topic of Thutmose. "He's back, I hear. How are you and your mother faring?"

I glance up at Thuiu's handmaid. I sent mine to her adjoining room, but Benerib is perched on a stool near the door.

Thuiu's wave speaks volumes. Whatever is said here, the old woman will hear it either in the moment or recounted later, so I might as well speak in her presence.

"Mother was furious."

"I'm sure." Thuiu takes a sip of beer.

"And he's bedding Teena. She's pregnant."

Thuiu's hand flies to her chest. "The doctor's girl? Why her?"

I shake my head. "That's a good question. It's not as if he'll talk to me about it. He despises me. I don't know what I ever did to make him hate me so much—"

"Well," she interrupts, "you were born the child of two pharaohs, while he's the child of merely one, and a weak one at that." She smiles at my shocked face. "Your father has been dead a long time. I think we can speak the truth about him, when we're alone at least, don't you?"

I weigh her words. "You didn't approve of him?"

She shrugs. "My approval or lack thereof isn't pertinent. He was born to power. He never did learn how to use it well."

"Unlike Mother."

"Yes, they were opposites in a sense. She was born to give her power away to some man, through her womb or through her titles. Yet she managed to wrench it away from not one but two pharaohs who outranked her from birth, if only because they were born men: your father and Thutmose. Oh, I know she's not the warmest mother." Thuiu snakes a bony hand out and rests it on my knee "She wasn't always so hard, you know. She learned to be tough. Perhaps she learned too well. She wouldn't have survived if she hadn't. In spite of all the obstacles hurled at her, your mother is a remarkable ruler. The country has been lucky to have her at the helm all these years."

"Yes," I agree. Yet as adept as she is at ruling, Mother's brand of motherhood leaves much to be desired. Her love is like a herdsman enamored of his own cows: it reeks of ownership. And I now know that her heart is heavy with misdeeds. "Thuiu," I say slowly, choosing my words. "Do you think my father's death could have been… unnatural?"

She sits taller. "Why would you ask that?"

"Thutmose—"

"Ah." She shakes her head and slumps. "Of course. He would want to turn the pharaoh he's most closely related to into some kind of victim. Thutmose has been dedicated to being a victim since he could walk. I remember him as a toddler. He once gave the floor a spanking because he stubbed his toe and felt the tile was to blame."

Inexplicably, the memory makes me smile. I loved him once, although it's hard to remember why.

"Is it possible?" I prompt her.

She tilts her head. "With the will of the gods, anything is possible. But I would rank that as slightly less likely than the god Hapi draining Iteru. Your father was sickly, in his heart and body. His death was natural, I'm sure of it."

Her words comfort me. If anyone alive today has insight into what happened at court in my father's final days, it's Thuiu. In spite of all I've learned, I want to believe Mother isn't capable of murder—Father's at least. At this point, it's undeniable that she tried to have Thutmose killed.

"Can I ask you about Grandmother's wisewoman and her scorpions? I have so many questions, and I have no one else to turn to."

Thuiu twines her fingers in her lap. "One question." Her nod is curt. "I will answer one question tonight."

I take a breath and spread my fingers wide against my thighs, sifting through words, trying to string the right ones together. I end up babbling. "I'm told Hathor and her band of scorpions believed they were fighting for the people. I'm told their purpose was to improve the lives of our subjects and that doing so sometimes meant marshaling resources to...control my family, I guess? They say she wanted to protect people when royal infighting became dangerous. Do you believe that's what motivated her? And could she really do that? If so, do you think she could help us now? I can't help but think maybe someone—someone other than me, I mean—could make Mother and Thutmose see reason before people get hurt."

Thuiu's eyes grow wider as I speak. "You're well informed, which isn't easy, given that woman's penchant for secrecy. Perhaps I shouldn't be so surprised. You've been sneaky lately, and you've become even more ambitious. I offered to answer one question, and you've asked me so many." Thuiu's smile softens her words.

I smile back. "Can we pretend it's one question asked several ways?"

Thuiu's grin widens enough to reveal a missing tooth. "I'm not certain I know all the answers. But as for her motive, yes, I believe Hathor felt too many people, women in particular, were born with the ability to lead and make improvements in their lives and the lives of those around them but weren't given the chance because of the stations they were born to. At the same time, she saw those, like your father, who were given everything at birth but never deserved it. People like your father never used the power they inherited wisely. I believe Hathor wanted to right some wrongs and give savvy women a taste of power in the doing.

"Power comes in many forms. Hathor collected power, in all its shades and varieties. I've never understood how she accumulated so much. But you're right about that too. She did in fact use her power to tame the tensions or, at times, to keep those who caused problems fighting amongst themselves so the people had a better chance at thriving."

"So she might be able to help me?"

Thuiu purses her lips. "I can't say, child. Royals are stubborn, and none more stubborn than your mother and half brother. Hathor does have unique resources. She's accomplished things that seem magical to those of us looking on. But whether she could or would intervene to craft some form of peace between those two, I cannot say."

"Why wouldn't she? It sounds like she knows more than most that royal mayhem endangers the people. And she seems dedicated to protecting them. Doesn't that mean she'd want to help me calm the waters?"

"One thing I've learned about Hathor is that she sees possibilities the rest of us don't. As a result, the paths that seem most rational to us don't always appeal to her." Thuiu pats my knee, struggling to stand. Benerib steps forward to help her. "That's enough for tonight. I'm too old for this plotting and scheming. I'll visit again soon. In the meantime, stay hopeful, child."

Thuiu clings to Benerib as they make their way out. I feel a stab of jealousy as I watch them toddle away. That could have been me and Iset many years down the road but for Thutmose's meddling and Mother's obstinance.

Exhausted, I drop into bed fully clothed, pulling my headrest close. I feel something attached to the wood. It's a scrap of papyrus. I hold it near the lantern. It has no addressee nor addresser, but it can only be from one person. The symbol of the goddess marks the top of the page, a sun disk flanked by two cow horns.

I am here. I will join you in your bedroom tomorrow night. Look for me after the sun falls.

Tears spring to my eyes. I squeeze them shut and breathe, thanking Amun for the excellent news. Finally, at long last, my wait is near an end.

ELEVEN

T HE GUARD ON DUTY AT MY DOOR BREAKS PROTOCOL, WHISPER-
ing to the old lady as I enter my room after morning ritual. I
think little of it, distracted by the speech I write in my head
to deliver to Hathor tonight, until the old woman rushes in and
hands me a scroll.

"It requires your immediate attention, Mistress." She bows.

I unroll it to find a request, written in an unfamiliar script, to
join Mother in Thutmose's quarters immediately. A feeling of unease
washes over me. Thutmose's rooms are the last place I'd expect
Mother to summon me. But ignoring a summons from Pharaoh
isn't an option, so I change out of my priestess robes and rush to
Thutmose's rooms, where I find Mother and Senenmut bickering in
front of the door.

"Why would I tell you to meet me here?" Mother frowns at the
scroll Senenmut hands her.

I peek over her shoulder, realizing it matches mine exactly.

"I did not send this. I suppose I can assume you did not ask me
to join you here either?" she asks Senenmut.

"I wouldn't dare," he intones wisely.

Mother waves the handmaids and guard away. "I've had enough of this trickster man-child."

Before her hand lands on the large cedar door, Thutmose opens it, welcoming us with a grin so disdainful it takes all my willpower not to slap it off his pretty face. I half expect Mother to twirl and march away at the sight of him. Instead, she storms past Thutmose to enter his quarters, head high and back stiff. Senenmut and I follow.

"Sit," Thutmose orders, pointing us to the cluster of empty chairs. I haven't seen his rooms in over five years. They're more elegant than when he was a boy, and irrationally, I wonder who's responsible for the updated decor, him or Mother.

Mother settles into the largest chair, adorned with carved lotuses. Senenmut and I sit next to her in high-backed wooden chairs with lions' paws for feet.

My heart is racing as Thutmose drops into a chaise facing us. He looks inordinately proud of himself, which is terrifying in a whole new way.

"I've invited you here—"

"Tricked us, you mean," Mother interrupts.

Thutmose starts again. "I've secured your presence in my quarters this morning so we can discuss my father's death—"

"Stop," I order, dread welling. "Stop talking."

He tilts his head to the side. "Is there a reason you believe I intend to take orders from you today?"

"Please, Thutmose," I beg. The moment I've dreaded since I heard him those months ago through the window behind him, framing him now, is here. Too soon, in spite of my scheming and sneaking, begging the scorpions for attention. Finally, I'm close to making progress—so close I can practically touch it. But once he makes the accusation aloud, we can never go back. Any chance of finding a peaceful solution will evaporate the moment he accuses Mother of this crime. "Please don't do this. For any love we once shared—"

He aims a raised, disbelieving brow at me and continues. "This morning's agenda also includes coming to agreement on how to punish the responsible party."

"Responsible party?" Mother snorts. "Responsible for your father's death? The only one responsible for that is your father, who was weak from the day he was born until the day he went to join his father, the sun. Perhaps the gods, who put an end to his reign, deserve some blame...if you dare."

Thutmose stares at her, mouth open, then drops his head back to stare up at the ceiling for a heartbeat before turning back to Mother. "Is it possible you're truly this ignorant?"

"Ignorant?" She huffs. "You little—"

"Oh, this is even better than I expected it to be." Eyes wide with glee, Thutmose sits taller. "You truly don't know. You, who claim to know all, who claim to be all. You, the conduit of the god, don't know you are sleeping with your husband's murderer? Your lover is the one who sent your husband to the netherworld. You've been sleeping with a killer all this time and had no idea?"

I inhale a ragged breath and hold it, stunned. This isn't what I expected. For a moment, I almost laugh, relieved that the accusation I've dreaded for so long isn't coming.

Imagining Mother murdering my father is one thing—she's fierce and ambitious and, as she's recently proven, willing to do what it takes to get what she wants. But Senenmut is gentle and kind. No one who knows him could believe he'd murder a pharaoh, or a peasant for that matter. What could Thutmose possibly hope to gain by accusing Senenmut rather than Mother? Is he just aiming at weaker prey, or does he actually believe this?

I turn to my tutor, and a chill runs down my spine.

Senenmut doesn't look one bit surprised by the accusation. His lips are pursed, body stiff, but he makes no defense.

"Senenmut?" I mutter.

"This is outrageous." Mother's words are clipped. "A lie of this magnitude cannot go unpunished. I'll have you arrested for spreading such traitorous falsehoods!"

"Delightful." Thutmose's smile is wide and genuine. "But before you toss me in a cell, let's examine the evidence, shall we? Allow me to present my first witness. Beetle," he yells.

I know who it will be before she walks in from the adjoining room, puffy eyes aimed at the floor. That at least is a wise choice: Mother might pluck them from her skull if Teena dared eye contact.

"Pharaoh," Teena whispers. She looks like a rag left behind by a chambermaid, her swollen belly a stark contrast to the lifelessness of her face.

"Tell them your story, Beetle." Joy rings in Thutmose's voice.

Teena falls to her knees before Mother, struggling to speak. Finally, she fixes her eyes on Mother's green leather sandals adorned with gold foil and says, "My father told me on his deathbed of a sin he carried for many years. He said the Devourer would eat his heart because he had...he had..." She rubs her belly, tears and mucus mixing with her black eye makeup and streaming down her face to soil her pale gown. "Father told me your brother and husband, the pharaoh Thutmose the Second, was poisoned. Father believed—"

"You lie," I yell. I'm on my feet, pointing an angry finger in her face, pulse racing. "You're sleeping with Thutmose. You're having his child. Thutmose told you to say this. Why would anyone believe you?"

Mother's eyes flash at that. "Conveniently," she grunts, "your father is dead so we cannot confirm your story."

"Fair point." Thutmose nods, fiddling with his dull blade. He holds the dagger's handle in one hand, running the fingers of his other hand gently over the blade like he's caressing a lover. "Fortunately, the doctor was not the only witness. Was he, Beetle?" He points the blade at Teena, prompting her to go on. "Tell them about the wisewoman who mixed the poison."

My eyes dart to Mother as I sink back into the chair, heart pounding. She's gone from enraged to confused, but she doesn't react to the mention of the wisewoman. Senenmut, on the other hand, leans forward, jaw stiff.

"That's where this all started." Teena stares at the floor. "A nobleman told Father that a tattooed wisewoman in the oasis cured him of some ailment Father had been trying to cure for years. At first, Father was angry. He didn't want to believe a woman had abilities beyond his. He was the court doctor after all." She hiccups. "He couldn't sleep. He wouldn't eat. He fell ill, refusing to leave his bed. I tried everything. I didn't understand why he was so disturbed by the information. His patient was better. I thought he should be happy. But the idea that the woman had the power to cure someone he couldn't was eating him alive. By the time Father told me who she was and what she'd done, he knew he was dying." Teena's eyes dart to Thutmose.

"Keep going," he commands.

"Father believed the wisewoman worked with someone in a position of high power, someone close to the old pharaoh, to poison him. But with the new pharaoh...pharaohs"—she corrects herself with another glance at Thutmose—"on the throne and with Senenmut's high position at court, Father held his tongue. He suspected one of you was involved. He only told me of his suspicions in order to clear his conscience before his heart was weighed."

"So you have a dead man who suspects poison but no proof, no suspect, and no actual witnesses. You don't know who administered this hypothetical poison or how. Yet you thought it wise to spill this ridiculous deceit to Thutmose. During a romp in his bed, no doubt," Mother says.

Teena hangs her head.

"Before, actually," Thutmose says. "Teena is the reason I came to court in the first place. She sent me a scroll when her father fell ill and started loosening his tongue. We've been friends since we were children, Teena and I."

Confusion runs through me. Since we were children? But Teena was the victim of Thutmose's crimes. "You know he stole the treats you were whipped for," I say quietly, pointedly glancing at her back. I want to hurt her. And this information is the only weapon I have at hand.

I'm disappointed when it doesn't land.

"I know what happened." She nods. "I don't know why you made him steal those honey cakes in the first place. He was such a sweet little boy. He came to me the day after I was whipped. He wanted to help but he was too little then. But he's not too little anymore."

The story takes my breath away.

Thutmose beams at me. It's a lie, but it's a lie that has served him well, and there's not a damn thing I can do about it.

"I let her share my bed after she told me what she knows," he gloats. "You might think of me as a reward for good behavior."

"I have more important things to do than listen to the details of your sexual conquests," Mother says. "You have a young woman, clearly under your spell, willing to lie for you. Even her lies don't implicate Senenmut. How far do you think that will get you?"

145

"Not far enough," Thutmose clips. The smile announces there's more to come.

My heart sinks. I think to the note I found—and burned—last night. There's no way he could know.

"The good news is," Thutmose teases, "thanks to Neferura's meddling, the old wisewoman returned to the palace just yesterday."

My stomach does a somersault.

"My men greeted her. Oh, Hathor," he calls. "Please come now, darling."

Senenmut sits taller. I look up at him, blood turning cold inside me. This situation just gets worse and worse. I follow Senenmut's eyes and gasp with surprise when I see her.

I've pictured Hathor a thousand times, and still she stuns me. Tattoos cover her body from head to toe, and large braids coil around her head like snakes. She's much younger than I expected. No less arrogant though. She perches on a chair and flings an arm over the seat next to her, like she's trying to take up as much space as possible. Not Thutmose's prisoner, clearly. She acts like the palace is hers.

"How are you here?" Senenmut's voice is low but steady. The fact that he's focused on the tattooed woman's presence rather than the accusation before him is telling. "I've looked for you. You disappeared. I thought..."

The guilt written on Senenmut's face is as clear as the tattoos marking Hathor's skin. Is it possible I've been worrying over Mother and Thutmose all this time, never suspecting my tutor was just as bad as them? Perhaps worse if Thutmose's accusation is true. The thought makes my heart ache. If Senenmut is not the kind, thoughtful soul who raised me, who is he?

No. I push the doubt away. There must be some explanation.

Please, mighty Amun-Ra, great god, let him be innocent. Let there be an explanation that will keep his heart light.

"I'm here because the goddess wills it, Senenmut." Hathor learns forward, reaching out to touch him on the knee consolingly. Her voice is deep and resonant. The art that covers her—symbols of the goddess Hathor—is muted by her sheer tunic.

"This is ridiculous," Mother insists, calling forth the strength of a djed pillar to mask the sheen of worry only I note in her eyes. "My husband was sickly his entire life. Even his wives made fun of his inabilities. It shocks me still that he managed to father any children who have survived this long. His death cannot have been—"

"Our guest will talk now. The next part of the tale is hers." Thutmose gestures for Hathor to begin.

She pats Senenmut on the knee as if he's a child, then sits back and directs her gaze at Mother. "You don't remember me?" she asks.

Mother looks more confused than ever. "I have never met you in my life."

"Ah, but you have, my child. I visited your bedside many times when you were younger. Surely you remember me curing the strange ailment of your youth? The sickness that struck you in childhood?"

I knew Mother was a sickly child. So many of her childhood mates died young, she's been terrified of the smallest sniffle ever since. Still, it's hard to imagine this woman caring for my mother in her youth. Hathor looks years younger than Mother. Of course, Grandmother too always looked uncannily young—a youthful look Mother has chased unsuccessfully her entire life.

Mother's eyes clear. "Ahmose. My mother," she whispers to Hathor before turning to her lover. "My mother did this?" she asks.

Senenmut's body droops in acknowledgment.

"Your mother did what had to be done." Hathor nods. "The

country was in turmoil. Your husband was weak. You and your mother were strong. We were very close, Ahmose and I. People believe she loved me and empowered me because my potions kept her beautiful. Well, looking young, in any event," she says with a shrug. "You and your mother were blessed with intellect and power. What woman needs beauty when she has those rarer, more precious assets? The truth is my relationship with Ahmose was about much more than potions and power."

Mother ignores the insinuation. "So Mother killed my husband." Her eyes dart to Senenmut as if she's hoping the information absolves him.

"We killed your husband." Hathor says this like she's bragging about ridding the riverbank of a child-hunting jackal. "Senenmut was just becoming a power player in the court at the time. Ahmose took a liking to him, as did I. Ahmose and I shared the same taste in many things, men included. I'm not surprised to see that you share it too." She flashes Mother a carnal grin. "In any event, Ahmose asked Senenmut to fetch the poison I mixed from my rooms on several occasions. Your mother administered it herself. After all, who would suspect the old woman of murdering her own stepson?" Her dancing eyes glance at Thutmose suggestively, like she might offer her stepson-killing services to Mother next. "And of course, even then, Senenmut's feelings for you were clear to anyone with a touch of intuition—Ahmose and I both had more than enough of that. Incidentally, she knew you did too, which is why she kept me away from you after I nursed you back to health. She believed you'd unravel our truths if you saw us together. Anyway, we tapped Senenmut to help us. Had we been caught, he was a lowborn man with motive and access, someone we could point to if it came to that."

"This is a lie," Mother thunders.

But Senenmut says different.

"I didn't understand what I was doing." His vacant eyes stare at the luxurious carpet.

My heart sinks lower at his confession, loss manifesting deep within me.

"Ahmose asked me to bring her potions from her wisewoman," Senenmut continues, "so I did. I was anxious to ingratiate myself with her; I didn't ask questions. It was months before I suspected what she was up to. Eventually, I realized the potions I fetched were killing him. I didn't dare confront Ahmose." He pauses like he's steeling himself, and I realize my body is rigid with tension. "And if I'm honest, I did want him dead. Perhaps my feelings for you clouded my judgment. But it was a political assessment as much as an emotional one—he was a terrible leader. You"—he finally looks at Mother—"are exceptional."

I release a heavy breath, trying to make sense of this new world, of this new man. This man I've loved like a father, the man who murdered my real father. He acted at his queen's demand. Does that absolve him? No. No, Senenmut knew the part he played in my father's death, and he chose to stay silent all these years. Every time he read me a story or soothed my pain or tucked me in, this lie was there, with us always, though only he knew it. If he's carted around a secret this big, what other secrets might he be hiding?

"I thought you were dead." Senenmut turns to Hathor. "There have been stories of you from time to time. I send a man to investigate every rumor that reaches me. It's never you."

"Or it is, but your little men are too late, too dense, or too easily paid off to confirm it." She grins, but her eyes flash to the blade in Thutmose's hands and crinkle in confusion. It lasts only a second—so brief I wonder if I imagined it or if she's also surprised he wields such a plain weapon.

"Senenmut, great steward of Amun," Thutmose trills. "The man of the people, fooled by a peasant woman." He grins at me. "Lucky for me, our little princess has been busy getting into other people's business. She lured our wisewoman back to court."

I shiver at the use of my old nickname—a nickname only he and Kamut would remember.

"I suppose I should thank you for revealing yourself to me," Thutmose says. "First at Beetle's door, then with that heartfelt confession about believing your mother murdered our father."

"Neferura!"

"If you hadn't tipped me off," he continues, ignoring Mother's outburst, "I would not have tripled the men searching for Hathor, and we wouldn't be here today."

I swallow the bile surging up my throat and lift my head in defiance. He's won this round, but the battle is still being fought. There must be something more I can do.

Before I can think of a single idea, Mother turns her rage on Hathor. "What did you get for this betrayal? By your own confession, you mixed the poison. You're more guilty than Senenmut, if this story is true. So what did you get to reveal this now, after all these years?"

"She gets to serve the better pharaoh," Thutmose interrupts. The candle next to him sputters. Even the flames react to his arrogance.

"You think this will ruin me," Mother spits at Thutmose. "You think this will give you the power you crave. It won't. I will deny these accusations. I will fight the battle publicly. The priesthood will stand with me."

"The military will stand with me," Thutmose responds. "And they're tougher than your flock of priests."

"Tougher, perhaps, but not nearly as wealthy. Besides, you only believe they prefer you because you're a man. You forget that I professionalized the army. I have enriched military leaders from one end of Kemet to the other. Yes, some may follow your lead. But much of the military will stay loyal to me. Most of the nobles as well. At best, the power you're so desperate to hold will be fractured. Our family's prestige will be battered."

"Your prestige will be battered," Thutmose says. "I was a child at the time. No one will blame me for this. You, on the other hand, are sleeping with the man who murdered Pharaoh, your own husband. Who will believe you were ignorant? You've convinced them you're omnipotent."

"No one will believe—"

"I have witnesses."

"Witnesses whose accounts will be denied." Mother's voice rises.

Thutmose sinks back in his chair, the picture of ease. "Your lover didn't deny the accusation. Is he going to change his story after confessing in front of five people? Do you think that will work? I don't. I think you'll be left claiming you were ignorant all these years—hardly an impressive display from an all-knowing pharaoh. You'll be viewed as an accomplice to Pharaoh's murder. But perhaps you're right."

Pinpricks slink across my skin at his dramatic sigh.

"Perhaps I do need something else." His pause is full of arrogance, pregnant with joy. "Fortunately, my little Beetle had her daddy write his confession down—"

"He didn't know Senenmut was involved." Mother's retort teems with desperation. "That won't help—"

"Yes, I was worried about that. I might have had him write a few versions, just to be safe. He might even have left off the bit about not being a witness." Thutmose snaps the trap shut tight. "He did want to make sure his heart was light."

"So he lied," Mother hisses. "Where is it?"

"The confession I like most is in a safe spot, guarded by people I trust. They will release it widely if anything should happen to me. I will release it if I don't like the way the rest of this conversation goes. If we can come to an agreement, I'll be holding on to it, to be sure you uphold your end of the bargain."

"What bargain? You'd be a fool to spread this lie. If this story is believed, it will damage our family, your family. You can't hurt me without hurting yourself too. What is it you hope to achieve with this villainy?"

"Finally," Thutmose says. "Yes, I have hopes. One might even call them demands. And you have options to choose between." He reaches out and pats Teena on the head. She sits near his feet, crying and rubbing her rounded belly while I try not to pity the creature who has caused such chaos. "First, I'm taking my rightful place on the throne and will have access to all resources. That part is nonnegotiable. But what happens to the three of you is yet to be determined." He sits back in his chair, reveling in the chase, like a cat that's trapped a scarab in a corner. Eyes on Mother, he lays out the options. "You have a choice to make, Hatshepsut. Option one: I destroy you. I go public with all I know. I make demolishing your legacy my top priority, for now and for all the years I reign as pharaoh. I'll chisel your image out of every temple and stela in Kemet. I'll forbid the priesthood and the people from uttering your name. Every cartouche in your House of Millions of Years will be replaced with mine. You will be erased. You will be forgotten. History will not know you. The gods will not welcome you. The future will not recognize you. When you die, your death will be complete and eternal."

Mother's breath is heavy. Thutmose has aimed wisely. There's almost nothing Mother wouldn't do to ensure that the legacy she's earned will flourish. "Option two?" she asks.

"You keep your legacy, and you lose them." He nods toward me and Senenmut.

"Lose them?"

"Lose them." He's serious now. "You're responsible for the death of those I loved. I will take those you love in return. For the peace you claim should be priority."

Senenmut's hand finds mine. I hang on to him, waiting for Mother to tell Thutmose that our lives will never be forfeit. It will be messy, but the alternatives Thutmose puts forth are not choices at all.

Mother swallows, the damp brow she tries to hide showing through her painted face. "There is a third option," she says.

I'm on the edge of my seat, ready for her to remind Thutmose that she wields the reins of power as masterfully as Thoth wields a stylus.

"You and I will share power in truth," she begins. "I will continue to manage trade, the patricians, and the priesthood. You can take control of the military. Senenmut will leave court. He can live out his days in peace, far from here." Her eyes find mine, narrowing momentarily as if weighing a final blow.

"Mother," I beg.

She ignores my plea. "And Neferura will be your queen—"

"Never," I hiss.

"She will bear your child," she adds. "She'll ensure your reign."

"Any woman can bear my child." He shrugs, motioning at Teena.

"But only Neferura's child will grant you the real legitimacy you crave. Not just the legitimacy that comes from your father, who was weak, but that of a much stronger pharaoh as well: me. Your child will have the lineage of the gods."

I can barely breathe. Is Mother truly proposing this? Bear his child? "I will not—"

Thutmose ignores me. "You would expect her to retain her position and estate, I assume?"

"I would." Mother nods. She's all business now, conceding, I assume, that she has well and truly lost. "Neferura derives power from me, it's true. But she accrues resources from her position. You will want access to both. Without her, the peace you mentioned will crumble. She's the bridge to the future you crave, the Isis to your Osiris."

Thutmose taps his fingers together and grunts. He leans forward, gaze piercing Mother. "I will let you keep your legacy. You can stay on the throne with me, but the real power is mine. Your campaign of lies, of sculptures and statues and opulence, can continue, as long as it makes me look good too. You'll deal with whatever I ask you to, nothing more, nothing less. But one point I will not concede. Senenmut will die. That is nonnegotiable."

Mother interrupts. "He will at least be celebrated—"

"No." Thutmose shakes his head. "He will be buried in the dirt like the peasant he is. His tomb will be destroyed. His name will not be spoken."

I squeeze Senenmut's hand. I can barely see through my tears. The fact that Mother is considering this at all is absurd.

"As for Neferura." Thutmose's gaze strays back to me, his hatred palpable, and in this moment, danger squeezes me tight. It's so close I gag on it. "Neferura gets one chance. I will take her as wife, honoring the traditions of our ancestors—traditions you changed to keep me from power. There is justice in that, I suppose. But I won't guarantee her life. She belongs to me the same way my horses belong to me. I will control her estate, her body, her time. We'll see how it goes."

His eyes turn hard, and a chill runs down my spine. "I expect you to follow my commands, all of them, without fail. If you bear me a child, perhaps you'll earn the right to live a little longer."

"You cannot be serious," I spit. "Mother, don't do this."

She ignores me, considering Thutmose.

My gaze finds Hathor. She holds my eyes, tapping her lip as if she's holding in a secret—a secret she wants me to know she has. I have no idea how she can reconcile setting flame to my family with the claim that she works in Kemet's best interest. At this point, I no longer care. Pinning my hopes on her was a mistake—a mistake Senenmut and I will both pay for.

The air is thick with tension, the two pharaohs glaring at each other, assessing the offer. I'm frozen next to Senenmut like one of the statues he's had carved of us posed side by side.

Finally, Mother nods her agreement, holds her head high, stands, and goes, leaving me and her doomed lover behind without so much as a backward glance.

TWELVE

I'VE PERFORMED THIS RITUAL A MILLION TIMES. EVERY JANGLE OF the sistrum, every flick of the wrist, every dip of the toe is written on my heart. But this is the first morning I've spent in the small, innermost sanctuary of the temple, alone with Amun, since Mother bartered my life and my tutor's off to Thutmose in exchange for power.

Today, everything is different.

Still, this feeling is more than the doom simmering inside me. I spin in a circle, barely hearing the distant beating and chanting as I search for something to explain the strange sensation that comes over me. The tall golden doors are shut tight. It's just me and the god in the tiny, incense-filled room, surrounded by white sandstone walls and stone floors. I drop to my knees, exposed before Amun, eyes cast down, hoping to earn a moment of tranquility.

"You're quite lovely, in your own way."

I jump at the intruder's voice. For a moment, I think Amun is speaking. I've waited years for him to animate his statue. I know he's in there. I've never seen the statue move, but it's not empty, although it is cold and still.

But that is not the voice of Amun.

It's the voice of the woman who helped ruin my life.

Hathor steps out from behind the god.

"You can't be here," I breathe, stunned by the sacrilege.

"I can be, obviously." She shakes a blue linen hood off her braided hair and perches on the god's altar. Her linen dress is slit high, revealing firm, bare thighs. A goddess's head marks each thigh, one with the mane of a lion, the other the head of a cow, two different personifications of the goddess whose name she shares. "Relax, Neferura. I'm here to help."

"Help?" I huff, pulling my robe tight around me. "You betrayed me."

"We don't have time for this," she scoffs. "I can't have betrayed you. I've never met you before yesterday, and I've certainly made you no promises. Perhaps some version of me you concocted in your own mind betrayed you. The real me has not."

"You said you would come to me."

"And here I am." She pats the space next to her with ink-covered fingers, inviting me to sit. Creatures of chaos—frogs, snakes, and scorpions—are scrawled across one hand. The other displays symbols of power: an ankh, a wedja, a Horus eye. The tapestry of chaos and power sums up Hathor perfectly. "Finding a private moment with you wasn't easy. I spent the entire night in this uncomfortable room."

"This uncomfortable room is the most sacred space in Kemet," I hiss, hot with rage.

"That may be." She rubs her neck. "But I'm getting too old for nights like this." She sighs and her face relaxes. "I really am here to help you, Neferura. I'm sorry if it is not the help you expected."

"You just helped Thutmose kill Senenmut. And me soon enough. Is that the kind of aid you think the people need? Please tell me how our deaths will force the river to rise or water to cover the fields? Or protect women in childbirth? Will forcing me into an unwanted marriage make the crops plentiful? Will slaughtering Senenmut deliver work to the poor man with children to feed?"

"I know how it looks. But appearances deceive," she says. "For some of us, deception is the currency of power. I am here for you. You summoned me. I came. That is a rarity, I assure you."

"You say you came to help me." My voice is too high. I should call the high priest and have her buried alive for this transgression. But I've waited so long to face her. I'm not about to send her away without answers. If Amun must look on, so be it. "You prove by your actions that you've chosen to side with Thutmose instead."

"An unexpected twist, to be sure." She shrugs. "But he did catch me red-handed in the palace, a position you put me in. I was captured responding to your request for a meeting. I was bound tight, by the way. I still would be if I hadn't given Thutmose what he wanted. Then I'd be in no position to help anyone. But I'm nothing if not nimble. I adjusted. I told him what he wanted to hear so he saw what he wanted to see. I had to make him believe I was with him, or I'd still be in chains rather than free to roam into your sacred space. He's arrogant, and arrogant people are easy to manipulate. It cost me nothing to convince him I'm pleased to put my services at the disposal of the handsome young pharaoh. He thinks I work for him now," she says with a snort. "Honestly, this may work out even better for us."

"There is no us."

"So you don't want my help?" One brow creeps up.

I release a heavy breath, pushing the anger away. The truth is, I need her help more than ever. I can't trust her, obviously. But if I'm to find some way to survive this and help Senenmut survive, I need allies and information—information she has. I may not get a chance like this again.

"If you really want to help me, why did you expose Senenmut at all? Why not keep his secret?"

She drums her fingers against her knees "Would you rather not know Senenmut helped your grandmother murder your true father?"

"That's not an answer," I retort, tired of her games and, if I'm honest, unsure of the answer.

"Then try this one." She crosses her arms, suddenly serious. "Thutmose believed your mother murdered your father. That's a far more dangerous theory—dangerous to the people I actually serve. It also has the pesky drawback of being untrue. So I gave him the truth. Senenmut's death will be painful, but only for those who love him. It's far less damaging for the country than one pharaoh accusing the other of murder. I had few choices, so I made the logical decision. I sacrificed Senenmut to save many more. The truth happened to be the least destructive option."

The logic of it stings, and my voice turns bitter. "I'm so happy that worked out for you. Now Senenmut is to be punished for the crime with his life, yet you, the one who brewed the poison that killed a pharaoh, roam free."

"As I should. I did the country a favor. Your grandmother was right. Your father was weak. His rule was doomed, and the powers coalescing throughout the country were dangerous. If he had lived, many others would have died. People less powerful, to be sure, but not less valuable. Your mother was the only one who could unite the country and lead us into peace. But your mother had a flaw many consider unforgivable."

"Yes, yes—she's a woman," I say.

Hathor nods. "I acted to promote your mother's rule and thus secure a long-standing peace. I've always been fond of your mother. I was impressed by her strength when I healed her in her youth. She's continued to impress me with the powers she's wielded so effectively in the years since. She's not much of a mother, I gather. But I'm not one to hold that against a powerful woman.

"My recent acts may seem at odds with my loyalty to her, but you may eventually thank me for convincing Thutmose he's won when, in truth, the battle has just begun. He was like a dog digging for a bone. He was never going to stop. Now, he believes he's gotten his reward. He'll stop digging. I've not only increased the odds of a peaceful succession once Hatshepsut's reign ends, whether your mother likes it or not, but by convincing him that he's won, I've bought you time. It may be an advantage in the battles to come."

"Battles to come? He's going to kill me the moment I step out of line. I spent years trying to please him. It's impossible. I'll be lucky to survive the week."

"That weak boy isn't going to kill you." She trails a finger over the disk and horns drawn on her chest. "Not yet anyway. He craves the heir only you can give. He doesn't want you to know it—he doesn't want to give you that power. But it's true. Besides, he's finally acquired the power he's always coveted—power over you. Why would he get rid of you so soon?"

"That weak boy is pharaoh," I seethe. "And a far more powerful one now that you've made him so."

"He's really not." She waves a hand, shooing the fact of Thutmose's status away like a pesky fly.

"Yes, he is. Really. He's pharaoh. You may have elevated him with yesterday's antics, but the god chose him in front of—"

"Did the god single out Thutmose?" She scoffs. "Or did your grandmother control the choice of the god by controlling the men who carried the float that spoke for Amun? Think, Neferura. Did the god choose you, choose your mother, choose any of the pharaohs of the past? Or was it people like me? Like us? Thutmose was selected by Ahmose, with my assistance and your mother's. That crime, she did commit."

I gape at her, shocked by the sacrilege. It's even more shocking than sneaking into the sanctuary for a chat with the high priestess. And Mother was part of it? Has she faked the will of the gods her entire reign? I think again of my ordained virginity, a tool rather than a decree from the gods. My anger simmers.

Hathor shrugs, unmoved by my alarm. "Thutmose was the obvious heir in any event. And his mother, Isis, was…bendable to our will, let's say. The choice made itself."

"Thutmose's mother was a scorpion?"

Hathor's brow raises, her lips quirking. "I didn't say that. Not everyone I have influence over works with me, Neferura. Some merely want to avoid a particular outcome or receive a prize. There are many paths to influence. The more paths you walk, the more effective you can be." Her narrow gaze studies me. "I'll give you a piece of advice, Great Royal Wife."

"King's eldest daughter," I correct.

"So far. But you'll be a queen soon too. In name, not just duties." She grins but there's kindness in her eyes. "If you are to survive this, Neferura, you must learn to curate your options. Stop confusing prestige with power. Don't wait for someone else to give you permission to be potent. The gods aren't going to tell you what to do. They don't speak to your mother. And they won't speak to you. But they are watching. You impress them by taking action to improve Kemet and the lives of its people." She shakes her head, and the jingle of amulets trills out in the small, confined space. "You're still so young," she sighs. "Perhaps you feel you've no choices, or perhaps you believe everything has been decided for you. But when it feels like you have no alternatives, you must create them. If you're creative enough, options are out there. Choices you haven't dared dream might be spun from nothing but air, intellect, and courage. And where there are choices, there is power. For you, there are so many paths you haven't yet considered. Becoming pharaoh, perhaps?"

"I hate the nobles," I admit. "I've watched Mother. I know managing the patricians is the largest part of her job. No. I don't want to be pharaoh. I certainly don't want the death and chaos that would ensue if I took the throne. Or tried to anyway. If I managed to take power, I'd be miserable and ineffective. Too many would die just for me to fail."

"Please tell me you're not always this humble."

"I'm not." It's true. I know what I'm good at. It's a reasonably long list. But sparring with the petty powerful isn't on it, nor do I want it to be.

"Then perhaps it's time to consider your mother's path. I have poisoned a pharaoh before."

I glance up at the god, shocked anew by Hathor's irreverence. The gold and lapis earrings dangling from Amun's ears sway as if they're reacting to her sacrilege. Even the fine linen draped across the statue stirs.

"I'm not going to plot to murder a pharaoh, or anyone else for that matter. I'm not you."

"Or your tutor," she adds.

I sigh, weighing her words.

"Or your mother. We both know she'd have killed Thutmose by now if he weren't so wily. Surviving appears to be that boy's true talent." She folds her arms, eyes sparkling with amusement. "You royals are a bloody bunch. You do realize, of course, your mother's plans just changed. Her plans to end Thutmose have failed, and she'll know better than to try again soon. The doctor's written confession gives Thutmose the upper hand. She won't be able to predict what would happen if Thutmose dropped dead. It's enough to end her attempts. So rather than disappearing Thutmose and handing you a throne you don't want, she'll focus on ensuring you produce an heir. Without you or your child, her bloodline dies. She's proven her legacy means more to her than, well, anything."

I think back to that moment. Mother had the choice to save me and Senenmut, and she chose her good name instead. "She cares for herself more than both me and Senenmut," I admit.

"She does indeed. And your womb is the only way to keep her blood on the throne—the only way that doesn't involve murder and mayhem, that is. That's how you stay alive. For now."

I drop my head in my hands. "I'm a broodmare. And even if I give them what they want, Thutmose is going to kill me the moment I give him a child."

"Count on it," she intones. "You need to worry less about my sins and more about your survival."

I study her. Her youthful skin, marked not by age but by the goddess's symbols. She's right about that, if nothing else. I must find a way to survive. And as angry as I am at her, if she's willing to help me, perhaps she's willing to help Senenmut first.

I lift my head to meet her dark eyes. "If you're really here to help me, you'll find a way to save Senenmut."

She nods approvingly, like I'm a small child performing a new trick. "That's better, Neferura. Think. Take the initiative. Don't wait for someone to hand it to you. I knew your mother's blood was in there somewhere. You may want to set it free more often."

"Senenmut," I repeat.

Hathor purses her lips and cranes her neck to look up at the face of the god. "Fine. I'll see what I can do. I can't promise anything."

"If you can't protect Senenmut from Thutmose, why should I believe you can protect me?"

"You need to protect you, Neferura. I'm just here to give you a push. For a start, stop overestimating Thutmose. But by all means, do make sure he believes you still do. He'll be easier to handle that way. And to survive, you will need to handle him." Before I can ask more, she stands tall to stretch. "You must finish the ritual. The high priest will get curious if your predictably timely performance isn't what he expects." She steps behind the god, out of my sight.

I don't bother to follow. She's right after all. And I'm glad to be rid of her.

I look up at Amun, trying to hide the anger still crackling in my gut. I force my arm to lift my sistrum high, willing the instrument to create Amun's favorite rhythms. I breathe in the smell of incense and the cooked meat sitting at the god's feet and call the movements to me. I swing my hips and embrace the familiarity of my routine's melodies as they rush into my body. As Hathor says, the god is watching. And if I am to survive, a happy god may be a useful resource.

Senenmut waits for me in my quarters when I return from the temple. My guard's staff bangs once fast, twice slow, warning me my old tutor is inside. He's in his chair, head bowed low.

I consider ordering him out so I can curl up in my bed to sleep this terrible day away. But I know from the night I just spent tossing and turning that crawling back into bed won't do me any good anyway. I sink into my chair facing him with the desk between us.

"I'm sorry," he says before I speak. "I'm sorry for the act. And I'm sorry for keeping such a secret all these years."

My heart crumbles at his defeat. "Why?" The single word feels too flimsy to carry the many questions and worries that flood my mind, but it's all I can muster.

I'm angry and disappointed and confused. Yet I have no idea if I'll ever speak to Senenmut again. If this is to be our final conversation, the thing I want most from him now is to understand why he did what he did and why he kept it secret from Mother and me.

He stares down at his long fingers, clutching bony knees. "I cannot speak to your grandmother's motivations. We never discussed what was happening. I assume she believed your father was unfit to rule, which he was." Senenmut glances up at me, then back down at his hands. "If he'd stayed on the throne much longer, your family would have been cast from power. It would not have been bloodless. The nobles were on the verge of revolt. Many people would have died in the battle for power that was brewing. But the nobles adored your mother. And Ahmose. And of course, your mother has always had the loyalty of the priesthood. Those two women were as strong as your father was weak. Yet the one thing he did manage to do was defy every bit of good sense the two tried to pass on to him."

"So you murdered him?" I push.

Senenmut drops his head back against his chair to stare at the ceiling. He's committed to looking anywhere but at me, apparently. "I supported your mother. I kept my mouth shut. I assumed Ahmose and your mother would hold on to power until Thutmose was old enough to lead."

"Even if that's all true, the crime you committed is unforgivable.

And the risk Grandmother took is inexplicable. Mother didn't have a son, only me. What if someone other than Mother had come to power when Father died? Grandmother's plot was risky—"

"Risky, yes," he agrees. "But your father wasn't going to live long. One way or the other, his time was nearing an end. Your grandmother worked to make sure his reign ended while she and your mother were at the height of their power, best positioned to assume control. Queen regents have ruled well and often since the time of the pyramids. Why wouldn't your mother be trusted to rule? She was visible and admired, the richest person in Kemet, aside from your father. She was god's wife of Amun and great royal wife, not to mention the host of other titles she bore. More to the point, she'd been executing orders throughout your father's reign. Thutmose had been identified as the heir, although he was a child still. And the tradition of regency was well established."

"What if Thutmose's mother, Isis—"

"Isis wasn't royal. She was an ornament. And she was terrified of Ahmose. I don't know what your grandmother had over her, but Thutmose's mother was in no position to push back. Thutmose was heir. Your mother was the obvious choice for regent. I have no idea if Ahmose expected Hatshepsut to take the reins of power as she eventually did." He stands to pace, watching his feet slap against my floor. "I do know that, as a woman, your mother was miserable. She was strapped to a man who could never give her the love she deserved. Your father was..." His eyes find mine before quickly darting away. "Cruel," he concludes. "In truth, dear one, your father was a monster, and not terribly good even at that."

I cringe at the accusation, although it may be true. Even so, Father was a pharaoh and a person. I'm not sure anyone deserves to be poisoned by someone they trust.

"Ahmose walked a path that I believed was in the best interest of the country and your mother—"

"And you," I add.

He pauses, then turns to look at me. "Yes. And me. I loved her. I couldn't stand watching her act like the abuse he inflicted was acceptable. So I walked your grandmother's path. And I've lived with the secret all these years, hoping to atone for the sin by being the man you both deserve."

"Why?" It's a question I've pondered often. "Why did you love her? Why do you still love her?"

He looks to the side like a spirit stands next to us, eyes bright with memory. "Your mother was fierce. She was like the goddess Sekhmet, the powerful eye of Ra. She wielded the power to kill or to mend, a warrior and a healer. Her abilities drew me to her. They still do. Most people would have crumbled when faced with the challenges she encountered. But your mother stood tall. She fought for herself. She fought for the people. She never let tradition stand in the way of progress. And she eventually won—"

"What did she win? Is a throne truly worth a heart as heavy as Mother's must be now?"

He looks down, flushed. "I am not in a position to judge the weight of another's heart."

I don't know what to say to that. I've spent so much time worrying about Mother's heart, heavy with misdeeds, or Thutmose, lashing out because he believed Mother already had. And here I sit, facing the man I should have been worried about all along. In some odd way, it's a relief to know Mother was as ignorant as me and that it was only Senenmut who betrayed my trust, not the woman whose path I may be doomed to follow.

I want time—time to work through my anger, disentangle

it from the grief that threatens to overcome me. I don't know if I can—or should—forgive Senenmut. But I do know I don't want him to die like this.

"You need to convince Mother to change her mind."

"Your mother will do what she must to maintain her legacy."

"She'll kill us both so the common man will remember her name—"

"You're not thinking straight, dear one," he argues. "She fights for her legacy so her name will be spoken. So she'll be powerful in the afterlife, as she has been in this one. So she'll be with us in Aaru, the heavenly Field of Reeds—"

"Us?" I gasp. "If Thutmose gets his way, you won't make it to Aaru. You'll die, name unspoken. What of your afterlife? She throws yours away so she can enjoy hers without you? I can't accept that. But she won't listen to me." I lean forward, pressing against the desk, fingers entwined. "You have to talk to her."

"I'll do everything I can to help you. You should not bear the consequences of my sin."

"And you? Will you advocate for yourself?"

He shrugs.

"This is twisted. This ridiculous choice," I sneer.

"Payback."

"Payback for what?"

Senenmut shakes his head. "A difficult choice she once forced on Thutmose, I suspect."

He doesn't go on, and I'm too tired to chase after another secret.

"The important thing is that you survive, Neferura. My life has been much more than I ever could have imagined. I'm ready."

"No." I let the tears finally flow. "Not like this."

"I did what I'm accused of. Death is a consequence I've deserved since the moment I chose complicity over honesty. But that was my choice. Not yours. And you should not have to pay for it."

I sob silently. Senenmut did a terrible thing, but I can't bear this consequence. What Thutmose has planned is the worst kind of death imaginable for a man as renowned as Senenmut. My tutor has been working on his elaborate tomb for years. He not only had his mother buried and his father's mummy moved to a tomb near his chapel, but his favorite horse was buried close too, so they'd all be with him in the afterlife. The entire point of Senenmut's well-stocked tomb and his stunning sarcophagus of yellow quartzite that matches Mother's is to set him up for a rich and plentiful afterlife. But this comfort is to be taken from him too. The chance for me to figure out how to move ahead with him will be gone, in this life and the next, unless someone does something.

I look up at Senenmut. Words fail me as he stands, kisses me on the head, and walks from my rooms.

He isn't going to save himself. And I don't dare trust Hathor again. It's up to me to make Mother see.

I roll into Mother's quarters like a cyclone.

"Out," I order the handmaids.

They scurry away as Mother glares at me through the reflection of her small silver mirror with the golden Hathor-headed handle.

"Feisty at last, I see." She tugs at the striped linen cloth on her head until the uraeus is centered on her forehead, then turns to look at me. "I suppose we have something to thank Thutmose for."

"Thank him?" I snap. "Is that your plan? To thank him for killing

Senenmut and eventually your only daughter while you pretend to hold on to the power you no longer have."

"The better question is," she retorts, "shouldn't you be thanking me rather than attacking me? If it weren't for me, you'd be days from dying rather than days from getting married."

"You auctioned me off," I roar.

"I saved you. I saved your life and your position."

"A position that is now Thutmose's in truth, as is yours. We'll have to go to him on bended knee for every little decision we want to make—decisions we've both made freely for years. He'll strip me of everything that matters. He'll starve you of power, me of priestesses, and the people of food." I sag, anger giving way to grief. "Worse, he'll starve Senenmut of life." I drop to my knees and look up at her. "Please don't do this, Mother. Don't give in. Let's fight. You command so much loyalty—"

"Loyalty I'll lose in an instant if people are given an excuse to abandon me. No matter how many obelisks I erect or men I employ, I can never change the fact that I'm defective. I'm a woman in a man's role. One misstep and the nobles who fall at my feet will eat me for dinner...with wine from my personal stocks, no doubt." Her anger too has vanished. She looks down at me, eyes wet with tears. I've never once seen Mother cry. As if she reads my thoughts, she lifts her head high. "If Thutmose gives the nobles a confession written by the court doctor, who was well positioned to know how your father died, people will turn on me. I won't get the benefit of the doubt. Second chances were for your father, and third and fourth and fifth chances. For me, it's perfection or expulsion. They'll happily believe I helped murder my husband. They'll think I'm under Senenmut's power, or worse, that I'm a fool. They'll believe I've been a fraud all these years. The prestige and clout I've spent a lifetime gathering will disappear the moment Thutmose's story gains traction."

"We won't let it—"

"Stop it, Neferura," she barks. "What do you expect me to do? He left me no choice."

"You do have a choice. You can choose us. You can walk away from power—"

"You want me to abandon my legacy?"

"In return for Senenmut's life? For my life? Is that not a fair trade?" I blink away the tears that sting my eyes. "Maybe it won't come to that. We have to try, Mother. I'll do what you want. I'll take the throne if I must."

She studies my face, then shakes her head slowly. "It's too late for that, daughter. We have lost. I salvaged what I could, as I have so many times before. And now we rebuild. I've done that before too."

"Without Senenmut?"

She turns away. I study her profile. The pain is unmistakable in her downturned lips and slumped shoulders.

"I saved you," she says quietly. "That was the priority."

"Priority? Why did you have to choose in the first place? What choice did you give Thutmose that was so awful he repaid it years later with this?"

She turns back to me. "What are you talking about, child? I never—"

"Senenmut believes it was payback. He said that you once gave Thutmose a choice..." I can tell by her furrowed brow she has no idea what I'm talking about.

For the first time in my life, I'm struck by her ignorance. I always believed Mother knew everything. But she didn't know about my father's murder. She didn't know about Hathor's existence. She doesn't even know if she once hurt Thutmose so fully he's waited years to pay her back for it. Perhaps she can't help Senenmut after all.

I blow a heavy breath, blinking fast to clear my stinging eyes. "How long?" I ask after a pause.

She stands tall, head high and face calm as she tells me I'll officially be queen in two days—there will be a celebratory dinner—and that Senenmut has five days to put his affairs in order. Apparently with Thutmose's permission, Senenmut will be allowed to take his own life rather than face being buried alive. Mother tells me this as if it's a concession worth cheering rather than the most horrific win imaginable. I close my eyes and pray that Hathor comes through with a miracle, but my faith is as faded as the desert horizons.

"And, Neferura," she says as I turn to go. "You're to do what Thutmose commands. And do stop meddling. I can't imagine why you'd tempt some old wisewoman to the palace for a chat. But there will be no more sneaking around behind my back. Understood?"

I barely manage a nod as I trudge out the door, heaving with disappointment, an unwelcome dose of guilt, and the suspicion that my sneaking has just begun.

THIRTEEN

I SET'S NEWS SOOTHES MY HEAVY HEART. NO ONE CAN REPLACE THE life that's soon to be lost. But knowing another life is just beginning reminds me that while my world is falling apart, elsewhere, the people of Kemet are thriving. It's not enough. But it is something.

I read the scroll Satiah passed me as I left the temple this morning one more time.

> *In life, prosperity, and health and in the favor of the gods and goddesses, I write with news. I assume you're in your study, sitting at your desk as you read this. I hope so. You'll want privacy and a sturdy chair to receive my news. It's come as quite a shock to me, and I suspect you'll be equally amazed.*
>
> *I'm with child! A girl! (Yes, wheat sprouted.)*
>
> *I tracked our trusty scribe down as soon as I knew and will get this note to Satiah once I'm able. Aside from Meriptah, you're the one person I'm most anxious to tell. In spite of my own mother dying in childbirth, I'm thrilled. I remind myself that every mother doing laundry, calculating household expenses, or*

worshipping at a temple today survived what I'm facing. If they lived through the ordeal, surely I can as well. I pray to Taweret daily and make all the proper donations to the goddesses.

As for other news, I worry about you constantly. I know Set is back. (A perfect code name for your chaotic half brother, by the way.) He's not done wreaking havoc, that much is certain. I've grown close with the scorpions who live in the village (would you ever have guessed they were here all along?), but their lips are sealed as tightly as the tombs of your ancestors whenever I bring up Hathor. There is one girl, younger than the rest, who has become almost a friend. I've plied her with beer, and some interesting news has spilled out. I've learned that there are five scorpions working in the palace at the moment. Apparently one girl is an accomplished forger, and another is gifted at disguise. They say she can even make Hathor's tattoos disappear. You are surrounded by powerful women. Never forget it.

You'll be relieved to know they were also true to their word. Father is working in the tombs, and I have a job with the seamstress, Maia. I am her assistant, which is second only to being your handmaid. I haven't met the wisewoman yet, though she did send word requesting a special commission. Whatever she's plotting now, a dress with secret pockets and a reversible man's kilt are on their way to her. I have no idea what she's up to. I do wonder if you know more.

This distance is untenable! To my never-ending horror, it turns out that gossip about court is not nearly as useful as court gossip.

Write soon and tell me everything. I've been dying to know if your hunch about the identity of the girl in the window panned out.

I hesitate to write back. My fate is sure to mar her happiness. But she'll hear the rumors soon enough. Better coming from me.

I tap my fingers against my desk, thinking, eyes stuck on the alabaster box full of old memories. Absently, I lift the inlaid lid, and scraps of the papyrus with the story of a shipwrecked sailor Senenmut once gave me as a gift—a gift little Thutmose tore to shreds in a fit of spite—fall out along with a small scroll. I unroll it to find the first passage I ever wrote on my own, an utterance from the pyramid texts, an ode to the sky goddess I liked as a child. My symbols are sloppy, but I still see my penmanship in the oversize birds' feet and precise beaks and crisp lines. I even added tiny eyelashes to my eyes.

O Great One who became Sky,
You are strong, you are mighty,
You fill every place with your beauty,
The whole earth is beneath you, you possess it!
As you enfold earth and all things in your arms,
So have you taken this king to you,
An indestructible star within you!

I return the old scroll to the box and notice Thutmose's final letter. I haven't read it since the day I got it, years ago. Mother sent him away to the barracks in Men-nefer the moment he was old enough to wield a khopesh sword. She didn't need an excuse to rid herself of the boy who shared a claim to the throne she coveted. I knew he was angry about the deployment, and I tried to keep in touch, let him know that I would still be here for him—a safe harbor at court. He'd turned angrier near the end, and I didn't know why. But every effort I made to reach him failed. He ignored my entreaties and my letters.

It was months before I finally got a scroll from him.

Then I read it.

And I never wrote again. His terse note made it clear that there was nothing more to talk about.

I unroll the scroll and scan his childish script, surprisingly similar to how he writes still:

Stop writing. I want you to leave me alone and know only that I'll hate you forever.

I'd like to burn it and add Iset's letter to the box, but that would be far too dangerous. If I'd had the good sense to burn the letter I wrote Kamut, she may be by my side still rather than working for the seamstress.

In the end, I burn Thutmose's scroll along with Iset's. I watch them vanish into the flame, then I congratulate Iset and pour my heart out on papyrus, first one scroll, then another, telling her everything that's happened since she left. I hold nothing back. It's the most honest and forthcoming missive I've ever penned. I may not have control of my fate—for now. But I can control this. I can share my pain with my closest companion. Mother would consider the letter—and the friendship, for that matter—a sign of weakness, which gives me some pleasure.

Because now, more than ever, I know I am nothing like her. And I fully intend to keep it that way.

My nuptial feast is a beautifully choreographed sham. I search the nobles' faces for friendly eyes. I can virtually hear their thoughts:

Pharaoh decided keeping power in the family is a good idea after all.

Why is the arrangement so sudden?

Where's Senenmut?

I hope she's pregnant by night's end.

Finally, Kemet is to get an heir from the country's most prestigious broodmare.

I spot Thuiu in the crowd. The concern written across her face does nothing to cheer me. Her glance flits across the head table where I sit. She's looking for Senenmut. Under normal circumstances, he'd be by my side.

Instead, he's nowhere to be found, and I'm sandwiched between Mother and my despicable husband.

I keep my eyes on the tables of nobles, heaped with meat and fruit and cups spilling over. The spiced duck on my plate smells like urine and blood in spite of the bouquets of roses, jasmine, and poppies surrounding me. Not that it matters. I couldn't eat if my life depended on it. My hands are in fists under the table; I don't want Thutmose—or Mother—to see how shaky they are.

Mother and I don't exchange a word. I know better than to look to her for comfort, even in circumstances as dire as these. I'd be a fool to expect her to help me. She agreed to this. She's going to let Senenmut die. She gave us both up in a desperate bid to ensure her legacy. I hope the guilt breaks her. I know it won't—she's convinced she did the right thing—but Senenmut's death might. Her plate, usually quickly emptied and refilled, is as untouched as mine. And while she's a master at feigning cheerfulness, surely even the dimmest of nobles can see the pain in her eyes now, note the fakeness of her smiles.

I search my memories for moments Mother showed me some warmth. Was she loving when I was small? Did she hold me on her lap? Comfort me when I cried? If she ever did such things, it was too long ago. All I remember are cold shoulders and judgmental eyes and snide remarks. It was Senenmut who hugged me and taught me and made me laugh.

Surrounded by pain on all sides, Senenmut's fate is the most excruciating part.

Why didn't he do something to stop Grandmother from killing my father? Why doesn't he do something to stop Thutmose from killing him?

"What do you say, nobles of Kemet?" Thutmose raises his voice and the harpists—a man and a woman who harmonize as they play—rattle to silence.

I imagine filling his wine cup with poison. I could do it, almost. I remind myself that life is short, the afterlife long, and Ammit's teeth sharp. And still, I'd give my toes and treasure to watch Thutmose drop dead right now while the court cheers him on.

All eyes turn to him—alive and in good health—and he yells, "Are you ready for an heir?"

The room erupts in delighted hurrahs. I glance at Thuiu, one of the few nobles not cheering their young pharaoh on in his tasteless boasting. I see Teena in the crowd. She's the other. Tears stream down her face. I have no pity to spare for her.

It takes every bit of willpower I can muster not to pull away from Thutmose as he turns my face to his and shoves his lips against mine. The kiss is hard and rough, a taste of what's to come.

The nobles cheer louder.

"If you insist," Thutmose bellows in response to their roar. "My bride and I will leave you now and get to work securing the future of this land."

Laughter twists around me, squeezing me tight. Thutmose's hands snake under my armpits, and he yanks me to my feet. I look at Mother; she's plastered a false grin on her face as if she's enjoying my humiliation.

"Now, wife," Thutmose hisses in my ear. His fingers dig into my arm as he shoves me forward with his other hand.

Someone starts a chant: *We want an heir, we want an heir.* I'm stunned by how quickly the crowd of nobles, usually so tame, has turned savage. It's a testament to how deep the influence of a ruler runs. Said ruler smiles and waves as he pulls me forward.

I'm stumbling, numb with anger, when I spot the servant girl with the tattoo on her neck—the girl I saw in the throne room the day Thutmose first returned, before I knew what the mark meant. I wonder if she's the forger or perhaps the girl who is gifted with disguises. Either way, I admire the way she glares at Thutmose. My eyes find Thuiu, lips turned down in a disapproving frown. These two women are as helpless as I am. But they see me. They know this is wrong. Their grim scowls acknowledge the horror of what's happening. The comfort of this silent sisterhood may not be much, but it's much more than nothing, and for that I am thankful.

The brief, painful rutting with Thutmose leaves me humiliated. And the knowledge that another day has passed, bringing Senenmut closer to his fate, fills me with such grief I long for the ignorant bliss of sleep. The sun is high in the sky when slumber finally forsakes me. I'm so weary I miss morning ritual for the first time in years.

I barely register my intentions as I allow the old handmaid to dress me. The second she places the wig on my head, I turn away, marching out the door, toward Senenmut's quarters, the old woman in my wake. I don't know if I can forgive him. I don't know if I can force him to do something, anything, to drag himself out of this mess. But I do know I only have a few days left to figure it out.

My pace quickens as I draw close, heart hammering.

Later, I'll wonder if the god was trying to warn me of what I'd find.

In the moment, I'm too stunned to make sense of the scene that greets me. Serious guards, talking in somber tones, spill from Senenmut's quarters. At first, I think Thutmose changed his mind and had Senenmut arrested, or perhaps Mother decided to fight the battle and these men are readying Senenmut for the war to come. I even wonder if Hathor came to the rescue after all. Perhaps Senenmut escaped and these guards are searching his quarters for a clue to his whereabouts.

My eyes find Kamut's, a recognizable body in the melee, and I know.

The pain written on his face tells the tale.

"Not yet," I whimper. "No, no, no. Not yet."

Kamut steps forward, eyes wet with tears.

I move toward him. I'd fall into his arms—and he'd likely let me, in spite of what it would cost him—but for the men flanking him and the old handmaid cackling at my back, who stop us both from the impulse.

The chief of guards places his body between me and Kamut. He bows low and begins reciting my titles. "God's wife of Amun, great royal wife, king's eldest daughter, lady of Upper and Lower Kemet, mistress of the Two Lands…" He continues—he must address me in full if he's to address me at all—but his words fade. I watch his lips move, numb with shock. My eyes dart to Senenmut's door just as two men emerge.

A figure, covered in a white linen sheet, lies on a stretcher. The two men carry it between them.

"Senenmut!" I run to him, draping my body over him. I try to pull the cloth off, but Kamut stops me.

"I'm so sorry," he whispers in my ear.

"Adoratrice, I regret to inform you…" The chief is saying that Senenmut is dead, that he died from poisoned food in his quarters and his body is being taken to the embalming priests now. Hands steer me away from Senenmut, and the men carry him away.

I close my eyes as they go, praying I'm still asleep, that I'll wake up and Senenmut will still be alive. The taste of natron stings my tongue. Senenmut's body will be drenched in it soon enough, his organs removed, his body wrapped in linen and amulets. But there's nothing the embalming priests can do to render Senenmut's heart light. There's no way to know if we'll meet again in Aaru or if I've spent my last moment with the man who has been like a father to me, the most loving and stable presence in my life, gone when I need him most, gone before I can resolve the conflict that now lives inside me.

I double over in pain. A moment later, I shoot up and march into Senenmut's rooms. Guards scurry to stop me, but Kamut's voice orders them to let me be as I enter my tutor's study and slam the door behind me, blocking the guards and my handmaid out. I sink into his chair, drop my head on the desk that still smells of him, and cry.

I don't know how much time has passed when I sit up. I've barely registered Kamut's voice, just outside the door, arguing with Mother's handmaid to give me space. I don't know what to do with myself. Grief and loneliness choke me. I pull a stack of scrolls close. These bits of papyrus were the last scrolls Senenmut would have touched. I read them, eyes blurry with tears, unsurprised by the last-minute instructions he penned, ensuring the many projects he oversees would stay on track on his death. I'm hoping to find one with my name on it, some final words of advice I can cling to, but there's nothing here for me.

Unless…

My fingers tremble as I worry open the latch of the secret compartment hidden in the desk leg. I don't know why I bother. A passing feeling, really. For a moment, I wonder if he could have known that I was in his study all those months before, that I'd learned of my chambermaid's disloyalty by reading the scroll hidden here. He hadn't seemed surprised when I asked him to dismiss her. And it wouldn't be the first time Senenmut feigned ignorance. I shake away the thought. He can't have known.

Yet my heart thumps and my hands tremble as I reach inside. Something whispers to me in my grief: he was always one step ahead.

I take in a breath as my fingers trace a jagged edge.

A single scroll, stamped with Senenmut's seal.

I hold my breath as I unroll it.

From the great steward, overseer of the treasury, Senenmut, to the god's wife, king's eldest daughter, and my cherished dear one, Neferura.

I clutch the fragile papyrus to my heart, count to ten, then lay it on the desk and smooth it open with shaky fingers. He knew. He knew I would discover his secrets, all of them, in the end.

In life, prosperity, and health and in the favor of Amun, king of the gods, I congratulate you on discovering my secret compartment. I suspect this missive will find its way to you—my confidence in you is limitless. I might have been angry about you sneaking into my study, but I was too impressed for that. You truly are the cleverest woman in all of Kemet. That truth, of course, only makes me feel worse for the fate I have forced on you. An afterlife of apologies will never be enough.

I have spent much of my life trying to be the father you

deserve. In truth, there was no way for me to make up for what I did all those years ago. The consequences of my folly now fall on you, which is my most piercing regret. Young, ambitious men are a foolish breed. If I could do it all over, I'd have kept myself out of schemes such as the one we both pay for now.

I write this last letter to remind you of my deep, abiding, and unfailing love for you. As a child, you lit up a room, filling it with your grace and energy. As a young woman, you not only filled my heart but challenged my mind as well, impressing me daily with your unique intellect. I wish only that I had the power to spare you pain—the pain I have caused, the pain I know you're enduring now, the pain to come. I'd happily give my life to spare you, but the gods have not granted me such power.

Know only that my love for you is real, my heartfelt apologies are genuine, and I shall strive still to protect you as I'm able. I have loved you with all my heart, and your mother as well. Enjoying life by your side has made every day worthwhile. I've had a long and full life, and aside from this one regret, I consider myself blessed. I hope Anubis will also weigh my good deeds, as I hope you do so that one day you might remember me fondly.

Remember, dear one, you are not alone, even when the world feels loneliest. If ever you find yourself in need of a true friend, write to the doctor Khui in Shedet. Leave the note where you found this one, and help will arrive. And do trust yourself and your intuition—if your heart believes in a person or their words, then go ahead and trust. Your heart is light. It will guide you. Until, by the grace of the gods, we meet again. I am yours, truly and forever.

FOURTEEN

K EMET'S PALACES AND TEMPLES ARE COVERED IN VIVID IMAGES.
I love the depiction of the gods and goddesses, but I avert
my eyes when I pass the war scenes that portray mounds of
corpses, sometimes just the hands or phalli of the conquered dead
piled high on an inscribed wall. I never imagined a rotting mass of
corpses piling up at the palace. It has never been a serene home, but
it did feel safe once. At least as safe as any place can be in a world
full of danger.

Now, less than a week after the death of Senenmut, another
corpse surfaces.

Teena died of poison in her quarters, exactly like my tutor.

The court buzzes with talk of two court members dying, alone
in their quarters, in such short order. Two cooks and three kitchen
maids are tortured, which is as useless as it is cruel. Two maids don't
survive the torment, rendering the mound of corpses higher.

I suspect Thutmose murdered Teena to show me he won't
hesitate to kill a woman, even a woman he's entangled with, even
a woman who carries his child. Of course, Mother is an equally

likely candidate, as Teena's death so closely mimicked Senenmut's, and Mother and I are the two people at court most broken by his. Neither explanation would surprise me.

Death holds me close in its cold embrace. It surrounds me, pressing in on all sides. Yet I barely have the energy to care. I've stayed in my bed since Senenmut's death. I should return to the temple, keep the god appeased so he's on my side. Senenmut would want me to fight. But every waking moment is anguish. I beg sleep to find me. I don't care if death is at its side.

"Get up!" Thutmose wakes me from a deep sleep. The sunlight bouncing off my walls tells me it's early, but his rage has had time to age. "Get out of bed, you lazy—"

"What do you care if I miss ritual? You've never shown interest in the gods—"

"I care if the god's wife—the figurehead of an estate that now belongs to me—does her job. I care if my wife plays the role of queen—"

"Then you shouldn't have killed him!" I'm on my feet, screeching. "You should have let him live." I fall to my knees, sobbing.

Thutmose yanks me to my feet. His fingers dig into my arms. Squeezing me tight with one hand, he wraps his other fingers around my neck—I'll be black and blue by the end of the day. "Unless you want to die too, you will grow up, and you will show up." He spits at me. "I'm perfectly happy to change my mind about you, Neferura. I don't need your child that bad. The country will settle for any royal brat once you're dead." He calms himself and releases me. "Speaking of dead." Rage sizzles under his words. "Did you kill her?"

"Kill...Teena, you mean?" I take a step back, shaking from the outburst. It's not the first time Thutmose has put his hands on me in anger. But he was a boy then. The man before me now reeks of danger. "Why would I kill Teena?"

"Revenge for Senenmut. Or envy. You want your child to be the first."

"I don't want your child at all. More to the point, I'm not a murderer. I'm not you."

"Senenmut was the murderer." Thutmose's gaze sears me. "Perhaps your act of piety is as fake as his. Maybe you were involved in Teena's death. Maybe it's time your favorite plaything meets the same fate."

"My play..."

Kamut.

My heart stops. How could Thutmose possibly know I have feelings for...? No. Thutmose knows nothing. He's fishing.

I force my shoulders to shrug, stilling my face. "Unless you're referring to the god, my real husband, I have no idea who you're threatening. To be honest, I assumed you'd murdered Teena to prove to me you're capable."

He laughs at that. "I gave up trying to prove myself to you years ago, Neferura. It's your turn to prove yourself to me now. So far, you're failing. You know what failure means, yes?"

I don't respond to the threat, but the fear that dimmed in the wake of Senenmut's death flares again.

"You will join me for dinner in the great hall tomorrow night. The nobles will see their real pharaoh dine with his great royal wife. Am I understood?"

The nod costs me, but I fear a refusal would cost me much more. Above all, I fear the punishment for refusal would fall on Kamut. It seems Teena's death has put another I love in danger. So I agree to Thutmose's demand and sag in relief when he leaves.

My reprieve is short-lived. Mother barges in shortly after Thutmose leaves, parroting his words, complaining that I've spent too many days in bed, avoiding my duties.

"What duties? My duties are now a sham, as are yours. We're his puppets."

"And we'll be his puppets forever if you don't join the fray." She drops onto my bed, where I returned after Thutmose's visit. "I don't want to dance to the rhythm he plays any more than you do. But for now, we must survive. To do that, we must carry on."

"I'm grieving, Mother. We can't even bury Senenmut properly. We can't celebrate him—"

"I loved him too," she reminds me. "I loved him enough to fight for the one thing Senenmut wanted more than anything else: for you to live."

I watch as the anger flows out of her, leaving a simple woman by my side. She could be any woman in Kemet in this moment—a housewife bereaved of her child, a young widow mourning a husband.

An unfamiliar well of tenderness blooms inside me. Maybe I'm too hard on Mother. I suspected her of killing Father. In the end, she was innocent. She did try to kill Thutmose though, I remind myself. And she sacrificed me. And Senenmut.

"Did you kill Teena?" I ask, praying that my suspicion is wrong.

Mother stands, waving my question away with a huff before yelling for a handmaid to fetch her wine. I wait for it to come, then repeat the question.

"Of course not, Neferura," she begins. "I have people who do those things for me. That girl deserved a far worse death for revealing Senenmut's secret."

"She spoke only the truth, Mother," I croak, heavy with the confirmation that Mother is a murderer. It's not a surprise, but it is unwelcome. "Do you think Thutmose is going to just accept that? You've killed his lover. You granted him power, then you provoked him."

"Don't be ridiculous, Neferura. He knew he was sacrificing that silly girl the moment he put her in front of me. He expected her death. I'd kill the wisewoman too if I could find her. Together they caused my downfall. And that girl was pregnant—"

"One would think that's a reason not to murder a woman."

Mother stands over my bed, wine cup in hand, looking down on me. "Your child must be the first. You must get pregnant, Neferura. As soon as possible."

"So Thutmose can kill me sooner? Why would I want that, Mother? Why would you?"

"It's the only way." She settles next to me again, earnestness oozing off her. "Can't you see? If you give him a child, he'll be appeased. We'll be all right. With an heir of your body, we can buy time and, more importantly, solidify the loyalty of the nobles. You'll be more beloved than ever. We can return to power in truth, not just this charade we're living now. But only with your child."

"How do you know Thutmose won't kill me the moment I give him an heir?"

She reaches a hand out, resting it on my arm. I freeze, then in spite of all I know, in spite of all she's done, I relax into her touch, aching for more. The last time Mother touched me, we were watching my father's mummified body be sealed in his tomb for the final time. "I promise you, daughter, everything will be all right. You just need to listen to me. Just do what I say, and we'll be fine. You and the child you bear will thrive. You'll have everything you deserve—"

"And you'll have your legacy."

Her hand leaves my arm. She doesn't deny it. "Yes. We will be pharaoh and god's wife, as we're meant to be. Our legacy will be secure."

"I want to believe you," I admit. It's true. But I can't shake the feeling Mother would accept my child in lieu of me if it meant keeping her lineage intact. "It's impossible. There have been too many secrets—"

"No more secrets," she vows. "I swear on the god we both love, in the name of Amun, that I will keep no more secrets. But, Neferura, you must bear Thutmose's child. I can return us to power. I've overcome threats and built power before. I can do it again. But only with your child. Promise me?"

I look into her eyes, heart aching. I want to believe my old life is still out there, waiting for me. But the ignorance that once comforted me has been shattered. And Senenmut is gone. There's no going back. Giving Thutmose a child will only bring my death closer.

In the end, I promise to consider her words and claim I need privacy. She walks out, head high, as if she's won the concession she sought, and I fall back into bed.

I wear my bruises to dinner the following night. It's not the most daring act of bravery, but it's what I can manage.

I haven't taken such care with my appearance since Iset left. I choose a pale linen gown that reveals the purple imprints marking my arms and neck. I add my finest bangles, designed to draw the nobles' eyes, slipping Iset's mother's bracelet on last to give me courage. I arrive late enough to be noticed, early enough for the light to shine brightly on me.

I want the nobles to see what their younger pharaoh has done.

Thutmose's pretty nose flares when he sees me. But Thuiu sits taller, head high and a fierce glint in her eyes. Her support bolsters my resolve, and I toss my shoulders back and stride to my seat next to Mother. Her eyes crinkle in confusion—I was covered in blankets when she saw me yesterday, so my bruises must come as a surprise. She recovers quickly, turning back to her gazelle, slathered in honey and herbs. My molested body is less interesting to her than the dead antelope on her dinner plate.

The court does what the court always does: takes a cue from its pharaohs and ignores me. The nobles go back to their gossip: Senenmut's untimely death, Teena's poisoning, Thutmose's growing influence at court, the possibility of an heir.

I fiddle with the whole salted fish in front of me, my favorite. I'm toying with the idea of eating it—I haven't eaten a bite in days—when a rough pinch on the back startles me. Irritated, I turn to rebuke Thutmose. But he's talking to the high priest, who is seated on his other side. Mother's hands are busy shoving food in her mouth. I look behind me to find the girl from Mother's quarters, the scorpion Hathor rescued as a child. She shakes her head once, a stern look on her face, then dashes off. I turn back to the fish, heart racing. Was she telling me not to eat it?

I push it away, fingers trembling.

"You definitely want to eat that," Thutmose slurs in my ear. "I had that one prepared just for you."

Poison.

Emotions swarm me, but I'm not about to let him see my fear. "I'm not hungry for spoiled fish." Amazed my voice sounds calm, I brave eye contact. "I'm surprised you went to such lengths, to be honest. Perhaps you're reconsidering the deal you made with Mother? Have you decided an heir of the blood has no value to you after all?"

"Any child of mine is a child of the blood, Neferura."

"Not Mother's blood. Not really. Not like a child of my womb would be. The people love her. They love me because they love her. And they'll love you much more if they believe you're with us rather than against us. A child of my womb gives you not only the legitimacy Mother carries but the loyalty we both command."

"Yesterday, you claimed you didn't want my child."

"I don't. But I do want to live," I say. "You've made it clear that's the price."

He leans close, so close I have to stop myself from scooting back. "Then I suggest you make sure your mother does not come for me or anyone I care about again. Because I will repay her, body for body. And from what I can tell, there's only one person left she gives a damn about. That means there's only one target left for me to aim at."

The high priest says something to Thutmose, who plasters his mask back on and turns away, leaving me shaking with anger, wondering how the scorpion knew to warn me and more desperate than ever to find a piece of me in the ashes of my old life.

Thuiu walks me to my quarters after dinner. I invited her for a late-night drink—she's a night owl, and I don't want to be alone right now.

Plus, tonight's incident reminds me life is short, and mine may be near an end. If I am to find any joy, I better do it now, before it's too late.

She grumbles, perched on the edge of my bed as Benerib serves her beer and me a large cup of wine. "Thutmose's behavior is unforgivable. You know, of course," Thuiu sighs. "Your marriage and potential heir are all the nobles will talk about for the next three months."

"When they take a break from gossiping about Senenmut's death." I don't bother to tell her about the poison fish. There's nothing Thuiu can do to protect me from my murderous husband.

"And Teena's. The doctor's girl finally captured the court's interest. And all she had to do was die." Thuiu pats me with a wrinkled hand. "I am sorry about Senenmut, my dear. He was a good man. I assume your mother has been forced to abandon him rather than celebrate him as one would expect?"

"She's abandoned us both."

Thuiu sighs again, louder. "I heard that silly Herneith say that if it weren't for Senenmut, you would have married Thutmose years ago and the country would have heirs by now. I'm afraid the nobles have turned against our old friend. He is to be blamed for the land's lack of heirs."

"Heirs," I mutter. "In the end, I'm just another broodmare."

"Aren't we all, dear?" She twines her fingers together on her lap as her eyes rove over me. "Have you seen the doctor?"

The sound that escapes my lips is part moan, part snicker. "Don't tell me you're anxious for me to breed too."

Thuiu's smile is forced. "Perhaps. But I want you to bear children for your personal happiness, my dear. Babies bring joy even in the darkest hours. And your best option is to embrace the life you've been cursed and blessed with. This is the role the gods want you to play."

Is it?

I thought I was to be a virgin for life. Now I'm to be forced to bear Thutmose's child. The truth is, I have no idea what the gods want of me. I'm not sure they have any plans at all for me. The doubt and humility are new and terrifying.

I gather myself and ask after her husband, Ineni, who continues to deteriorate. He's now too sick to enjoy his garden, and she prepares his tomb, readying for his imminent departure. It's kind of her to visit, under the circumstances. I promise to do everything I can in my role as god's wife to ensure Ineni's peaceful and successful transition to the afterworld. That's one duty I presume I'll still be allowed to perform.

Unlike her sickly husband, Thuiu is in excellent health, and her mind is as sharp as ever.

She stands to go, and I reach out to grab her hand, beckoning her close so Benerib can't hear the words I whisper to her.

"The young man with the scar, my guard, Kamut, is standing outside my door right now. Will you tell him to come to me? Tonight, if he can."

Her wrinkled face scrunches.

"Please, Thuiu."

"This is a dangerous game you play, girl," she warns.

"I was born to this game," I retort. "Don't you think it's past time I actually play it?"

Worry written on her wrinkled face, she nevertheless nods an agreement, then toddles out at Benerib's side.

FIFTEEN

I DREAM THAT I'M IN BED WITH KAMUT. HIS LIPS ARE WARM ON mine. Our legs are entwined. He slides his hand down my thigh, and I moan, pressing myself into his palm. "Little princess," he sighs. I'm a queen now, but I prefer my old nickname, so of course Kamut knows to use it. It's my dream after all.

"Neferura."

My eyes snap open.

I'm still dreaming, but now Kamut is by my bed, on his knees, his face so close I feel his breath on my cheek.

"Don't scream," he whispers. "It's me."

I lift up onto my elbows, shaking the cobwebs from my mind, my body still slick with desire. But this is no dream. It's real. Kamut is here, next to me. "You're here."

"As summoned." His smile is sweet, but there's a hunger in it too.

The words I'd planned flee. In this moment, I want only one thing. I want to remake my dream in reality. I want Kamut inside me, washing away Thutmose's touch, replacing him in my bed and in my body.

Wordlessly, I toss the blanket aside, inviting Kamut to my bed.

He doesn't hesitate. He slides in beside me and I pull him close, press my lips against his, feel the length of his body against mine. He makes love to me. It's slow and tender and everything Iset once hinted at.

He holds me afterward. I don't want to break the spell—I could stay like this forever—but I called Kamut here for a reason. And as lovely as the night has been, this isn't it.

"You need to leave Waset," I whisper.

He moans quietly, rolling onto his back, fingers twined in mine. "Before Thutmose kills me, you mean?"

I turn to my side to face him. "You know?"

He stares up at my ceiling. I can tell by the curve of his cheek that he's smiling. "He's made it rather clear. He even brandished my father's dagger at me today—"

"The blade he's always fiddling with? It's your father's?"

"Not much of a blade for a sword master, I suppose," Kamut says. "But it was my grandfather's before Father inherited it, and his father's before that."

"How did Thutmose get it?"

"The dog incident."

"Thutmose's dog, Anubis? When he attacked you, you mean?" I prop myself up, curious. Moonlight streams in through my open wall, dappling Kamut's face with light. "What does that have to do with your father's blade?"

Kamut's eyes stick to mine. "Father killed the dog with that blade." He turns onto his side so we're facing each other. "You know your mother had the dog put down after it attacked me?"

A feeling of dread creeps over the bed that was nothing but bliss just moments ago. "I didn't know. I suppose I didn't think about the dog. I was too worried about the two of you. You'd taken such a risk protecting me from Thutmose—"

"I'd take that risk any day." He smiles. "It wasn't nearly as terrifying as what came next."

I wait for an explanation.

"I was far more worried about what you'd think when you saw me with this ugly scar."

I grin at the memory, reaching out to run my fingertips over his scar. "I felt awful about what happened. The only good thing that came out of that terrible day was Senenmut making you my guard."

"I'll never forget the terror I felt that first day, standing outside your door, waiting for you to see me. You hadn't seen me since the dog attacked me…"

"I was thrilled. Elated you were going to be so close. I felt safer, having you near."

"Your smile was enormous." He pulls my hand to his lips. "I've loved you ever since the moment I saw that smile."

I lean in to kiss him slowly, then pull back and blink away tears. "I didn't know…about the smile. Or the dog."

Kamut grimaces. "Poor beast. Thutmose and that dog adored each other. It was bad enough your mother had the dog killed. Worse still, she forced Thutmose to choose between killing it himself or watching my father saw its head off with that damn blade. Thutmose couldn't kill it, so he was forced to watch every bloody moment, the dog squealing and whining through far too much of it. It was horrendous for me. I can't imagine how awful it was for him. Your mother's punishment was far worse than the attack."

"The choice," I gasp, falling to my back. That's what Senenmut meant. And the cruelty. It's no wonder Thutmose hates us. Mother exiled him from the only home he knew, trapped him far from court, leaching away the power he believed Father and the gods granted him. The dog's death can only have deepened his resentment. Clearly the choice Mother gave him stuck with him all these years.

Kamut traces my cheek, then my breast, and finally rests his palm on my stomach. "Thutmose hated you both long before the dog died. I'm sure the poor thing's ugly end didn't help. But if it wasn't the dog, Thutmose would loathe you for some other incident. It's not like your mother didn't give him reasons."

"Maybe I should have done more."

"Maybe you did too much." Kamut pulls me closer. "You were too good to Thutmose for far too long. He had reasons to be angry at your mother, not you. He never had the right to treat you as awfully as he did."

We both fall silent. I know without asking that Kamut is thinking the same thing I am—I'm now married to that angry little boy. Thutmose can treat me however he likes. And if I react at all, my life is at risk.

After a while, I ask Kamut where he'll go.

"I don't know," he admits. "I intend to stay close, find some way to help you. I'll stay in the palace if you—"

"No." I snuggle into him. "I can't lose you too."

"There must be some way we can..." He doesn't finish. We might both want this more than anything in the world, but we are an impossibility. "At least let me help you. I can't just walk away and leave you. Don't ask me to do that."

I close my eyes, considering the options before me. None feel safe or right. Hathor may have failed me by not saving Senenmut, but her scorpion did just save my life, and Hathor is right about some things. I do need to find a different way forward. I must stop choosing between paths others have laid.

"Stay in Waset," I say at last. "Make sure you're safe. But stay close. I will ask for help when I need it."

"How? It's nearly impossible to talk when we're near each other. How will we communicate if I'm hiding out in the desert?"

I think for a moment, then remind him of the eight flagpoles in front of the first temple pylon. "Tie a red streamer around the last flagpole when you want to communicate with me. I'll do the same if I need you. Then wait for a priestess to find you near the Kushite brewer's stall. Wear something red so she can spot you. The priestess will tell you what to do next. Trust no one but Iset, your brother, and the priestess I send."

He draws me close, breath heavy. "As you command." His voice is husky. "I do aim to please you." He kisses me once more and then draws away, his voice wistful. "You could come with me. We could disappear together."

I close my eyes, imagining it, then release a sigh, heavy with regret. "Thutmose would never stop hunting us. He'd tear the country apart searching for me. There would be no peace, for us or for Kemet."

He rubs his nose against my cheek. "So we give Thutmose a different wife and I can take his," he jokes.

"If only we could." I smile, imagining a life with Kamut, far from court. It's a beautiful thought, until I envision Thutmose's soldiers bearing down on us, destroying whatever we'd managed to build, the country in constant chaos, worried over its missing god's wife. And then, of course, there are my duties. It's my job to care for the people of Kemet. How could I do that without my titles and the resources they grant me?

Disappearing would be wonderful. If only it were possible.

My musings are interrupted as Kamut's hand slips down my

spine. This time, the lovemaking is fierce and desperate. When it's over, we hold each other until dawn. Then Kamut kisses me one final time, agrees to deliver a message to Iset, and disappears onto my deck.

I stare up at my star-speckled ceiling, breathing in the scent of him, still on my linen throw. I may never see Kamut again. Yet my body feels light. In spite of the grief that still sits in my gut, my thoughts are clear. My resources and options may run thin. I've lost so much already. But I've gained something too—the will to live, to survive and thrive. That means finding a way to live that doesn't involve Thutmose owning my body and will, a way to avoid the death traps he'll continue to seed. I must claw back my power and find a way to help the people of Kemet as I always have.

I don't have much to fight back with, but I have far more than nothing, including friends who can help me forge a new path.

Three days later, Iset flies into my arms, wrapping me in a warm, happy hug. I return the embrace, inhaling her scent: mint with hints of lotus and beer. Satiah hurries Nebtah inside and closes the door behind them, locking the four of us in my small temple office alone.

"I was so happy to see Kamut," Iset whispers. "I've been praying you'd find a way for us to meet. I can't believe Kamut isn't going to guard you anymore. Still, he looked rather happy." One side of her lips turns up, her eyes hungry with curiosity.

I grant her a small smile, which makes her squeal, then pull her down onto a chair next to me. We're not here to discuss romance, although I can't get to the topic at hand without asking Iset about the pregnancy. "How are you?"

She touches her belly, grinning. "Less sick than I was. Happy to be here."

Satiah and Nebtah pull chairs close so we're in a small circle.

I turn to Satiah. "Did anyone follow you?"

She shakes her head. "No one paid us attention—"

"No one paid me attention," Iset interrupts. "They assumed I was one of your priestesses, dressed as I am." She gestures at the white robe she wears, adorned with gold thread. It matches Satiah's and Nebtah's exactly. "Everyone stares at pretty Satiah, but they ignored me and Nebtah entirely."

"You get used to it," Nebtah jokes.

Iset grins at her, then turns to me. "Did you call us all here because you have a plan?" Her face falls. "I do hope so. Your last letter broke my heart. I'm so sorry you had to marry that vile man. And Senenmut..." She pauses, eyes brimming with tears. "It's all Thutmose's fault—"

"Iset," I interrupt, glancing at the two priestesses. Their eyes are wide and curious. "Before this goes any further," I say, "I want to be clear about a few things. Just being here puts you all in danger. I'm in danger. I want to find a way out of it, but right now, I can't protect myself, much less the three of you. You don't have to have anything to do with this. You can stand up and walk away now. I will never hold it against you. Nothing between us will change. You have your own lives to live, your own families to worry about. You don't need to worry about mine. You have a choice. But if you stay, your choices will soon be limited, and your lives will be at risk."

Nebtah leans forward, eager. "If I hadn't joined the troupe when I did, well, let's just say you gave me a purpose when I had none.

And more than a job, I watched you work every day to help people. You're one of the three most powerful people in Kemet. You could sit in your palace stuffing yourself with honey cakes and date tarts. But you're here with us, working to keep the god satisfied, to allocate more of the priesthood's resources to the people—"

"No one works harder than you, Nebtah," I remind her.

She grins, pleased by the compliment. "I had a good role model, Adoratrice. You gave me the opportunity, and you showed me how to make smart use of it."

"Yes, yes. We are all fiercely loyal." Satiah smiles. "And you know Nebtah and I aren't scared of a little danger. I assume that's why you chose us?"

I nod, impressed by the observation. Many of my priestesses are loyal. Fewer are loyal and brave. Fewer still are loyal, brave, and keenly observant.

"If you're in danger, your estate is in danger, which means we're in danger too. And I'm assuming many others would be in danger along with us," Nebtah reasons.

"So how can we help?" Satiah finishes her thoughts.

The two are close. In some ways, they're as different as fish and birds. Satiah is sleek and beautiful; Nebtah is chubby and plain. Satiah loves to joke and laugh; Nebtah takes the work seriously, pushing the troupe to do more, do it faster, do it better. Satiah likes to surprise; Nebtah believes in order and predictability. Yet they share a passion for service. More to the point, they are both risk takers, comfortable with questioning authority.

That's another reason I chose them—they'll both disagree with me, sometimes loudly and passionately, which too few of the priestesses feel comfortable doing. I trust them to be loyal, but I also trust them to be honest.

"I don't have a final plan quite yet. I don't know how this will all play out." I tilt my chin up. "But I have ideas, a place to start. First, we must find a way to discover what Thutmose is up to. We need a spy in his quarters—someone who can get and stay close to him."

My eyes flit to Satiah, turning over what I need to ask her to do. I've played many scenarios out in my head through the past few sleepless nights. Some lead to death, sometimes hers, sometimes mine. But the first step toward safety, toward survival, is always the same: eyes on Thutmose. I take a soothing breath.

"Iset." I turn to her. "See if you can learn more about the scorpion with skills at forging. Oh, and I'm going to order new gowns for the priestesses and for myself. I'll make Maia a rich woman. And it will give us an excuse to see each other more often."

Iset nods happily.

"Nebtah." I turn to her. "We need new instruments. Go to the one-eyed jeweler. Have him make a new sistrum." I explain the design—it's my own idea, but it's influenced by the many contraptions Senenmut collected. "Keep an eye out for a red streamer tied to the eighth temple flagpole." I tell her what to do if she sees it.

She nods her agreement, and I turn to the most difficult task of all.

"Any plan with a shot of working will hinge on you, Satiah. I'm considering punishing you for all that beauty." I grin, hoping to soften the threat. But I also want her to take it seriously.

"Who am I to bed?" Satiah's grin is naughty.

"No one yet," I retort. "But eventually, perhaps…" I take another gulp of air before I say, "My husband, which means danger."

Her eyes widen at the prospect of getting close to Thutmose, but she shakes it off and shrugs. "I've been in danger since the day I was abandoned as a child. If bedding some poor fool makes you—us— safer, it's a small price to pay."

"This fool is a pharaoh," Iset points out.

Satiah's lips curve into a grin. "Pharaohs are just men. Well, most of them are men anyway."

My stomach churns at the thought. "We'll see if it comes to that." I nod, replaying my plan to ensure the risk will be worth my while—and hers—in my head, reminding myself that Satiah is my best chance at infiltrating Thutmose's inner sanctum so I can learn his moves before he makes them. If I'm to succeed, we'll all have to pay some price. "We're quite a team," I continue. "I'm lucky to have you three. I intend to find a way to survive and use the power the gods gave me to help people as I always have. With your help, perhaps I'll succeed."

The two priestesses offer curt bows and walk outside, leaving me alone with Iset. They're waiting just beyond the door to escort her home. We don't have long, but there's time enough for a final hug. I whisper in her ear. "I may not have Hathor's scorpions, but I have the three of you. It may be enough."

"And Thuiu," she reminds me. "And Kamut. You have to use all your resources, Mistress. We can't let vile Set win. If he does, everyone will suffer. I know you well enough to know it'll help to remind yourself it's not about you. Not really."

My hand falls to her belly.

She presses her hand over mine. "I'm so sorry about Senenmut."

I pull her close and we stand still, holding each other. I wait for my tears to stop, then step back again. I worry her mother's bracelet off my wrist and hand it to her, anxiety simmering as she slips it on.

"Thank you for keeping it safe," she says, fondling the scorpion amulet, now dangling from her wrist. "It's going to be all right, Mistress. We'll find a way. Wait and see. In the meantime, I can't wait to dress you all." She grins, then turns to go. Pausing at the door, she looks back. "By the way, the crocodile dung we took from the doctor's rooms is in the bottom drawer of the big cedar chest. You might need it after all." She nods, opens the door, and leaves me alone with too many what-ifs to contend with. What-ifs that, if not handled correctly, could threaten the whole country.

At least one piece of the plan is clear.

Back in my quarters, my feet aim themselves at my large cedar chest. I drop to my knees and rummage through my bottom drawer until my fingers find something hard amid my linens. I pull it out: the jar full of crocodile dung. I hurry to my study to find the scroll that contains the right potion and spell, then mix the tonic that will ensure I am not with child. There's enough to last me for a year, perhaps more. Mother and Thutmose can want an heir of my body all they want. Only I have the power to give it to them. It's a power I intend to use to advance my agenda, not theirs.

PART
THREE

SIXTEEN

S TOP IT, MOTHER!" I SCREECH AS AN ALABASTER POT FLIES PAST
my head to strike Mother's handmaid.

The woman doesn't even duck. She just stands there
and lets the thing hit her, then goes back to her duties as if it never
happened. A big red welt blooms on her forehead as she fiddles with
Mother's cosmetics.

"That's enough." I scoop up the pot and slam it down in front
of Mother. It contains a lotion of palm and nutmeg oil for her face,
a concoction she's used on and off for years to treat a skin inflammation she claims to have inherited from her father.

At least Mother has the good sense to look ashamed. I suspected
she's more embarrassed of her emotional outburst than of harming
the poor old lady, who's served Mother since I was a child on the
knee. I'd like to say this is an isolated incident. But it's been nearly
two months since Senenmut's death, and in the past few weeks,
Mother's outbursts have grown increasingly common. She has
wandered out of a ritual, leaving me and the high priest gaping in
shock, punished a farmer for the death of his own goat, assigned a

harlot to the priesthood, and given one of her least favorite nobles a small fortune.

"I'm going to summon the doctor—"

"You are not," she insists with a lisp.

Mother's body is failing her. She pronounces words oddly as if her mouth can't quite form sounds. Her tooth pains her, as does the inflammation around her joints. Her skin is blotchier and rougher than ever.

"Yes, I am. And you will do what he says."

"I do not need Hesi-Ra, Neferura," she says. "His spells and curatives are useless."

Unlike Inhapi, the new doctor, Hesi-Ra, doesn't lay claim to magical unguents that will keep Mother looking forever young, which renders him worthless in her opinion. She has a point. Mother looks older than even her advanced age—many don't live to their forties, and few who do look as old as her. Of course, Hesi-Ra's inability to stop Mother from aging doesn't mean he can't help with whatever ails her, but I'm too tired to remind her of that now. It wouldn't move her anyway.

Instead, I lean close, nearly gagging on the smell of sickness that surrounds her, to whisper, "You are giving Thutmose the excuse he needs to strip you of those last vestiges of power you're so desperately clinging to. Unless you want to lose even the pretense of being pharaoh, I suggest you do what you must to get better. And that means letting Hesi-Ra examine you."

"Mind yourself, Neferura," she huffs. "You look scraggly, by the way. One would think a woman hoping to conceive a child would make some effort to beautify herself." With that charming observation, Mother turns to read a tablet—upside down, no less—putting an end to another short, futile conversation.

Not long ago, I would have suspected Thutmose of poisoning her, especially after he poisoned my fish. After years spent longing for peace between Thutmose and Mother, their tense truce now chafes me. Mother just grins and looks the other way as Thutmose plunders the treasury, doling out resources for his military objectives while she deals with the nobles he wants to avoid. She treats the relationship as normal, as if he didn't kill Senenmut, as if he's not planning to murder me the moment I give him a child. Yet that's exactly what Mother wants me to do. They're united by their desire for an heir. My body is the scroll on which their truce is written. My will is irrelevant—to them at least. I continue to take the potion, set on denying their wishes. The three of us have survived, but I'm the one who pays the price of their truce.

And Senenmut, of course. He paid the largest share.

The thought of Senenmut decides it. I march out of Mother's quarters and rush toward my old tutor's rooms, leaving the old handmaid to waddle after me. She falls farther behind every step I take. It's cruel—the old woman moves like a snail. But I've lost my taste for enabling Mother's spies.

Relieved to find Senenmut's quarters unguarded and empty, I slink behind his desk and pull his old writing palette close. I need to get Mother help before she drops dead, or worse, finds some new, even more humiliating way to reward Thutmose for murdering the man we both loved. So I scrawl signs across the page, roll it, stamp it with my glazed steatite seal ring, and slip it into the empty cubbyhole in Senenmut's desk.

Senenmut recommended Khui to me in his deathbed letter. And he is a doctor, presumably a man Senenmut trusted. If Mother won't allow Hesi-Ra to inspect her, perhaps this man Khui will be more palatable. Hopefully my missive reaches him soon. If I'm lucky, he'll appear and claim he has the power to make the old look young again. Appealing to Mother's vanity may be the one way to cure her.

The court doctor comes unbidden. I know who's at my door from the guard's coded knock. I dare hope Hesi-Ra's unexpected visit means Mother is finally letting him treat her. I know at a glance that's not why he's here.

The new doctor is a small, tidy man with a long nose and sharp eyes. Right now, his eyes are fixed on mine. It doesn't last—he knows better—but in that brief glance, I read grief, pain, sadness.

"Mother?" I fall onto a stool—my trembling legs won't hold me.

"No." He shakes his head, then looks at the chair across from me. When I motion for him to sit, he sinks down and sits stiffly, a single scroll in his hand. "But it is bad news, I'm afraid."

Kamut? Iset? No, the doctor wouldn't know them, and he wouldn't know to come to me if he did. For a moment, I dare hope it's Thutmose, but the doctor's grief is too genuine.

"Thuiu," I sigh.

He confirms my guess with a curt nod. "She followed her husband to Aaru last night. I learned of it right after you left your mother's side earlier today. I came as soon as I could." He hands me the scroll. "The messenger who brought the news asked that I give you this. Apparently Thuiu left instructions to deliver it to you on her death." After a pause, he clears his throat. "I saw her two days ago. She was in excellent health. She was a truly remarkable woman. Her heart will be weighed, and she'll be ushered into the Field of Reeds. If we're lucky, when our time comes, our hearts will be as light as hers. We'll see her then."

He stands awkwardly, as if he's anxious to leave as I struggle to process the news. Yes, Thuiu was old, far past the age most live. But she was so…so…young. "How?" I manage.

"In her sleep. It was painless and natural. It was her time."

I bow my head and stare down at the scroll in my fist. Did she write me a farewell letter? Did she know her death was near? Or perhaps she left me one of her favorite passages from the wisdom texts.

"I'm sorry, Adoratrice." Hesi-Ra bows as he backs slowly toward the door.

Worried about crushing Thuiu's final words, I release my grip, blinking to clear the blur from my eyes. My chest aches as I unroll it.

I scan the signs—it's written in Thuiu's small, neat script. It's nothing I'd ever expect. Thuiu was nothing if not predictably unpredictable.

From the noblewoman, Thuiu, to the god's wife, Neferura, in life, prosperity, and health and in the favor of the gods, I've a gift for you, my dear, although this gift is not truly mine to give away. Benerib has agreed to serve you when I pass. If you are reading this, I have passed at last. Ineni will be so pleased to see me. And Benerib will need a new project to keep her busy while she waits to join me and our husbands. She'll spend some time with her daughter once I'm gone, but she'll join you after a visit to Behdet. Serving you will be a balm to her. She is not the handmaid you once loved—my old heart knows true friendship when I see it—but she is the handmaid I have cherished for nearly five decades. And she brings with her far more than skills at warming a bath or braiding a wig. I believe she'll be a valuable resource to you, as she has been for me. Above all—and please believe this—you can trust her completely. She is not shy with her opinions, and her word is as reliable as the sun. When you join me in the Field of Reeds, many years from now, I'll be waiting to hear of the adventures you find together. I am yours in true friendship, in this life and the next.

The familiar grief wells in my throat. The pain of losing Senenmut comes and goes, unbidden but familiar. At times, it's even welcome. I feel my old tutor in those moments. Even after what he did, I pray that his heart will be light enough, that his good deeds were so weighty that he'll make it to Aaru. Perhaps he's there now, peppering Thuiu with questions. The thought makes me smile.

I look down at the letter. I'll be happy to replace Mother's old handmaid with Benerib, but shouldn't the woman have a chance to rest? She's earned it after all these years. Surely she agreed, or Thuiu wouldn't have offered.

The sound of the door opening for Hesi-Ra's exit startles me. "Hesi-Ra." I stop him. When his eyes land on mine, I blurt out a question that's been stuck in my heart for months now. "Did Thuiu have any tattoos?"

Is it a trick of the light, or does his face harden? "No." He shakes his head. "I assure you, Adoratrice, Thuiu was unmarked."

The searing sense of loss still accompanies me, haunting me like a spirit, as I face the crowd days later. The long white dress, once too tight, now fits me like a glove. If only this headdress were as comfortable. I have to keep my head tilted just so to keep the vulture head centered on my forehead, not an easy feat as I set wax figures of Kemet's traditional enemies on fire one after another.

It's my duty as god's wife to burn our enemies in effigy a few times a year. Usually I enjoy the ritual, one of the few I perform before the people outside of festivals. I wouldn't want to do it often, but the occasional public ritual reminds me, and I hope the people, of the bonds we share.

Nine bows line the stage in the temple forecourt, representing Kemet's enemies, and nine additional foreign enemies are painted on the podium under my feet—even the insides of my sandals are etched with images of foreign enemies—so I trample our enemies as I burn them. The people cheer as I set each little figure on fire and watch them melt, one after another.

Today, the ritual pains me. In addition to mourning Thuiu, I'm aware that the last time I stood here, rather than the dour old soldier who watches me now, Kamut was on duty at my side. I recall fretting over spoiling the pure white dress. I was bleeding and terrified by the thought it might show...

Bleeding.

I crush the wax figure in my fist.

My monthly blood. I haven't had it since.

That was around the time of Senenmut's death, just before Kamut left.

Months ago. Too long.

Could I be...?

No. No, that's impossible. I've taken the potion religiously. And I've lost weight.

Yet my body has shown signs. I've been nauseous and tired. Smells make me queasy. My breasts have been sensitive.

My breath hitches.

Have I ignored the warnings, embracing ignorance out of desperation to avoid giving Thutmose a child?

The crowd twitches, confused that I've altered the tempo. They're superstitious like that. One beat out of line and the children of Waset will cry themselves to sleep tonight, convinced the Heka Khasut are creeping over the border. One of the priestesses behind me, Nebtah or Satiah, stirs, prompting me to focus. I owe the people a proper ritual, whatever my personal situation may be.

Heart racing, I set the figure in the flame. I feel like I might be sick, a sensation I've noticed a lot lately, although I assumed it was loss and stress and the constant dread that comes with being forced to take a man you detest as partner—a man who is as likely to murder you as pass you the wine. Or, if the past is predicate, may just poison the wine, then hand it to you.

A child is the last thing I want now. I want to prove to myself that I have some power—power over my own body. I want to defy Mother and Thutmose. I want to make one decision about how I live my own life.

But there's nothing I can do about that in this moment. I stand taller. Either I'm pregnant or I'm not. Either way, our enemies must be vanquished, which means this ritual must be finished. Causing a scene will only trigger questions I'm not ready to answer.

I lift the next little enemy, and with my head held high, I set him into the fire to burn.

Five days after the suspicion that I'm pregnant hits me during a public ritual, Hathor sits in the small, opulent boat that waits to take me back to the palace on the west bank after a long morning spent at the temple.

The guards watch me, oars at the ready, but they don't push off, confused by this new twist in our morning routine. I'm usually joined by my handmaid, but the old lady was sick this morning. Suddenly, I wonder if that was a coincidence or part of some plan concocted by Hathor.

"They promised to throw me in the river if I lied when I claimed you asked me to wait for you here," she says, grin precocious.

I grunt—her presumption is expected by now—then nod at the guards and step inside to sit facing Hathor, so close our knees nearly touch.

My permission secured, we move away from the shore, advancing to the rhythmic sounds of oars dipping in and out of water as I struggle to find my voice. "You're back. And you've helped yourself to my personal space again," I say, low enough to be heard by her and not the men who sit on nearby benches, just beyond the shade of the umbrella that covers me and Hathor.

"I am. I did. And hello, Neferura. You summoned me?" She holds the counterweight of a menat necklace in her hand. The long, beaded faience strings dangle down to bunch on her thighs. Perhaps she clutches it tight for luck—it amuses me to believe the clever wisewoman can't swim. But for all I know, she's about to serenade me: the thick strands are designed not only for protection and wear but to play. The rattle is as essential to Hathor's priestesses as the sistrum is to my troupe.

I take a deep breath, looking out at the river's surface slipping past, to steady myself. Exposing my anger won't get me where I need to go. "I did summon you." My voice is miraculously calm. "I asked Iset to convey that I wanted to speak with you over a month ago now actually." I didn't expect Hathor to respond to my message immediately. But I didn't expect weeks to pass either.

"Have you been pining for me?" She lifts a brow. "Apologies for the slow response. It may be difficult for you to believe, but my task list sometimes includes duties that are even more important than jumping the moment the great royal wife tells me to. But I'm here now and willing to help. I'm told you want to borrow my forger?"

"I do," I admit, glancing at the rowers.

"You may speak freely. These men cannot hear us."

For a moment, I wonder if she means it literally. I'd hardly put it past her to replace the men who row me to and from the temple with deaf men, but a man who has rowed my small boat for years—his name is Tahu, and he's the father of a newborn son—grins over at me, jiggling a bag, full of gold, no doubt, and my fears settle.

"Do you buy my guards often?"

She shrugs. "In their defense, they took my money and agreed to stay silent, but only if you wanted them to."

I can't tell if they hear us over the splash of oars, but if so, they're doing a good job pretending not to.

"And even if they were bought, it would only be fair, no?" she continues. "You have a spy among my scorpions now after all."

"You knew Iset and I were close before you invited her to join your ranks," I retort. "I didn't send her. You drew her in. It's not the same as buying off my guards."

She grins. "Who needs palace guards when one has my more capable resources?"

"Scorpions, you mean?"

"Exactly. They're everything your guards are not. Small. Overlooked. Deadly."

"Ubiquitous," I add.

She smiles proudly, then her lips dip. "I heard about Thuiu. I'm sorry, by the way." She looks genuine. "A gem of a woman. I held her in high esteem. I understand she was very fond of you. That's something you and I have in common. We both earn loyalty from our devotees—"

"I don't have devotees."

She laughs at that. "Tell yourself what you will. What matters is that your priestesses are thriving. I'm delighted to learn one of the royals I've championed has the good sense to promote and elevate women—"

"You do know Mother has added more priestesses to the priesthood than any pharaoh in history."

"Quantity counts," Hathor admits. "Quality counts more. You've an eye for both. And you've invested in the women. I can't help but wonder how you intend to use the loyal troupe you're growing."

"I'm making them tattoo Amun's scepter on their asses and spy for me," I deadpan, earning a high, clear laugh. A few men look our way, but most keep their eyes on the far bank, arms moving back and forth, up and down, in tandem.

"How original." Her eyes run over me, from my head to my toes. "You're thinner."

For a moment, I consider asking Hathor to bring me wheat and barley. Clearly I'm in need of a pregnancy test. But I know in my heart the seeds would sprout, and I'm not anxious to trust the wisewoman with another secret. Plus, I have a more important boon to ask of her. I didn't summon her to test my urine but to help me position my spy.

"Are you well?" she prods, gaze lingering on my torso.

"Terrific," I drone, ready to change the subject. "Mating with a man who wants to poison you does wonders for your diet. I suppose

I should thank you and your scorpion for alerting me to his plans. How did the girl know my fish was poisoned?"

"I have your food tasted, Neferura. It's a redundancy to be honest—your mother does the same. The poor man who tasted that fish dropped dead. You were lucky my scorpion got to you in time."

I swallow, feeling the fear in my gut, as I too often do, but now guilt mingles with it. "A man died? I thought you were the protector of the people. It's wrong that he died of poison meant for me."

"Two men actually. Your mother's and mine. The family of the man who worked for me has been extremely well compensated. He knew the risk. But yes, it is wrong. I'm not here to right every wrong in Kemet, Neferura. I aim only to minimize them where I can."

"And the man who worked for Mother? Has his family been compensated?"

She doesn't answer, but her pinched mouth says it all.

I turn away, craning my neck to watch the shore recede behind me, wishing I could disappear inside the market that fades from sight, lose myself in its twists and turns and immerse myself in its cast of colorful characters.

"Is there something you'd like to tell me? Perhaps you have news of the heir your mother and Thutmose have their hearts set on?" She taps her fingers against my knee.

I'd move away, but there's no space to maneuver here. So I shake my head, withholding the information she so clearly wants.

"Hmm," she hums. "Well, that is your business and your decision, of course. I'm not one to blame a woman for controlling her destiny. I've chosen to remain childless these many years. How could I move freely, practice my trade so effectively, with brawling brats tugging at my shift? I expected you to avoid conception out of fear of what your husband will do to you if you bear a child."

I keep my face turned away, eyes on the market, so she doesn't see the flush creeping up my neck and cheeks. I need to confirm my suspicions. But if I ask for Hesi-Ra's help, Mother and Thutmose will know hours later. If I ask Hathor, she'll have yet another secret to add to her pile, and who knows what all she does with them?

"Do remember, whatever your situation," she says, and I feel her gaze on me, "there are always options. I'm here to help, whatever you decide, whatever you need."

I turn back, glance flitting over the rowers, praying they don't hear or at least stay silent in return for the gold Hathor paid them. Finally, I meet her curious eyes. "If the gods want an heir, I suppose I'll give them one."

Hathor scoffs at that. "The gods will get their heir, one way or another. I hear tell of a princess of Retjenu being groomed for the role of secondary wife now. Oh, it's not the grandchild of the great Hatshepsut—no doubt the country would prefer that. But it is your body. You do get the final say. In the end, any child the system deems the heir will be the heir. You royals take your blood far too seriously. Trust me, I've seen royals bleed, and your blood is the same as everyone else's."

I take a deep breath, calming my mind. It may be months more before I have a moment alone with Hathor again. I've waited too long already. "About your forger. I need to borrow her."

"She's yours. But may I ask what you want her to do for you?"

"You may. And I'm going to tell you, mostly because I need more than your forger. I need to know which noble family I can bribe."

"Because?" She leans forward, intrigued. The beads of her menat rattle as she moves.

"I need to improve someone's status, give them a prestigious family tree."

"The person you need to promote is lowborn?"

I nod.

"How prestigious do they need to be?"

"Very," I say. "As prestigious as, well, not me perhaps, but as close as one can be to royal without being one. So close they may one day advance."

Hathor's eyes glitter with intellect. "A woman, I assume?" I nod, and she continues. "You're right. You will need more than a girl who can fake anyone's script—the girl can't read a sign, by the way. But when it comes to symbols, her art could make the artisans who chisel your mother's propaganda across Kemet weep with envy. She's yours to use, of course. More importantly, I know the perfect patrician for such a scheme. You won't have to bribe him either. He'll be happy to play along. It's his nature. Plus, he owes me. Still, I best check my assumptions. I can do that soon and send word back through the seamstress—"

"Iset." She has a name.

"Iset," Hathor parrots.

I wriggle, annoyed that she'll know exactly what I'm up to. But Satiah's safety is the most important thing. I wasted weeks trying to advance my plan without asking Hathor for help, but the wisewoman is better positioned to secure Satiah a new status safely than I am, so I agree.

"Excellent," she says. "I'll report back soon. In the meantime, is there anything else you need? I'm here now and I do aim to serve."

"So anxious to help me now," I grunt. "You may recall that I asked for your help once before. I'll count myself lucky if you help me secure a safe family tree and the papers to back up the fiction I have planned. My first request didn't work out well." I should leave Senenmut out of this—I need her help. But the anger is still with me, as constant as my shadow.

Hathor's eyes crinkle in confusion. She blows a heavy breath and shakes her head. "Your mother truly does disappoint me at times."

A bark of laughter escapes my lips. "Mother warrants blame enough, but she didn't let Senenmut die alone. She wasn't the one I asked to save him."

"Didn't you?" Her gaze is intense.

I turn away. Of course I did. I begged them both. And both failed me. Yet every other path to upgrading Satiah's family background puts her in more danger. I need the wisewoman's help. It galls me to ask—again—but hopefully she'll come through this time.

Hathor's sigh is heavy with displeasure. "I have spent a lifetime educating and elevating women. Sometimes I forget that others prefer to smother them with blind loyalty and ignorance. Nonetheless." She sighs again, even heavier this time, "I have a gift for you." She turns to look behind her, where the palace looms larger as we approach. "Start tonight. Your mother will be back to her charming, scheming, deceiving self within weeks."

"What—"

Before the question is out of my mouth, Hathor plucks an alabaster pot from under the menat necklace she holds, then steps past the nearest guard and jumps into the river, clutching the menat.

I jump to my feet and the boat shifts. Tahu leaps up to steady me, and by the time we're all safe and sound, Hathor is gone. I'd worry she's drowned, but given her abilities and connections, it's entirely plausible Hapi himself protects her.

I look down at the pot and read the small scroll tied to it.

Administer the remedy in this vase to a linen bandage and wrap your mother's neck with it each morning. Slather the potion thickly, and make sure to cover the back of her neck. Have her

drink pomegranate root in water with a dose of honey while
you chant the prayer on the vase's base over her nine times each
evening for nine days.

I grip it tight as I scan the river. There are people and birds and fish and boats but no sign of the wisewoman, nor can Iteru tell me what she meant about Mother disappointing her. I quiet the suspicions that tickle my mind, determined not to let Hathor's antics distract me from the plan I intend to execute.

SEVENTEEN

THUTMOSE SITS IN MY CHAIR. I PULL UP SHORT WHEN I ENTER my study and see him behind my desk.

"We need to talk," he begins.

I swallow my emotions. Revealing how disturbing his trespass is would only inspire more unsanctioned visits. So I nod and sink into the old chair Senenmut once claimed.

"What are you planning to do about your mother?" he asks.

I breathe in through my nose, then release the breath slowly. "Hesi-Ra is handling it. She should be well soon." I can hardly admit I summoned some doctor my dead tutor referred to me and gave her a potion snuck to me by a wisewoman Thutmose believes is loyal to him.

His slump is heavy and dramatic and reeks of disappointment. "You know, I could be ruling alone, without either of you dragging me down." He sets his blade—the blade that once belonged to Kamut's father—on the desk, aimed pointedly at me. "I do wonder why I bother keeping you."

The *alive* remains unsaid. It's unnecessary, really.

"Because the country is more attached to me and Mother than you are," I point out.

"Until they're not." He shrugs. An awkward silence swells. Thutmose picks up the dagger, cleans his nails with it, then waggles it in my direction. "I want you to move the honey and oil production out of your estate. The House of the Adoratrice will shift that production to my personal estate."

I ignore the weapon. Thutmose has had a weapon pointed at me—figuratively or literally—for months now. "Are you planning something that requires more resources than you have available to you now?"

"No."

"Then why are you asking?"

"Because I want it, Neferura. And I'm not asking. I'm telling. Let me rephrase so you understand. The god's wife's estate is no longer in the business of producing honey or oil. That production will be signed over to the pharaoh who matters. Me. Immediately."

"My steward will—"

"Do what he's told," Thutmose finishes. "As will you."

"I am not—"

The words aren't even out of my mouth when he grabs me.

He yanks me by the hair—a wig, thank the goddess—out onto the deck.

Dragging me to the railing, he shoves me against it, lifting me onto it with one arm and pressing my head forward with the other.

I manage not to scream, but I can't stop the tears.

"Look down."

I don't look.

"Imagine a little Neferura, broken on the ground below. One

giant shove and I'm rid of you. Then I'll take the damn oil and honey. Give me a single reason not to—"

"I'm pregnant." I spit the words at him and regret them the moment they tumble out of my mouth. Not because they're not true. I'm certain they are. My belly is growing while the rest of me shrinks. But after the terror he's wrought in my life, the last thing I want to do is reward him with his heart's desire.

His hold slackens enough for me to stumble off and away. I realize my gown is ripped and I pull it up, covering myself.

"How do I know you're telling the truth?" he asks.

I stand tall, swallowing the bile that creeps up my throat. "If I'm lying, you can come back and throw me to my death another day."

He smiles at that. "Finally. A reasonable offer." He smooths his kilt. "Tell Hesi-Ra to come see me tomorrow. I need proof that my heir is on the way." With that, he swaggers toward the door.

I watch him go, knees shaking. Dropping onto the deck as soon as he's gone, I press my back against the rail and cry until my tears dry up. The old handmaid appears. I have no idea if she saw the entire episode or slept through it—her naps grow longer. But for the first time since she attached herself to me, I'm happy she's here. Benerib would be better, but she's still in Behdet, visiting family. I don't expect her for another month at least. So I let this old woman help me up and put me in bed, where sleep mercifully takes me.

I dream of eyeballs. Giant round eyes, shifting and darting and watching my every move. When I wake, I'm more desperate than ever to see what Thutmose is doing behind closed doors.

Hathor's concoction works. Mother's health and senses return as if the illness of the past months never happened. She's ecstatic about my news.

"You must take care of yourself." Mother nods her approval. "With this child, our return to true power advances. I'll have word of the soon-to-be heir sent throughout the country. The crops are bursting forth. The land is fertile, and the queen is fertile. The people will be pleased."

"And the crown is pleased to know it will be a good tax year."

"Of course I am pleased—"

"I was talking about Thutmose, the true ruler." It's petty, but the fact that Mother is so happy I'm pregnant and so unconcerned about what it means for my future prospects makes me angry. And of course, I can't forgive her for Senenmut's death. Hathor's strange behavior when I brought Senenmut up has stuck with me. I've come up with all manner of theories to explain it, but theories can cloud the eyes like mist, so I force the temptation they hold away and pull my anger close. Mother's illness may have distracted me from blaming her temporarily, but she's well now, and my rage simmers again. Pointing out that Thutmose has the real power is a small victory, but it's what I can manage.

"You're with child. That's all that matters," Mother says and beams.

"And if he kills me after he gets his son?"

"This is about legacy, Neferura. My legacy is your legacy," she reminds me. "And with a son of your body, our legacy can't be denied. The scales of power inch in our direction. Trust me."

Her satisfied grin is nauseating. I'm done trusting Mother or anyone else who's shown themselves to be untrustworthy. Thutmose was not my friend, even when I believed he was. And Mother will never be the mother I've too often pretended she is, no matter how successfully she rules Kemet.

Struggling to hide my contempt, I excuse myself and return to my quarters to work. Mother isn't the only one making plans to return to power.

My schemes finally advance a week later. Iset drapes a blue tunic adorned with leopard trim and protection symbols that circle the neck over me as priestesses laugh and drink and twirl white linen gowns all around us. Iset's employer, Maia, hands them new robes, festival gifts from me. The royal pleasure barge rocks under our feet. The rowers keep their eyes on the river, but I'm sure they're enjoying the view.

I spent my morning accompanying the god's statue. My band of priestesses chanted and played their sistrums as priests carried Amun, hidden in his veiled shrine of cedar and precious stones, past cheering crowds and staring sphinxes on his visit to the smaller temple. Waset still hums with excitement. People line the riverbank, enjoying dancers and musicians along with food doled out by the temple— milk, cakes, bread, beer, and meats. Iteru is packed with ships, large and small, all decorated for the festival. I invited a small group of priestesses to celebrate with me, arranging for Iset and Maia to come along under the guise of ensuring the new gowns fit properly.

The hoopla, great as it is, doesn't distract Iset. "What's wrong?" She pulls me under the shade sail, hand warm on my arm.

I shake my head, anxious to ignore the fear that haunts me and embrace the distraction the day offers. But Iset is my closest friend. Even with our new arrangement, I rarely get to speak to her alone. So I whisper news of the pregnancy, pulling her close to be heard over the melodious sounds of the musicians I hired for the day: a band of three women, playing a lute, a lyre, and a double pipe. Their sheer dresses will soon be covered in wax from their perfumed hats, sure to melt quickly in this heat.

"I'm sorry. I know this isn't what you wanted." Iset rubs her rounded belly, eyes warm with compassion. "Who would have imagined us having children that will be almost the same age? Did the barley sprout or the wheat?"

"Both," I admit. I urinated on wheat and barley for the doctor, who confirmed my diagnosis. "I don't know if it's a boy or a girl."

"What if…?" She drops her voice to a whisper and leans close. "What if the baby is Kamut's? That's possible, right?"

I hush her. Even the quietest whisper of my night with Kamut puts him in danger.

The thought of Thutmose welcoming Kamut's child almost puts a smile on my face, until I think of what would happen if Thutmose ever discovered the truth. He'd murder me, Kamut, and the baby. Besides, surely it's Thutmose's child. Wouldn't the gods want an heir of the blood? Or is Hathor right that the gods don't care about blood and royals at all?

It seems the faith I once had in my ability to read the will of the gods vanished when I learned Mother's displays of piety are just power grabs masked as religious belief.

I settle for shaking my head, unsure.

"I'm going to believe what my heart wants to believe," Iset whispers just as the song rattles to a stop. She drops her voice lower. "I hope it's a girl. Thutmose seems like a man who'd cling to a son and toss a daughter aside."

"Perhaps. But Mother will claim any child of the blood. She'll own them just as she's owned me. Besides, at least a boy will be pampered and raised as the heir. Thutmose will keep a son safe. A girl will be a commodity to him. She'll be forced to breed against her will, as I have been. And Thutmose will insist I bear him children until I conceive a son. Unless he just kills me instead."

"We won't let that happen," she vows.

"I'm not sure we can stop him." I see myself shoved against the rail of my deck, imagining the fall—soft flesh meeting hard ground—and shiver. I almost tell Iset about Thutmose's most recent threat. But it would only make her worry more. "The pregnancy buys me time, but once this child is born…"

"We're going to figure it out, remember? We can do this. Young women are an underestimated group. But we don't need to underestimate ourselves." Iset scans the gaggle of priestesses. Tall Tasherit, wise Beketamun, and our wittiest priestess, Hui, huddle together, whispering, just beyond the shade sail. "Speaking of powerful women, I have news from Hathor. She sent a scorpion to the shop yesterday to deliver it. You're about to get your spy."

"Hathor finally secured Satiah's new family? Who?"

"She's to be Ahmose Pen Nekhbet's niece."

"Impressive," I admit, wondering how Hathor managed to get such a prestigious noble to do her bidding. Ahmose Pen Nekhbet is one of my favorites; he's my other royal tutor, although in name only. The other nobles tease him for being older than Horemakhet, the Great Sphinx. An absurdity, of course, although the man's stare is nearly as stony. In spite of the fierce visage, he's quite benevolent and endlessly entertaining. His tales of battles with my father and grandfather are too outrageous to be true but no less amusing for that.

"Does Satiah know she's going to be a noble soon?" Iset asks.

I shake my head. "Not yet. I wanted to be certain I could make it worth her while to spy on Thutmose before roping her into a scheme that could get her killed."

"Well, let's see what she thinks of old men with hearing loss and a silly sense of humor," Iset says just as the music starts back up, drowning out the clashing melodies emanating from the busy river.

I wave Satiah over and pull her under the shade sail for privacy.

"Adoratrice." She nods at me, flashing a conspiratorial grin at Iset.

"I have news," I begin.

"I hope it means I finally get to do something." She winks. "I've been dreaming of becoming a spy. I'm convinced I'll be good at it."

Her enthusiasm should be reassuring, but instead it gives me pause, and I second-guess the plan. Thutmose's recent threats have left me uneasy, which is no doubt the intention. Still, the fact is, unless I want to help him succeed, I must take some risks. Unfortunately, this risk puts Satiah in danger too. Who knows if it will even work? Thutmose may surprise me. Perhaps he'll be immune to her charms. But that would just leave me where I am now—ignorant about his plans for me, unable to discern what his next move will be. If he does what I expect and falls for Satiah, I'll have eyes and ears in his quarters. Of course, if he discovers our ruse, he'll kill us both.

Satiah reads my hesitation for what it is—nerves. "I want to help," she says quietly. "I can't say I've acted as a queen's spy before, but you know I raised myself from a young age. Even before joining your troupe, I'd managed to build myself a decent life. I learned to listen, to really hear what people say and, more importantly, what they don't say. I know how to choose my words wisely and how to summon the information I need. I can do this, Adoratrice. What's more, I want to."

"Even if it means giving your body to my husband and putting yourself in danger? This is not a game, Satiah. Thutmose is dangerous."

"The world is dangerous," she insists. "We need to know what he is up to. I can get close to him if you give me a chance. You're not asking me to do anything I'm not comfortable doing. Men are all the same. I'll act like he's perfect. He'll believe it and want more of me. I can seduce a pharaoh as easily as a bartender or priest."

"I'd like to hear that story," Iset mumbles.

Satiah and I stare at each other, listening to the lutist's solo and the laughter of priestesses and the rise and fall of music from nearby boats. Finally, desperate for information about what Thutmose will do next, I tell her that she's to be a noble. "Congratulations. You're now the niece of Ahmose Pen Nekhbet." I put my hand over hers. "He's as kind an uncle as any girl could want. And has the prestige you'll need—"

"Why do I need prestige?" Her eyes crinkle in confusion. "Surely Thutmose beds peasants as well as nobles. I don't need to be a patrician to spy on your husband."

"I don't want you to just spy, Satiah. I want him to make you a queen. I want you to have some of the power that comes with the position. You told me once that's what you wanted most. If you're to do this, I want to be sure it serves your goals, not just mine." I don't add that she'd also be an excellent replacement for me as queen and high priestess and, if it comes to that, as my child's mother.

"You want me to be a secondary wife?" Her eyes open wider. "To live in the palace with you?"

"You did say you envy my position. I don't know if the reality will disappoint, but if you're willing to make this sacrifice, the least I can do is ensure you get more than pretty jewels for the risk you're taking."

She stares at me, speechless, which is a first. "Thank you," she stutters. "And don't worry about me, Adoratrice. I can handle the job and the man. Your trust is safe in my hands. Thutmose will be like clay I mold to my will, I promise you."

She nods and walks toward Nebtah, her chin up, posture strong. I watch them whispering, heads together, hoping I'm right about this. Because Satiah is my one chance to know exactly when and how Thutmose will strike against me. She's my first alarm and she may be my final blow if, after all this, I fail, leaving Kemet in need of a new god's wife and great royal wife.

Thutmose may be culling my estate of resources and influence, but I'm still the queen and high priestess. He can hardly stop me from throwing a dinner party. He almost seems pleased when I invite him to dine with some of the nobles I'm closest to, especially when he learns that he's invited and Mother is not. I tell him I'm trying to improve our relationship so we can work together, pharaoh and god's wife, in the years to come, as I've always hoped. He seems to believe it. He's in a better mood now that his heir is en route and he owns the honey and oil production that formerly belonged to my estate.

What matters tonight, though, is that he falls for my plan.

Mercifully, he does. Soundly.

His eyes practically leap off his face when old Ahmose Pen Nekhbet toddles in with Satiah on his arm.

"Who's that?" Thutmose's voice is throaty.

I lean close to him. "One of my priestesses. Highborn, beautiful, and good at what she does." I try to sound envious—he'll like her more if he believes I'm jealous of her.

"I bet she is good." He doesn't hide his lust.

I roll my eyes, pretending to be put off, hiding the glee that fills me.

As if on cue, Satiah looks up. She meets my eyes and bows. There's not a hint of warmth there, nothing to suggest we are close or share a shard of affection. Her eyes flit to Thutmose's. Her lips part, eyes steamy before she drops them to the ground, then she turns back to the old man, glancing shyly at Thutmose. Her performance fills me with confidence. She will play him like a lute. Hathor once told me I overestimate Thutmose and that he'd be easier to handle once I stopped. Now I see how right she was.

I raise my cup to my lips, savoring the sweet red shedeh and believing, for the first time, that my plan may work after all. This sense of confidence makes me too bold when Thutmose follows me to my bedroom after dinner.

"Do you need something?" I step behind my bed so it's between us.

"I'm merely confirming my heir is safe and sound. I was considering visiting the front now that your mother is well, but I think I'll remain at court until the child arrives," he vows. "I must ensure you're taking care of my womb."

"Your womb," I echo, anger creeping up my spine. "Yes, you should certainly see to that. But then what?" His blank look invites more. "Once you have the heir you crave, will you leave me be?"

His eyes are cold. "Once I have my heir, you won't matter. Surely there's a girl somewhere in Kemet who could take your position. Someone capable of pleasing the god and me. You're expendable, like that old tutor you were so fond of. Who knows? Once the child is born, maybe you can join him. I understand you miss him, although I can't imagine why. He was a perjurer and a pretender. Ammit probably choked on his foul heart—"

Rage drives me forward.

One moment, I'm on the opposite side of the bed. The next, I'm holding his knife, pressing it to his exposed neck until a trickle of blood kisses the blade, feeling full. It's a sensation I've experienced a few times during ritual. It's like Amun is entering me, lending me his strength.

Maybe the god approves of willfulness after all.

Or maybe the gods don't care about our petty human squabbles at all.

"What do you intend to do? Slit my throat?"

I grip the plain handle harder. My hand is sweaty, but power surges through me. "I intend to survive. I intend to live my life free of your yoke. If you want your heir, you will agree to leave me be once he's delivered."

"And if I don't agree to your terms? Are you going to murder me right here and now?" Thutmose shifts away from me.

"You're not the only one who can poison a royal," I spit. "Or toss them off the palace wall—"

"Or plunge a knife into their cold, hard heart. Or strangle them with your bare hands. Or smother them while they sleep. Or release poisonous snakes in their quarters. There are many ways to kill, Neferura."

I ignore him. "If you want this heir, you'll back off and leave me to my work."

He breathes out through his nose, shifting his shoulders back as he considers me. There's something new behind his eyes.

"You're more like your mother every day. Perhaps you are a killer," he says. "All right, wife. You've earned a reprieve. You shall live. Time will tell if I make a different decision after my heir is secure."

He pivots to storm out, and I drop to the bed and pull the blankets over me.

A turquoise monkey greets me the morning after my row with Thutmose. It sits on my desk, snuck there, I presume, by one of Hathor's scorpions. A few days ago, I found a cowrie shell girdle in my bed. A week before that, an alabaster statue of the goddess Taweret was in my sedan chair. The symbolism of these fertility icons is unmistakable. Hathor is sending them. She knows I'm pregnant— she probably knew even as I was denying it. The question is, what does she hope to achieve with this meddling?

EIGHTEEN

THE WATER OF THE SACRED LAKE IS WARM AGAINST MY SKIN. Priestesses splash and chatter around me. When I first began these monthly group ritual cleansings, the women were quiet and shy. But in the months since, they've become bold and boisterous, flicking each other with water, laughing at the priests who pretend not to see us, sneaking off when we're done to prowl the market and drink wine on the riverbanks.

Originally, I just wanted to see if any of my priestesses bear tattoos. They don't, as far as I can see. But spending time with the larger troupe outside ritual has turned into much more. There's more joy in the work. Our rhythms feel more in sync, our chanting richer, the *shake, shake, shake, pause* of our sistrums more pleasing.

I've learned more about the priestess's personal lives as well. Many of the women are close friends. Some are mothers; others are caretakers for mothers and fathers and even, in one unusual case, a great-grandfather. Most hail from families who boast of rich histories, working in the priesthood for generations. Some, like Nebtah, are the first in their line to serve the god. And a few, including

Satiah, have no families to speak of. They come in every imaginable variety—various shades of brown, fat and thin, from dour to hysterical. Each woman is unique and valuable.

At the moment, several women circle around Meri, whose belly is rounded enough to announce she's expecting. She's a bit further along than I am, less pregnant than Iset. The water laps at her hips. One hand rests on her stomach as a tear winds its way down her cheek.

"Adoratrice." Satiah swims up, Nebtah beside her.

"Is Meri all right?" I ask, nodding at Meri and her protectors. "Can we help her with something?"

"We can help," Nebtah says. "But unless you have the power to magic up a family for her or at least tell her who the babe's father is, Meri is going to be raising that child on her own."

"I see."

"I told her to be careful," Satiah sighs.

"That's rich coming from you," Nebtah chides. "You're not exactly the paragon of abstinence."

"No," Satiah agrees. "But I do what I do for my own pleasure. Meri is seeking to fill the holes in her life and bind her loneliness. She'll never find peace that way."

"Maybe the child will give her the peace she's looking for," Nebtah says, although she doesn't sound convinced.

"Let's hope so," Satiah agrees, swirling water with her hands.

"Speaking of men." I drop my voice lower. "Is my husband in love with you yet?"

"He's moving in that direction quickly," she assures me. "His defenses are falling. I listen to him talk and talk. I act fascinated. I make an excellent audience, leaning in, gasping, clapping my hands, touching him like I'm enthralled. It's progressing perfectly."

"Does he ask about us?"

She bobs her head. "I speak of you with respect but no warmth. He asked how I thought you'd react to a secondary wife."

"That was fast. What did you say?"

One side of her lip quirks up. "I said you would be jealous if the new queen was more beautiful than you."

Nebtah grunts her approval, and I manage a brief but genuine smile. "He must have loved that."

"He will make me a secondary queen soon. If my charms alone aren't enough, my fake uncle adds layers to my appeal. Thutmose is desperate to get closer to Ahmose Pen Nekhbet. You're still certain this is what you want?"

I nod. "And you?"

"I do. I want to know what he's up to. And I want to be in a position to help." She dips lower in the water. "Unlike my future husband, my new uncle is a lovely man. I must thank you for that. And for this opportunity."

"I hope you don't come to regret it, Satiah. As for Ahmose Pen Nekhbet, you have Hathor to thank for that. The wisewoman is efficacious. When she wants to be."

"She showed us that women make good spies." Nebtah splashes water over her shoulders. "I do wish someone would tie a ribbon around that flagpole so I can do a little sneaking of my own. I'm envious. I'm a much better sneak than Satiah. I should get to have some fun too."

"Until then, I have a bit of information," Satiah says. "The argument you and Thutmose had the night we met still haunts him. He hasn't told me the details, but he mentions it often. He's moody when it comes up. But he's equally pleased he's going to have a child. Once I change the subject to his son—he believes it will be a boy, of course—Thutmose is malleable again."

"What happens if it's not a boy?" Nebtah asks.

"The better question is what happens if it is?" I remind her.

The question puts a frown on Nebtah's face. She's worried. But the thought of what Thutmose will do to me once he has his heir makes Satiah angry. Her eyes flash fire.

"Is there anything else?" I ask, resting a hand on my growing belly.

"Not yet. But I'm seeing him again tonight. And tomorrow night. He's greedy." Satiah rolls her eyes. "I'll learn what I can and report back."

They move away—it wouldn't do for me and Satiah to be seen talking too much—and I sink under the water, watching the sun dapple the surface with its light. The priestesses' voices are muffled from here, like I'm in a dream. I hold my breath as long as I can, removed from the world. But the world is not ready to release me—not yet anyway—so I surface and watch the carefree play of the women who surround me, snatching little bits of joy as I can.

Benerib finally arrives. I'm prepared for a confrontation, but I meet her puffy eyes and see only a woman mourning a friend we both loved.

"I'm sorry," I mumble, inviting her to sit in Senenmut's old chair.

She hesitates only a moment. No other handmaid would be so bold, but surely she and Thuiu didn't stand on ceremony when they were alone. I see no reason to pretend this relationship is anything other than what it is.

"You loved her too." Benerib's voice is solemn, but her eyes are dry.

"I did. And I do appreciate her intention here, sending you to me. But I must be direct, Benerib. I'm not convinced this is a good idea."

She tilts her head to the side. "It is your choice of course, Adoratrice. But I'm happy to serve. I was..." She pauses, biting her lip, until I ask her to speak freely. "I was under the impression you'd benefit from a handmaid whose loyalty to you could not be questioned."

I lean back, studying her round cheeks and narrow eyes, the short wig that hugs her head, the large gold heart scarab amulet dangling from her fleshy neck. It rests above her heart. If I flipped it over, I'd find a spell from the Book of the Dead reminding Benerib's heart to be silent when she stands before Osiris to be judged. I do hope she doesn't intend to stay silent today. "That's rather the point," I admit. "I fear your loyalty may already be spoken for."

She looks down, shaking her head, then lifts her chin to meet my gaze. "You're like her, you know?"

"Thuiu?" I ask. "Or Hathor?"

I'm certain Benerib works for the wisewoman. I suspected Thuiu when I found Hathor's note stuck to my headrest after she visited my quarters. But once the doctor assured me Thuiu was unmarked, my suspicion shifted to Benerib.

"Both," she says blithely. "Both women are smart, inquisitive, insightful. You may find this hard to believe, but I'm rather relieved you've brought this up. I was debating whether to tell you I was once a scorpion. How did you know?"

Determined to keep the secrets I can, I ignore the question. "I do appreciate your honesty, Benerib. And I know how much you meant to Thuiu. But the truth is, I have no interest in trading Mother's spy for Hathor's."

"That was not my arrangement with Thuiu." She shakes her head. "And I certainly wouldn't expect it to be my arrangement with you. It's up to you to accept my service or not. But I would like to help you if I can. It's what Thuiu wanted."

"Exactly what was your arrangement?"

"Beyond the usual duties of a handmaid, I can reach Hathor if needed. I worked with your grandmother those many years ago. You might say I'm retired from service. But I maintain my contacts, which means I hear things others don't. On occasion, Thuiu found it useful to use me as an intermediary. Hathor can communicate to you through me if she asks to, assuming you agree to that."

"She doesn't have trouble finding me when she wants to."

Benerib smiles at that. "Yes, she is resourceful. Having me just makes any communication between you two quicker and more discreet. And you can rest assured that I would never spy on you. If you'll forgive the boldness, Adoratrice, Hathor does not need me for that. The wisewoman gathers the information she wants. Oh, she'd rely on an old lady if she needed to—never doubt that. She's an old lady herself, though she doesn't look it. But if you accept my service, my loyalty is to you and you alone."

I study Benerib, thinking back to the times I questioned Thuiu about the old wisewoman. I should have directed my questions at her handmaid. Odd that it took me, a uniquely educated woman, daughter of Kemet's most successful female pharaoh, so long to recognize the many capable women who surround me, to acknowledge they aren't always born to their roles. They often need to work for them, sometimes from the shadows, toiling unnoticed but not ineffective.

"I want to trust you. I want to trust the words of Thuiu's last note to me. She vowed that you are true."

Benerib shrugs. "Then trust it. After all, no one knew me better. Thuiu knew me like you know Iset. This life we share is unique. It binds us in ways others might not understand."

"Did you spy on me for Hathor while you were with Thuiu?"

"I did not. My loyalty was to Thuiu then, and she'd never have asked that. I did sneak a note under your headrest once though." Her grin reveals a gap-toothed smile. "In my defense, I was under the impression you would welcome that."

"I suspected Thuiu," I admit.

"We thought you might."

"Thuiu once told me she believed Hathor and her scorpions worked in good faith to empower people and maintain peace in Kemet. Is that what you believed you were signing up for?"

"It is."

"And the danger? Did you sign up for that?"

She purses her lips. "I did. I was comfortable with the danger from the beginning. I never did warm to putting others in danger, unless they chose that for themselves. Hathor is less queasy about such things. But she's also mindful of how others feel. That's one reason she's been so successful. She has a knack for matching people to tasks."

"Did she match you and Thuiu?"

"She did." Benerib's smile is so joyful it's almost childlike. "Hathor didn't foresee the bond we'd forge, of course. But she intuited we'd connect." Benerib leans forward, intense now. "I don't want to mislead you, Adoratrice. I'm terribly fond of Hathor. I would even say I love her. My loyalty will be to you, but I do hope you don't ask me to work against the wisewoman. That would put me in an uncomfortable position. I say that in case you are angry at her—"

"For Senenmut's death, you mean?"

She looks down at her fingers. "I need to…" She pulls a small scroll from the pocket on her shift dress. "I wasn't certain I'd tell you about my past today. But I did plan to reveal a far greater secret. I have something for you." She sets the scroll on my desk. "This scroll would have made it to you with or without me. I am only involved because I visited Hathor last night. I felt it was proper to tell her I was coming to you myself, although she'd heard tell already. But to my surprise, she was not alone. She was with, well, I suppose I'm to call him Khui."

"The doctor?"

She snorts. "That man is many things, but he's no doctor, nor magician." She pushes the scroll toward me. Her posture is stiff, eyes glittering with concern. "He asked me to give you this when he learned I was coming here today. He's in Waset. Hathor told him she'd seen to your mother's illness, but I'm afraid he could not be dissuaded from staying. He misses you—"

"Misses me? I've never met the man."

She gestures toward the scroll. "Prepare yourself."

A strange sensation creeps under my skin as I pick up the scroll. For a moment, everything feels fuzzy, like I'm back in the sacred lake, beneath the water. I feel like I'm descending, drowning, as I unroll the papyrus. It's not addressed. It doesn't need to be. I'd recognize the script anywhere.

I must apologize for another betrayal. For I am Shedet's doctor, Khui. The tale of how this came about is too long to confess here, for I received your missive and…

I drop the scroll. My eyes are blurry, and my stomach aches with the shock of seeing Senenmut's familiar script, as if he writes from the afterworld.

I turn to Benerib, and she nods. "It's true. I watched Senenmut pen the note myself. He is alive."

Impossible. The letter must be forged. Could Hathor's scorpion have done it? For what purpose? Or perhaps it's from my tutor's spirit. I rub my scalp with my fingers. No. Spirits read letters; they don't write them.

"He's alive, Neferura," Benerib whispers.

Has Senenmut been alive this entire time?

I feel the pain rise. Wouldn't he have let me know? Then again, he's not exactly the man I thought he was. He didn't tell me he helped Hathor murder my father. And he is the one who gave me Khui's name.

Trembling with shock and a dose of anger, I rest the letter on my desk, wipe my eyes, and read.

I am in Waset. I'm working on a way to see you safely. I will inform you when I've worked out a solution. In the meantime, I don't know if this missive will be welcome by you, but all I can do is try to make amends for my trespasses. I should have either refused the offer that led to this deceit or insisted you be consulted. The wisewoman claimed it was your wish. And my conscience was compromised when the plot was hatched. Time and distance have cleared my vision, and now I see my mistakes in vivid detail and wish only to make them right.

I do hope you are well. I worry about you constantly. Perhaps I no longer have that right. But I understand the terror of your situation. I once watched your mother struggle with similar trials, which have led us all here. The secrets I've kept so long feel a burden to me now. Know that I'm committed to being brutally honest with you, even as I lie to the world about my very existence.

I will see you soon, I'm sure of it. When we're face-to-face, you can tell me goodbye forever or accept my apologies so we can find some way to stay in contact now that my secret is revealed. In the meantime, my desk leg is a safe way for us to communicate. I don't have the heart to leave Waset until I have a chance to apologize in person. More soon, dear one.

Heat creeps up my neck.

He's alive.

And he lied. Again.

I've excused his first betrayal, but am I now to overlook another? What of my vow to stop trusting the untrustworthy?

Another thought hits me, driving the wind from my chest.

Mother.

My eyes snap to Benerib. "Does Mother know?"

Benerib purses her lips, jaw tight, like she's holding words in.

"You are to speak your mind with me, Benerib. Or this will not work."

She nods. "It is not easy to be direct when one is considering criticizing a pharaoh. But if I must, then yes, Pharaoh knows. She was there when Senenmut made the decision to run. She urged him to make the choice. She's always known."

My blood runs cold. Mother knew Senenmut was alive this entire time, and she didn't bother to tell me. How could she? Mother has watched me mourn the man we both loved and done nothing to ease my pain, even after she vowed to stop keeping secrets. The guilt I've ascribed to her is a fantasy. No wonder she's been able to ally with Thutmose. Unlike me, she's never blamed him for Senenmut's death…because she's always known he's not actually dead.

The scroll flutters to the floor. I watch it settle on top of painted stone. My head is thumping. One thing is clear.

"Hathor did this."

Benerib nods. "She did. She told me you asked her to save him. Is that not true?"

I think back to our conversation in the sanctuary. It would have been mere days before Senenmut's death, or what passed for his death. Did Hathor save Senenmut because I asked her to?

"She should have told me."

"Why?" Benerib asks. "She believed your mother would do that. She assumed you knew until, well, I'm not sure what you said to her recently, but it alerted her to your ignorance."

"My ignorance," I scoff. "It's practically legendary at this point. Does everyone but me know?"

Benerib shakes her head. "No. I assure you, this is one of the court's most well-kept secrets. I know far more than most, and I hadn't heard a whisper. Nor had Thuiu. I almost died from shock when I saw your old tutor's face yesterday."

I scoop up the letter and smooth it out on my desk. "Your wisewoman even brings back the dead, it seems."

"Ahmose Pen Nekhbet can attest to that." A small grin spreads across her face.

"Is that what she uses to tempt him to her will? Does Hathor claim to know the secret to eternal life?"

"Her spells and potions can extend life at least. They helped Ineni. Thuiu might be alive still, but she refused to take them after her husband died." Benerib dabs her eyes with one of the new dresses Iset made me, tossed carelessly across the back of Senenmut's old chair.

Curious, I ask if she uses Hathor's potions.

"No." She shakes her head. "I'm ready to join Thuiu and my husband. Until then, I'm here to serve you however I can."

I nod, skin still hot with surprise and confusion. "I'm glad you're here, Benerib. Thank you for coming and for telling me what you know."

"I'm not sure I proved myself trustworthy. Yet. As I said, Senenmut was determined to reveal himself to you, and Hathor was as committed, although she does want him to leave Waset, if only because it's dangerous here for him." She purses her lips. "But I'm glad I'm here too. You can trust me, Adoratrice. Now, do you want me to communicate anything back to them on your behalf?"

"No." I shake my head. I have nothing to say to Hathor. And I now know how to reach Senenmut directly. What I don't know is if I want to.

NINETEEN

I'M TRAILING BEHIND MOTHER AND THE HIGH PRIEST. BENERIB
and Mother's handmaids are at my back as we wind through the
temple complex. Two slow weeks have crept past since I learned
Senenmut lives. The knowledge that Mother knew, participated in
the entire charade, and didn't tell me simmers in my gut like lava.
She promised not to keep secrets if I'd bear Thutmose's child. But
here I am, pregnant and still fooled.

Yet as angry as I am at Mother and Senenmut, it's a relief to
know my old tutor lives. I haven't left him a message yet. I will when
I'm ready. I want to look him in the eyes when I ask why I should
forgive him for another, most brutal lie. I take perverse pleasure in
making him wait on my response.

"Adoratrice," Nebtah rushes up. She notices Mother and the
high priest and pauses. It only lasts an instant before she's back to the
confident priestess I know, going about her temple business. "You
forgot your sistrum."

She holds a sistrum out to me, and my breath catches.

That sistrum can only mean one thing: Kamut is here and alive
and has something to tell me.

Nebtah must have finally seen a red streamer on the flagpole and put whatever message he wants to deliver inside this sistrum. I tasked her with this duty. I've been waiting months for this moment. Yet somehow, it's still unexpected.

I reach out and take the instrument from her. My hand is trembling, but hers is steady as an obelisk. I nod a thanks, then tuck the instrument in the pocket designed to hold it—Iset's invention, included on all our newest gowns—and walk forward like the world didn't just shift beneath my feet.

After months of my companions falling out of my life, now phantoms are returning. Miraculously, I manage to make small talk with Mother as we're rowed back to the palace, where I rush to my quarters the moment I can excuse myself.

I lay the sistrum on my desk. Made of metal and painted blue with a goddess head at the top of the stem, it looks like an innocent instrument any wealthy woman would be proud to possess. I shake it. It's not quite as tuneful as my usual sistrum, but it's not meant to play. It's meant to communicate. It was inspired by Senenmut's seal ring, which also had a hinged bottom. He kept, of all things, ink in the small hidden compartment within.

My fingers tremble as I work the small door at the base of the sistrum open, then shake out the scroll and unroll it, worms twisting in my belly. The handwriting is Kamut's brother's. My breath hitches as I scan the page.

From the royal guard Kamut to the little princess, in life, prosperity, and health. I don't know whether news has reached you that Iset's husband Meriptah died in an accident on the site yesterday. I'm told Iset has taken it hard—so hard the villagers worry she risks losing the child, perhaps even her own life.

She's too fragile to send word to you, so I'm sending it via our arrangement to be sure you're informed. I've sent word to the wisewoman as well. Hopefully Hathor will rush to Iset's side once the news reaches her. Iset is strong. I pray, as I know you will, that she gets through it and delivers a healthy child to ease the pain of Meriptah's loss.

I do wish I were writing with better news or could at least be with you to provide some comfort. I'll keep an eye out for a response. If there's anything I can do for you, do send word. I'll reach out if I have more to report. I think of you always and, as always, serve you as I'm able, although I wish I was doing more.

"Benerib," I cry out as I scan the letter again, wondering how long ago it was written. Yesterday, most likely, which means Meriptah died two days ago, and I'm just learning of it now.

Benerib opens my study door.

"I need to get to Iset." I'm on my feet.

"What's happened?"

"Her husband. He's dead." I hand her the letter. "And Iset is in danger. I need to go to her. Now." I rush into my bedroom and grab a shift to cover the priestess robe I still wear, stepping toward the door.

"Adoratrice." Benerib doesn't follow. "Let's take a moment to think. We only get one chance to make a good choice here."

"There's no choice to make. Iset needs me—"

"Yes. You must go to her. I do wonder, though, if you need to go in that." She nods at my gown. "If you slow down, I can get you there undetected, if, that is, you have reason to believe Iset could be in some danger if your fondness for her was widely known."

I suck in a breath, like I'm absorbing a punch in the gut.

Thutmose.

Iset would be another target for Thutmose to aim for if he knew how much I cared about her. I gape at Benerib, who reads the scroll in her hands. I'm surprised to learn she's literate, though given her friendship with Thuiu, perhaps I shouldn't be.

"You're right." My mind clears. "He can't know how much I love her."

She nods. "Then let's be smart about this—"

"But I need to go now. Kamut must have written that yesterday. I can't wait—"

"It won't take long. I've made preparations in case the need arose."

She ducks into her small bedroom that opens to mine. I follow her in and watch her drop to her knees and retrieve something from under her bed. When she has it, she marches out onto my deck. I follow her outside. Hand to mouth, Benerib trills a series of birdcalls. She waits to hear the call returned, then turns to me.

"Come." She leads me inside and drapes the blue cape she brought from her room over me, pulling the hood low.

I'm jumping out of my skin, on fire with fear. I have no idea what's happening with Iset right now, and the ignorance sits in my gut, heavy as a mastaba. I'm about to ask why we're wasting time with this silly robe when the guard announces visitors.

Benerib opens the door and ushers two women in. They're dressed in the same blue robe I'm wearing. "The queen needs a massage. Expectant mothers do require extra care," Benerib tells the curious guard as she shuts the door. She pauses to flash me a small smile. "I knew your pregnancy would come in handy."

I shift from one foot to the other as I watch one of the women remove her blue robe. She wears a dark blue tunic with red rosettes underneath. It matches one Iset made for me weeks ago.

"I was about to send word to you both," the other girl says. Her eyes dart to me—they're full of worry. "I assume you've heard about Iset and the child?"

My blood runs cold. "What—"

"They're fine." She holds her hands up, shaking her head. "Hathor has been with Iset since last night. She delivered the child. She sent word an hour ago, asking me to see that you were informed."

"Is Iset all right? And the baby?"

The girl grins. "They're both fine. It was a difficult labor. The baby is early, but with Hathor's help, the little girl will be fine."

I exhale, and the release flows through my body, from my head to my toes. She's fine. The baby is fine.

And then I remember, Meriptah is still dead. Iset may not be in danger, but she's certainly in mourning.

I turn to Benerib. "I'm still going. But I need to keep Iset and the babe safe. What exactly is your plan?"

She nods at the girl who just spoke. "This is Tentamun." Benerib motions toward the other girl, the one who wears a dress that matches one of my own. "And this is Neith."

Neith isn't just dressed like me. She looks like me. She has my light brown skin. She's the same size. She even shares a rounded belly, although I'm not sure if that is real or fake. Her wig is in her hand, revealing rows of short braids. She holds the wig out to Benerib, who takes it and turns to me.

"You're both scorpions?" I ask, dipping low so Benerib can swap the wig I'm wearing with Neith's.

"And friends," Benerib says as she shifts the unfamiliar wig into place, handing mine to the girl. "Tentamun knows Iset well. She lives in the village too. She'll take you to her. Neith and I will stay here until you return. I'll say you've decided to spend the day in your rooms. You must be back in time for dinner with your mother this evening. We can't keep this ruse up longer than that. Are you ready?" she asks.

I bob my head, fear replaced by nerves.

"Head down. Let the hood and hair cover your face," she advises me quietly as she opens the door, lifting her voice as if she's chiding the women. "Next time you come to the queen's quarters, be better prepared. Go now. And be back later this afternoon. Be ready to please her this time."

I follow Tentamun out, head bowed, wondering if she's the village girl Iset mentioned in her letter. I don't say a word as she leads me through the palace, out the front gate, and into the back of a cart. A silent driver whistles once, and the donkey pulls us forward.

The village isn't far. The ride is short but bumpy, and it entails another costume change. Tentamun hands me a rough-hewn garment. We change silently, and she pulls a different hood over my head as a guard waves us into the village gate, where a group of boys hit a small circular disk with bent bats, jeering the poor boy who just missed a shot. We pass them quickly, and I turn my attention to the small homes that line the straight street, running from one end of the village to the other. Less than fifty houses stand in this small, gated community, home to the artisans who work on the tombs, including my own, under construction now. Although I know about the village, called Set Maat, the Place of Truth, by the locals, I've never been inside.

The driver crosses a road that runs perpendicular to the one we're on before stopping before an unremarkable mudbrick home. Its red door and the two clay serpents that flank it guard the home from evil. *Not well enough*, I muse as I follow Tentamun inside. She opens the front door and waltzes in like she lives here.

A blood-soaked Hathor greets us. Her eyes widen with surprise, but it passes quickly and she nods with a grunt. "I should have known to expect you, Adoratrice. One would have thought Tentamun would have sent word."

"Sorry, Mistress," the girl says. "Benerib gave the signal. There was no time—"

Hathor waves away the explanation. "It's fine. You did well. You can go, but stay close—you'll need to see the queen back to her rooms later." She excuses the girl and turns to me. "I'm glad you're here." She looks tired. For the first time, her true age is evident in the lines around her eyes, the droop of her lips. "Iset is doing well. It's good I was informed so quickly. She was in shock when I got here. The baby was early. This could have turned out very differently."

"Meriptah is still dead," I point out.

"Yes, Neferura. But we averted the tragedy we had some power over. Let's give ourselves permission to make an impact where we can without feeling guilty for all the things we can't control."

"I didn't say I felt guilty," I quip, stung by her criticism.

She relaxes into a heavy sigh. "I'm sorry. It's been a long night."

"I'm sorry too," I say. "I've just been so worried. Can I see her?"

I glance over at the small cubby, built into the wall of the front room. It's painted with a colorful image of the god Bes, protector of childbirth. I can see a covered figure and assume the low breathing I hear is Iset's.

"They're finally asleep. We can wake them, but let's speak for a moment first." Hathor motions toward two small, low benches that hug the wall near the altar erected to honor Iset's and Meriptah's ancestors. I slump on one, and she lies on the other with her knees bent so her feet are on the floor as she stares up at the ceiling. "Are you worried about Iset alone? Or are you worried about yourself too?" she asks.

"I don't need to be reminded that he's going to kill me when the child is born," I sigh. I can't hide my exasperation. It's tiresome, this ever-present threat. "But I do have more important things to worry about before I get that far."

"I was thinking of the upcoming birth. Pregnancies are dangerous, Neferura. That can hardly come as a surprise to you."

I pull my eyes off her bloody gown and rest a hand on my swelling stomach, anxious to avoid the topics of bloody pregnancies and Thutmose and all the terrifying things he might do to me once he has his heir and I'm expendable. "I'm aware. I suppose I just don't care."

She sits up. "Don't care about yourself or your offspring?"

I glance over at Iset, sleeping soundly. The painting of a rotund Bes, with his large ears and long beard, floats protectively over her. I assume the child sleeps next to her, but I can't see her from here. "I want my child to be safe," I admit. "I'm trying not to get too attached to the idea of a baby to be honest. Any child I bring into the world will be scooped up by Mother and Thutmose."

"A pity," Hathor says. "You're a far fitter parent than either of them."

"Speaking of parents." I change the subject and Hathor tucks her legs under her and sits tall in scribal pose. "There's a priestess in my troupe. Her name is Meri. She's pregnant and alone. No family. Can you check on her? Make sure she's cared for?"

"As you wish, Adoratrice." Hathor nods, the small grin adding a hint of sarcasm to her words. "I'll see to your priestess and to you."

"Will you sneak fertility figurines into her home too?"

"I certainly will." She smiles wider. "It's a dangerous business, bringing people into the world. You expectant mothers need all the protection you can get."

I relax at that. Perhaps Hathor's meddling is well intended. She just saved Iset after all. "Thank you." We're silent for a moment, the appreciation hanging in the air. The pile of things I have to thank the wisewoman for is growing. "Thank you for saving Iset. And for finding Satiah the perfect uncle." I pause before adding, "And thank you for saving Senenmut as well."

"You're welcome. I'm sorry you weren't informed." Her lips curl into a snarl. "Sorry and disappointed." She blows out a breath. "To be honest, I had half a mind to rescue him before you asked me to. He didn't deserve the fate Thutmose demanded. I kept reminding myself that Kemet is full of people who suffer fates they don't deserve. But I was relieved you asked me to intervene. It gave me the excuse I needed to take the risks necessary to pull that trick off—"

"Teni?" Iset turns over in her bed, and the bundle cuddled tightly in her arms squawks.

I stand up, and Iset gasps.

At first, she looks happy to see me, but her brow instantly crinkles. "What if you get caught?" She goes right to the point, direct as always.

"I couldn't stay away." I move toward her and the baby. She swings sideways so her feet rest on the steps that lead up to the small cubbyhole. Soon my feet are on the bottom step, arms around Iset and babe. "I'm so sorry," I croon.

The baby gurgles, and Iset breaks into big, racking sobs. I hold her as she cries. Hathor comes to take the baby, but Iset waves her off. "My dearest friend will want to meet her. Won't you?"

"Of course I do."

Iset scoots over, and I climb into the pigeonhole—there's barely room for the two of us in this elevated bed—and take the child gently into my arms, cradling her to my chest. She's so small and fragile, I'm worried I'll break her.

"I named her Neferu," Iset says.

Now I'm crying. And Iset is crying again. And soon the babe is crying.

"I'll leave you two," Hathor says. "I'll check on you tonight, Iset. If you feel anything strange or have any reason at all to be concerned about little Neferu, send Tentamun to fetch me sooner."

Iset nods and thanks Hathor, who walks out, shoulders drooped in exhaustion.

"I'm so sorry about Meriptah," I say when the door swings shut, examining the bags that ring Iset's pretty brown eyes.

She sits up, resting her back against the wall, head nearly touching the ceiling, and stares down so her long, black braids fall over her face like clouds covering the sun. "I didn't expect to see you. Hathor said Kamut sent word to her. I don't think Neferu and I would have survived if she hadn't come."

"Was it terrible? The birth?"

"I lived." She shrugs. "That's more than my mother got."

I reach out a hand and twine my fingers through Iset's.

She gives them a squeeze.

"What can I do for you?" I ask.

She shakes her head, eyes bright with tears. "You're here. That's enough."

I run my finger down the baby's cheek, then lean close to take in her scent. "My estate will cover the funerary costs. We'll see that Meriptah's funerary goods are perfect."

"Thank you. That would help. Meriptah worked so hard on our

tomb. It would make him happy to know it will be well supplied. We were just beginning to…" She swallows hard, picking at the hem of her gown as she begins, slowly at first, talking about the shock of learning Meriptah was dead, much like what she'd experienced when her mother and baby brother died.

I know what grief feels like, having mourned both Thuiu and Senenmut. The latter uselessly, as it turns out. "I wish I could do more."

"You're here," she whispers, taking the baby to feed her. "That's more than enough. I hate the risk you're taking, but a visit from my closest friend is the best possible balm." She smiles down at Neferu, suckling at her breast. "I remember the first time we met. I thought I was the luckiest girl in Kemet. I was full of fantasies of a life spent at your side."

"I thought Mother would boot you from the palace before nightfall." I smile at the memory. "I was stunned you were so young."

"And a commoner."

"A commoner with a flair for luxury. Who would have guessed that we'd reunite? Once again, you're making me up in a wardrobe that could make the most well-dressed noblewoman weep with envy."

"As if you care about your wardrobe," she says. Her voice is lighter now, less heavy with grief for the moment. After a pause, she asks if I learned about Meriptah from Kamut, and if he'd sent a letter through Nebtah's sistrum according to my scheme.

I confirm her suspicion, and then I tell her about Senenmut.

"Alive?" she gasps.

I squirm with guilt. She's just lost the man she loves, and here I am talking about my father figure's resurrection.

"It's a second chance," she says.

"If I can forgive him."

"Of course you can forgive him," Iset chides me. "Even Anubis weighs our good deeds against our bad after we die. No one's heart is weightless."

"He let me mourn him for months," I remind her. "I thought he was dead."

"What should he have done? He was leaving, and your mother was staying. She obviously didn't want to tell you. If she'd wanted you to know, you'd have known months ago. Was he to disregard the woman who birthed you—a pharaoh no less—even as he planned to never see you again? When one has no good options, even their best option is bad."

"We don't know that Senenmut wanted to tell me either."

"He told you about the doctor, Khui. Maybe that was his way of telling you."

I reach out and touch Neferu's toes, then lean close to press my lips against the soft skin of her cheek. "When someone shows you who they truly are, you have to believe them." I say it as much to remind myself of this hard-won lesson as to inform her. "You can't pretend like they're someone they're not just because you want them to be."

"Senenmut has shown you who he is a million times. I'm not saying he's perfect or blameless. But he is a good man."

I weigh her words in my mind. "I said the same of Mother. And Thutmose when we were younger."

"Did you? Surely they both showed themselves to be selfish and cruel long ago. I understand if you can't forgive them. But Senenmut is different. No one is all good or all bad. But he's much more good than bad. Can you say the same of your mother or husband?"

"No," I sigh. "But—"

"Girl."

I flinch as a man barges in, shattering the intimate moment.

Iset sits up, pressing the baby into my arms. "Father. You shouldn't be here—"

"It's my house."

"No," she reminds him. "It's my house. I'm in mourning. I've just given birth. Is it really too much to expect privacy—"

"I heard voices. Who is this?"

I should follow Iset's lead. But I'm so irked by his attitude, I can't stop myself from putting him in his place.

"Neferura," I say as I turn to him. The shock on his face is priceless. For good measure, I add, "The queen."

He drops to his knees, prostrating himself.

"This isn't necessary, Father—"

"You may rise." I speak over Iset, voice as commanding and arrogant as I can make it.

He stands but keeps his eyes down. I'm already regretting my rash behavior—I'm here to help Iset, not create new problems for her to manage once I'm gone. I glance at her, and the small smile dancing around her lips gives me courage.

"I cherish your daughter. Our relationship is private—she would be in danger if my fondness for her was well known, so do not go bragging about it, whatever you do. But I will see to it that she's taken care of, and you as well."

"What does that—"

"Father!" Iset hisses, stopping the man from haggling, I suspect.

"As you wish, Great Royal Wife." He backs up, eyes on the floor, leaving through the door he entered through.

Iset and I snuggle back into position, the baby between us. We lie face-to-face. She cries quietly and I hold her hand, crooning whatever soothing words come to mind until Tentamun returns and calls me back to the palace.

Two nights after I meet Iset's child, I wake with a fire of determination filling my belly. The palace is dark as I creep through it, Benerib quiet as a spirit behind me. Only guards are awake at this hour, and they believe Benerib when she claims I need to feed my pregnant belly in the middle of the night and want to raid the kitchen myself. The court falls over themselves to make my stomach happy.

Fortunately, no guard stands at Senenmut's door.

Benerib follows me into his study, holding the lantern to light our way. Her eyes crinkle in confusion when I drop to my knees to stick the scroll in Senenmut's secret compartment. The scroll contains few words:

Kamut is still in Waset. See that he's protected. I'm making plans to see you. I'll tell you more when I'm ready.

TWENTY

NEBTAH HANDS THE SISTRUM TO ME AGAIN A WEEK AFTER I write to Senenmut. I'm thinking about Iset and the baby, and it takes me a moment to realize what's happening. I don't even wait to get back to the palace this time. I march to my small temple office and pull out the scroll. It's longer than the last one, and Kamut's brother's handwriting is messier, like he was running out of time. I scan the page, heart pounding.

From the royal guard, Kamut, to the little princess, in life, prosperity, and health. I'm told you already know Senenmut lives—I cringe saying it aloud, even in front of just my brother. I can only assume you were as shocked as me. I wouldn't have believed the man who approached me with the story, but he carried a message so personal I can't imagine any other way he could have come by the information. I can hear you asking what it was, so I'll tell you. Remember the little clay tablet I used to distract Senenmut so you could sneak out of his study? The man who found me—his name is Ameny—used the phrase that was on it—"Writing is more enjoyable than a basket of beans." Who but your old tutor could have known that phrase would mean something to me? Ameny also claims you asked Senenmut to check on me, which is believable, although I'm not sure you'll like the direction the conversation took.

Apparently, Ameny has spied for Senenmut for years. He has reason to believe you would recognize his script, so I've included a scrap with a greeting from him to check his claims...

Recognize his script? I shake the instrument, and a scrap of papyrus falls out. The script has the same elongated signs I saw on the note I found stuck in Senenmut's desk leg, the note that revealed Thutmose was to blame for Iset's banishment. Its message is simple enough:

Life, prosperity, and health to you, Great Royal Wife, God's Wife of Amun, King's Eldest Daughter, Lady of Upper and Lower Kemet, mistress of the Two Lands, God's Hand...

I drop it, and turn back to Kamut's letter.

This man not only tells me your old tutor lives and wants to ensure my safety, but after some persuasion, Ameny admitted that he's stationed in the desert where Thutmose's private troops are mustered. He can get me a position with the men. Before you refuse that idea, think about it. These are the men your husband turns to when he needs something done. And this is our chance to know more about his next moves. It's a chance we can't afford to pass up.

I don't want to commit to something without your agreement.

But I don't want you to warn me away from this just to protect me either. I love you. I'd do anything to be with you. But we both know that's never going to happen. What I can do is work to protect you and help you as I'm able. It could give us insight into what these men—and the man you're married to above all—are doing. It's worth it. But I'll wait for your approval before I make a move. I do hope it comes soon. I'm going out of my mind hiding from the action. I beg you to stop worrying and let me help.

I read the note again, heart pounding. It's no surprise that Senenmut revealed himself to Kamut—I practically ordered him to. But the thought of Kamut putting himself in more danger is terrifying. Yet I can't move forward without taking risks. Kamut is a grown man. More to the point, he's right—knowing what Thutmose's men are doing may prove useful. So I agree to his plan, remind him I love him back, and outright refuse his tempting offer to stop worrying.

"Do you intend to avoid dining with me forever?" Mother waltzes into my study unannounced, interrupting me and my steward, who flees like a mouse scurrying away from a hawk.

"Apologies, Mother," I grunt. "I haven't been feeling well, as you no doubt know."

"I do not know that, Neferura. For I am left getting updates on your health from Hesi-Ra, as if keeping your mother informed is too much for you, and the doctor must do your job."

My eyes drop to the scroll in my hands, a list of goods on order for my tomb. Seems wise to prepare, under the circumstances.

Mother taps her toes, and I wonder how many times the painted fish under her sandal has been stomped on over the years. When I don't speak, she adds, "I am your pharaoh as well as your mother. I've every right to know how the pregnancy progresses."

"The heir grows inside me as bid, Pharaoh," I report drolly.

She sighs loudly and drops into Senenmut's old lion's paw chair. "Do you intend to maintain this attitude until the child is born? What is it you're so angry about anyway?"

I blink quickly. After a deep breath, I meet her eyes. I should keep my mouth shut, but anger and exhaustion and my growing belly make me bold. "He's alive. And you knew that. And you didn't bother to tell me."

She freezes, blinking fast a few times, before her face scrunches into an angry red ball of wrinkles. "Why would I have told you, Neferura? The agreement was between me and Senenmut."

"You didn't think I'd want to know?"

"I wasn't aware Pharaoh was required to ask her little girl for advice. Quite honestly, I did not give it much thought."

"Of course you didn't," I mutter tiredly. "Did he want to tell me?"

"Senenmut wants to tell you everything, all the time." Mother fans herself, and the skin on her arms jiggles. "But you are my child, Neferura. I have every right to reveal or withhold information as I please."

"And your vow to stop keeping secrets? You promised me—"

"And there haven't been any new secrets since. You should be happy he is alive. Now, do you care to tell me how you learned of this? Don't tell me Senenmut has been in touch?"

"You think after all this I'd tell you a thing? I won't." I lean forward, my growing breasts pressed uncomfortably against my desk. "And that response is not good enough, Mother. I am not a child anymore. I have rights too."

"Rights?" Her rebel brow crawls up, pausing high above her crooked nose.

I take a deep breath, inhaling the scent of cedar and papyrus and the potpourri from Punt Mother gave me years ago. Her lectures on my mounds of responsibilities and my dearth of rights are legendary.

"You are the queen, Neferura. You serve the country. No one cares about your feelings—"

"He cared." The words slip from my lips like a sigh.

"And look how that turned out for him."

We stare at each other, both holding words in. I know from experience more words will just waste my time and trigger her temper. Mother is incapable of acknowledging when she's wrong, and she lashes out anytime anyone displays an iota of disapproval. She doesn't deserve the effort it would take for me to explain the emotions that churn inside me. Venting won't make me feel better. So I shake my head and take a cleansing breath in an effort to quiet my face. I decide a change of subject is the best strategy.

"Did Father hurt you?"

Senenmut's note suggests as much. The idea of Mother young and vulnerable is difficult to embrace. But if I knew her history, perhaps I could decode her terrible choices.

"What kind of question is that, Neferura? Your father was pharaoh. His behavior is not to be questioned. I was a queen too. It's our duty to conceive. We're not required to enjoy it. And I'm not going to discuss my marital duties with you." She sits taller. "Focus on your own duties. Nurture the heir you bear, and bring it safely into the world."

"What then? Once I give Kemet the heir it deserves? Whose child will it be? Mine?"

"Of course not," she jeers. "The child of your womb belongs to—"

"Who will raise it? Who will care for it?"

"I will choose an appropriate wet nurse, appropriate tutors. The heir belongs to Kemet."

"And what belongs to Kemet belongs to you. Yes, Mother. How well I know that. But has it dawned on you that Thutmose may have different ideas?"

After a pause, she says, "Your job is to deliver the heir safely. I'll handle the rest." Her eyes roam over me. "But for that belly, you're too thin. I do hope you're taking care of yourself."

I chuckle at the absurdity of this conversation. "I'm tired, Mother. If you don't mind, I'll retire for the evening. The heir must be tended to after all."

I drop my head to my desk and don't look up again, although I can feel her eyes boring into me. I sit like this for what feels like an eternity, waiting for her to leave. When she finally does, my mood shifts; the tears I've struggled to hold inside pour out, leaking onto my steward's tidy papyri. What will the poor man think when he sees his work spattered with tears rather than the questions and corrections he's used to?

The array of canopic jars laid out inside my burial chamber is staggering. There are plain limestone canopic jars that look like they hail from the time of the pyramids; one set has lids that look like my face; others sport the heads of protective gods. They're made of alabaster, aragonite, stone, even glazed porcelain. My fellow countrymen would rejoice to know their innards were destined for such vaulted containers. But I'm not sure I care whether my lungs and liver end up in stone or porcelain. I certainly don't care at the moment. I'm not here to pick out tomb goods. I'm here to meet Senenmut.

I made a plan—albeit a plan I couldn't have executed without Benerib's help. Senenmut and I have communicated through his desk leg, and today is the day.

He's to meet me inside my tomb. Reviewing the progress that's been made is an excuse for me to be here. But now, the artisan who lays these options before me needs an answer.

"Perhaps if you give the queen some time alone," Benerib suggests. "It's such a personal decision."

My tomb chamber is small. It's also half-finished. Half a dozen men sketch or chisel or paint the images I've approved on the walls. Other men stand waiting for me to select the proper resting place for the bits of me that won't be mummified to live out their eternity. Benerib shoos them all out.

"The queen needs to be inside, alone. We'll call you back when she's made a decision."

The men keep their eyes down as they stream out. If I weren't watching them so closely, waiting for a sign of Senenmut, who promised to be among them, I wouldn't notice one stooped workman step into a niche, disappearing into the dark as his colleagues trickle out. Benerib shuts the temporary wooden door that guards my tomb chamber behind them.

"I'll guard the other side." She gives me a tremulous smile. "If you need anything—anything at all—just knock. I'll be right here. We can't have ears pressed against the door."

She leaves and I turn to the niche where my old tutor hides. He steps out, and the light of the lanterns that pepper the small space shines on him. I've know Senenmut my entire life, but the man before me now is a different man entirely. He's been gone months, but he's aged years. His hair is completely gray, his shoulders are bent, and he walks with a limp. An act, I'm sure, but it's so convincing I can't tell what's real and what's affect. Senenmut was always known for being impeccably and richly dressed, and he had the most proper posture imaginable. This lame, disheveled servant could walk past any old acquaintance and never be recognized.

"Dear one." He holds his arms open, inviting me into his embrace.

I hesitate for a heartbeat, then throw myself at him, holding him tight. I let the tears flow.

"I'm sorry," he mumbles over and over.

"You keep lying to me." I step back. I want to look in his eyes. I hope they'll reveal more than his words. His words have too often been misleading.

"I should have made a better decision. I intended to die. I was ready. But Hathor came to me. She told me you'd asked her to save me. She had this plan and I…" He stops talking. "I should have come to you at that very moment. I don't know whether I deserved to live or die—the gods will judge that. But I do know I should have told you everything."

"Did you want to tell me?"

He grimaces. I see the answer in his eyes. He did, but Mother didn't. And now he's deciding if he should finally admit Mother is damaged, not the perfect divine specimen we all pretend she is, or lie to me again.

"It was not my choice," he admits. "Still, I could have insisted. I could have refused to go along with the plan unless you were involved. I didn't."

"Yet you did tell me the doctor's name. Why that but nothing more?"

He shakes his head. "It was a difficult time. The worst part about it—and this was true whether I chose to die or disappear—was leaving you. I knew how difficult things would get for you. I wanted to be here to support you. In the end, that's why I chose Hathor's path. I wanted to be alive in case you needed me. I suppose I thought hiding a letter—a letter you may or may not discover—with the doctor's name was leaving it to the gods." He reaches out a hand, running his finger down my cheek. "And to you. You could find the letter or not. You could reach out to Khui or not. I convinced myself I was giving you some agency." He shakes his head. "A half measure, and far less than you deserve."

I step close and rest my head against his chest. "I'm still angry. I hate that you lied. But I do love that you're alive."

"I know." He wraps his arms around me. "Be angry for as long as you need to be. I truly am sorry I didn't consult you. I suppose it's hard to reckon with the fact that you're no longer a little girl sometimes." His eyes drop to my stomach.

I maneuver clumsily onto the step at the base of the red quartzite sarcophagus my mummified body will one day occupy and rest my back against the cold stone. Senenmut falls to his knees in front of me, setting the lantern between us. The light is eerie, which seems right somehow—we are in a tomb, and I am talking to a man who has returned from the dead.

"How did she do it?" I ask. I don't want to talk about my growing belly or my evil husband.

He twines his fingers behind his neck. "She gave me a potion. It made me appear dead long enough for Hathor to replace my body with another's before the embalming priests began their work."

"She swapped your body inside the temple?" The woman has no boundaries. I shouldn't be surprised. "That means the priest embalmed, what, some poor tomb worker? A fisherman perhaps? Did you care about that? Does anyone other than Mother and Hathor know this?"

"The man they embalmed died of natural causes. His mummi-fication wasn't nearly what I expected for myself, but it was more than he could have afforded. It will serve him well in the afterlife." Senenmut exhales. "And no, only the three of us knew the entire truth. And now you."

"We're not the only ones who know you're alive. Benerib knows. And Kamut. And Iset. And your man, Ameny. You trust him?"

"With my life, which he's saved more than once, by the way."

"You know Kamut is in the desert with him?"

"Ameny shouldn't have told Kamut that was an option. Of course Kamut jumped at the chance to spy for you. That boy always has been devoted." Senenmut sighs, shaking his head. "Ameny took a liking to him. I didn't expect that—Ameny dislikes people in general. But once he attaches to you, he's fiercely loyal. He'll toss himself in front of a sword for Kamut if it comes to that. Still, they're in a very dangerous position."

"Is it worth it?"

Senenmut shrugs narrow shoulders. "Time will tell. But Thutmose's private army isn't there to do good. Best we know what it is there for."

Benerib's voice rings out from the other side of the door. Talking loudly with the artisans is meant to warn us that the men grow restless.

"Time is short, dear one," Senenmut says. "Tell me how I can help."

"Go back to the oasis," I say. "Stay safe. Communicate with me when you need to. I'll check the desk weekly, or Benerib will. I'll leave a message if I need to—"

"But it will take time to get to me. If I'm here, I'm close at hand."

"And in greater danger. I need just one person in my life safe from the threat of Thutmose. You're the one he thinks is dead, so you're the one who can stay safe."

His jaw is tight. He doesn't like this request, but he can't deny me so soon after tossing apologies at my feet. "I'll leave in the morning. But I will return the moment I'm needed. You'll tell me if I can do anything for you, won't you?"

I promise to keep him informed and wave him back into the cubby to hide until the men return. It's only when he's inside, beyond my vision, that I whisper one last question—a question that's been in my heart for most of my life. "Am I the child of your body, Senenmut?"

The pause feels eternal, and when he answers, I'm not sure if I'm relieved or disappointed.

"No, dear one," he whispers from the dark. "You're not the child of my body. You're far more than that. You're the child of my heart."

TWENTY-ONE

A T FIRST, SATIAH IS HER CHARMING SELF DURING TODAY'S meeting with my troupe leaders. The women listen to Tasherit's story about her brother, a priest, who was recently chastised for letting stubble sprout on his head during vacation in the north.

"Baldness is cleanliness," Tasherit says, mimicking the high priest.

Nebtah snorts as the others laugh, but Satiah catches my eyes and frowns.

Alerted by the look, I beckon her to join me near the rail as the others lounge on the deck, dipping their feet in my pool and drinking spiced wine. We slip behind a column for shade and some privacy.

Satiah wastes no time. "He's planning something."

"What?" The familiar worry blazes.

She shakes her head. "I'm not sure. But something happened yesterday. I know it. He was exultant last night. I asked why and he wouldn't tell me. But I have a bad feeling."

"What do you think it is?" I trust Satiah's intuition. She certainly understands Thutmose and what moves him better than I ever have.

"I think he learned something new. I got one hint out of him. He said the day was going to cost him a lot. I think he meant it literally, like he was going to have to pay for something in gold. I fear he's bought a secret and that it may have to do with you."

"Could he have figured out you're not who you say you are?"

"No." She shakes her head. "It's not that. I'm safe. It's something else."

I press my back against the column for support. What if Thutmose found out Senenmut is alive? What if he captured Kamut? Or Hathor? She knows everything. She's revealed secrets before when it behooved her to do so. I believe she's working in Kemet's best interest, but her idea of what's best for the country and mine don't always align. It wouldn't even have to be Hathor. Maybe he paid off a scorpion, perhaps even Iset's friend.

I make an effort to relax my face as witty Hui wanders close.

"Be careful," Satiah whispers, then stretches and grins like we weren't just discussing the many ways Thutmose could inflict pain on me and the country.

"Thank you for your work, Satiah," I say. "The orphans will be better off for your ideas." It's not a lie exactly. "Do remember to take care of yourself too."

Satiah takes Hui's arm, leading her away with smiles and whispers. I stare out at the river, bursting with people fishing and sailing, going on about their lives as I sit, counting the many paths Thutmose could take to my ruin, before ambling into my study where I write a quick note to Kamut, which I pass to Nebtah on her way out, telling him to stay alert and stay safe.

Benerib holds up an intricately beaded tunic with small faience and gold beads that form large ankh signs around the skirt and sleeves. "Iset sent it today," she says. "It's a bit heavy. But she thought it would look lovely with your dark hair."

"It's perfect," I say. Iset should be resting, but I know the work eases her heart, and I'm pleased to have something of hers to wear to tonight's feast, especially when I'm greeted by Thutmose's snide grin the moment I walk into the great hall.

"Should you be here?" he asks.

"Why shouldn't I be?" I may hate palace events, but I can't keep an eye on him from inside my room.

"You are carrying my child, Neferura."

"And you think that means I can't walk and talk? You do realize women have been bringing children into the world since before King Narmer unified the country. We're not rendered helpless by pregnancy. One might argue it's a sign of our strength."

"It's not your strength I'm worried about. It's my heir's." He runs his eyes to my toes, then back to my face. "You've been quiet lately. Docile, almost. It makes me think you're up to something. Is there anything you want to tell me."

Is he being sarcastic? I'm reaching for a response when Nehsi strolls up, arms spread wide in greeting. He's blissfully unaware that he's interrupting a marital spat. I love him more for it. "It's been too long, Adoratrice. I haven't had a chance to congratulate you."

I return his smile and turn my back on Thutmose to walk with Nehsi. Small talk has never been my strong suit, but Nehsi is a man of few words. He's easy for me to spend time with. Still, the smells of sweat and wine and perfume quickly overwhelm me. I'm rarely nauseous as the pregnancy progresses, but this is a lot to take in. I excuse myself and head for the courtyard where I sit on a bench, watching lotus blossoms float serenely across the small pool and taking deep calming breaths.

"Adoratrice."

I recognize the voice before I see her. She sits next to me. I'm less surprised to see Hathor wandering through the palace than I am by her skin. It's smooth, pale brown, unmarked.

"Iset told me you had a makeup expert in the palace. Perhaps I should borrow her sometime. It's impressive work. I can't see a single tattoo."

Hathor shrugs. "Our greatest strengths can sometimes be our greatest weaknesses."

"Do you consider your tattoos a strength?"

Her laughter sounds like bells. "I consider my relationship with the goddess Hathor a strength. As, I suspect, your relationship with the god Amun is for you. The tattoos are merely an expression of my dedication."

"So your dedication to the goddess is a weakness?"

"You must admit, the outward expression of my dedication is memorable, no?"

I snort. It isn't very queenlike, but I'm not feeling especially elegant at the moment.

We pause as a group of nobles wanders through the courtyard. They move away and I ask her why she's here. "Thutmose could see you," I chide.

"Thutmose sees what he believes he will see. If he managed to notice me, I'd just pretend I was here to see him." She shrugs. "Benerib tells me you have reason to fear he's planning something. I wanted to learn more. So here I am."

"I liked it better when you snuck into the temple."

"We could have met in a tomb, I suppose."

I turn to her, irked by her knowledge.

"Senenmut and I spent time together before he left. It was a clever plan, by the way. Yours or Benerib's?"

"Ours," I say.

"Funny," she says with a grin. "I asked her the same question and she said it was yours alone. I do love that you give others credit, but it's so much simpler to be honest."

My jaw drops. "You are not lecturing me about honesty."

"I might be." Candlelight from the lantern on the bench between us glitters in her brown eyes. "It pays to be honest. It just pays more to be bold."

"You are that," I admit grudgingly. A slow dirge of music floats on the breeze, punctured by sounds of laughing nobles. I pause and listen to the words of the blind harpist, struck by his message: make the most of today, for tomorrow is not guaranteed.

Follow your heart as long as you live!
Put myrrh on your head,
Dress yourself in fine linen,
Anoint yourself with exquisite oils,
Which are only for the gods.
Let your pleasure increase,
And let not your heart grow weary.
Follow your heart and your happiness,
Conduct your affairs on earth as your heart dictates.
For that day of mourning will surely come for you.
The weary-hearted Osiris does not hear their lamentations,
And their weeping does not rescue a man's heart from the grave.

Enjoy pleasant times,
And do not weary thereof.
Behold, it is not given to any man to take his belongings with him.
Behold, there is no one departed who will return again!

"I'm afraid you've wasted your time," I say as his voice fades. "I don't know what Thutmose is plotting. Satiah is worried. And Thutmose just implied he thinks I'm up to something."

"Are you?"

"Does trying to survive count?" The blind harper wouldn't approve of my pessimism. But "increasing my pleasure" feels like a lot to expect.

She grins. "My sense is that you're aiming for far more than mere survival. My sense is you want your power back. Am I wrong?"

I gulp lotus-scented air, then blow it out. Hathor knows too much about me already. She doesn't need the details of my plan, so I change the subject. "I'm worried about Senenmut."

"He's safe," she assures me. "He's on his way to the oasis."

"Do you know about Thutmose's secret troops? They're in the desert—"

"Yes, yes. I have men on the payroll. I checked with them today. If Thutmose's plans involve them, my men have not been informed."

"Any ideas?"

"One." Her nod is curt. "I believe you've met my scorpion, Senseneb. I sent her to answer your questions about me before we met, when you were first looking into me. She spoke to you at the temple, inside the chapel your mother builds to honor Amun."

"Oh, I remember her." Mostly I remember her suggesting the rituals I performed aren't, what was the word she used? *Tangible*, I believe.

"Senseneb is a skilled fighter. She may not look it, but she could battle a field of men and come out on top. I'd like her to stay with you for a few nights. She'll stay out of the way. But you'll have extra protection—"

"I doubt Thutmose would have me murdered in my own rooms."

"How do you think your husband will kill you when the time comes? Because the time will come, Neferura. The babe you carry may protect you now, but it protects only your life. Thutmose would happily chop off a few fingers or torture Benerib in front of your eyes if it meant putting you in your place and maintaining his power."

I watch a lotus flower sink slowly into the water, its fragile life snuffed out by the unassuming waves that ripple across the pool. "Fine," I agree. "Anything else?"

"See that your priestesses are warned. Pretty Satiah is in danger. That was a clever move, by the way. Are you sure you can trust her?"

I don't bother to deny that I've put Satiah in harm's way to spy on Thutmose. Hathor has too much vision into that plot to feign innocence. "I trust her completely."

"I will abide your judgment. For both our sakes, I hope you're right. You are setting her up to have an enormous well of power. And she knows your secrets—"

"Satiah is true," I say simply.

Hathor nods, then plucks a pair of miniature symbols from the braids piled around the perfumed wax mound atop her head and claps them together. A long, sweet note peals out, just loud enough to fill the courtyard. A servant girl rushes up. She's a few years younger than me with slick black hair cropped at the chin and a sheer sheath dress that falls to her bare feet. She's vaguely familiar, one of the many palace servants I've passed in the halls.

"I'm enjoying the party. I think I'll attend to more business while

I'm here. Make arrangements for me to stay a while. I may need to leave on short notice. Make sure my route is prepared."

The girl nods and pivots prettily to do Hathor's bidding. A small scorpion, tattooed on the back of her calf, peeks back at me through the slit in her dress as she walks off.

"Send word through Benerib if you hear more. I'll do the same," Hathor vows.

"Will you?"

"I will." She bobs her head. "Stay alert. And stay in touch."

I wake to Kamut by my bed. This time, I know it's no dream.

Pulse racing, I sit up and take in the scene.

Senseneb has Kamut in a choke hold. He's kneeling at her feet, struggling to breathe.

"Release him," I command just as Benerib marches out of her room to stare open-mouthed at the tableau.

Senseneb steps back. Kamut falls onto his hands and knees, sucking in great gasping breaths. "Nice to see you have protection," he chokes out.

"Sorry, Adoratrice." Senseneb shrugs.

I don't think she's sorry at all. I have a feeling she enjoyed that.

"Why are you here, Kamut? What's so important the safe channels we've established to communicate aren't good enough? You could have been caught."

Revived, he rolls onto his buttocks and wraps his arms around his knees, looking up at me. "Hello, little princess."

His smile sends the old birds fluttering around my stomach. I'm not sure how they fit with this child growing inside me, but I've half a mind to send Benerib and Senseneb away and pull him close.

"To answer your question," he continues, pulling his eyes off my rounded belly, "something happened tonight. I would have used the usual channels, but your note... I didn't want to wait for..." He pauses, eyes darting to Senseneb and Benerib.

"Senseneb works for Hathor, and Benerib is loyal. Would you prefer I send them away?"

"Do you want the wisewoman to know what you know?" he asks.

I pause for a heartbeat, then nod. "I do."

"Good. She may be able to help. Ameny heard a rumor that someone important was coming to camp tonight. I thought it might have something to do with the warning you sent. So we stayed close to the camp leaders to see who they spoke with. There are fewer than a hundred of us—it's not hard to know everything that goes on. I didn't expect Thutmose himself, but that's exactly who came riding in. It was odd—Thutmose has never shown before. Soon enough, an old man was led out to Thutmose. The man had his head down. He looked terrified. I thought maybe Thutmose caught a spy. You and Senenmut both have men inside. I assume Hathor does too. Perhaps your mother and who knows who else? But that wasn't it. The man was scared, but he seemed to be negotiating. He shook his head a few times. Then he finally nodded, and Thutmose spoke. Eventually Thutmose motioned at one of his men, who handed the old man a bag. I assumed it was of gold—it looked heavy. The man dropped to his knees, thanking Thutmose, until he was pulled away."

"So you don't know who he was or what he said?" My heart is racing.

"I'm not done," Kamut says. "Ameny and I figured we'd follow the man, maybe find out what he was up to. Even from a distance, he looked familiar, and I needed to get a closer look. It took us some time to wiggle out of camp unseen, but we picked up the trail easily enough. Only it didn't lead back to town like we expected."

The pause is dramatic.

"It led to a corpse."

"The man's?" I ask.

"Yes." Kamut nods. "They'd walked him into the desert, slit his throat, and left him there."

"Without his gold, I assume?"

"Correct." Kamut nods. "But that's not the problem. The problem is I knew him."

I steel myself, worried about where this is going. When I learn who the man was, I know I wasn't nearly worried enough.

"It was Iset's father. I don't know what he said to Thutmose, but…"

Nerves drive me to my feet. I twine my fingers above my head, swallowing a scream. "He told Thutmose I visited her," I spit. "I had to see her when I got your note. I wanted to comfort her, and see the baby. He found us, and I was so angry about how he treated Iset I revealed myself just to intimidate him."

Silence reigns for a heartbeat, then Kamut growls. "The man sold his own daughter for coin? I'd have slit his throat myself—"

"We need to warn Iset." I turn to Benerib.

"I'll go," Senseneb offers. "I can get there quickly—Teni can help if I need it. I'll take your friend somewhere safe."

"Hurry," I say. But nowhere is safe for Iset now. I might as well have scrawled a target across her face. My rash act has put her in danger. And the child.

"There's a baby."

"I know. I'll report back. If necessary, I'll send Teni to update you so I can stay and protect Iset." Senseneb turns to Kamut. "You'll stay to make sure the queen is safe?"

"I'll hide here until we learn more," he agrees.

"Hurry," I repeat.

She nods, grabs her sword from the cot where she was sleeping, and zooms into the night.

TWENTY-TWO

WAITING FOR NEWS IS AGONIZING. KAMUT SITS NEXT TO me on my bed, holding my hand. Benerib pours wine, drinking more than Kamut and I combined, though it doesn't seem to affect her. This is the second time Iset has been in danger. Only this time, it's my fault.

"She's here," Benerib finally whispers, back stiff as a was scepter.

Kamut and I stand, skin prickly with fear as Senseneb reappears. My heart drops when I see her.

Kamut wraps an arm around me, pulling me close.

"She's gone," Senseneb says simply. "Her house is empty. There's no sign of Iset or the baby. Teni saw them earlier tonight. She says they were fine. She swears Iset planned to stay home tonight. Teni promised to bring her breakfast in the morning."

"Thutmose has her." I choke on the words, on the knowledge. If only I'd kept my mouth shut. I shouldn't have revealed my identity to Iset's father. "Where would he take her? And what does he want from her?"

"I know where he'll take her." Kamut's hands are tight on my shoulders. "There's a cave. The men use it to torture people. That's where she'll be."

"You think he's...?" My hand flies to my belly. How odd that my instinct is to protect the unborn child I hadn't even hoped to conceive.

"We'd be fools to put anything past Thutmose. If he knows you went to the trouble of visiting Iset in the village, he'd assume she's important to you. That alone may make her worth torturing, especially if he doesn't know why she matters to you."

"He thinks I'm up to something. Just the other night, he said..." I stop and put up a hand, ordering the world to still. I need a moment. Just a moment to think, to plan. I blow a heavy breath, then turn to Kamut. "Take me to the cave. Now."

He shakes his head. "It's too dangerous. Thutmose would be perfectly happy to torture you too."

"Not tonight." I touch my stomach. "Not while I'm carrying his heir."

Kamut's eyes fall to my stomach, then jump back to mine. I see the question lingering behind his gaze, but there's no time for that now.

"I need to go to her—"

"How are you going to help her exactly?" he interrupts me. "Can you kill the men who torture her? Because there's a good chance that's the only way we can rescue her. In all those hours we spent in the yard with my father, I don't recall you wielding a sword."

"I can't just sit here, wallowing in luxury while Iset is tortured on account of me."

"No one is asking you to—"

"I need to alert Hathor." Senseneb says, loudly enough to drown out my argument with Kamut. "I'll go as quickly as I can."

"No." I turn to her, mind clearing. Kamut is right. This is about Iset's safety, not my ego. Senseneb and Kamut can help Iset now better than I can. "You two go to the cave. Find Iset. You can fight. I assume you're willing to kill if necessary?"

"I'll kill the men with my bare hands if I must," she swears.

"As will I." Kamut's voice thrums with rage.

"Go," I say, rigid with fear. "Rescue Iset if you can. Benerib and I will fetch Hathor. But how will she know which cave?"

"Tell her it's the one with the old graffiti," Kamut says. "She'll know it."

"Fine. Go." I push Kamut away.

He cups my cheeks in his hands. "Stay safe." He kisses me on the forehead, whispering "I love you" in my ear.

My heart aches as I watch him walk away, Senseneb at his side. Hopefully she's as fierce as Hathor claimed. The thought of losing Kamut and Iset both tonight is too much. But if I dwell on imagined losses, I'll be frozen. I can't afford inaction now.

Benerib shoves my warmest tunic into a bag. "The desert is cold at night."

"How are we going to get out of the palace?"

"The hard way," she says.

I pull my light tunic tight around me and follow her through the open wall and into the night. Fear courses through me like tides flooding the river. Benerib turns right and drags herself over the short wall separating my wide deck from the narrow, pillared deck that runs the length of the palace. I follow her, weaving past pillars, staying near the wall, where we're less likely to be noticed by the guards who prowl the grounds night and day.

She pauses when we reach the end of the long row of pillars where the palace's deck ends, scanning the empty space before turning to me. "I hate this part. It's been years." She sighs. "I suppose there's no way forward but ahead."

I don't have time to ask what she means before she holds her nose and steps off into thin air. I bury a scream, hurrying to the edge to look down, relieved to see that she's landed in the water, where the river juts into the shore. The royal barge is parked in this small pond of river, moonlight bouncing off the white sail. I'm relieved when Benerib's head pops out of the water. She motions to me, and I hold my breath and jump, shocked by the cold that swallows me.

I struggle against the water until Benerib grabs my arm, hauling me to the surface. We hold on to each other, moving forward, into the river. Finally, she pulls me to shore, where we crawl onto a small boat, choking on river water until we catch our breath.

Iteru is silent as the temple before the dawn ritual. It's just the two of us and a bright moon as Benerib pulls our dry cloaks from her bag. I shiver as we sail down river before docking, then weave our way to a small, indistinct hut on the west bank.

"Stop." Hathor steps out from behind a small shrine behind the hut. Seeing it's us, she waves us into the shrine.

The space is small. It's an ancestral shrine, dedicated to a local family. Their names and titles and images are carved into the walls, mounds of offerings shown in front of them, sustenance to ensure their healthy afterlife. There's barely room for the three of us. It's private and dim, lit by a single lantern.

"Speak," Hathor commands.

Benerib speaks for us, reporting on the night's events in clipped, organized sentences. It's clear they've done this a million times, a soldier reporting to her general.

I lean against the dirty wall, still damp and vibrating with fear.

When Benerib's recitation is done, I stand taller. "Benerib must return to the palace with Neith."

Hathor nods.

"Adoratrice, I—"

I raise a hand to stop Benerib's argument. "We don't know what the night will bring. We may need a cover by morning. If we can save Iset and make Thutmose believe it wasn't us, that would be the best possible outcome. You can keep everyone out of my rooms. Let Neith be seen from afar—even I'd believe that girl is me."

Benerib frowns, but after a heartbeat, she nods and turns to Hathor. "Can I use the doctor?"

"Only if you need to."

"Hesi-Ra reports to you?" I ask.

Hathor shakes her head. "I told you before, Neferura. Not everyone who owes me favors enjoys doing them. He'll cover for you if he must, as long as he believes we're helping you and not putting you in danger."

"You'll take me to the cave," I say to Hathor.

"I will," she agrees. "But I'll remind you that I'm an expert at all the things tonight may bring, and you're a novice. If you come, you're to follow my commands. Agreed?"

My fear combined with the flicker of candlelight must be playing tricks on my eyes: the goddess's head tattooed on Hathor's chest seems to spring to life, examining me with a wary stare.

"Let's go." I sidestep her question. She's not wrong—she's more experienced than me at sneaking and fighting—but I'll decide what commands I follow and what I choose to ignore. I only want to see Iset safe.

Benerib drifts back into the night to find Neith so she can take my place in my rooms as I follow Hathor out to greet the two donkeys tied behind the shrine.

I've never ridden a donkey. I'm uncomfortable as we make our way through the white cliffs. The clip-clop of my donkey's hooves matches the hammering of my terrified heart.

The peak looms large. It hugs the bodies of my father and grandfather tight, protecting their tombs. I pray it holds Iset tight tonight too.

Ages pass, stuffed with countless terrible thoughts of the things that could be happening to Iset as the beasts plod forward. Hathor finally stops her donkey. She dismounts gracefully, then helps me slide off mine. My stomach is big enough to render me clumsy.

"The cave is close," she whispers.

Scurrying sounds erupt to our right, and I startle, only to be soothed by the tattooed woman.

"Snakes and other desert creatures. The real danger is ahead."

I rub the bulge of my belly.

Hathor's eyes shift to my stomach briefly, then she flashes a commanding glare. "Stay silent. And stay close."

Close, I manage, but silent is beyond me. I have no idea how the wisewoman moves through the night so soundlessly. Nor do I know how far we've gone when Hathor pulls me to the cliff wall.

She peers around soft stone into a valley far beyond where my sore feet have traveled before. "We're here."

Iset! I want to spring into the night and dash to my friend's rescue, but Hathor wraps long fingers tightly around my wrist, holding me in place.

She whispers low before I can move, "Recite your favorite maxim three times, silently, then join me."

"But—"

"Do as I say, Neferura." She's imperious as she yanks her shoulder straps to the side and steps out of her clothes. She stands straight and regal—her body looks like that of a nubile young woman rather than the old lady I know she is—and she steps around the corner out of view.

The night grows darker and tighter now that I'm alone. My heart is full to bursting with questions and fears. I take Hathor's advice and close my eyes, muttering to myself, "Cleanse yourself before your own eyes, lest another cleanse you. Let your name go forth while you are silent with your mouth. When you are summoned, be not great of heart because of your strength." I imagine Senenmut chastising me for mixing the words of two wise men. Senenmut's voice in my ears strengthens me.

"Anyone want to play with me?" I hear Hathor, followed by masculine voices. Their laughter is soon cut short by a grunt, a curse, then silence.

I grab Hathor's shift. Attempting to mimic her perfect posture, I step into the valley opening.

Two bodies lie on the ground in front of a small cave.

Hathor is standing in the cave opening, moonlight bouncing off her naked back. She sheathes a long, sharp needle in a wedjat eye amulet that dangles from the gold cuff circling her upper arm. The amulet houses poison, I assume.

Something moves to her right, and my heart jumps into my throat.

"Hathor!" I cry.

"It's me." Kamut jumps down from a ledge, wiping a blade on his kilt, which is covered in blood.

"There were six more nearby." I don't know where Senseneb came from, but her sword is in her hand, drenched in gore. "They're not nearby anymore."

"Is that all of them?" Hathor asks.

Senseneb looks to Kamut.

"I think so. I can't be sure." His eyes dart to the cave opening.

"I'll stand guard," Senseneb says.

Before I can force my terrified feet to move, Hathor rushes in. I follow to find her on her knees in the dark cave—it smells like evil. Iset's head rests in Hathor's hands.

I drop down and struggle to loosen the ropes that bind my friend's legs and arms. One arm is turned in a painful angle, and her face and hair are covered in blood. Bile surges up my throat. My hands tremble as I touch the small tattoo on her thigh, barely visible in the dim light—I didn't even know she had one. The delicate scorpion is curled up, unlike the others I've seen with the creatures shown poised to strike. I push Iset's clotted hair aside to examine her pale face.

"Is she alive?" I ask, voice shaky with fear.

Hathor holds Iset's wrist, eyes closed in concentration.

"Barely." Hathor shifts to inspect another woman, lying unconscious at Iset's side. "The seamstress."

"Maia?" I ask. "Why? Iset's employer is an innocent. She knows nothing—"

"Thutmose doesn't know that," Hathor points out. "He doesn't know what you're doing or who might be loyal to you. He'll torture all Waset if he thinks there's a chance you can take his hard-won power away from him."

"Where's the baby?"

"Here." Kamut steps forward, Neferu in his arms. "She's fine."

I breathe a sigh of relief, reaching for the child.

"Neferura." My name slides from Iset's mouth like a fish slipping from a fisherman's fingers. Her eyelashes flutter, then her eyes flicker open: one eye is familiar but the other is a stranger, bright red with blood.

291

"I'm here." My vision blurs. I wipe blood off her cheeks with filthy fingers. "Hathor is with me. She's going to help you. You're going to be fine—"

"We said nothing." Iset's voice is low and scratchy. "Poor Maia."

"I know. That doesn't matter now. You—"

"They wanted information from her she didn't have. They asked about you. A million ways they asked. She told the truth—she knew nothing. I stayed silent."

Iset sees the child and whimpers. Kamut drops to his knees to set the child gently on her chest.

She closes her eyes, like she's concentrating on feeling the child's skin against her bloody torso. Her voice is weak. "Take care of Neferu, Mistress. I know you will... Find somewhere safe." Her voice fades, and her eyes blink shut.

"Iset!" I grip her shoulders, willing her to wake up. I can barely see past the tears and blood. Everything is blurry, fuzzy.

Let her live. Let her live.

The words course through me.

Hathor pushes me gently aside, running her hands over Iset's stomach, up her arms, down her neck. Irrationally, I realize Hathor is clothed again, and I wonder when she managed to pull on her shift. She turns to me and shakes her head; a wave of dizziness rolls over me.

"She'll be fine," I stutter.

Hathor places a tattooed hand on each of my cheeks. "Iset is dead."

"No," I mumble. I can't see. I can't breathe. I can't think. "We're here now. You'll save her, like you saved Mother. And Senenmut."

"I can't. It's too late for Iset. But we can save her child. And Maia. And ourselves. And we can bar your husband from feeling the joy of Iset's death." Her voice is as cold as my husband's heart. "Breathe, Neferura. And come."

I'm not going anywhere. We're going to save Iset. I fall on my friend's body, chanting ritual words that aren't supposed to be uttered outside the most sacred chamber of Amun's temple. I don't know why I do it. Perhaps I'm used to believing the god hears me. Perhaps I think if I get his attention, Amun will intervene to save my dearest friend.

Kamut's arms are around me, his heartbeat banging against my back as his hands cradle my stomach. This is the second time his presence has brought me comfort me when someone I love died.

But Senenmut wasn't really dead.

Maybe Iset will return to me too.

"Neferura." Hathor's voice strikes me like a lash. "We don't have time to mourn now. You must think of the child."

My hand falls to my stomach, and Kamut twines his fingers in mine.

But the tattooed woman shakes her head. "Little Neferu is now motherless. We must act now before your husband's villainy spreads."

She's right. Iset wanted me to focus on her child. Her last words... But I can't accept this. She can't be gone.

Kamut shifts away from me, and my back is suddenly cold with the loss of him. He's back a moment later, the babe in his arms again.

"Kamut, you must get Maia and the baby to safety," Hathor tells him. "Neferura, you must—"

"No," I sob. "We have to help Iset."

"We cannot." Hathor is stern. "And unless you want to add to the pile of bodies tonight will bring, we must go. We're all in danger here. There are more guards in the hills nearby. They'll figure out their friends are dead soon. They'll notice Kamut is gone. When they realize what he's done, they'll come for him. His position is exposed. He will be their next target."

No. I can't be the cause of Kamut's death too. My fingers tremble as I release Iset's body and push myself up. Tears slide down my cheeks.

"Breathe," Hathor repeats.

Kamut puts one hand on my shoulder, babe sleeping in his crooked arm. "I'll see to the child. I promise I'll keep her safe." He leans in and breathes deeply, like he's taking in my scent. "Be safe, Neferura," he whispers.

And then he's gone, vanishing with the babe he cradles. Senseneb appears to scoop Maia up gently and follow Kamut into the night.

"You can do this," Hathor vows.

"I can't—"

"You can. And you must. For Kamut and Neferu, if not for the two of us."

"Iset is dead," I say, voice cracking with grief.

Hathor nods. "She is. And her heart will be light. You'll reunite, but tonight we must act to save her daughter."

Neferu.

She's right. I must save the child. "What do I do?"

The wisewoman whips out commands—commands I follow as if she truly is my pharaoh. My actions are a blur. My mind is like mist drifting over the marshes. I have no idea how Hathor summons the donkeys, but they're back. We secure Iset to one and Hathor insists I ride the other while she walks.

My eyes won't stop wandering to Iset, limp on the donkey in front of me, as we plod through the night. Images play before me: the wholesomeness of her face the day we met, her feigned innocence when I chastised her for being presumptuous, the looks of joy dancing in her eyes when we were reunited. I hear her hushed voice, teasing me about my crush on Kamut, and her concern when I explained the pain her joke caused. I see the letters she dictated, telling me she was married and then with child. I recall her enthusiasm when I gathered my friends together to make a plan to stand up to Thutmose. I remember her chiding me when I appeared at her house and her proud grin when she told me she'd named her daughter after me.

Now, because of me, the child is alone and in danger. Thutmose knows I care about the baby—I snuck out of the palace to visit them. He'll kill Neferu without losing a moment of sleep, if only to cause me pain.

I'm worrying over the babe's fate when we finally reach the shrine. A pink sun is peeking over the horizon. Hathor helps me off the donkey and carries Iset's body inside, setting her gently on a bench that stretches the length of the far wall.

She puts her hands on my shoulders, steadying me. "Kamut will get Neferu to safety. My scorpions will see to Maia. In the meantime, Thutmose must not know you were here tonight. He must not know that you know about Iset's disappearance. Do not let on that Iset is dead. Don't give him the satisfaction."

That demand penetrates my fuzzy thoughts. I look over at Iset, her lifeless body—bruised, bloodied, and crooked—slumped on the dirty bench. "No. No, I won't give him that." The promise settles in my gut, igniting every part of me with determination.

"I'll have someone lead you back to the palace when it's safe. You were wise to send Benerib back to cover for you. It buys you time—"

"For what?"

"That's up to you, Neferura. Hesi-Ra might grant you a few days alone. You can trust him, with your health at least, but there's no reason to share anything that went on tonight with anyone but Benerib. That includes your mother."

The snakes squirm in my belly at the thought of Mother. "Was Mother involved?"

Hathor shakes her head. "No. This was Thutmose's work. And I don't think Iset and Maia were the only victims. Because of Satiah's warning, I sent a scorpion to keep eyes on Iset. I suspect we'll find my scorpion dead too."

"Iset's friend?"

"No. It was another." Hathor squeezes my shoulders. "You need to rest here until one of my girls returns to fetch you. I need to go. Sleep."

Hathor mutters a spell under her breath. Suddenly, I'm too tired and sore and angry to keep my eyes open. I sink into a chair.

"Sleep," she repeats, and the world goes dark.

It's late morning when I wake to find Iset's body clean. I slip her mother's bracelet off her arm and onto mine. She's with her mother now after all. Iset would want me to keep the bauble to remember her by, I think as I lay myself over her and cry until a girl I've never seen before comes to lead me back to my bed, where sleep takes me again.

When I wake, a single desperate thought burns bright in my heart: Thutmose did this. And if he gets the chance, he'll do it again—to Kamut, to Neferu, to me, to everyone I love. If the child I carry is a girl, quite possibly to her as well.

TWENTY-THREE

HESI-RA BUYS ME THREE DAYS. THREE DAYS TO AVOID EVERY-one but Benerib, pretending I must stay in bed for the safety of the child I bear. Three days to plot a way to keep me and my baby safe, ensure Iset's child is loved, and keep Senenmut and Kamut out of Thutmose's reach. Three days to ensure the work I do for the people continues, in one form or another, and to take my life and my unavoidable death out of Thutmose's hands. Because if Iset's murder taught me anything, it's that Thutmose will not stop until I end up just like her.

On the evening of the fourth day, Mother arrives. And she's not alone.

Normally the smells would delight me. Today, the barrage of scents makes me want to vomit as servants place mounds of culinary delights onto a long table. Others carry in a smaller table and two chairs, setting them up by my bed. Mother strides in behind them.

"Do see that the wine that arrived yesterday is brought," she orders her royal handmaid as she perches in the chair next to me.

I'm too exhausted to argue. I struggle to get up and shift into the other chair.

"What are you doing?" she asks.

"I assume we're dining together," I reply, confused.

"Obviously." She's droll. "But I didn't have the dining room shifted to your bedside to get you out of bed."

I look at the second chair. "Then who—"

"Thutmose, of course."

I drop my head back onto my wooden headrest, wrapped in soft textiles with amulets tucked in the folds to ensure my safety. I barely have enough time to still my face before Thutmose arrives. He's taken extra care with the kohl around his eyes tonight. An effort to impress Satiah, I'm guessing.

"Are you well now?" he asks.

I ball my fists and force myself to sit and shrug nonchalantly. "I'm fine. Hesi-Ra is not worried. He wants me to rest, but all is well." No need to mention it's my broken heart the doctor has tended to for the past days rather than the pregnancy.

"You must take care of yourself." Mother sips from the cup of red wine she shifts from one hand to the other while Thutmose devours honey-roasted goose.

I will my hand to pick up food and deliver it to my mouth, then force my mouth to chew and swallow. It tastes like dry mud.

"More importantly, you must take care of the child in your belly," Thutmose adds.

I lean back in my bed, rubbing my stomach. Thutmose examines me as if I'm as fascinating as a new lover. Does he suspect I know something about Maia and Iset? I took to bed, the doctor refusing to let anyone see me, the morning after Iset died. Does Thutmose really believe that's a coincidence?

I blow a heavy breath, determination steeling my spine. It's essential that he believes I'm ignorant. I can't give Thutmose the gratification of my pain or any hint of my knowledge. I listen quietly while the pharaohs talk about disciplining a pesky noble; a rift among the elites of Kush triggered by our tight control of their mines; Mother's most recent building program, which Thutmose feels is excessive but Mother argues honors the gods and employs men who need the work; and the recent unrest in the land of Naharin.

When they fall silent, I speak. "I have news about the heir." I coerce my mouth into a grin.

Mother's eyebrow crawls up. Thutmose freezes, glowering at me over the piece of meat he holds halfway between his plate and his mouth.

"Good news?" Mother leans toward me, and I pull the linen throw higher, take a deep breath, and make my head nod agreeably.

"It's a boy."

"Are you sure?"

"Hesi-Ra confirmed it."

The doctor said no such thing. But Thutmose doesn't need to know that.

"Why didn't Hesi-Ra tell me?" Of course, Mother's initial response is to be annoyed that someone in Kemet knows something about me before her.

"He had me take the test today for a second time. He wanted to be sure. You're pleased I hope, husband?"

My heartbeat speeds up as Thutmose studies my face, searching for deception. "Of course it's a boy." He shrugs. "And lucky for you it is. I plan to expand my progeny soon. Your child will not be the only one."

"Will you take another wife?" Mother's voice is casual, but I can see the worry she hides. Another wife renders me even more dispensable. And, more pertinent to Mother, a second wife with no loyalty to her could further weaken her tenuous hold on the limited power that remains to her.

If only she knew how little I care about that now. If she knew of my plans, she'd see how essential Satiah is to me. I remember Kamut joking once—the two of us were wrapped in a blissful embrace—about giving Thutmose a different wife. He asked me to disappear with him. The idea was absurd of course. The god's wife of Amun cannot simply disappear. A great royal wife dying in service to Kemet, on the other hand, may be a different story.

"I will marry again soon." Thutmose twines his fingers around his wine cup, raises it to his lips, and takes a large gulp.

"The priestess you've been spending time with?" Mother asks. "I didn't even know Ahmose Pen Nekhbet had a niece."

Thutmose snaps, "I don't need to explain my plans to you. I'll marry who I want to marry. And I'll mate with whoever I choose to mate with. Do you need a reminder of how our agreement works, or shall I tell the artisans to start chopping your image out of temples and shrines now?"

Mother's grin, once haughty, is forced. "Do as you will, of course. I was just hoping to welcome her to the family. I've never met the girl. She works with you, Neferura, yes?"

"One of my troupe leaders actually," I say as if I'm bored. "She's…" I draw the moment out, let them think I'm working hard to find something nice to say about her. "Capable."

Thutmose laughs at that. Then, to my relief, he stands to go, sending servants scurrying to do his bidding. Mother follows him out.

I stand and retreat to my study the moment the last servant leaves my room, carrying the remains of a feast that grows stale in my belly. "Benerib," I call as I settle at my desk.

She shuts the study door behind her and turns to me. "Adoratrice?"

"I have a proposition for Hathor. Tell her I'd like to speak with her. As soon as possible." Benerib nods and I continue. "Summon my troupe leaders. I want them to visit me here in three days. Given Satiah's new position, all eyes will be on her. She'll be hounded by gossip now that people know she's to be royal. I trust these five women, but I would like a few moments with Satiah alone without drawing the attention of the others."

"I'll see to it. Is there anything else I can do for you?"

I shake my head. "That is all for now, Benerib."

She nods, eyes worried, and leaves me alone with my thoughts and a heart full of unanswered questions. I turn my chair so I can look out at the river. I watch a bird dive for a fish as I utter a prayer to the god I've spend a lifetime serving, begging for him to approve my plan.

Amun-Ra, great god, bull of your mother, please bless the plan you've written on my heart. Safeguard your land so Kemet doesn't pay for the trespass I intend.

Make certain Hathor agrees with my wishes and does your bidding, o great god, sacred of arm. I cannot do this without her.

And please, mighty Amun, protect the people of Kemet. See that they're cared for even after the god's wife of Amun, great royal wife, king's eldest daughter, lady of Upper and Lower Kemet, mistress of the Two Lands, is gone.

Hathor comes the following night, waking me from a deep slumber.

"Neferu?" I ask the second I open my eyes and see the wisewoman hovering over me.

"Kamut is taking the girl to safety." Hathor perches on my bed, running her hands over my body. Her age is evident in the light that shines up onto her face from the lantern on the floor near her feet.

She's worn down, a fact I intend to use against her.

"And Maia?" I ask.

"Scorpions are caring for her. Her body will heal. Her heart and spirit...more slowly."

"How do you intend to keep Thutmose from finding out what happened?"

"How could he? There's no one left to tell the tale." Hathor's face is still.

"Won't he suspect you? Who else would have intervened like that but you? Or me of course. But Thutmose doesn't think I have the kinds of resources needed to carry out such a feat."

She shakes her head, lips turned down. "Thutmose has no idea what happened or where either woman disappeared to. He won't think you're capable. And he believes I'm in the delta on a mission he sent me on."

"What if he discovers your deception?"

"Why would he? The scorpion who took my place is adequate for the task."

"You are"—I hesitate, searching for the right word—"unique. Surely you're easy enough to distinguish from another—"

"How many tattooed women do you think do his bidding, Neferura? Another woman with markings like mine, under my orders, would deceive every fool in Kemet. Your husband is not nearly as clever as he believes he is. For the country's sake, I hope his wisdom grows with his age."

"You're right, of course. I suppose I just keep thinking of the many ways our secrets might come out. Like Ahmose Pen Nekhbet for example. Are you certain he'll keep our secret?"

"He's rather excited about it, to tell you the truth. He adores Satiah. Her position will only boost his, not that he needs a boost. He's as noble as they come and too old to fear Thutmose. He's still feisty though and enjoys his little games. He's reliable. You should worry more about your priestess. Is she making progress?"

"She is."

"She'll be a second queen soon, I hear."

I wrap my arms around my belly, bracing myself. "I've changed my mind about that." After what happened with Iset, it's clear I won't survive long after the birth of this child. I've grappled with this undeniable reality, shifting my plans accordingly. Now I just need Hathor to agree to a plan that will, I'm certain, go against her every instinct. "I have a different plan for Satiah now. And for myself," I begin.

"I assume this new plan has something to do with this proposal you have for me?"

"It does. I need your help. And I believe you need mine as well."

I watch Hathor's face as I tell her what I have in mind and listen to her suggestions when we get to the snags I can't solve alone. The idea is my own, but such treachery would never have occurred to me if Hathor hadn't barged into my life, if I hadn't witnessed the path to power she walks and seen the uncommon ways she uses her position to help the people of Kemet.

"The plan could work," she finally agrees. "Possibly. But are you truly prepared for that? You're talking about sacrificing your very life—"

"I have no choice. I can't let anyone else get hurt. Iset is dead because of me. As long as I live, Satiah and Kamut and Senenmut and Neferu and Nebtah—perhaps even the child I carry—are in danger. My sacrifice will be worth it. I know I'm asking a lot of you.

But it's the only way forward. And I can't do it without you. Will you help me?"

She folds her arms, tapping her fingers against the swirls of her tattooed arms, considering me through kohl-outlined eyes. I'm braced for a refusal. What I'm asking her to do is tantamount to surrender, which may be the one thing Hathor has no experience with.

"I will," she says at last. "And I'll accept the help you offer as well, although, to be honest, I was under the impression my need was a well-kept secret. I don't know if I'm annoyed or impressed that you've uncovered the worry that keeps me up at night." She stares out at the full moon sliding across the night sky.

"Perhaps it's time to stop carrying your worries alone. You've spent many years helping others. It's time you take some help for yourself, no?"

She turns to me. She's smiling, but something about her grin feels sad. Heartbeats pass; I begin to doubt she'll speak again. Finally, she leans close and kisses my forehead, whispering a single word in my ear before disappearing into the night, her "together" humming in my heart, filling me with the faith of an answered prayer.

My troupe leaders cluck around me. I'm perched in a chaise on my deck. My usual view of the river is blocked from where I sit, but the breeze is strong today—so strong I sent the girls who usually fan us away, although one left her ostrich-feather fan behind, which Nebtah now uses on Tasherit, who is almost too tall for the chaise she lounges in.

I've taken extra care to walk each of the priestesses through my hopes and expectations, plotting the coming months more tightly than usual. I expect they assume I'm preparing to be stuck in my quarters, busy expanding and birthing and feeding and burping. They're not wrong. Entirely.

"Adoratrice." Benerib appears at my side. As always, her timing is perfect.

"Thank you, Benerib. I do need to take a break." I roll my eyes and smile at the women, jesting about the inconveniences of my advancing pregnancy as Benerib helps me up. "Satiah," I call. "Would you mind helping me to the bathroom? Benerib's back has been bothering her—"

"I'm fine, Adoratrice," Benerib pretends to argue.

I ignore her, beckoning Satiah close and slipping an arm in hers, letting her guide me inside. Because of her change in status, if I tried this in front of the larger troupe, tongues would wag. News of Satiah's growing influence at court has rocketed through the ranks. The women are, by and large, pleased they'll be led by two queens soon. Given Satiah's legendary beauty, the only surprise is that her lineage wasn't well known. Predictably, a few of the usual troublemakers claim they knew all along. I do enjoy seeing the women who have triggered such headaches over the years unintentionally pitch in to help my cause.

"He's planning to harm you," Satiah whispers the moment we're in my bathroom, door shut tight and Benerib on the other side for good measure.

"How do you know?"

"The other day, I teased him about being a mere secondary wife. Thutmose told me the status wouldn't last long. He said that I'd be great royal wife soon enough. He laughed it off when I acted surprised. But it wasn't a joke—"

"I know."

"And Benerib said Iset is…" She licks her lips, eyes wet with tears. "I'm so sorry, Adoratrice."

"I'm sorry too." I hug her close for a few heartbeats, feeling the grief that now lives inside me rise in my throat. I release her before it overwhelms me. "We don't have much time, Satiah. It will get harder and harder to find time and space to speak alone. You're to be a queen soon. You'll find privacy is the one treasure that's too often out of reach. And you need to understand that what happened to Iset could happen to you too." I swallow the lump in my throat. There's no time to fall apart now. "The danger is no longer hypothetical. It's real and it's deadly. Are you sure you want to move ahead with this?"

"I still want to help. But I'm worried. If we can't speak, how am I to help you? What's the point of spying if I can't report what I learn?"

I push a stray braid off her face. "You once told me you wanted a position of power to help people. Is that no longer true?"

"It is." She nods. "I still want that, and of course being a queen puts me in a position to do that. But this was about helping you. I fear I've put you in greater danger. I think Thutmose believes he can replace you with me and the nobles will go along with it. He's convinced the country just wants a queen and heir. If Thutmose believes I can give him that…" She doesn't finish the thought. She doesn't have to. Thutmose's intentions are clear. Indeed, I'm counting on them.

"I know all this, Satiah. There's something I need you to know now." I put my hands on her shoulders, steadying her. "If I die, there's no one I'd rather leave my responsibilities to than you. It was always about having a spy in Thutmose's quarters of course, but it was also always about my succession. You can be more than a secondary wife.

You would make an outstanding great royal wife and an equally brilliant god's wife of Amun."

"Stop. Don't talk like that."

"You will care for the troupe and the people. You share my passion and dedication. I suspect you'll be more efficacious than I have been since Thutmose gained power over me. We don't do as much for the people as we used to, but you can solve that. You can bring Thutmose along, convince him to do things he'd never agree to if I were asking."

"You are not going to die. The country will not stand for him murdering his wife and heir." Her voice is too loud.

I hush her. When she's calm, I continue. "We can't go on like this. Yes, the nobles would rebel if they believed I was murdered. But you are too smart to believe that would be the story, Satiah. There are plenty of ways for a woman to die."

"I can't be great royal wife." She shakes her head. "That's impossible."

"No one doubts the lineage Hathor created—"

"It's not about that." She looks down, shoulders drooping. "I should have told you this when you first asked about it. But I imagined being one of many secondary wives, another ornament. I hoped I could help you and perhaps grow enough influence to do more for the troupe and the priestesses. Maybe I could help the orphans somehow, help the children who have nowhere else to go, children who've been abandoned like I once was. I never imagined being great royal wife. It wouldn't be fair to the country—"

"You're worried you weren't chosen by the gods." I lean back against the cool stone wall. "I've come to believe none of us are chosen. I don't think the gods put us in these positions. I think we earn the approval of the gods—or not—from whatever perch we're born to. It is powerful men who determine who rules. Or in this case, powerful women." I manage a small smile. "Kemet would be lucky to have you."

She shakes her head. "It's not about the gods. It's me. I'm… It's that I can't have children," she whispers. "I didn't think it would matter. I didn't imagine…"

I blink fast, startled by the news. My plan, so carefully thought out, unwinds. "I'm sorry," I mumble. "I had no idea."

She shakes her head. "It's fine. It's been a convenience, mostly. I have the orphans. I figured one day I'd take one home. Or five," she jokes.

I pull her close again, mind whirling. It's unexpected news. I assumed she could produce an heir. Yet I've come too far down this path to change course now. Besides, the value Satiah brings stems from her character and capabilities, not her womb. As Hathor once told me, the system will find its heir, one way or another. "It doesn't matter, Satiah," I whisper. "You can do this."

"I pray I never have to."

I don't respond. She will have to. I know it. And I know too that the time draws close.

A moment of peace settles over me when I learn of Neferu's fate today via scroll. Benerib has checked Senenmut's desk the past few days. The scroll comes as no surprise. I knew where Kamut would take the child, and enough time has passed for Kamut and Neferu to get to the oasis and for Senenmut to send a letter by his fastest carrier.

From the doctor, Khui, to the god's wife, king's eldest daughter, and my cherished dear one, Neferura, in life, prosperity, and health and in favor of Amun, king of gods. My heart breaks at the news of your loss. I learned of the situation only this morning when Kamut arrived with a sweet bundle in his arms. I am overcome, thinking of your suffering.

They're both sleeping now as I write this from the veranda of my small villa, a lovely shedeh in the cup next to my scribal kit. The priest in charge of Amun's local temple gave me a dog as a gift. I named the beast Khufu, and he lies at my feet, tongue hanging out, panting in this heat, although the breezes here are sufficient to cool those of us who aren't covered in hair. It's been years since I shared my life with a dog, and I find him a terrific companion, a balm to the loneliness that creeps in from time to time.

I write to send condolences and, more usefully, to assure you that I am of course willing to take the little one in. I will do everything in my power to soothe her. An old man is no replacement for what she's lost. All I can do is be present and kind and reliable. You won't be surprised to learn that your old guard is a natural with her. He'll make a fine father one day. He's an easy man to like. Of course, his dedication to you is the best of his many good qualities.

As saddened as I am for her, I'm equally heartsick thinking of you and what you must be going through. I know how much Iset meant to you. True friendship is one of life's greatest gifts, and yours ended far too soon.

I will keep you updated as often as I can. I wish I could do more for you, now more than ever. I'm afraid all I can offer is a true dedication to caring for the one you've sent to me. I will not fail you in this. If there is anything else I can do, you have only to ask. And do take care of your health, dear one. I leave offerings daily, but it is a poor substitute for sharing time and space with you.

As expected, Thutmose takes Satiah as secondary wife. Mother is furious that their marriage feast outshines mine. I'm wondering how I can use the event to sneak a private moment alone with Satiah as Mother paces across my floor, pivots, then trudges back to the bed.

"That girl thinks she can replace you. Once your son is born, we'll find a way to make Thutmose declare him the official heir. She'll learn…"

I watch Mother closely, rambling on about the threat Satiah poses to my life and to Mother's power. My head swerves from side to side as I watch her pace, fear curdling in my stomach.

"Sit, Mother," I say at last.

She turns on me, preparing to lecture me on our relative power for the umpteenth time. Something in my face must give her pause.

"Please," I add.

She pulls a chair next to the bed and perches stiffly.

"I am going to say this one time, and I am going to make myself very clear. And for once, you are going to do what I say."

"Neferura—"

"Stop talking." I put a hand up. I suspect her immediate silence is due to surprise rather than submission, but I'll take it. "You will not, under any circumstances, harm Satiah. She has done nothing—"

"She aims to replace you." Mother leans into me, angry.

"Stop!" I yell it this time, then drop my voice low. "Be quiet and hear me." I wait for her to still, then continue with a lie. "I know where Thutmose keeps the doctor's letter."

"What? Where?" Her eyes are wide.

"I will not tell you. Suffice it to say, I know where it is. I heard the confessions. I know everything Thutmose knows. And I will use it against you myself if I must."

"You'd never—"

"I would. You've made your choices. You've put your needs first over and over. Now I'm making a choice to put my needs first. But unlike you, I expect to use my leverage to help others as well. First and foremost, Satiah."

Mother sinks lower, understanding washing over her. "She's yours. You set this up. She's your creature."

"No, Mother." That's not a lie. Satiah is no one's creature. Still, Mother doesn't need to know about my relationship with Kemet's new queen. "She is not. But others are. And they have enough information to act in my stead. If anything should happen to me and you make a move against that woman, it will cost you." I pause, weighing her reaction.

She stares at me like she's never seen me before. Perhaps she hasn't. Perhaps Mother only sees those in the act of wielding power over others. "You are in danger, Neferura. Once your son is born—"

"I recall you once promising to protect me if I had a son."

"That's what I'm trying to do," she exclaims. "But the people love her. Even the nobles adore the girl. The woman works with orphans in her free time. I don't need to tell you she's beautiful and you're not."

"You don't." I smile at that. I take some pleasure in the fact that her words no longer wound me.

"She will have a son. And her power will rival yours, even without her royal blood. People are stupid for beauty. No one will make a fuss when you die once she's—"

"She will not have a son." A bit of honesty will do more to stay Mother's hand than any threat I could make.

"Of course she will. Eventually. A few daughters may buy you time but—"

"She will not have a daughter. She will not bear children, Mother."

Mother stiffens, examining me like I'm the latest inscription detailing her divine statue. "She's barren," Mother gasps.

"You will follow my lead. You will leave Satiah alone. She has enough to deal with, strapped to Thutmose. You will not make it worse for her. I will haunt you from the beyond if you do and see havoc wrought in the living world against you from whatever side of the veil I'm on."

After a long pause, Mother calms her face and nods. "As you wish, daughter. But really, this talk about dying is a bit dramatic. You're not the first woman to bring a child into the world."

And I wouldn't be the first to die doing it, I think. But I have the vow I asked for. I must hope she actually means it this time.

TWENTY-FOUR

I DREAM OF ISET. THE DREAMS ALWAYS INVOLVE SCORPIONS.

The first time it happens, I think it's real.

Iset's mother's bracelet, which I wear constantly, springs to life and strangles me. I wake screaming. Poor Benerib was scared out of her wits.

A week later, I wake to find Iset sitting on my bed. I drink her in with my eyes, my heart bursting with joy. A scorpion tattoo covers her neck. I gasp when I see it and she laughs, then takes my hand in hers.

"I've come to thank you," she whispers.

I sit up, pulling her to me and holding her close, my tears mingling with her braids. I realize as I release her that her amulets are now golden scorpions, squirming with life.

"I failed you," I sob, dropping my head onto her lap.

"You're my truest friend." She puts her hands on my head. "And you're going to do what I can no longer do."

I sit back up, and we're in front of my polished bronze mirror. She stands behind me, braiding my hair, a happy smile on her face as she hums softly to herself. "You have some now too," she giggles. I look closer and realize she's fastening wriggling golden scorpions in my braids. I toss my hair and the living amulets screech.

My eyes fly open, and I shoot up, sweat pouring down my body, now swollen beyond familiarity. I rub my round stomach, wondering if the child feels it too.

A few nights later, I dream of her again. This time, she stands by my bed. The venomous creature on her neck squirms in concert with the amulets in her hair as if their moves are choreographed.

"I miss you." The words escape before I can grant them permission.

She smiles, then lifts a hand to her braid, plucks out a scorpion, and places it on my forehead. She whispers a prayer I can't understand, and I feel the creature slink under my skin. It fills my body like the god has on rare occasions, animating me and bending me to its will until I'm more scorpion than woman.

I scream.

We're in front of my mirror before my cry dies. But when I look into the bronze, Senenmut's face stares back at me, a scorpion tattoo stained on his head just where Iset's pet entered me.

As my time draws close, Hesi-Ra caves to my request and orders me to keep to my bed and limit my visitors. I spend my hours sitting and waiting and studying.

Aside from Benerib, I see mostly Hathor. She visits when the moon is high and the palace is quiet. Some nights, Hathor and I talk for hours, debating a wide range of topics until the sun threatens to rise. Her visits leave me exhausted, physically and mentally. She seems old during these nights spent alone, her age on display when the privacy of the night surrounds us. And still, she challenges my mind much as the words of our wise men once did, although her wisdom is as different from that of the wise men as her power is from Mother's. In some ways, she reminds me of Thuiu. But Hathor is more irreverent and much more dismissive of traditional education and didactic literature than Thuiu ever was, although Hathor is nearly as learned. The wisewoman taught herself to read and write, if her claims are true. I can't imagine how one would accomplish such a feat. But I'm convinced it's true when she forces me to memorize more names and personal details and data about Kemet than Senenmut ever did. I'm happy to have a project to take my mind off the fears that plague me.

Senenmut's letters appear in the desk leg every few weeks. The latest letter brings a smile to my face, which is rare nowadays.

From the doctor, Khui, to the god's wife, king's eldest daughter, and my cherished dear one, Neferura, in life, prosperity, and health and in favor of Amun, king of gods. Your latest letter made this old man very happy. I'm pleased to report that the little one thrives. She's like a flower blooming in the sun. She fills my heart like a balm, and I'm reminded of the remarkable power little girls carry within—a strength I've been privileged to experience once before. Indeed, the child reminds me of that other young girl I've loved truly. I can tell already that little Neferu will be bright and curious and creative just like you. Once again, I vow to be the best caretaker I can be.

My only complaint is that my disloyal beast, Khufu, has forgotten I exist. He dedicates himself to the baby. He seems to believe it's his job to guard her. He watches her sleep. He sniffs the poor wet nurse again and again each day, confirming she's safe. The child seems to love him right back. She coos up at him, smiling. He responds by snuggling close and licking her. They adore each other.

My friendship, on the other hand, grows strained. My friend the priest grows cross with me. I can't focus on senet, and he finds the child an unwelcome distraction. In truth, it wouldn't matter if I could focus, for the man is a master game player and he's too rarely defeated. Thank the gods I'm well stocked with good wine—my bold reds keep him coming back in spite of the dog and the little girl and the bad game play.

I pray daily for you, wishing only to know that you heal like little Neferu does. I hope news of her improvement brings you some relief. I'll continue to report on her—or perhaps I should write "their"—adventures just as I'll continue to pray for you. I intend to keep sending missives to you, whether you reciprocate or not, for as long as I have the child at my side.

I have done it again! I dropped my pen, and my finger flew to my own head, tapping three times, after I wrote those words, as if to alert you that someone was dissembling. Me! For that is not true. I intend to keep working away at earning your forgiveness until the day I take my dying breath, child or no child.

Mother insists on joining me in my quarters for dinner once a week. Week after week, it's the most tedious hour. She's convinced herself the chill between us is due to the child growing inside me and that it'll magically dissipate once the babe is born.

I long for release. I want to be away from her, by any means necessary.

It's our third dinner together since the doctor sent me to bed, and finally, some strong emotion stirs me. It isn't Mother who triggers it though. It's our unexpected guest, Hathor.

She drifts in like mist and stands still, in all her glory, at the foot of my bed.

Mother leaps to her feet, sending her chair toppling over. "How did you get here?" she yelps.

Hathor smiles and rubs her arms as if my room is cold. "The same way I get anywhere. I came."

I smirk at her nonsensical utterance. I'm used to her appearing at my bedside unannounced. Mother, on the other hand, is not amused. Her head whips around, searching for a guard or a handmaid.

"We're alone," Hathor says, waving an inked hand around.

"Why?" Mother shrieks.

"Because no one else is with us."

I don't bother to hide the smile her sarcasm elicits.

Hathor smooths her face and sighs. "I come to inform you that the doctor, Khui, has died," she says softly. "He was found dead in the oasis. I learned of it only yesterday. I thought you'd want to know."

I suck in a ragged breath. My eyes are glued to Hathor. Time slows as she raises her right forefinger to her forehead and taps three times.

Senenmut's signal!

She's lying.

"I'm sorry," she utters.

Mother howls and I turn to her, wrapping my arms instinctively around her. To my surprise, she holds me too. In spite of my anger, it hurts to witness her pain. And it doesn't escape my notice that I'm doing to Mother exactly what she once did to me: allowing her to believe the man we've both loved is dead even though I know it isn't true. I'm surprised how easily I stomach it. Does that make me an awful person? Will my heart be made heavier? Or will the gods see justice in me giving Mother back exactly what she once gave to me? After all, how long am I expected to care for the emotions of those who've never shown a care for mine?

I don't bother to turn back to Hathor. I know she's gone.

I worry over my pending delivery, now mere weeks away. The fear is made more real when I invite my priestesses for a bedside visit. I may not get time alone with Satiah, but seeing the new queen should give me some sense of how she fares.

Turns out she's not faring so well. I can tell the women are shaken the moment they trail in, Satiah in the lead, and sit in the chairs Benerib has arranged by my bed.

"What's wrong?"

They exchange glances, uncharacteristically shy.

"Satiah?" She's a queen now. Her status outranks the others, so her responsibility does too.

"We've had bad news this morning," she begins. She takes a moment to gather herself, holding back tears. "It's Meri." She licks her lips, scared of telling me the bad news.

Her fear tells the story.

"She died in childbirth?"

Satiah nods, and poor Tasherit bursts into tears. Nebtah pats her leg, hushing her.

"And the child?" I ask.

"A boy," Satiah reports. "Alive but motherless."

My chest tightens at the news, the weight heavy as I rub my hand over my swollen stomach. Another child left behind by the mother who would have loved him. I think of poor Meri, of what she wanted for her son. I think of little Neferu and the dreams Iset had for her. I think of Satiah, who was abandoned as a babe, left to fend for herself far too soon. So many motherless children. The idea of my child ending up as one more babe raised without its mother sears me. I push the thought away. Fear will not serve me well now.

"Her heart will be light," Hui wails, red eyes on me. "Won't it, Adoratrice? You don't think Ammit will...will?"

"The Devourer will not take Meri's heart," I promise. "Meri had her struggles, to be sure. Perhaps in Aaru, she'll finally find the peace that always eluded her here."

The women share stories about Meri and, eventually, some of her more colorful priestess friends. Benerib offers honey cakes and spiced wine, luring my troupe leaders away from the bed long enough to buy me a moment alone with Satiah and Nebtah.

"You're all right?" I ask them.

Nebtah grunts and Satiah nods. "I've wanted to visit. I couldn't find an excuse, and the situation has not yet turned desperate enough to force it."

"Do you have anything to report?"

She shakes her head. "Only that Thutmose has been in a good mood. I've never heard a single whisper about Iset or her child. Or poor Maia. I'm afraid my usefulness has—"

"We've discussed this, Satiah. You are useful to me and, more importantly, to Kemet. That will last. Have faith."

She frowns, but Nebtah leans closer. "We are here for you,

Adoratrice. Our loyalty is unshaken. We're heartbroken over Iset, but we will not be cowed. Our spines are as stiff as a djed pillar."

"I've never doubted you," I say just as the others return.

There are more tears, additional updates, and soft consoling words. Finally, Benerib sees them out and turns to me, face tight with worry.

"Is it Meri?" I ask, wondering what's bothering her.

She sinks into the chair Satiah occupied moments ago. "Yes and no," she says cryptically. She scoots the chair closer, eyes narrowed in thought. "I'm sorry to hear about Meri. Childbirth is…" Her eyes fly to mine, and she shakes her head. "You'll be fine, Adoratrice. You're strong. I survived the ordeal three times." She grins but there's sadness in it—of Benerib's children, only one still lives. "But I was thinking about Hathor. Why didn't she come to inform you? She could have at least sent word."

I consider her words. She's right. Hathor has been diligent about keeping me informed of Meri's health. I would have expected her to update me immediately. Still, the wisewoman's ways are mysterious even now. "Perhaps she was too tired? Or had some other calling that kept her from coming?"

"Perhaps. Or perhaps I'm being paranoid," she sighs. "Your time draws close. I can't help but worry. I'm a silly old goose."

I grab her hand and pull her closer. "You're no goose. And you're rarely silly," I say with a smile. "Thuiu was right to send you, Benerib. She knew what I needed even when I did not. You've been an unexpected blessing, a true friend when I needed one. I will miss—"

"Stop." Tears spring to her eyes. She examines my face, then pulls me close.

The bitter taste of fear stings my throat as I squeeze her tight.

The morning after I learn Meri died in childbirth, pain floors me. It's like a lightning bolt going off inside my body. Thank the goddess Benerib is here, cooing in my ear, telling me she too felt this pain, hours before giving birth.

"The baby is coming," I grunt. Terror ripples through me. "It's early." I lean so heavily on Benerib I nearly topple the poor old woman.

"Hathor is close. I'll summon Hesi-Ra too." She helps me waddle to my newly constructed birthing pavilion, situated next to my pool. Vines crawl across the roof for shade, and the plaster walls depict images of nursing mothers and the traditional hair-dressing scene. The images of successful delivery are designed to help me bring the child into the world safely. Just last week, Hathor drew a protective circle with her curved ivory wand, promising I'll be protected.

The pain recedes and I breathe in the scents of mint and eucalyptus, another concoction Hathor delivered. Benerib rushes out, promising to send word to the wisewoman. Hathor will be here soon. She'll drape my body in amulets—frogs, locusts, monkeys, and cowrie shells—as she chants to Hathor, Mut, Isis, and Taweret. I cling to the knowledge that she's coming and that she understands my wishes.

Before the pain strikes again, Benerib is back. She sits by my side, voice soft and encouraging. She tells me about the birth of her first child, the fear followed by joy. I hear my door fly open, footsteps on the floor, then Hesi-Ra rushes out from my open wall.

"Let me see you."

I toss the blanket aside, prepared for inspection. I meet his eyes just as the crippling pain returns. It's so intense I'm certain I'm about to breathe my last breath.

"Don't worry, Adoratrice." He runs his hands over my bulging stomach. He can't hide the fear in his eyes. I'm not sure if he's scared of losing me or the future heir, but his hands, usually so steady, tremble against my thighs.

I lean my head back and close my eyes. My body contracts with pain, surging through me to the tips of my fingers and toes.

"Just breathe," the doctor says.

I try to suck in a breath, but it's as if my lungs have stopped working. Blood is everywhere, the smell and taste of it surrounding me.

"You must breathe, Neferura." He sounds desperate now.

I manage short, shallow breaths, but I can't escape the pain. I look down and watch the blood flowing from my birthing bed onto the deck. And suddenly, I don't feel it. I don't feel anything at all. It's as if I'm in a dream, watching my own body from above.

The pain recedes.

The space grows dim.

Hesi-Ra's voice fades away.

And as the world grows hazy, I know, as surely as I know the maxims of my favorite wise men, that the god's wife of Amun, great royal wife, king's eldest daughter, lady of Upper and Lower Kemet, mistress of the Two Lands, will not survive the night.

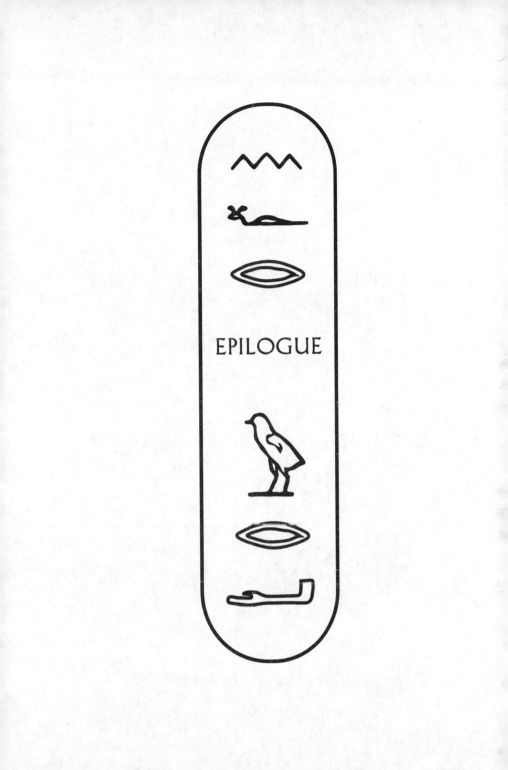

EPILOGUE

L IES. SECRETS. SCHEMES. DECEPTION.

These are the wares of my trade, the currency of my nest. Perhaps that's why the cottage appeals to me. To the untrained eye, it's another charming home in Per-Bast. But the abode deceives, and the illusion of dullness it spins draws me in. For those uninitiated in espionage, the home offers a lovely view of Iteru's green waters snaking past. But I see the curve of the river, bending around the property, hiding the visitors who jump on and off quiet boats floating close to the riverbank from prying eyes. Others may appreciate its panoramic view, but I value the outlook it creates, a vista that invites the viewer to spot enemies coming from the north or south. Some may find the cottage cozy, the way it hugs the low cliff, practically embedded in the stubby crag. I see the protection its position offers, the narrowed danger zone that is easily observed by scorpions hiding in the trees that surround the small home, shading it from the raging sun.

Of course, that also means they know I'm coming.

I huff up the hill, listening close. I want to hear the oars of the boat that just dropped me off splash in and out of the water. But my hearing, once exceptional, has faded. I hear only my heavy breath and the too-loud crunch of my sandals on rocks, joined, as I near the house, by the sounds of a babbling child.

I turn the corner and see the old man holding a cup of wine out to greet me. A baby sleeps in his other arm and a dog slumbers at his feet. The toddler who rests her head on the dog's back, staring up at the sky, stops gibbering when she realizes she and her grandfather are no longer alone.

"For you." The old man lifts the wine higher, smiling so wide wrinkles branch out from his eyes to touch his temples.

I take the wine—it will be earthy and rich and very welcome—and sit in the empty chair next to him. "You're getting predictable in your old age, Ameny."

It's not his name. He adopted the name, his third that I know of, to honor his childhood friend, murdered by Thutmose's men after Kamut's betrayal became known. Like Iset, Ameny stayed quiet. And like Iset, he died for it.

"Predictable isn't so bad," he claims. "I like being dependable. I suspect you secretly like that about me too. We can't all be moody and mysterious."

I offer him one of my most studied grins—the one that says I'm amused by him but not too amused. He ignores me, and Iset's daughter returns to her nonsensical gabbing, convinced by his demeanor that she's safe.

"Do you bring news?" he asks, changing the subject.

I huff—he could let me rest before asking. Still, the wine is worth rewarding. So I hand him the pouch.

He opens it to thumb through the collection of amulets. The ankhs and djed pillars and scarabs hide messages of noteworthy feuds and shifting alliances and the needs and surpluses of Kemet's various regions. The amulets were Nebtah's idea. Inspired by the sistrum Neferura once designed to sneak messages to Kamut, Nebtah, now in charge of all scorpion communication channels, devised them to pop open with the right combination of pushing and pulling. The hidden messages keep the new mistress of secrets well informed.

"The child?" He places an ankh amulet back in the bag and sets it on the ground.

"Little Amenemhat is fine," I say. "The queen adores the boy. You'd think the new heir of Kemet was Satiah's own child rather than a boy orphaned when his mother died in childbirth."

Ameny shrugs. "Orphans love orphans."

"Satiah loves orphans," I retort.

"Because she was an orphan. Until you gave her a family. It's no surprise she's taken to the babe." He releases a dramatic sigh and kicks his feet up onto a nearby log. "Rather incredible how things worked out, isn't it?"

I turn to him, alerted by the undertone of his voice. He avoids my gaze.

"Do you have something to say, Senenmut?"

"Ameny," he reminds me as he refills my cup. "Just musing on the mysteries of life, like how Meri died so conveniently just when you needed a newborn boy with no family."

"I'd never murder a new mother under my care, if that's what you're suggesting." I make an effort to look offended. I'm not, of course. I've done worse than allow a mother to die in childbirth to save the country. Although in this case, I did nothing. Well, not exactly nothing. I didn't stand idly by and let Meri die—I couldn't have saved her if I'd wanted to. But I did speed up Neferura's delivery. How was I to pawn Meri's son off as the child of Thutmose and Neferura, the grandson of the great Hatshepsut, if he was weeks old when I presented him? No, that would not have done at all. The goddess gifted me a boy child right when he was needed—Hathor provides, and as her servant, I act. And this boy wasn't just any babe.

He was a babe the new queen would be desperate to care for, close as she was to the child's poor mother. So I snuck into Neferura's rooms, bloody and exhausted after Meri's death, without waking Neferura or Benerib and called on Heka, god of magic, to aid me as I performed the spells I knew would trigger Neferura's labor. I didn't expect the early labor to pose a risk to the queen. Poor Hesi-Ra was in over his head when I arrived.

My eyes fall to the girl sleeping soundly in her grandfather's arms.

"Of course you wouldn't," he grunts. "And what of Thutmose? Is he still enamored of his son and new queen?"

"Pharaoh finally has everything he ever wanted." I pause, swirling the mention of Hatshepsut's death, mere weeks after she was informed that her daughter died bringing a son and heir into the world, around my mouth before I speak. I'm not known for restraint, so I ask how he's handling the loss.

"I loved her once." He gazes out at the river.

"All of Kemet loved her once. She was a remarkable woman."

"Yes, and it cost her. She lost herself to the struggle to be so remarkable." He sighs. It's heavy. "Perhaps I did as well, for a time. You may not believe this, but I find that I finally have everything I want now too. I'm at peace."

"Truly?" I find that hard to believe. I feel my eyebrow shift up as I turn my chair to face him. "You're not bored playing grandfather?"

"Never," he says. "And on the rare occasion I get a bit antsy, there's always another amulet to keep me busy. I'm happier here than I ever was in the palace. And I dare say she is too."

I search the trees for signs of scorpions, proud that I can't see them. I taught them well. "Where is she?" I ask.

Neferura is usually the first to greet me, although she now goes by the name Amunet. Fitting that the former god's wife of Amun would take the female aspect of the god as her alias, a name that literally means "the hidden one." Her long list of titles has been replaced by a singular label, created and bestowed by me: mistress of secrets.

"She'll be along shortly. She doesn't leave the babies for long."

I reach out and take the baby from his arms. I run my hands over her small body. I listen to her breath and feel her heft. She's as healthy as a child could be. A remarkable achievement, given all she's been through in her short life.

I think back to the day Neferura asked me to help her fake her own death and the death of her child so she could escape Thutmose and the viper's nest of a palace. The request came as no surprise—I'd considered offering my services to do just that. But her second request did surprise. She wanted my job. She argued that her position and experience made her the logical successor to my nest. She all but said I'm too old to go on as I have been. She said it was past time for me to pass on what I've built. She wasn't wrong. But releasing my power has been painful at times. At other times, it's surprisingly pleasant.

The baby cries, and I hold her closer, replaying the arguments I had with her mother in my mind. I was the one who insisted on substituting Neferura's child, boy or girl, with a male infant, though at the time, I wasn't certain where I'd find him. Still, I knew the country would release Neferura more easily with an heir in the arms of their beautiful new queen—an heir Satiah could never give Kemet. Thankfully the goddess provided the perfect child at the perfect time. And still, Neferura argued. She only agreed to pass Meri's son off as her own after I convinced her the boy's life would be even worse outside the palace than inside, where at least he'd be fed and cared for.

Senenmut clears his throat, bringing me back to the moment. "What about you?"

"What about me?" I ask.

He rests his fingers on my tattooed arm. "Don't you deserve some peace? Have you considered settling down? You're supposed to be retired. Amunet can handle your web of spies. She has Nebtah and Benerib. She even has the queen of Kemet when she needs Satiah's help. And there are plenty of other women who can travel from one end of the country to the other as couriers. The job is a bit pedestrian for the great tattooed wisewoman, no? Perhaps it's time you stayed still."

His hand is warm against my skin. I narrow my eyes on him. "Are you flirting with me? We're a bit old for all that, no?"

His grin is tempting. Senenmut always was an attractive man, in mind and body.

"Perhaps I am flirting. A little. As for our age, the great mysterious wisewoman doesn't age, or haven't you heard? She's magical like that. I'm quite sure, however, she could do with a little companionship, especially companionship that offers a remarkable view and the best wine in Kemet."

"And babies," I remind him.

He laughs. "Yes, and babies. But really, my dear Hathor, who better to help raise two young women than the woman who's rescued girls from Abu to Sai and everywhere in between? You should think about it."

"Should I?" I look down at Iteru, wide and slow here, its green waters shimmering under a sun so bright it would burn but for the shade of the cottage and its lush foliage and trees.

Perhaps Senenmut is right. Maybe I should stay still for a while. I can always make a different choice later. But even I won't live forever. And the one thing I haven't yet experienced in my long life is a real home. I can't remember a time when I wasn't wandering. My mother was a wanderer—a habit that killed her young. When she died, I just kept going, gathering other young women to me. At first, it was instinct. Later, I became more intentional, manifesting pathways and resources for the girl I had once been. I dedicated my life to creating options for girls like me—options I wanted but never had. Hasn't that earned me a few years of home and family and tranquility before I die?

Laughter startles me. I look up to find my favorite pupil, hugging one daughter while her scarred but handsome husband lifts the other high.

"You're back." The mistress of secrets beams down at me. "Will you stay a while this time?"

I meet Neferura's eyes, then glance at Kamut and finally turn to Senenmut. "Perhaps I will," I say, unsure. "Perhaps."

Sometimes, it seems, the choices of the tattooed wisewoman are unknown and unknowable even to me.

AUTHOR'S NOTE

While this is a work of fiction, many of the people, artifacts, and beliefs represented here reflect the true history of ancient Egypt.

The pharaoh Hatshepsut ruled ancient Egypt during the New Kingdom's Eighteenth Dynasty. Her rule started in the late fifteenth century BC and lasted more than twenty years. It is widely regarded as a period of peace and prosperity, celebrated for its impressive building programs and heralded for its advancements in international trade. While Hatshepsut was not the only woman to rule Egypt, her reign was the longest of the female rulers and was, by all accounts, remarkably successful.

Hatshepsut's mortuary temple, Djeser-Djesru and its surrounding complex, is a popular tourist attraction today, and for good reason. The depictions of her trade expedition to Punt alone are worth the long flight. In addition, she left twin obelisks at the nearby temple at Karnak, one of which still stands and is the tallest ancient obelisk in the world. Another obelisk of Hatshepsut's is in place in its quarrying site in Aswan, known as the Broken Obelisk, to name just a few of the building projects she's left behind for history to enjoy. But although the monuments referenced in this story are real, they are referenced without consideration to building dates, as the timeline in this story is unfixed.

As noted in the story, Hatshepsut was often depicted as a man with a king's bare torso and false beard. Although this strikes modern observers as odd, it's less so when one realizes that pharaohs are the personification of a male god, Horus, on earth and that ancient Egyptians, pharaohs included, were generally idealized. Our modern notions of portraiture and individuality would surprise ancient Egyptians.

We know nothing of Hatshepsut as a woman or as a mother, but princess Neferura seems to have been her only child. Neferura had the rare distinction of being the child of two pharaohs: her father and her mother. Her father, Thutmose II, died when she was still quite young, although her exact age is unknown. Officially, her mother served as co-ruler with Neferura's younger half brother, Thutmose III. Hatshepsut's rise to power is often linked to the rich and prestigious religious role she held, the god's wife of Amun, a position she passed to her daughter. This is one of the ways Neferura stepped into the role traditionally played by a queen: as a woman, Hatshepsut had no queen, so her daughter was elevated accordingly.

The title of god's wife was used in earlier periods, and with different gods, but the Theban-based office of the god's wife of Amun grew in wealth and power at the beginning of the Eighteenth Dynasty with the dynasty's first queen, Ahmose-Nefertari. The increased status of the role may have been designed to shift power from the local priesthood of Amun to the royal family, which was extending its control at the time, on the heels of national unrest and the expulsion of the Hyksos, foreign rulers who had temporary control over some areas of the country. Some queens, including Ahmose-Nefertari and Hatshepsut, privileged the title even over that of great royal wife, which is to say queen, underlying the title's prestige.

It's clear that the title included both political and financial clout, but the daily routine of the god's wife of Amun is not well understood, and my depiction of Neferura and her troupe is speculative. Similarly, celibacy, which may have played a role with gods' wives in later periods, was not part of the tradition at this period. The title likely did involve some kind of ritual, sexual stimulation of the god. Indeed, the related title, god's hand, is a not-so-subtle reference to masturbation, an act linked to the creation of the world in some ancient Egyptian creation myths. We get a glimpse of Neferura in her ritual role in her mother's Chapelle Rouge bark shrine at Karnak, where the princess is shown in a ritual that seems to involve castigating enemies. The god's wife is depicted elsewhere participating in cult liturgies, being purified in the sacred lake of Karnak, participating in procession, accompanying priests inside the most sacred areas of the temple, and presenting food to the god, who she entertains with her sistrum. After Neferura, the title was stripped of wealth and power, perhaps as a protection against future royal women using it to launch themselves further, as Hatshepsut seems to have done. But although the title lost some authority, it remained in use for royal woman for generations to come.

In addition to her god's wife title, Neferura held other titles, including the lady of Upper and Lower Egypt, mistress of the Two Lands, king's eldest daughter (princess), and god's hand. The title of great royal wife (queen) is not attested for Neferura, but interestingly, Neferura's name does appear inside a cartouche, an unusual honor for a princess.

Beyond her titles, virtually nothing of Neferura's life is known to modern scholars. We don't know when she was born, how long she lived, if she married or had children, or how and when she died. We have no idea how she felt about her mother or half brother, or, for that matter, the nobles and servants and priests that surrounded her. Still, the fictional account here is built on a few scholarly theories, such as the theory, proposed by Peter Doman, that she married Thutmose III and bore his first son, Amenemhat.

Neferura is also, despite her near invisibility, uniquely featured in an unusual series of statues. Her royal tutor, Senenmut, had figures of the two of them carved and erected throughout the country. The statues are unusually, and charmingly, intimate: Neferura, always a child, sits on Senenmut's lap, pokes her head out of his cloak, or basks in his embrace. These should be understood, in part, as propaganda pieces designed to advertise his prestige and high position in the court. Senenmut was of humble birth but ascended to be one of the most powerful men in the country. Showing off his close relationship with the royal family would have been an excellent way to herald his clout. The statues of Senenmut and Neferura may, of course, also reflect genuine affection, as depicted here.

The idea that Senenmut may have been Hatshepsut's lover is suggested, some scholars argue, by graffiti found near Hatshepsut's mortuary complex, which appears to depict a pharaoh being penetrated from behind by an unnamed man. Senenmut's name and image were also included behind a door at Djeser-Djeseru, an unusual token of royal affection if the artwork was indeed approved by the pharaoh. He was shown as a bachelor in his own parents' tomb, suggesting that if he made a match, the match was not officially recognized, as one would expect of the consort of a female ruler. Mysteriously, Senenmut's Theban tomb, which contains the earliest known star map of Egypt, was unfinished, as was his nearby mortuary chapel. Although none of this is clear-cut evidence that he was Hatshepsut's lover, or that he was unceremoniously cast out of the court, as represented here, it is atypical enough to invite speculation.

Like Senenmut's, Neferura's death is a mystery. The last date definitively associated with her is year 11, which means she was certainly alive in Hatshepsut's eleventh year on the throne. Neferura was depicted on her mother's funerary temple, leading some scholars to believe she was alive at the time of Hatshepsut's death. A tomb some scholars associate with Neferura was discovered in the Valley of the Monkeys, sandwiched between the Valley of the Kings and Queens, near a rock-cut tomb excavated for her mother when she was still queen. The archaeologists who investigated this tomb believed that she died before her mother. Other scholars have argued that she outlived Hatshepsut and may have been the mother of Thutmose III's first son. The tradition of brother-sister marriages between members of the royal family was well established by Hatshepsut's reign, and one would expect Neferura and Thutmose III to be paired per the custom of the day. Thutmose III's first son, the prince in question, Amenemhat, appears rarely in historical records and certainly died before his father, who left the throne to Amenhotep II, one of Thutmose III's other sons. If Hatshepsut truly did want Neferura or her child on the throne, ultimately, her wish was not granted.

Although this story does not address the mystery, it's worth noting that late in Thutmose III's reign, a widespread effort to erase Hatshepsut from memory was carried out. This *damnatio memoriae* included tearing down and smashing her statues, chiseling her name and image off walls, and even walling up her obelisks at Karnak. Some scholars believe Amenhotep II, the son of Thutmose III who became coregent late in his reign, carried out this program, perhaps because his own royal lineage was not closely linked to Hatshepsut. But such an effort is so rare, one cannot ignore her sex when we interpret it. Indeed, an earlier generation of scholars assumed Thutmose III tried to erase her out of resentment, believing she usurped his throne. But it's become clear that the erasures occurred more than twenty years after her death, and it's difficult to understand why, if it was some kind of emotional outburst, Thutmose III would have waited so long to carry it out.

The supporting cast in this story is made up of attested and fictional characters. Queen Ahmose was Hatshepsut's mother. There truly was a noblewoman nicknamed Thuiu—her real name was Ahhotep. Her husband, Ineni, was a renowned architect who did indeed brag about his extensive gardens in his tomb. Ineni's tomb was also one of the few places Hatshepsut's image was not erased, perhaps out of respect for a man who had served such a long string of pharaohs. Hatshepsut did have a Nubian general named Nehsi. He was depicted in the Punt reliefs at her temple in Deir el-Bahri, as was Senenmut, and is credited with leading the expedition. Ahmose Pen-Nekhebet was a nobleman whose autobiography sheds light on the history of the period. He lived through many reigns and claimed to be one of Neferura's tutors. He may have been the father, or at least a close relative, of Satiah, who was Thutmose III's queen. She bore the titles of king's wife, great king's wife, and god's wife. Amenemhat may have been her child, but that is speculation and no children are securely attested for Satiah, who died during Thutmose's reign. Other characters—including Kamut, Iset, Nebtah, Teena, Benerib, and Hathor—are fictional, although Hathor's character was influenced by the recent discovery of heavily tattooed, mummified woman from Deir el-Medina believed to be a magician and holy woman. Her many tattoos link her to the goddess Hathor. The role of tattoos in ancient Egypt is a fascinating topic. Our understanding of what tattoos meant to the ancient Egyptians, especially women, who bore them has evolved from a belief, common among earlier scholars, that women with tattoos were low-class prostitutes to more recent, nuanced beliefs that tattoos might be linked to religious roles, fertility practices, inscriptions of power or protection, or something else entirely.

A word about words: the ancient Egyptian language doesn't map neatly to English. Selecting the right words—words that would be faithful to the period but meaningful to a modern audience—was a challenge. For place-names, I chose terms that would be familiar to an ancient Egyptian, although probably, by and large, not to modern readers. The Nile, for example, evokes ideas of Egypt, ancient and modern. But it is not a term the ancient Egyptians would recognize. They referred to the Nile simply as the river, Iteru. But although I often chose ancient words, there are times where I opted for words more familiar for my readers. Pharaoh is a key example. The word stems from *per-aa*, great house, used a bit like we use White House today and eventually used as a synonym for king. It was not, however, used in this period. Similarly, I chose Adoratrice as a term of address for Neferura even though she did not carry the title of divine adoratrice. The title, associated with the god's wife, appears later. And yet the god's wife estate, the *per hemet-netjer*, literally translated as "the House of the God's Wife," was sometimes collo-quially referred to as the *per duat*, "the House of the Adoratrice," even in some early Eighteenth Dynasty documents.

Finally, many of the small details such as Hatshepsut's skin condition, the pregnancy test, the food, the religious practices and beliefs, and the quoted texts are based on historical evidence and primary source documents. Other details, such as the way letters are addressed, are simplified with a nod to authentic practices. And some details, such as the description of the palace or the priestess gowns, for example, are educated guesses. In all cases, I've worked to represent the people and culture of the period as authentically as I'm able. It is my hope that the spirit of ancient Egypt imbues the pages of this fictional tale of court intrigue, friendship, abuse, and the universal trials and realities women have faced throughout history.

READING
GROUP GUIDE

1. At the beginning of the story, Neferura learns that her half brother, Thutmose, is returning to court. What happened between Neferura and Thutmose to make her wary of his return? Then, discuss the political reasons for why Hatshepsut and Neferura don't want Thutmose back.

2. Neferura holds many responsibilities as the daughter of a pharaoh. What specific roles does she play within her society, and how do they give her power? Did you learn anything about women's roles in ancient Egypt while reading?

3. Neferura has a tumultuous relationship with her mother, Hatshepsut. Discuss their mother-daughter dynamic and some events that showcase their relationship. How did this relationship make you feel?

4. What reasons does Thutmose give for his return to Kemet, and how does this affect Neferura? Do you think his reasons were justified?

5. Neferura learns of an old wisewoman and her network of spies while she is digging for information on Thutmose. Who is Hathor, and how does she wield power throughout Kemet? Then, discuss how her relationship with Neferura evolves throughout the story.

6. When Thutmose learns the truth of how his father was killed, he doesn't hesitate to use this knowledge to his advantage. What ultimatum does Thutmose give Hatshepsut, and what is her reaction? How are Neferura, Senenmut, and the people of Kemet affected by the decision these two pharaohs make?

7. How does Neferura's character evolve throughout the story? Do you think she changed by the end of the novel? Why or why not?

8. An important lesson that Neferura learns is that there is more than one way for a woman to hold power. Who does she learn this lesson from, and what does it mean? Then, compare the ways in which the women of the novel (Neferura, Hathor, Hatshepsut, Iset, and Satiah) all hold different forms of power and how they might choose to wield it.

9. Near the end of the story, a terrible event takes place. What happened to Iset, and what did Thutmose have to do with it? How would you have felt if you were in Neferura's position?

10. Thutmose is the main antagonist of the novel, but his character is quite complex. What were your feelings toward Thutmose? Do you think the events of the story were entirely his fault? If not, who might have also been a villain? Why?

11. Compare and contrast Neferura's and Satiah's views on bodily autonomy and sexuality. How do these views lead them to the decisions they make in the end, and how did these actions make you feel?

12. After Iset's death, Neferura realizes that she cannot stay at court. Describe the plan that she makes with Hathor and Satiah. Were you surprised by this ending? Do you think Neferura had any other options?

13. Discuss the epilogue. Where do each of the characters end up after the final events of the story? Did you find this ending to be satisfying?

14. *Neferura* is a historical novel inspired by real people who ruled in ancient Egypt. Were you familiar with any of these historical figures, practices, or places? How did you like reading a retelling from this part of history?

A CONVERSATION
WITH THE AUTHOR

You hold a PhD in Egyptology. How did your academic background help you in writing this novel?

I couldn't have written this book, at least not in the way I did, if I hadn't spent so many years in academia studying the language and artifacts, traditions and beliefs, of ancient Egypt. As a historian by training who's learning how to write fiction, the knowledge those years embedded in my brain freed me up to focus on the fictional aspects of the story. And I needed that. My early drafts read a bit like a dissertation—not a lot of fun to read. Finding a balance between history and storytelling didn't come easily, but having a background in the history of the period helped me imagine the building blocks of the story. The setting, conflicts, characters, plot points, and even the themes my tale explores were influenced and animated by my understanding of the ancient world and the Eighteenth Dynasty in particular.

Why Neferura? What about her life inspired you to write a story about her?

Even for one looking to write a novel about a formidable ancient Egyptian woman, Neferura is not the most obvious choice, in part because so little is known of her life and in part because she's overshadowed by so many other fascinating women, including a number of intriguing women from the same dynasty. And still, she called to me for years before I tried putting pen to paper. Her mother, Hatshepsut, would have been seen as remarkable even in her own time. Queen regents were common enough, but Hatshepsut set herself apart when she chose to declare herself pharaoh. And she dragged her daughter along for the ride. It doesn't take much imagination to envision the daughter of such a woman having mixed feelings about, or a fraught relationship with, her inimitable mother. And while I suspect some may not appreciate my unflattering depiction of Hatshepsut, it's worth remembering that much of what we believe about the rulers of ancient Egypt is the result of what was, in their own time, pure propaganda. It's not terribly difficult to envision the powerful ruler of an authoritarian country in narcissistic terms, even if such a depiction may make her modern-day fans, including me, a bit uncomfortable. And while there's certainly no reason to suspect Neferura would have been opposed to her mother or the propaganda she perpetuated—Neferura benefited from it, after all—it's more interesting to imagine what it might have been like if she were aware of, and at times even at odds with, the privilege she was born to and the hype that surround her. Did she see her mother's claim to divine parentage as disinformation, or did she believe it was true? Surely plenty of accomplished people today have children who aren't as impressed with them as the outside world is. Could that have been true then as well? How would the belief that her family was anointed by the gods color her relationships with others? Would she have given any thought to the fact that, in a world where many women were free to choose their own partners, her choice of romantic partners was dictated by her position? What might she have made of the irony that in some ways she was disempowered by the very power she alone inherited? These questions and others made Neferura an appealing protagonist. And although her story eventually took me to very different places than I first imagined it would, I enjoyed the ride, and I like to think she did too. After all, ancient Egyptians believed they were made stronger in the afterworld when their names were spoken. It pleases me to imagine that somewhere, somehow, Neferura revels in a bit of extra strength every time I type her name.

Historical fiction is always a fine line between fact and fiction. How did you achieve this balance? What are some events in the story that are more fiction than fact?

Emotions and relationships are the heart of all stories, and everything about the relationships in this story is pure fiction. To my mind, the most important relationship in the story is the friendship between Neferura and Iset. I knew from the beginning that I wanted to write a story about love. Not about romance but about the kind of love close girlfriends share. So Iset was a key character from the beginning. And everything from her position to the way she addresses Neferura to her duties is pure speculation.

This, of course, is the kind of fabrication any reader of historical fiction expects. But when I first imagined what this story would be like, I faced a more fundamental clash of fact versus fiction— the tension between the most authentic presentation of the past I could muster and speaking as clearly as possible to the audience I was writing for. It was the brain that plagued me early on. Not the brain as we know it, but the brain as they understood it and the many implications their understanding has for the language I share with my audience. Ancient Egyptians imagined the heart as the locus of feeling and thinking. We, on the other hand, see thought (brain) and feeling (heart) as separate, which creates a kind of dichotomy between emotion and knowledge that's enshrined in our language in countless ways. Thus we say one follows their heart or their brain. The English language is littered with references that would confound ancient Egyptians, who would never have "run over a thought in their mind," or "racked their brain for an answer," or "focused their mind on a problem." At first, I wanted to acknowledge this difference for readers. But if the English language can be adapted to convey that difference in a way that isn't downright clunky, I'm not the writer to manage that hefty task. There came a day that I had to choose—true to thought categories of the past or understandable for today's readers. That day, dear readers, I chose you. (Although, as a nod to this conundrum, I left in a scene where Senenmut taps his chest as he speaks about knowledge and wisdom, a subtle reference to the conflict that appeased me, even though it may be invisible to most readers.)

You retell a piece of ancient history through a feminist perspective. Why do you think this new lens is important?

Hatshepsut has long been a darling of women's history. For those looking for powerful women in our past, she's an excellent example. And of course, intriguing details such as her gender-bending depictions, peaceful reign, and powerful religious position only invite more interest and speculation. Here, I wanted to speak from a woman's perspective, widening the lens to tell the story of three powerful historical actors who ring out across the millennia as unique—Neferura, of course, but also her mother who ruled and her tutor who seemingly used his relationship with the two of them to boost his own status.

I also wanted to explore what it meant to *be* a woman in this specific time and place by depicting some of the rights, limitations, assumptions, practices, and challenges they faced, some of which resonate still today while others are idiosyncratic and unfamiliar. Contrasting the kind of hard power Hatshepsut, and to a lesser degree Neferura, would have certainly wielded with examples of softer power, like that employed by Hathor and Iset, was a way to explore the invisible ways women impact the world they live in. This kind of influence is particularly hard for historians to capture, in part due to the nature of soft power and also because of the dearth of evidence scholars have to work with. Unlike royals and patricians, ancient Egyptian commoners didn't leave a lot behind to tell us about their lives, and women left less evidence behind for Egyptologists to study than men, in part because they were less likely to be literate. This contrast also depicts a truth I suspect is rather universal: it's easier to achieve a thing if you see others who share the attributes you were born with, such as gender, managing it first. In my story, Neferura can't envision a different way to be powerful in the world until Iset and Hathor model the path. She makes it her own, but the influence of these women, neither of whom were born to power like Neferura herself, showed her—and I dare hope reminds some of us—that we can all make a difference in the world around us and be a positive influence for those who come after us.

What do you hope readers get from your novel?

As a historian, it sometimes frustrates me that history is too often framed as progressive. American history, for example, is often depicted as a straightforward march toward a more inclusive nation, which ignores all the times people won, and then lost, rights. Of course I want to give readers a glimpse into what life was like in this ancient African civilization and highlight some of the ancient discoveries that influence our life today, not least of which is the alphabet I'm using to write these words. To my mind, ancient Egypt doesn't get the credit it deserves when it comes to understanding the roots of our modern world. But I also hope this view into what life was like thousands of years ago reminds readers that humans have gained and lost personal freedoms again and again throughout history. Women in the Eighteenth Dynasty, for example, wielded more legal authority and autonomy than many women in early American history. (One might argue that in some ways, they had more bodily autonomy than some American women do as I write this.) The social issues we grapple with today are often assumed to be inherently modern somehow. But many of these issues have been faced by humans for millennia. The battles we fight, or ignore, today have already been won, and lost, by those who went before us and can be won, or lost, again now and in the future.

What is your writing process like? Are there any ways you like to get creative inspiration?

I'm a busy single mom, so my writing process is mostly about sneaking in writing hours where I can. I've become adept at writing in short bursts, although I prefer four- or five-hour, uninterrupted windows. For years now, I've woken early on weekend mornings to write while the house is still quiet. And when I need inspiration, dog walks help. Also working with my hands while my mind is free to roam, crocheting or needlepointing, for example, often helps me think through problems. When these tricks don't work, a sleepless night mulling over my protagonist's challenges usually does the trick. It's not the most relaxing way to move forward, but there is a certain kind of pleasure found in going to bed with a problem and waking up with a solution.

What are you reading these days?

Predictably, I love historical fiction, especially stories set in the ancient world. Two recent favorites have been *Kaikeyi* by Vaishnavi Patel and *Clytemnestra* by Costanza Casati. Natalie Haynes's *Stone Blind* is next up in my to-be-read pile. I adored her other books so I have high expectations. I also absolutely love young adult novels. Amanda Joy's *A River of Royal Blood* and its sequel are recent favorites, and I can't wait for Rosaria Munda's *Gods and Gamemasters*, a YA retelling of the Trojan War. I've also been revisiting some classics, especially recently banned old favorites. I've enjoyed rereading Toni Morrison's *The Bluest Eye* and Laurie Halse Anderson's *Speak*. I'm reminded of why I loved them both so much the first time I read them. And to my delight, I've discovered some books I didn't know existed. I've never spent much time with graphic novels, so I hadn't run across *Maus* by Art Spiegelman. But I'm glad I found it—it's a powerful tale and well worth a read.

ACKNOWLEDGMENTS

Sometimes an author's path is as topsy-turvy as her protagonist's. Looking back, the long list of people I should thank for contributing to this book begins in the early '90s. I was graduating from college and hoping to embark on some kind of career. I'd learned plenty as an undergrad, but college didn't teach me how to find a job. Not sure which way to turn, I braved a phone call to a professional woman I respected but barely knew. She didn't hesitate a beat. She took me to lunch, drew out plans, and helped me land my first job at a local radio station.

Before long, that first job rewarded my hard work with a real client. And in our initial meeting, the new client I was so desperate to impress ran his hand up my thigh. I ran back to the office in tears only to have an older colleague drag me into the boss's office where she explained to the general manager exactly how the situation would be managed to my benefit—a plan he didn't dare disagree with.

And so it began.

Again and again throughout my life, when I've been lost or stuck or scared or alone, a woman has appeared by my side, lifting me up and helping me navigate obstacles, march forward, and problem solve. These women inspired me and my story. As I began to imagine what Neferura's life might have been like, how it might have felt to be the only daughter of a woman so remarkable and the custodian of such an esteemed religious role, I wondered where an ancient Egyptian princess might turn for help. What if the powerful characters around her didn't understand her fears and ambitions? What if, instead, she had access to a network of women as fierce and determined as the diverse women who have supported me throughout my life?

This is pure fantasy, of course. Still, I like to imagine Neferura had a Susan Spivey or Susan Andrews, the women who helped me begin and navigate the early years of my career. Or a Liz Cullen who helped me transition to a new city. Or a Janet Johnson, who tucked me under her wing and helped me plot a course through graduate school and the rigorous dissertation years that followed. Or an Esther Hershenhorn, who gave me my first lesson in how to write a book worth reading. Or the many brilliant women who have touched my life in more ways than I can count, including the book friends who have read and reacted to various iterations of this story and others: Darlene Jacobson, Amy Potts-Ostrowski, Naomi Milliner, Rosaria Munda, Franny Billingsley, Sarah Hammond, Amanda Caverzasi, Nancy Goodfellow, Julie Golden, Carrie Evans, and others. And of course, even an Egyptian princess could benefit from the support of my wise and patient agent, Liza Fleissig, who championed this story from its anemic first draft, guiding me through ups and downs as we zigged and zagged *Neferura* toward the perfect editor. If Liza found the manuscript a house, my editor, MJ Johnston, made the house a home. MJ and her amazing editorial assistant, Olivia Turner, have pushed and encouraged and brainstormed tirelessly, matching my dedication to Neferura's story at every turn. The team at Sourcebooks has been an author's dream, supportive and collaborative throughout the very long process of editing and producing a real-life book. I am full of appreciation for Cristina Arreola, Anna Venckus, Tara Jaggers, Heather VenHuizen, Stephanie Rocha, Jessica Thelander, Maddie Herr, Cameron Kirk, Laura Boren, and the rest of the Sourcebooks team, including, of course, the woman who started it all, creating new pathways for authors like me, Dominique Raccah. I'm grateful to Andrew Davis for the beautiful cover, which perfectly captures the ancient-meets-modern themes in my story. And last but definitely not least, my heartfelt appreciation goes out to the readers who will give *Neferura* their time and attention. May your scales be forever in balance.

ABOUT THE AUTHOR

Photo © Erin Harris

Malayna Evans was raised in Utah and spent her childhood climbing mountains and reading sci-fi. When she was in her early twenties, she moved to Chicago, where she earned MAs in the ancient history of the Mediterranean and the Near East and a PhD in ancient Egyptian history. She enjoys sharing her passion for the ancient world with readers, adores travel, and plays a mean game of cards. A single mom, Malayna lives in Oak Park, Illinois, with her two children and two very spoiled Frenchies. You can learn more about her at malaynaevans.com.